THE MAN SHE MARRIED

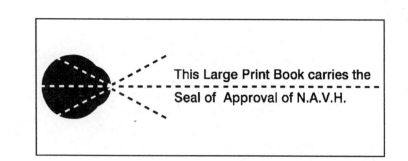

This Large Print Book carries the
Seal of Approval of N.A.V.H.

THE MAN SHE MARRIED

CATHY LAMB

THORNDIKE PRESS
A part of Gale, a Cengage Company

GALE
A Cengage Company

Farmington Hills, Mich • San Francisco • New York • Waterville, Maine
Meriden, Conn • Mason, Ohio • Chicago

LIBRARY OF CONGRESS CIP DATA ON FILE.
CATALOGUING IN PUBLICATION FOR THIS BOOK
IS AVAILABLE FROM THE LIBRARY OF CONGRESS

ISBN-13: 978-1-4328-5684-7 (hardcover)

Published in 2019 by arrangement with Kensington Books, an imprint
of Kensington Publishing Corp.

Printed in the United States of America
1 2 3 4 5 6 7 23 22 21 20 19

To Jim and Bette Straight's kids,
Cindy Everts, Jimmy Straight,
and Karen Straight
With love always and forever

PART I

CHAPTER 1

He had lied.

He lied about his past, he lied about where he was from, and he lied about what he'd done before I met him.

All of it.

"What *isn't* a lie, Zack?" I heard my voice pitch straight up, a screech and an accusation in one.

"Natalie, I —" He closed his eyes for a second, his face pale.

"Answer the question!" I slammed my hands down on the granite island in our kitchen. It hurt, but I didn't even wince. The coffee machine gurgled. It gurgles every morning. The gurgling is usually comforting. Today it sounded as if it were choking, which was exactly how I felt. "Answer it!"

He ran a hand over his eyes, his expression exhausted but determined. So determined. "What I told you from the time I lived in Alaska is all true."

"And before that?" I had had enough lies already in my life; they had stalked my childhood, and I didn't need any from him.

"What I told you about my life before Alaska is not true."

"Is your real name Zack? Zack Shelton?"

His jaw tightened. "No."

I hit the granite countertop again. *I can't believe this.* My husband of five years, whom I had made love to, in the bath, last night, whom I had also made love to during halftime of the football game, *was not named Zack.*

The morning had started out right and warm and ended up cold and wrong. We'd been in bed, the dawn light sneaking around the edges of the curtains. I had turned, naked as usual, to snuggle into Zack. He was always cuddly, and I loved hugging him. I didn't want to go to work.

I'd decided that morning sex would be a splendid idea and rolled on top of him and smiled, my messy blond curls spilling onto his chest. Yes, I'd smiled on top of Zack, but he had not been smiling.

"Zack?"

He'd had his cell phone in his hand and he placed it, slowly, on the nightstand next to our bed. He closed his eyes for long seconds and swore. He can swear with the best of them when something ticks him off. In the years we had been together, he had never, ever sworn at me.

"What's wrong?" I figured something had gone wrong with his home construction business. Lumber not delivered. Appliances lost. A plumber not showing up.

"Baby," he'd said. "I need you to trust me."

That's when he told me what I didn't want to hear and my life spun in a spiral and flipped upside down. I peeled myself off him, stunned. I grabbed my pink lace robe and headed to the kitchen to get away from him, to get away from what he'd told me.

And now we were here, and I was freezing, and reeling. I dragged in a breath. It was breathe or pass out. I studied my husband. Zack has brown hair, not a soft curve on his face, and light green eyes, with fine lines fanning out from them. He has a long scar on the right side of his ribs and a smaller one on the top of his left cheekbone from when he was a fisherman in Alaska. His face is Marlboro Man type, only he does not smoke. "What is your real name, Zack?"

He hesitated. I saw it. Infinitesimal.

"Devon."

Devon? "Devon what?"

"Devon Walton."

Devon Walton?

"Natalie, sit down, please, for a second. You're shaking. You look like you're going to faint."

"Of course I'm shaking, Zack." I wrapped my arms around myself. "Or Devon. Oh, my God. Two names! It's not every day you find out your husband is not who he has told you he is."

"Natalie, I am sorry —"

"You are not sorry enough." I put my hands to my head. What was going on? Was this real? Was this a nightmare? He hadn't lied only about his name, either. My God. The worst came *after* he told me about his fake name. "You are wanted by the police."

"Yes."

"For murder."

"Yes —"

"And for evading the law."

"Yes. Honey —"

"Don't you 'honey' me!" I was furious, and I was scared. He had killed a man? Zack had never been violent, though he's built like a lumberjack. He didn't even have a temper. He got along with all of his employees. He had four best friends from college. He laughed a lot. He did *crosswords*. He played chess with me.

12

"We don't have time to talk right now, Natalie. We need to leave."

"Oh, heck, no. I'm not leaving." I glared at the vase of white daisies that Zack had brought me. I wanted to throw them against the wall.

"Yes," he said, his voice low, insistent, "you are, Natalie."

And there was the steel. The strength. His voice was quiet, hard. Zack, my Zack, was an incredible man whom I fell in love with on the Deschutes River, a fly rod in my hand, but I sensed that steel the first day I met him, and I had seen it many times since. It's what helped him build his company. It's what made him Zack. But I was not letting him push me around.

"We are leaving together," he said. "Now."

"No." My whole life was crumbling, which sounded totally melodramatic, but it was true. My reality as I knew it was not my reality. My marriage was a myth. "This is my home." *Actually,* a little voice said in my head, *it's not your home, it's his.*

"Natalie, I would not tell you that we have to leave unless we did. I will take care of this problem, but I can't take care of it until I get you someplace safe."

Safe? *Safe?* I'm an accountant. That's a safe occupation. I co-own an accounting

13

firm. That's a safe business. I like numbers. Numbers can be brought to order. They are safe. They tell the truth. You can trust the numbers.

I drive a blue truck built like a tank. That's a safe way to go. We have a home in Portland, Oregon, with my collection of hummingbirds hanging from the ceiling and a towering oak tree in the backyard. That's a safe place to live. I like driving tractors and playing poker, reading books and fishing. I like home decorating and choosing paint colors. I love making necklaces when I have time. These are safe hobbies.

I have worked hard so that I will never be poor again, because being poor makes me feel unsafe. I have tried hard to be a normal woman and to fit in because I spent a lot of years not feeling as if I fit in and not feeling equal to others or loved. Those are safe neuroses. I am working on them.

But today I woke up and my husband told me he's not who I thought and he killed some man a long time ago and apparently someone wants to kill me because of it.

Kill *me.* Natalie Deschutes Fox Shelton.

That does not make me feel *safe.*

"I'm not going anywhere with you, Zack. I have no idea if you're telling me the truth."

"I am telling you the truth." His jaw was

rigid. He might crack his teeth.

"You just told me you killed a man. Why did you kill him?"

"I will tell you later. We don't have time now. It'll take too long."

"And after hearing that I'm supposed to trust you?"

"Yes."

He came toward me, and I put a hand up to stop him. "Stay away from me. You are not going to tell me what to do. I don't even know who you are, and that sounds so . . . so . . ." I struggled because I couldn't think through the shock. "Stupid. Ridiculous. Like we're in a badly written movie. But it's true. Who the hell are you?"

"I'm your husband. I love you. You need to do what I'm telling you to do."

"No. I am not going with you." I turned to the bathroom to get in the shower and ready for work. I am never late for work. I had clients. I had columns of numbers to examine. I had tax codes to study. Profit and loss sheets to explain.

He followed me to the bathroom and said, "You don't have time to shower. Get dressed. Grab your purse, your computer, and your phone. Hurry. You have to hurry."

I slammed the bathroom door in his face and locked it. I stared into my worried blue eyes in the mirror. They are an odd blue. Some people say they have a smear of lavender in them. My mother has told me they are "too large — try to lower your lids, dear, so you don't resemble a guppy fish."

I have a crooked smile, but it takes up half my face. My teeth are big. Let's just say I have no problem eating steak. My nose is ever so slightly off-center. I'm told that no one notices it, but I do. It looks as if my nose were plopped on my face and then squished to the left side. I have blond curls that do what they want to do no matter what. They stop midway down my back.

I stared at my reflection, which was utterly stricken, until the bathroom door was kicked open with a bang, the hinges flying off, wood splitting.

"You broke the door, Zack," I protested, my hands over my head for protection.

"I did. Baby, come on." His voice was gentle.

"No." He pulled me out. "Stop it. Let go of me!" I pushed him away and got dressed for work while he followed me and told me we had to be out the door in two minutes. I ignored him. I would go to my office, find a difficult file, and concentrate until all this stuff stopped buzzing in my head and I could figure out what to do.

When I was dressed I went back to the kitchen to grab my briefcase, my phone, and my purse. I glanced at my late grandma's antique perfume bottles on a shelf. She would know exactly what to do here, but I sure didn't. "I'm not running, Zack." I faced him across that granite counter in the black suit I'd pulled on, black heels, and sheer tights with two black butterflies on my ankles. I had not brushed my hair or teeth. That's how confused and furious I was. "You run, not me." I glanced at the clock. I was going to be late for work! I grabbed my purse and headed to my truck in the driveway.

"Natalie, for God's sakes —" He grabbed my arm, and I pushed it off.

I said a bad thing to him that started with an F and ended with a "you," and I ran to my truck as fast as I could and climbed in. I locked the doors before he could yank them open. He yelled at me to stop, but I didn't. I was living with a liar. I was living with a man I didn't even know who had lied to me. Repeatedly. For years. I could not trust him or what he was saying now. He had admitted to *killing* someone. His name wasn't even Zack.

And now I was late for work.

I reversed out of the driveway in my safe

truck. He ran after me, and I headed down the street of our safe, quiet neighborhood in the hills to my safe job with numbers. Fall leaves — scarlet, gold, yellow, and green — spiraled in front of me, as if it were a normal autumn day. I started to cry. I cried so hard it felt as if I was going to choke.

I saw Zack rush to his black truck.

It was in that state that I drove to work, Zack right on my tail, honking. I stopped at a stop sign, and when I was waiting for a school bus to cross, he got out of his truck and raced to the door of my truck and banged on the window. "Natalie!" he shouted. "Pull over —"

I kept driving and stopped at the next intersection, two blocks from my home. I should have looked. I always look. I am a cautious and safe driver.

A flash caught my eye. Someone had his lights on. But that wasn't what I remembered last. The last thing I remembered was the driver of the van, seconds before he rammed his car into mine. He was driving way too fast and smiling.

Yes, the driver of the van — heavy, bald, with beady eyes — was smiling.

Oh, my God, I thought, before our explosive impact. *Zack was right. Someone* is *trying to kill me.*

Because of him. Because of Zack. Because of the man I married.

CHAPTER 2

I hear screaming noises.

It's sirens.

My head has exploded, I think. Maybe my brain is in pieces all over the steering wheel. That would explain why I'm being crushed by pain. There's a white pillow against my face and chest. Why is there a white pillow there? There's red paint all over the white pillow, all over my blond curls. It smears when I touch it. I glance up and can see only broken glass. Broken glass is so pretty. Tiny fissures. Elegant lines. Geometric and organic shapes.

I hear people yelling. Why are they yelling? Someone hits the door of my truck, but I don't look at who it is, because if I do my brain might shatter. I picture my brain, like a puzzle, all broken.

Wait. Is that Zack yelling? Yes. It is. He opens the door of the truck with his key. "Natalie! Natalie! Hang on, honey." I want to hug Zack. I want to be with him. I love Zack.

"I love you, Zack, I love you," I whisper.

Something in my head pops, one final blast of sheer pain, and the broken glass on the windshield of my truck, such an intricate design, starts to fade and blur. It's getting smaller, pulling away from me. Wait. Maybe I am pulling away from the glass.

Yes, it's me. I'm pulling away. I'm moving backward in a soft, warm tunnel. I don't understand how there can be a soft, warm tunnel in my truck. The steering wheel is getting smaller, and for some reason I am in the backseat and I can see that the white pillow is the airbag and my blond curls and the blood are still on it. How can I be looking at myself in my own truck?

I don't have much time to think about that conundrum, because I'm soon outside of my truck and floating. I watch Zack lean in toward the other me, the "me" with her face on the bloody airbag, his head close to mine. I can tell he's panicked; there are tears on his cheeks. People are around us, trying to help, two on their phones, yelling. I see a few of my neighbors running toward my truck. A fire engine is down the block, lights and sirens on, an ambulance screaming in from the other direction, a police car speeding through the neighborhood. I watch them arrive from way up in the sky.

I am leaving the scene of my accident like a bird. They think I'm still in my truck because my body is there, but I am moving through the tunnel, nice and smooth. My head doesn't hurt anymore. Nothing hurts. I think I can hear music. Ah, yes. Beethoven's Fifth. My very favorite. Then country music. I hear my dad's voice, too. He's singing me songs from my childhood. Johnny Cash's "Ring of Fire." "Old McDonald Had a Farm." The Beatles' "Let It Be." My mother never sang to me, so it is not surprising I don't hear her voice.

I feel someone with me, holding my hands. I feel love. Peace.

The morning light is a golden circle around my truck now, the circle getting smaller as the tunnel pulls me back. The paramedics are getting me out of the truck, a brace on my neck. Zack is talking to me, anguished, earnest, but I can't hear him. He's holding my hand. I'm put on a white stretcher. The sirens are silent now.

I hear my dad sing, "My hummingbird, you are my life, my love. . . ." He often calls me Hummingbird because when I was little I loved them and told him I wanted a pet hummingbird farm.

I float upward, through the trees with their burgundy and pumpkin-orange leaves, above my home, farther into the blue sky and the white cotton puffs of clouds. I am rested. I am calm now, in the clouds. Happy.

Is that . . . ? Oh, my gosh, it's my grandma Dixie, my dad's mother. She's been dead for years. She taught me how to play poker. I love Grandma Dixie. I run to her and give her a hug. In the background I see the love of her life, Howard, grinning, waving at me. I wave back.

She gives a cry of delight and hugs me tight, a drink in her hand, the ice clinking. "Good to see you, kid." Her eyes flood with tears. She puts the drink down on a table beside a red 1967 Chevy. The hood is up. She's in her blue mechanic overalls. She places her hands on either side of my face. "I have missed you so much, honey."

"I've missed you, too, Grandma Dixie." She smells like her rose perfume.

My grandma was a ball-breaker. She was popular in Lake Joseph, our small town in eastern Oregon. She was *the* mechanic. Everyone said she could get a car without an engine to drive. She shot darts, bluffed her way through poker, and won the rifle shooting contest every year. When she swore it was like listening to a poem or short story.

She'd left me all her antique perfume bottles.

"I'd like you to stay and play poker, kid, have a beer, but you have to go back."

"What?"

"Your dad needs you. Zack needs you."

"I don't understand."

"Go back, Natalie." She hugs me again, cheek to cheek, then lets me go and says, "Go back now."

"Go back where, Grandma Dixie?"

"I mean, get out of here, quick as a hot cat. It's not your time."

"Not my time?" And then I get it. I know where I am. Oh, hell. Not that I am in hell, but *hell.* I do not want to be here, that's for sure.

"Fight, baby. Fight for your life. I love you."

She takes three steps back, then rushes forward and shoves me as hard as she can, right in the chest.

I fall straight back through the soft tunnel, Beethoven's Fifth whirling around me.

CHAPTER 3

I can't breathe. I can't move. I can't see. I can't talk. It's dark in here. I'm in pain. My head is throbbing, every cell shrieking. I need to breathe.

What is going on? Where am I? What happened?

"Clear!" someone shouts.

Ouch! That hurt my chest.

"Clear!" someone shouts again.

Ouch! Hurts again.

"Natalie."

It's Zack. He's upset. Is he crying? I think he's crying. He rarely cries. Only a few times, when I told him I loved him, when he asked me to marry him, our wedding day . . .

"Natalie, breathe, honey. Please. Take a breath. . . ."

I feel my heart flip. This is freakin' scary. I feel it flip again; it's out of rhythm. It's weak.

"Her heart is beating," someone says,

panting.

I force myself to take a breath. And another one.

"She's breathing," a woman says. "She's breathing!"

I'm lying down and I'm moving fast. I can hear people shouting around me. There's something over my mouth and nose.

They're telling one another what to do. Medical terms and "stopped breathing" and "blood pressure plummeting . . ." and "severe brain injury . . ." They grab my arm and stick it with a needle. It hurts, but I can't tell them that. Something stiff is around my neck. Lights are flashing. Bright. My heart is still flipping around. Like a suffocating fish.

Obviously, something is very, very wrong. I remember having sex with Zack at halftime during the football game last night. We had sex in the bath, too, after he'd undone all the buttons of my white lace negligee. We went to bed, and I gave him a kiss good night. What happened after that? Why am I not at home? Why am I not at work? Am I late for work? I am never late for work. I have clients. Why am I here? Where is *here*?

I start to scream. They clearly cannot hear me.

I don't know how long I scream. I hear

someone shout, "She'll be out in three, two. . . ."

I wake up in a bed. I am lying flat. My eyes are closed, or I am blind. I hope I am not blind. I cannot move. Not my head, my hands, my toes. Nothing.

Where am I? I hear people talking. It's fuzzy at first, then it becomes clearer, as if my brain has shifted, or turned on, and now it can listen, evaluate.

It's a hospital. I'm in a hospital. I hear doctors and nurses talking in urgent, sharp voices to one another. They are using medicalese I don't understand. There are at least six voices. I hear what I don't want to hear: Brain swelled. Blood on the brain. Brain injury, moderate to severe. Operation went better than expected, but we'll have to see . . .

Then someone talks to me. "Mrs. Shelton, my name is Dr. Tarasawa. You've been in a car accident and you are in the hospital."

A car accident? I was in a car accident? When? What happened? Oh no. Did I hurt someone else? I hope I didn't. I feel ill. I didn't hurt anyone, did I? Tell me. Please tell me.

"You sustained a head injury. We operated. The operation went well."

You operated on my brain?

"Mrs. Shelton, I want you to squeeze my hand if you can hear me."

I try. I cannot squeeze.

"No movement," he says to someone.

I try for movement. No go.

"Mrs. Shelton," Dr. Tarasawa says again. "I need you to squeeze my hand."

I try to squeeze. I can't.

The doctor mutters, "She should be awake by now."

I am awake, I try to shout to Dr. Tarasawa.

"She shouldn't be in this coma," another doctor says.

I am not in a coma! Am I?

"I don't know what's wrong," Dr. Tarasawa says.

I know what's wrong! You can't hear me!

"We're consulting with other doctors. We'll figure it out."

"Damn," Dr. Tarasawa mutters again. "Mrs. Shelton. Can you hear me?"

I can hear you.

I can't see you.

I can't talk to you.

I can't move.

But I am here. In here. In this body, this nonmoving body with a brain that's been operated on. It's me, Natalie. I am in a coma. It is a Coma Coffin, because I am trapped and stuck.

I am hooked up to machines. I can hear them beeping. There are IVs in my arms. I can feel them.

I am locked in my own body. Locked in. Locked inside.

I try not to scream in fear, in terror.

It doesn't work.

I scream.

Dr. Tarasawa doesn't hear me.

No one hears me.

The next time I wake up, Zack is with me. I can feel him. I can smell him. He smells like the wind. He smells like mint and soap and fir trees. Somehow he reminds me of my grandma's apple pie, my favorite. I always tell him, "You're my apple pie," and he laughs.

"Hey, baby," he says, so quiet, so depressed. He kisses my limp hand, and I hear him start to cry.

I want to hug him. I want to talk to him. But I can't move. I can't talk to him. I can't say, "I don't remember any car accident and the last thing I remember is going to bed with you last night, Zack, so what happened? What's going on now?"

Zack, I cry inside this bleak hole, this

bleak place, this waiting place, maybe a dying place. *Help me, please, baby. Help me.*

He cries on the side of the bed.

I cry in the bed.

I remember seeing my grandma Dixie recently. I remember smelling her rose perfume. I remember she had a drink in her hand. She was working on a car, a red 1967 Chevy, in her blue mechanic's outfit. I remember her giving me a shove, which wouldn't have happened. Grandma Dixie would never shove me.

Plus, Grandma Dixie's been dead for years. This is so confusing. I would love to have one of her apple pies, though. She loved baking pies. Didn't like to cook. Her cookbooks gathered dust, but she found peace in making apple pie crusts and mixing brown sugar and cinnamon and nutmeg together.

Why do I feel as if I recently gave Grandma Dixie a hug?

"Hummingbird, it's time to wake up."

It's my dad. My lumbering, grizzly bear dad. "Darling Hummingbird, please. Open those blue eyes of yours and smile at me. One smile, only one . . ."

Next to Zack, my dad, Scott Fox, is my

favorite person. I adore him. He's six foot four, ironically the same size as Zack, and built like a human tractor. He's a man with a barrel chest, black and white hair, and dark brown eyes. He has been a metal-smith for a famous outdoor artist named Margarita Hammer for a number of years. Before that he was a roofer.

He cries when he watches *Pride and Prejudice,* says Jane Eyre is one of his best book friends, reads voraciously in all subjects, and loves to hunt and eat whatever he killed that afternoon or hooked on his fly rod that evening. He was trained to shoot by my grandma. His shot is excellent.

"Oh no, oh no, oh no," my dad cries. "Please, my hummingbird. You are my life. Wake up, wake up."

My dad holds my hand, his hand hard and rough from years of working outside, putting roofs on houses, working in our orchard, and taking care of our animals. He says, "Open your eyes, my blue robin. Open those bleepin' eyes. Come back to your daddy."

Zack and my dad sit beside me in my hospital room. They have always gotten along. The atmosphere is grim. Heavy. Depressing.

My dad sings me a song. "Old McDonald

31

Had a Farm." In choosing that song, a song he sang to me as a kid, I know he's lost it. His voice breaks and cracks, but he does all the animal sounds, and inside my coma, all trapped and stuck, I cry.

Who knew the sound of a goat could cause such emotional wreckage?

I hear many doctors coming in and out of my room. They do not know I can hear every word they say.

"She was hit by a van," one doctor tells another. "Hit-and-run. The van was stolen, driver wasn't caught. Police have been here."

Ah. So that's what happened. I must have been on my way to work when I got in an accident. I don't remember being on my way to work, though. I remember hugging Zack last night — was it last night? — and that was my last memory before I went to sleep. But I would have been going to work in the morning. I am always on time.

I am furious that a driver hit me and drove off, but I am so relieved that I didn't hurt anyone I can barely catch my breath. I have always known that I could not live with the guilt if I hurt someone else. I couldn't bear it.

"She took the full impact," the doctor says. "Truck totaled. Flatlined. Paramedics

32

brought her back."

I want to scream at them to do their jobs, to save me, to pull me out of this.

"Mrs. Shelton!" they say to me. "Can you hear me? Can you squeeze my hand?"

I can't answer and I can't squeeze.

My brain is trying to tell me something. It's like when you have a word in mind but you can't get it, can't grab it. My brain has something on the tip, something that I can almost remember, something I need to know, but then . . . poof. Gone. It has something to do with Zack. It has something to do with the accident. I wish I could remember the accident. I feel as if the thought is dangerous. It's . . . scary. But how can that be? Zack never scares me.

This does, though. This coma scares the heck out of me.

That night I have a nightmare in my Coma Coffin.

I don't know how this is done. Anyone seeing me would think I was in the deepest sleep of all without being dead. But sometimes I wake up inside my coma and I realize I've been asleep.

In my nightmare I see a man. He's white, he's heavy with a round face, his skin fleshy. He's bald. He has tiny, dark pig eyes and a mocking slash of a mouth with teeth like a crooked picket fence. His nose is bulbous, red veins shot through, scratchy like a crow's claw.

The worst part is the evil rampaging through that man. He is laughing, one of those sick people with a smiling smirk who are the most dangerous of all.

He is trying to kill me.

Zack says to me, in a broken voice, "I am so sorry, Natalie." My tough, reserved, protective, smart, loving Zack is trying not to cry.

I don't know what he's sorry about. Why is he sorry? He didn't do this. I heard the doctors talking. I was hit by a van. I don't remember it, but I know Zack wasn't driving the van, so it's not his fault. We don't even have a van.

I wish I could see him. I am petrified.

I don't want to live like this. I don't. I know that.

But I don't want to die. I am too young to die. Of course, I will think I am too young to die when I am ninety, too, and part deaf and walking with a cane and wearing a diaper, but I want to live.

Zack and I are going to have kids. A bunch of them. A gang of kids. We are going to build our dream house. *One day.* We are going to plant a ton of white daisies because they're my favorite flower.

But wait. Zack . . . what's wrong? He's on his cell phone. He's furious. He's threatening someone. He's swearing at them as he leaves my hospital room. Come back, Zack, come back.

When Zack comes back, he holds my hands in his and cries like I have never heard him cry. I cry because he's crying, and it hurts me to hear.

"I am so sorry, Natalie. This shouldn't have happened to you. It should have happened to me. This is my fault. All my fault."

I don't understand. What is his fault?

"Natalie."

I hear my voice being called. I have to come up through a fog. Was I asleep or was I dying? I don't know. But I do know Chick's voice. I would know Chick's voice anywhere. I've been hearing it since kindergarten.

I picture her. Reddish hair, the sunlight glinting through it, turning some of it golden. Chick is curvy and, as her husband says, "sexily lush, that's my woman." Brown eyes, sharp, smart, they take no crap. Her personality is somewhat tractor-ish, as in, she will mow you down if she needs to.

"Natalie, can you hear me? It's me, Chick."

Hello, Chick, I think, deep inside my Coma Coffin. Chick's real name is Esther Thornton-LaSalle. She was given the name Chick by her brother, Jed, because they had little chicks when they were kids. She raised them in her bedroom and loved them and would only cluck like a chicken for weeks and refused to speak English. Chick is married to Braxton, her high school sweetheart, and they have six kids.

"And me, Natalie. It's Justine. Please open your eyes."

Hello, Justine! I picture Justine, too, my other best friend, who I also met in kindergarten. Justine and I co-own our accounting firm Knight and Fox in downtown Portland. She's the rainmaker, the hand shaker, the one who brings clients in, and I handle the numbers and accounts. It's a perfect business marriage. We have four employees. Five. Three. I can't remember.

Justine has black hair, long, fashionable. Hazel and gold eyes, a blend. Gorgeous, naturally, and knows it but isn't snooty about it. She can't help what she was born with. She's a brilliant accountant and the oldest of eight kids.

She is desperately in love with Chick's brother, Jed Thornton, and has been since we were seven. She has a secret. I know the secret; Chick does, too. The secret hurts her every day, like a tiny, searing knife cut.

"Open even only one eye," Justine pleads with me. "One. That's all we're asking. One eye. Even half an eye."

Inside I laugh at Justine's plea that I open "half an eye."

"Come on, Natalie," Chick says. "Buck up and wake up. Rooster's crowing, rise and shine." Chick has always liked farm phrases.

They are tearful, their voices desperate. They are begging. Justine, Chick, and I are the Moonshine and Milky Way Maverick Girls, and one of them, me, is dead and not dead at the same time.

I try to open "even half an eye," but I can't. I'm living in my body, but my body is not living. It's hard to explain, but we are two separate beings in here. My body, which doesn't work or respond, is one, and then there's me. I am a brain and a heart and a soul stuck inside bones and skin.

"Please, Natalie, you're our best friend," Chick pleads. "We're the Moonshine and Milky Way Maverick Girls. It's the three of us. You have to fight. Fight like a you-know-what-bad-word that starts with an M and has an F in the middle. Fight like a bull is chasing you down a field, like that one time when we were fifteen." I remembered that. That bull was fast and snorting. "Fight like a wild cat."

"I love you, Natalie," Justine whispers to me. Her tears drop on my cheeks.

"I love you, too," Chick says. She hugs me, gently. I am covered in tubes, a collar around my neck, something over my head, bandages; you name it, I have it. I can't see myself, but I can imagine.

"This is all gonna end soon," Chick says. "I mean, it's not going to end, in your death. Don't think that. Didn't mean to freak you out, Natalie. I mean, this is all gonna end when we see that smile of yours again. Bring it on. Bring the smile over the horizon."

"Yes, we'll take the smile. And the dimples in your cheeks. Not the dimples in your butt cheeks." Justine makes a sad, gaspy sound. "Those are cute, the butt dimples, but we don't need to see those. I don't know why I said that. Why am I talking about her butt dimples? Why? I'm so upset! I can't breathe. Is there air in here? Is there?"

I am fortunate that my best friends don't need to see my butt dimples. We have seen one another's butt dimples. We used to skinny-dip.

We used to jump off The Rocks at the lake, too. We haven't done that in years, as we've all had jobs and responsibilities and blah. Plus, we've all chickened out. If I get out of here, I'm jumping again. I am stuck between life and death, where no one should ever live, and that jump will tell me that I'm alive and well.

I hear the Moonshine and Milky Way Maverick Girls crying.

I feel terrible for the pain that Zack, my dad, Justine, and Chick are going through. This is not fun for me, but it's killing me to hear their pain.

Ha. Killing me. This is my strange sense of humor boiling up through my corpse.

But if I do not use humor in here, I will have a total and complete nervous breakdown.

Justine Knight and Chick Thornton and I met in kindergarten.

On the first day of school Justine came in and promptly fell asleep at her desk across from me, her long black hair a mess. I learned later that she was up most of the night because her mother had a baby in a swimming pool in their living room and she had to help take care of her twin three-year-old siblings. She was asleep for most of the morning. The teacher woke her up for art time, which is when we met.

"You slept for a long time," I said to her as we both glued white cotton balls onto a piece of blue construction paper to make lambs. My lamb looked angry and mean, definitely dangerous.

Justine's lamb was cute. We had those roly-poly eyeballs, and she glued them onto her lamb's face just right. One of my lamb's eyes was an inch higher than the other. He had five legs and a hump on his back like a gargoyle.

"We had another baby."

"You had a baby?" I gasped. She was pretty young to have a baby! Only five years old. I looked at her stomach. She was skinny. That baby must have been as small as a squirrel.

"My mommy had a baby. She had it at home in our living room in the swimming pool."

"She had a baby in a swimming pool?" This was getting better and better. I stopped working on my dangerous lamb.

"You have a pool in your living room?" Chick asked.

Justine nodded. "That's how she likes to have babies. Then she doesn't have to go to the hospital and get shots. She pushed it out in the water so it could go swimming, and she screamed a lot."

"How big is the swimming pool?" Swimming in your living room? That sounded like fun. "Is there a slide?"

"Is there a diving board?" Chick asked.

"No. It's a small pool. With whales on it. For kids. But we're not allowed to swim in it. It's only for the new babies."

I thought about the screaming part. "Why did she scream?"

"She told me it's because she's trying to push something the size of a watermelon out something the size of a grape and it hurts. I like grapes."

"I like grapes, too," I said. "I stuck one up my nose one time. It fit."

"I like watermelon," Chick said. "I even eat the seeds." Chick had made three cotton ball lambs. The mom lamb had a beer and her nails were painted pink and red.

Justine glued more cotton balls down. "I'm not going to have a baby ever."

"Me, either." I didn't want to have babies if it hurt. "How did the baby get out in the pool?"

She pointed to her privates. "Right there."

"What? Are you sure?" I was suspicious.

"I'm sure," Justine said, nodding. "I've

seen it."

Chick pulled up her dress, pulled down her underwear, bent over double for a close-up examination, and said, "There's no room for a baby down there." She stood back up. "I'm going to get a zipper on my tummy and when a baby wants to come out then I'll unzip the zipper and she'll walk out in her dress and get on a horse. I have a horse."

Wow. That was a good idea. Chick was smart.

"They don't wear clothes," Justine said. She wriggled her nose. "There's no zipper. They come out all red and slippery and crying and sometimes they're sort of purple. It's gross. They're gross. My mom wears a white lace dress when she has the babies."

"My mom paints women's fingernails," Chick said. "She says they tell her all their secrets." She leaned forward and whispered to us, "You know Mr. Toberton, the mayor? Mommy says at night he comes when everyone else is gone and gets his toenails painted pink with yellow flowers."

"I didn't know men polished their toenails," Justine said. "But my dad has handcuffs."

"My dad doesn't polish his nails," I said. "But he can wrestle down a pig."

"And Mrs. Leonard is pregnant again," Chick said, "but it's the wrong daddy."

I didn't know what that meant. What's a wrong daddy?

"My mommy told my daddy that he needs to keep away from her at night or she's going to have a herd of kids," Justine said. "Like a herd of goats or a herd of cats. I think he puts the babies in her tummy at night when she's not watching him."

"But doesn't she wake up?" I asked.

"How does he get them in there?" Chick asked.

Justine shrugged.

"My mommy says that she only wants one kid because I can be a big brat," I said.

"I don't think you're a brat," Justine said. "But your lamb is sort of scary."

"Yeah, I don't think you're a brat," Chick said. "I think you're nice. Like my chickens."

I couldn't believe it. These girls didn't think I was a brat. They liked my lamb.

Justine had a mom who had babies in a swimming pool with no slide in the living room. Chick's mother put nail polish on men's toenails. I had a mother who often screamed at my dad and threw plates and plants, an occasional chair and, another time, our cat at my dad's head. He caught the cat.

She would sometimes roar off in her car for days at a time. She would come home with shopping bags full of clothes and my dad would look sad. Sometimes she came home all wobbly and would stumble over furniture. She would go to bed for days on end, and cry and not eat and not talk, then all of a sudden she'd get up and pretend that she hadn't been sad.

She always wore pretty dresses and heels and said I had to dress pretty too. "We're not white-trash poor people. It's not like you live in a shed, Natalie, or in our car, so don't dress like it," she'd tell me. "My parents were wealthy. They bought me beautiful clothes." Her parents had died before she met my dad. "If you look poor, people will treat you like you're nothing and we're not nothing! Do you hear me? I'm not nothing!"

All our moms were sort of weird.

I fit right in!

We were friends from that moment on.

The Moonshine and Milky Way Maverick Girls had met and bonded over lambs.

"Natalie," my husband, my Zack, my fly-fisherman, says to me as I am lying flat, machines beeping around me, trapped inside my nonresponsive body. "You have to wake up so we can fish together on the Deschutes. Remember, baby. We've already planned the Deschutes trip for spring. I bought you that new pack for your waist. You can put all your flies in there." His voice breaks.

My middle name, Deschutes, is for the Deschutes River. I grew up fishing it with my dad, and I definitely want to go and fish it with Zack again.

"Come on, sweetheart. Open those blue eyes for me."

I can't open my blue eyes. I want to. I am in here, alone, and it's dark and scares the hell out of me. It's like drowning without the water.

"You're getting better, and everything's okay."

I'm trying, sweet Zack, I'm trying.

"Natalie, I can't live without you."

I can't live without you either, Zack. I can't. We didn't even get to live in the dream home we've always planned on living in. *One day.* Inside my dark shadows I start to cry.

"Can you squeeze my hand, honey? Can you? Try. Please try."

I try. I can't. I can do nothing.

"We have to do our crosswords together," he chokes out. "I can't do crosswords alone."

We are so nerdy. We do crosswords together. When we started dating, I introduced him to crosswords. We do them on Sundays. We also read books together. We each have a copy of the same book. We call it the Deschutes Family Book Club. We discuss the book as we go. We read fiction, nonfiction, memoirs, and biographies, with a few thrillers thrown in.

The crosswords and books are like mental foreplay, I suppose. I'm a math person, he's a construction engineer. I like numbers. He likes blueprints. I like analyzing complex tax returns. He likes building with his bare hands. We like to make love in the afternoon. It's the best time. Everybody's rested and fed.

"I want to do a crossword with you, honey." His voice crackles and breaks again and that's it. Zack starts to cry again. "I want to do a crossword with you. I want to do a crossword with you, Natalie." He says it again and again, my poor Zack, he has lost it. "I want to do a crossword with you."

I want to do a crossword with you, too, Zack, I do. I so desperately do.

My strong husband is falling apart.

Inside, I cry with him. I can't stand knowing he's in this much pain.

Then Zack drags in a ragged breath.

"That son of a bitch," he whispers, ferocious in his quiet fury. *That son of a bitch.* He slams a fist into a table of some sort. I hear it crack.

Whoa. Who is a son of a bitch?

I don't know how long I've been like this, in my Coma Cof-fin. Doctors and nurses come in and out. My mind comes in and out. One time I heard I've been like this for three days. The next time I woke up I heard it was five.

I try to add numbers in my head here in my hospital bed to distract myself and get my brain working. They flip and bounce and disappear.

I try to name all the animals I can think of. I am up to twelve.

I name states and try to match them to their capitals. I think I reached thirteen.

I name countries. Eleven.

I have started to make up poems about my condition.

Natalie is under the weather.
She will soon get better.

A food tube gives her tea and toast.
This is definitely not a funny roast.

There she lies in a coffin bed.
Darned if she will end up dead.

Wake up, Natalie, do it now.
Or else you'll have a permanent frown.

I never said the rhymes were going to be well written. This is how I entertain myself. If I don't, I'll cave to my panic.

The next day I cave to my panic. Inside my dark Coma Coffin I start to have a panic attack, all by myself. Alone. Is this going to be my life? Is nothing going to change?
I am locked inside myself.
No one knows I am alive.

Oh no. Gall. Sheesh.
It's my *mother.*
She's crying. I feel her hand on my forehead. This is surprising because my mother is not affectionate. At all.
"Talk to her, Jocelyn," my dad says. His voice is calm, encouraging. He forgave her instantly for what she did; he does not have room in his heart for anger. I did not forgive her instantly. I'm not sure I've forgiven her yet. "The doctors say she might be able to hear us."
"What do I say?"

Ah. There's my sparkling mother.

"Tell her you love her."

"Natalie knows I love her." Her voice is snappish through her tears. "I've already told her that, Scott."

Have you, Mom? Recently?

Jocelyn Miller Fox Andretti Moscovitz Chavez Smith leans over me. She lives about four hours away from here on a ranch in eastern Oregon with Husband Number Five, Dell. She took Husbands Number Two, Three, and Four to the cleaners when she divorced them. Her home is about an hour away from my dad's, the home I grew up in, in Lake Joseph.

She has thick blond hair that curves into a bell around her face and blue eyes, like mine, but hers are brighter, which she often notes to me, as if we are in a competition to see who has the bluest eyes. Every piece of clothing, every handbag, every heel is designer, labels prominent. Her "social status" is important to her. She has no women friends, probably because she flirts with their husbands. You never know when you'll need a new husband! Must keep your options open!

My mother is still in love with my dad. When I do talk to her, she always asks me about my dad. What is he doing, how is he doing, and, in one way or another, is he seeing anyone?

My mother has convinced herself that my dad has been pining for her forever. That is not true, but she believes what she wants to believe, regardless of facts. My dad has had a few relationships, all long-lasting, and I have liked all of the women. He does not miss my mother.

I can smell her overpowering perfume. Her mouthwash. And . . . brandy. Yes, brandy. Had to have a shot before coming to see me. I don't blame her on that one.

She sighs. Then she says, her voice wobbling, "I love you, Natalie."

Whew! She did it!

I haven't seen her in months. She calls now and then, and sometimes I call back, sometimes I don't because I'm not up to it. It's like dealing with a lipsticked Godzilla.

"I'm sorry, baby." She puts her hand to my cheek, which, again, startles me. More affection!

"And I'm sorry. I'm sorry for . . . for everything." At that, her voice sinks into nothing. I hear her inhale. I hear a sob, the sob turns into more sobs. She is holding on to my bed rail, and I can feel it shake.

My dad says nothing.

My mother cries and cries.

I don't hate my mother. But I don't want to be around her. She hurts me every single time I'm with her and has since she deserted my dad and me with a cheery wave as she drove off when I was seven.

In her bright blue eyes, brighter than mine, I don't dress "fancy enough." My hair needs to be highlighted. I have the wrong bra on and I need more "boob lift." I look pale. I look sickly. I should think about Botox. "Image is everything, Natalie. Never forget I told you that. Dress the part. Always look your best. Don't dress like you're poor and stupid."

The worst? She repeatedly lied to me as a child as to when she was coming to see me.

But maybe I feel a pinch of pity for her today. She is a mother looking at a daughter in a coma. My mother is crying over me as if her sobs are going to kill her.

As my body lies as flat as roadkill, my brain fluttering, I feel my heart swell a tiny bit. Maybe that tiny swell is a tiny bit of forgiveness.

Then she snaps at my dad, "My God, Scott, has no one washed her hair? It looks awful. Get a nurse in here. I can't have my daughter looking like white trash."

Inside, I sigh.

I wake up to Zack arguing into the phone. He calls someone "one sick shithead." He does not anger easily, but he is swearing, his tone furious. Zack is usually calm and controlled. He's a measured, mature man.

As if he realizes I might be able to hear something, and he doesn't want to upset me, he gets up and leaves my hospital room.

Maybe this has something to do with his construction business, a contractor who didn't show up? Maybe there was a lawsuit? Was Zack being sued for the first time ever? But there was a threatening tone to his voice. This is personal.

About five minutes later, he comes back in. He kisses my forehead and says, "Hi, honey," then he starts to pace. I feel him staring down at me sometimes. I love that man and I know he loves me, and the way he has been with me, almost all day and all night since this happened, whenever it happened, proves to me once again that my husband loves me.

But I also sense something else: Fear.

I know he's scared. I am in a coma. He's scared I'll die. But there's something else here, too. The fear is coming from someplace else. I can feel it.

What is it?

I thought about that for a while, inside my coma, trying to catch an answer that kept slipping away, hiding in the darkness of my injured brain, before everything went dark again. I wish I could remember the morning of my accident; it bothers me that I lost it. Something's there. . . .

I am having a bad night. My heart keeps racing, then fluttering, and my blood pressure plummets down, then shoots up, then back down again. There are doctors in and out all night. Zack and my dad beg me to hold on.

I hold on.

Oh, joy. I have finally realized that I have a catheter up my va gi gi that is hooked to my urethra like a plastic snake. I don't know how I missed this part. Maybe it's the crush of all kinds of bizarre things going on with me at the moment.

The catheter is now my special snake friend. I am all IV'd up, so clearly the liquid has to leave my body or my bladder will inflate like a balloon and pop. It's reassuring that I have a snake catheter, because I definitely want to keep my bladder.

In addition I believe that I am in a diaper. Yes. A diaper. This is what my life has become. You don't know how much you love a toilet until you are unable to see one anymore.

I am also being tilted and flipped around like a human side of beef so that I do not get bedsores. I do know that every day I lie here my muscles atrophy. I am also getting a shot a day so I don't get blood clots that can kill me. My teeth are cleaned by nurses, and drops are plopped in my eyes to keep them moist.

I could worry about this snake catheter, or I could worry about the feeding tube into my stomach, where I am undoubtedly getting mushed-up filet mignon and banana cream pie, or the diaper or the shots, but they are the least of my problems.

No, I have a much bigger problem in that I am still alive, in a nonmoving body.

I have identified three doctors by voice: Dr. Tarasawa and two doctors I call Dr. Doom and Dr. Hopeless. Dr. Doom and Dr. Hopeless are the two who stand over me and say hopeless and doomy things about me such as, "She should have woken up by now . . . could be permanent brain damage . . . we should let her go . . . talk to the family . . . her life may well not be worth living even if she does wake up . . . the longer she's in a coma, the harder her death will be if they decide to stop treatment . . ."

These are the types of things that set me to screaming inside myself again.

Dr. Tarasawa says, "Let's wait and see if she gets the golden miracle."

I want the golden miracle.

So my vagina snake and my diaper hardly make a blip of discomfort in my mind.

It is smart to prioritize what is really a problem, and what is merely an inconvenience, in life.

A snake catheter, for example, is an inconvenience; listening recently to two doctors say that I should be "allowed to die" is a problem.

An enormous, earth-quaking problem.

CHAPTER 4

My nightmare comes back that night. I see a bald man chasing me, laughing. I am running in place as fast as I can, panting. He catches up with me, puts an arm around my neck, and slits my throat. My blood spurts out until I dissolve and disappear.

To get me to wake up, my dad sings me a loud, booming song about a trucker and a barmaid and how they fell in love and got married and had half a dozen kids. His voice is deep and resonating, flowing through many rooms on this hospital floor, I'm sure.

I loved that song when I was a kid.

He then sings me "Kentucky Woman" by Neil Diamond. He loves Neil Diamond.

Next he sings a song about a mermaid who fell in love with a captain of a ship. The captain kept waving at her and leaving her, no matter how long she followed the ship. One day she jumped up, grabbed him, and drowned him. It was actually a funny song.

It would have been funnier if I could move.

Later I hear a nurse say to someone else, "Who was that man in here? The singer. Is he a professional?"

"He sort of looks like an older rock star . . . maybe he was in a band? He's got that rebel quality to him. That *yum.*"

I laugh. My dad never thinks of himself as handsome. Ever. In fact, it's hard to get him to remember to brush his hair.

My dad inherited his toughness, and his softness, from Grandma Dixie, who had him when she was eighteen. My dad's father promptly ran off to "find freedom." Dixie worked with her father in his auto repair shop in our hometown and became a mechanic. Dixie had people coming in from hundreds of miles away with their special cars for her to fix. They said she was magic with engines. "I swear the woman is a car witch," one man muttered to me when I was helping out at her shop. "She could build an engine with her bare hands, blindfolded, slamming down straight shots."

In our small town we would often have Porsches, Ferraris, and Lamborghinis locked up in my grandma's shop. She'd told me that her favorite cars to work on were 1967 Chevys.

Grandma Dixie was almost attacked one night when she was working on a Ferrari.

Two men came in. Their intent was rape and they probably would have killed her, based upon the fact that they were wanted in California for these particular crimes. She heard them come in. She knew every inch of her garage and she knew where she hid the guns. When they smirked at her, said something about "being alone and having some fun with this slut," and advanced, she pulled one out from under the old blue coffeepot. A .45.

One of them had a gun, but he was slow on the draw and he was up against Dixie Fox.

Both of them were shot through the thigh, blood gushing. She stood over them and told them if they moved she'd shoot 'em again.

"I did not shoot to kill," she proudly told the policemen and the police chief, all friends of hers. She had known one of them, Norman, since kindergarten, and the other, Sherman, as a fellow baker. They enjoyed baking pies together with Sherman's "friend" Santos. "I shot to maim so that for the rest of their lives they will remember me, Dixie Fox."

The police chief and officers nodded respectfully.

"It was an inspired idea," the chief, Howard MacIntosh, said to her.

Other people from town crowded into her shop, alerted by the police officers' cars and swiveling lights. It's a small town. People wanted in on the excitement. Everyone was impressed with my grandma's marksmanship as the two men writhed on the ground. Yes, those two would remember Dixie Fox.

My grandma then swore at the criminals as if every swear word out of her mouth added another year to her life, I'm told.

Chief MacIntosh said, with fervent admiration, "Dixie Fox, I don't know if I have ever fully expressed to you how impressed I am with your cursing. It's like listening to a short story."

"Thank you, Howard. I appreciate that. I'm teaching my son, too."

"I can almost hear a poem," her kindergarten friend, Norman, said to her. "I bet you learned it when you were studying poetry in fourth grade with Mrs. Kerns."

"Mrs. Kerns knew how to make a poem come alive," my grandma Dixie said in admiration. "Alive."

The criminals moaned on the floor.

"I must also say that I am impressed with your shot, Dixie," Chief MacIntosh went on, his hat in his hands. He had only arrived in town a year ago. "I have heard about your reputation as a deer hunter, but this raises your reputation yet another notch. Two men shot, not killed, deliberately saved, so they can suffer for their attempt on your virtue, your dignity, and your life."

"Pride is a sin," Grandma Dixie intoned. "A sin. But defending your life is not, and I am proud that I am still here. I have a responsibility to my son."

The townspeople around them nodded sagely. She was a mother, after all! Not replaceable.

"They deserved it," Sherman the pie maker said. "A man should suffer if he harms a woman."

The criminals semi-screamed in pain and begged to go to the hospital.

"Don't interrupt," the chief told them. "If I can offer up a final compliment, your son, Scott, is a fine young man. I hear that he's an excellent athlete and has perfect manners. You know my cousin, Charlene, is his English teacher at the high school."

"Yes, I do. Tell Charlene hello. I appreciate her attention to the works of Jane Austen and Charlotte Brontë."

"Fine women," the chief intoned. "As you are a fine woman." He blushed.

"Chief, I have to have you over more often. I'm getting more compliments this evening than I've had in years."

The criminals screeched in pain again. A bullet in the leg does that to a man.

"I'm free on Friday night," the police chief said, his tone hopeful.

The pie-making pal grinned. The kindergarten friend's face lit up. Why, these two would be perfect together! And they could say they were here when the love affair began! They could speak at the wedding, give a toast, tell the tale!

Grandma Dixie studied the chief. He was a few years older than her. He was widowed a few years back, she'd heard. Honest. Employed. Strong teeth. "Will you bring dinner? I have my momma's cookbooks, but only because I loved her. They gather dust. I don't cook well."

"I sure will. Thank you, Dixie. I'm already looking forward to it."

"I will make an apple pie."

"I have also heard that your apple pies are the best in the county."

"Oh, that is the truth." Sherman nodded. There was no arguing with Sherman on this.

"I do my best," my grandma Dixie said

modestly. She smiled at the chief. I'm told he smiled right on back.

"I like the smell of your perfume," he said.

"It's pink roses. I'm a mechanic and a lady who enjoys a floral scent. I save all my perfume bottles. They'll be antiques one day."

The criminals begged again for the conversation to be done with so they could get to the hospital before they bled out.

The criminals were taken to jail after their operations. Research was done, phone calls were made. They were serial criminals; they went after women. They never got out of jail. My grandma received eight letters from victims and their family members who praised her for shooting those men and giving them "what they deserved, may they rot in a fiery hell, the devil prodding at them daily with his pitchfork."

"Pride is arrogant and obnoxious," she told me when I was older when I asked about this particular well-known event in our town. She raised a finger in the air. "But I have avenged their victims, and for that I am grateful that our holy Lord gave me a better than average shot."

The chief wanted to marry my grandma, but she declined. She didn't want to get married. Too conservative. Too restrictive.

Plus, the chief had teenagers and she didn't want to upset them. So they kept separate homes and the love affair commenced.

The chief died first, and Grandma organized a funeral for him. It was held in the school gymnasium because so many people wanted to come. My dad gave one of the eulogies, talking about how Howard had become a father to him, the father he never had, and his children, who had moved away, the siblings he had always wanted. The siblings nodded and blew him kisses.

I gave a eulogy, too. Grandpa Howard was my "real" grandpa in every sense. He was strong and courageous and welcoming. He would make up stories for me, off the fly, about magic and witches and goblins and lost cats. I told everyone one of his stories, and I saw people wiping their eyes.

My grandma had met the love of her life. Lucky her.

I thought of Zack. Lucky me.

I picture my grandma shoving me again, her rose perfume wafting by, a red 1967 Chevy right next to her. Crazy stuff goes on in a coma.

That night, late, I sense someone near me. I know it's late because it's quieter in the hospital as a whole and my family and friends are gone. Earlier I heard the nurses insisting that my dad and Zack leave. "We will take care of her, we promise. You both look like you're going to collapse. Go sleep."

I can't see whoever is near, stuck in my unmoving corpse, but I smell him. He smells like beer and sweat and a slight bit of urine.

The nurses and staff here do not smell like beer and sweat and urine.

I hear a grunt. Heavy breathing. I feel him staring down at me.

I am instantly scared. Instinctually scared.

He laughs, dark and rumbling.

Who is it? Why is he here? Is he going to attack me? I've heard of sickos who attack people in hospitals. But how could someone bad be in here? I don't know hospitals well, but I do know that there's security here, especially in the ICU. You have to be buzzed through the double doors by an employee to even get in. You have to speak to someone at the reception area. Or you have to have a tag on you, as an employee of the hospital, that allows you to pass through.

The grunter puts something on the table beside me and giggles softly. At least, I think it's a table. It may not be. It could be some medical apparatus thing, I have no idea. I haven't seen the room. Something breakable, it sounds like a glass, falls and shatters. He swears and grunts again. His breathing is ragged, heavy. I want him out of my room.

I can feel my heart rate rising. My body can't breathe well with him here. I feel like I'm struggling to bring air in. I hear a bell ringing by my bed. He swears again, his voice harsh, bitter, and I can hear his thunky footsteps. He's leaving.

"Who are you?" I hear a nurse ask.

I hear him mumbling.

"I asked you a question. Who are you? Let me see your tag. Hey! That photo does not match your face. I asked you a question. Who are you? Where are you going? Stop running! Cassandra, get security. Now!"

The nurse runs in to check on me. I know her. Her name is Bettina. She's from the south. She checks me, checks my vitals. She always talks to me when she walks in the room, says hello, says her name, tells me what she's doing. Sometimes, when no one else is in the room, I hear her praying for me.

"Everything is okay, Mrs. Shelton. It's me, Bettina." I hear the worry in her voice, the anger. "We're getting everything taken care of . . . I don't know who that was, but we'll

make sure he doesn't come back again. . . ."
She pauses, then she yells, "Oh, my God.
Oh, my God!"

I freeze up. Why is Bettina yelling, "Oh,
my God"? What happened?

"I called security, Bettina, they're after
him." Another nurse. This one is named
Darrell. Deep voice. I like Darrell. When
he's in my room he tells me about his wife,
his three boys.

"What is it, Bettina?" Darrell says. I hear
him move toward her. "Oh, my heck, that is
demented."

I'm scared. I am really scared. What happened? What did they find? Who was that?
What did he do?

"This is sick," Bettina says.

My room is soon filled with people. They
all have the same horrified reaction.

"Don't touch it," Bettina says. "There will
be fingerprints."

"Is that a Barbie doll?"

"Her head is on backward . . ."

"Those are cuts on her body . . ."

"I think the cuts were made by a knife . . ."

"There's red ink for blood . . ."

"Look between her legs. There are stab
marks . . ."

"There are two letters on her stomach. . . .
Oh, this is awful. It's NS."

"It's for the patient! Her name is Natalie Shelton."

What?!

"Get the head of security on the phone," someone says, her voice rigid. "Get Shea Zogg. Tell her to call the police. We need to look for this man. He may still be in the hospital. . . . She'll take a look at the cameras, the tapes. . . . We need a guard outside this door twenty-four seven starting right now!"

"This is a crime scene," someone else says. "Everybody out except for Bettina and Darrell, who will care for Mrs. Shelton. Out, out, out!"

Apparently, the man who was in my room, a supposedly secure room in the ICU, has left me a gift.

It's a Barbie doll. Her head has been screwed on backward. She is naked. Someone has taken a knife to her, and she has cuts all down her body. He has used a red marker for blood. There is a lot of red on her vagina. My initials have been carved into her stomach.

I am more scared than I've been since the first days.

The grunter cut up a Barbie doll and put it in my hospital room.

Who is he? Why would he do that?

The police come. Security comes. I'm counting the voices, and there's at least six of them in my room. One of them is a detective named Macy Zadora. A police officer was assigned to the hit-and-run, mine being one of zillions of hit-and-runs, but when it elevated to a hit-and-run plus an assaulted Barbie, we got a detective.

Detective Zadora has a low, authoritative, competent voice. I'd put her about fifty.

Detective Zadora and Shea Zogg are clearly the ones in charge. Dr. Tarasawa doesn't usually work at night, but he had an emergency operation and is here, too. His job is to check me, which he does. He whispers, "Mrs. Shelton, I am sorry this happened. We're going to protect you better than this. You'll be safe, I promise. Hang in there."

Zack and my dad arrive. I hear them running down the corridor. Zack kisses my cheeks and cups my face. My dad hugs me, panting.

"Everything's okay, baby," Zack says.

"My hummingbird," my dad says, his voice wobbling. "We're here."

"We don't know who was in Mrs. Shelton's room yet," Shea says to Zack and my dad, one on either side of me, holding my limp hands.

"We've determined that he stole a white coat and a doctor's badge to get through the locked double doors here," Shea says. "He was in blue scrubs. Could have gotten those anywhere. He was trying to impersonate a doctor, and he did it well. The cameras showed him confidently entering the hospital and the ICU, although his head was down. Now we know why."

"But how did he know her room number?" my dad asks.

"It would have been easy for him to find out what room she's in, as she was not made anonymous by our security staff when she arrived. People call every day, all day, and they need the room numbers of family and friends who are here. We give it to them unless that person, or the family, or law enforcement, has requested that we not for whatever reason."

"What did he look like?" Zack's voice is quiet now. Steel and control over anger.

"Tall. Big. White," Shea says. "We're getting a photo of him. It'll be brought to the room so you can take a look at it."

Geez. Sounds scary. Sounds like the man from my nightmare.

"He was wearing thick-rimmed glasses,"

Shea says. "We think he was bald under the surgeon's hat, because there was no hair on the lower side of his head or neck. When the alarm sounded, he ran down the hall, headed into the stairwell, ran out a side door through the parking lot, and headed into the woods behind the hospital."

I can feel Zack tightening beside me, his hand gripping mine. I can feel his tension . . . and the fear again, that white-hot fear.

"We thought Natalie," Shea says, "was in a typical hit-and-run. We had no reason to believe she was in danger."

I hear Zack swear softly beside me.

"What do you mean, in danger?" I hear my dad's confusion, his fear. "I don't understand. You called and told us there was an intruder in her room —"

"There's more," Detective Macy Zadora says.

"What do you mean, more?" Zack says.

"I was going in to check on Mrs. Shelton because her heart rate was up," Bettina says. "That's when I ran into him and saw the Barbie."

The what?" my dad and Zack say together loudly. Obviously, they had not been told about the Barbie when the hospital first called about the intruder.

Detective Zadora tells them about the Barbie, which the police already have in an evidence bag.

Zack's hand freezes in mine. I think that man of mine is about ready to explode.

My dad asks, incredulous, "Are the Barbie and the hit-and-run related?"

"They could be," Detective Zadora says.

"You're telling me that someone is after my girl? That the car accident was deliberate? That the son of a gun did it on purpose? That the Barbie . . . Oh, my God . . ." His chair flies back. I know he's standing, because my hand is in the air in his. "Who would do this? You find him, I'll shoot him."

Inside my Coma Coffin, I have to laugh, even though this whole thing is a cauldron of evil. That's my dad. Threatening to kill someone in front of police officers.

"Please don't, Mr. Fox," Detective Zadora says. "If you even attempt it, I will have to arrest you."

Zack is breathing heavily beside me, like a bull ready to charge.

They discuss the incident, the man, and the Barbie as I lie like a scared-to-death corpse. The Barbie thing, combined with the hit-and-run, has frightened me to my bones.

"Mr. Shelton," Detective Zadora says, "I

need to speak with you."

"All right," he says, but it's through gritted teeth.

"Can you step outside?"

"No. I will not be leaving my wife."

"I understand," the detective says. "Who do you think would do this?"

I hear Zack hesitate, for a second. "I don't know."

"Is someone angry at you? At your wife?"

Infinitesimal hesitation again. "No. Not that I know of."

"I understand that you build homes. Your company is Shelton Construction, and your wife is a CPA. She is a co-owner of Knight and Fox Accounting. Do either of you have employees who are angry with you?"

"I don't know of any."

"Have you fired anyone recently? Has Mrs. Shelton?"

"No."

The questions went on about our jobs and any arguments or disputes we'd had with other people, neighbors, any ongoing conflicts . . . then they got personal. How long have we been married? How was the marriage? Was Zack having an affair? Was I? Both of those questions infuriated Zack.

"No, I am not having an affair and neither is my wife."

Are there money problems?

"I'm a homebuilder. Hit a rough spot."

He had? What was wrong with his business?

"Do you owe someone money?"

Pause. *Why the pause?* "No."

"Does your wife?"

"No."

Someone else enters the room and says, "Here are the photos of that guy."

Detective Zadora says thank you. "Who is this man?"

I think the question is directed at Zack, but my dad says, "Never seen him before."

Zack says, his voice gruff, my hand squeezed tight, too tight, "I don't know."

"Are you sure?" Detective Zadora asks.

"Yes."

The questions continue as I listen.

There are three mind-numbing problems, besides the nearly decapitated Barbie, that I detect from my Coma Coffin.

One, Zack didn't react with shock, as my dad did, to learn that the Barbie and the hit-and-run could be tied together, as far as I could tell. He wasn't surprised.

Two, Zack isn't telling the whole truth. I don't even know what he's lying about. All I know is that he is. I can hear it. Feel it. He knows something about the Barbie.

And three, I can tell that the detective knows he isn't telling the truth, too.

Eventually the police and security guards, the nurses and Dr. Tarasawa, and my father all leave. Zack's fist suddenly hits the table by the bed. The same table — at least, I think it's a table — the man put the Barbie doll on before knocking over a glass.

I feel the fury burning off him in waves. Then he cries, one gasp, and I know he's had it. I'm in a coma and my husband is breaking. He's at that point we all get to when we can't take any more. He swears and cries and I want to hug him tight.

My beaten brain is struggling to tell me something. I try to find it, but I can't; it's darting into the shadows, like a dark secret. My brain knows a secret and it wants to tell me, wants to let me know, but it can't because it's damaged, like I am damaged.

I am moved to a new room that morning as soon as it's "set up." I hear Shea Zogg telling my dad and Zack that I will now be directly across from the nurses' station. No one can call the hospital and get my room number. I am officially "anonymous"; I have been flagged. The hospital will not even admit that I am here.

Zack spends the next three nights sleeping in my room, despite a guard who is posted outside my door for the duration of my hospital stay as, Ms. Zogg says, my safety is "clearly at risk."

In the middle of my third night in the new room, Zack takes a phone call that enrages him. He stalks out, the phone to his ear, his voice low and threatening.

What in the world?

A hit-and-run car accident. A coma. A knifed Barbie in my hospital room. A snake up my yaya. A feeding tube in my gut. Someone might be trying to kill me. Not the best time in my life.

I wake up to Justine. I can tell she's drinking beside me. I hear her silver flask clinking on the side of the bed. We all have a silver flask. Chick had them made for us. The inscription? Maverick Girls Moonshine.

"I wish you'd wake up, Nat. You've had a long-enough nap. Like a grizzly bear. Only you're not. Not a grizzly bear. Roar!" She drops the flask, and I hear her grunting as she picks it up. "You're my best friend. You're who I jumped off The Rocks with into the lake. We need to jump off The Rocks again. We'll spread our wings out and fly like ostriches." She hiccups.

"And this Barbie thing. Who the heck would do that to you? Who would kill Barbie? Chick and I are so upset about that." She hiccups again, then she sobs. She's had way too much to drink. When she visits me she always has a drink for herself, and for me. Then another drink for herself. "I'm going to pluck your chin hairs out just like we always promised one another if this very thing happened. Here."

I wish I could move. Right at that second. I'd open my eyes and yell, "Boo!" at Justine. It would freak her out and she'd scream and fall back in her chair and probably land on her skinny tush, the flask and her four-inch heels flying up in the air. I do appreciate her efforts, though. I do not want Zack to see my chin hairs.

"I'm going to brush your hair, too, not only your chinny-chin-chin." I picture her pushing her black hair back from her face as she plucks. "I'll be careful on the shaved spot with the scar. Hang on, hold on, holler around. I have to cry because of your scar."

I wait while she cries. Not that I have a choice. And I have heard that my head scar is long and frightening. It will probably make me cry when I see it.

"I can't believe they have you in this ugly

hospital gown. Why do you have to wear a hospital gown in here? You would hate it. If you had to wear it in your real life, you'd add a scarf and a bunch of beads and a cool belt with silver stars." She burps. "Excuse me. You hippie-hip-hip dresser, you. Hip hip."

It's true. I may be an accountant, but I have a distinct hippie/bohemian/country girl style. When I'm not in a suit for work, I'm in loose cotton blouses with ruffles, shirts with sequins, and colorful jeans. I like long, flowing skirts in pastels and short skirts with tights. I like embroidery, I like shirts that look as if they've been painted, and I like shirts with iconic rock stars on them, like Janis Joplin. I love lace.

I like wearing multiple necklaces that I've made myself and earrings that make statements. I like bright colors and bangle bracelets and boots. Leather boots, but boots in purple or red are my kind of jive, too. I like belts with bling and scarves with silver or gold threads.

Justine, on the other hand, likes modern, classic, and expensive. She is sleek and stylish. As the oldest of eight kids she did not receive many new clothes, or used ones for that matter, and she was expected to keep them as nice as possible so they could be handed down to her sisters.

"The firm is stumbling and bumbling and everybody is sad, so sad, which is why I'm having some sad scotchy scotch tonight," Justine says. "They've all come to see you and they come back to the office and they cry."

I knew they were upset. I lay like a dead sausage while they cried, and it upset me that they were upset.

"You are the brainiac of our business. Brains. Brains. Brains you have." She hiccups. "You are the brains behind the numbers and our most delusional and spooky clients. I miss you so much there. I can't even walk by your office without feeling like I'm going to . . . to . . . roar like a crying grizzly bear."

She sighs, she sobs again, she gurgles down another swallow. The flask hits the bed.

"Okay. I have to talk about something else. So. Jed. Judicious. Juicy. Jacked-up Jed."

Ah yes. Jed. The love of her life. Chick's brother and a prosecuting attorney.

"Can you believe he might be a judge soon? I can."

I can, too. Jed had left our hometown of Lake Joseph for the Ivy League for undergraduate and law school. He missed one — *one* — question on the SAT.

He is tall and lanky, about six two, with short brown hair that's conservatively cut and wears glasses. He has high cheekbones and dark brown eyes. He is quiet, reserved, brilliant. He is single. He works in the city, lives out in the country. He has twenty-five acres, three horses, two dogs, a bunch of sheep, and chickens. He has a city job, but he's a country kid — an eastern Oregon man at heart. Like me. Like Justine. Like Chick.

Justine makes a sobbing-choking sound, and the Maverick Girls Moonshine flask hits the side of my metal bed again.

"I can't tell him about . . . about . . . you know, Natalie."

I know what she's talking about.

"I wouldn't be able to tell him. But I should tell him. If we were together I would have to, right? We shouldn't have secrets. But I have a bad secret. If he knew my secret he would think I was bad. Bad, bad, bad."

No, he wouldn't think that, Justine.

"He would think I had no heart." I hear her pound her chest.

No, he wouldn't think that, either, Justine. That's you thinking that about yourself.

"I would rather not be with him than tell him and have him think I'm a drunken and mean grizzly bear." She burps. "Excuse me."

And there is the problem. Justine is so in love with Jed. I think he loves her, too, but he is, despite his high-profile profession, a tiny bit shy about it. Justine pulls away because she doesn't want to tell him the secret. Their timing has been off for years, too. She's been in a relationship, or a marriage, or he has. Like two triangles hitting each other in the corners and bouncing away.

"Wake up, Natalie. Please, for God's sakes. And for my sake, more importantly, mine. I need a pickle. And peppermint ice cream. You do, too, my friend, but I won't eat them without you. We'll eat them together again, it's our Moonshine and Milky Way Maverick Girls tradition."

It is. Justine, Chick, and I eat peppermint ice cream and pickles together. It started when we were young and a baby was born in a pool in a living room.

"Now, hold on there, Natalie!" she suddenly shouts. "I missed one hair. I'll pluck it off your chinny-chin-chin."

She plucks it straight out.

"I'm going to get a taxi and then I'm going to sling my head over a toilet like a drunken sloth, my friend, a drunken sloth. I have had way too much scotch to drink. Too much scotch. It's the only way I can cope with you like this. Sleep tight, Maverick Girl. I love you."

Sleep tight, Maverick Girl. I love you, Justine. It was good of you to pull my chin hairs out. I knew I could count on you to do that.

And you'll be with Jed one day, you will.

I hope.

"Listen to me, Natalie," Chick says the next day, leaning over me in my hospital bed like a friendly vulture and holding both of my hands in hers. "I can't take this any longer. You have to wake up and help me. I am so stressed out with you in this coma. I mean, what the heck? You're my sanity. You're my best friend.

"The doctors say you might be able to hear, so I'll talk about the kids and all the trouble they're causing me. Ellie, the mad scientist, is growing bacteria under grow lights in the garage. I wouldn't think she was so odd if she was growing pot, but she's not. She says she's going to take pictures of the bacteria at each stage to show it to you to make you feel better. What a strange kid.

"Hudson is mad we won't let him up here.

Sorry, son, no go. I mean, I can hardly look at you without losing my ever-lovin' mind. You know how sensitive he is. He'd have nightmares for weeks. His new business idea is to sell frogs. We now have a frog farm in our backyard. Yes. You heard me. We have a frog farm.

"Joshua told me he wants to come and sing songs from Broadway shows to you. He's gay. I know he is. His love of purple pants and his insistence we buy him a pink bike with a flowered basket were my first clues. He wants a flowered coat.

"Ally made up a dance that she said was named 'Natalie, the Angel,' and she jumped around like a stoned elephant for a while. You know how honkin' big her feet are. Unnaturally big for a girl. She should be a swimmer with those feet. She could get a scholarship.

"Timmy and Tessie snuck out of the house on their trikes. Timmy was wearing his Batman outfit, complete with that black mask you gave him, and Tessie was wearing her warrior woman outfit. She'd attached a toy sword to it. They told me they were going to find Aunt Nat."

Chick fell in love with her husband, Braxton LaSalle, when we were sixteen. He had been waiting for that glorious moment since their third-grade hopscotch days when he let her win so she would like him and stop throwing chalk at him.

Braxton was wide and lumbering, played football, and was super easygoing, which was perfect for her tractor-type personality.

The wedding took place the summer after we graduated, Braxton smiling the whole time, happy as could be. After the vows he threw her over his shoulder and walked down the aisle.

All of the kids were "whoops" kids, as Chick likes to say. As in "Whoops. We're knocked up again." Chick wasn't able to take the pill because her blood pressure shoots sky high, she gets migraines, and she feels nauseated. They relied on condoms, to which Chick had said, "Sometimes we forget. It's easy to get carried away in the passion. I mean, look at Braxton."

I thought of friendly dough-boy Braxton, with a smile that brightened his cute face, a football body getting fat without the football, and a balding head.

"Who could resist him?" Chick had said, shaking her head. "I mean, who? The man is shakin' it."

Well, I could. So could Justine. Easily. But we'd nodded our heads anyhow when she said that. One has to be polite.

"I see what you mean," I'd said.

"He's irresistible," Justine had added.

"I can't get pregnant again, not one more time," Chick said to us after the twins, who showed a penchant for trouble early on. "I told Braxton to go and get neutered. He hemmed and hawed and said something about his manhood and a rooster being made into a chicken, and I cut him off. This barn door is closed, I told him. The tractor is out of gas. The silo is locked. I slept well for a week, and he sighed and went to see the doctor for the ol' chop-chop."

When Braxton and Chick have a fight he gets upset because he's sensitive and "Chick is my chick." He goes out to his workshop and carves an animal until he stops snuffling. He's extremely talented, and after seventeen years of marriage they now have shelves full of carved wooden animals in their rambling, blue Queen Anne home in Lake Joseph.

They own LaSalle Hardware, which is a destination place in eastern Oregon now. Chick saw that home furnishings sold well in other stores and knew there was a place for that in Lake Joseph. She wanted to cater to women shoppers. "We're the ones who make the decisions about décor, right?" She started ordering curtains and outdoor furniture, pillows, plants, pretty tiles, flooring, carpets, lighting, kitchen counter materials, seeds, flowers, indoor and outdoor plants, etc. It was one-stop home shopping. You could come in for pliers and walk out with an outdoor fireplace, a fountain, and a tasty coffee from their in-house coffee shop.

"I need you, Nat. The kids need you. I love you. Please wake up."

I want to reach out and hug Chick when I hear her crying.

Jed, Chick's brother and Justine's secret love, is up next. He holds my hand. "Hey, Natalie. It's Jed. You've always been the sister of my heart. You're one of the only people I trust, you're one of the only people I really like. Please pull out of this. Please fight in there. Please try to wake up. Remember how we swam in the lake that one day in summer and you went out too far and I swam out to get you?"

Oh, yes, I do. Jed literally saved my life. He jumped in, grabbed me, pulled me to shore, then pounded me on the back until I stopped coughing up lake water.

"You thanked me for saving your life, but you've saved mine, Natalie. You and Chick and Justine. You're all my little sisters. Well." He coughs. "You and Chick are. Not so much Justine."

Yep. There is the love.

"You're all family. You know I didn't have a father, but by extension I got your father and a brother in Zack, and all of Justine's gang."

That is true. Chick and Justine and I got one another's families when we became friends. We were all "chosen family," or, as Justine liked to say, "extended crazy family members with normal neuroses," and as Chick liked to say, "family by love, beer, and tractor races."

"If I could save your life now, Natalie," he says, his voice a whisper, filled with tears, "I would. Please, Natalie. Save yourself. We need you. We love you."

I make up another poem:

Natalie is in a coma.
She can't stand her own aroma.

She has a snake up her Vee Jay.
She can't go out to play today.

Her brain is a mess.
Her thoughts are less.

And she's worried she'll never have sex.

In my room are Dr. Doom, Dr. Hopeless, and Dr. Tarasawa. Dr. Doom and Dr. Hopeless are talking about "letting me go" again.

It would probably make this a more exciting story to say there was a "bad doctor" who wanted to do away with me as quickly as possible. We could have a villain! We could have evil, good versus bad, that sort of thing. I could wake up at the very last second and we'd have a dramatic ending!

But it's simply not the case.

The doctors are doing their jobs. Part of me wants to smack Dr. Doom and Dr. Hopeless, who are advocating pulling the plug on me, so to speak, to let me die. The other part thinks, if I don't wake up, if I'm stuck in this lifeless body, I do not want to live. As terrifying as it is to die, it is more terrifying to live like this. No one deserves this.

Dr. Doom and Dr. Hopeless could be my best friends. My saviors. The people who will prevent me from being stuck in a dead body, fed through a tube, for decades. Lost and alone in here, panicked and trapped, loneliness shredding me.

They don't know why I'm not moving, not talking, not dancing in my bed. Well, not the dancing part. I am a medical mystery, and I am a vegetable. An untasty vegetable, unless one is a cannibal and likes to gnaw on humans.

The words *moral* and *ethics* come up as the doctors talk. Is it right to continue this? Should we let her go? What kind of life will she have even if she does wake up?

I don't disagree with them.

I am being kept alive by advanced medical technology.

I want a miracle, but I don't want to be unreasonable or irrational. Hearing myself think like this almost makes me laugh. I am in a coma. And I am talking to myself about being unreasonable and irrational when I am in the most unreasonable and irrational place I can think of to be.

"We need to end this," Dr. Doom says.

No, we don't!

"We need to talk to the family," Dr. Hopeless says.

Oh no. Don't do that.

"Let me do it," Dr. Tarasawa says, "when it's time."

Not yet. It's not time.

Dr. Doom and Dr. Hopeless agree, but they say that time is coming.

Let's wait this out for a while, I think. Please.

Dr. Hopeless mutters, "Better you than me with that husband. He will never agree to letting his wife go."

No, Zack won't. Not now at least. He will give me time to recover, time to fight.

"Oh, hell no, but neither will the father or the girlfriends."

My dad will threaten to shoot you, that I guarantee. Chick will literally roll up her sleeves and start punching, and Justine will threaten legal action and have a scary attorney here in an hour.

"We're in for a fight," Dr. Hopeless says.

"It's not a fight I want." That's Dr. Doom. "I did not become a doctor so I could pull the plugs on a woman who has everything to live for."

"Me either," Dr. Hopeless says. "I want Mrs. Shelton to wake up. But I would not want to live like that, and we all know the longer she's like this, the poorer the eventual outcome."

I feel them staring at me. In the silence I want to yell at Dr. Doom and Dr. Hopeless and Dr. Tarasawa, "Save me. Reach me. Haul me on out so I'm not stuck in this coma. Inject me with something. Electrocute my brain so it will wake up. Shoot me up with any kind of new 'wake me out of my coma' medicine ya got."

"Mrs. Shelton!" Dr. Doom shouts at me.

"Natalie," Dr. Hopeless semi-shouts at me.

"Can you squeeze my hand?" Dr. Tarasawa says. He sighs. "We still need the golden miracle for this one."

I do not respond, rude thing that I am, swimming in hysteria.

I am sure I look like a corpse.

And that's what I am: a nonmoving corpse.

I don't know how long I've been like this, but this is what I know: My time is coming to an end.

CHAPTER 5

I hear Zack's footsteps coming down the hall of the hospital.

I long to see that man's face. Those light green eyes that stare right at me as if I am the last living being on the planet Earth. That square jaw, the lines here and there that speak of a man who spends a lot of time outside, in the sun. That smile. The special smile that is only for me.

I can smell him. Mint. Wind. Man. Lust.

Can you smell lust? I think I am projecting. I want to wrap my arms around his neck and pull him down, preferably naked. I love sex with Zack, and he loves sex, too. We are a match. The last thing I remember is sex in the tub and at halftime. Not a bad memory at all!

He kisses my forehead, wrapping my face in his hands.

"Hey, baby," he says, so quiet. "How are you?"

When I do not answer, he settles on the side of my bed and holds my hand. I feel him staring at my face. I wish I didn't look dead. It's simply not sexy.

He sighs. I know he's crying, because his tears drop on my hand.

"When you're on the Deschutes, you can believe there are billions of stars and galaxies. You used to say it made you feel tiny, Natalie, but you have never been tiny to me. You've always been my whole life. *My whole life.* You are all the stars up in the sky for me."

Wow.

I mean, *wow.* This is my Zack. He has always been affectionate. He tells me he loves me all the time. That I'm beautiful, smart, etc., but to say, "You are all the stars up in the sky for me"? That's poetic.

"I will never fish again if you're not with me, Natalie. I can't. I will look for you on that river and it'll kill me. The Deschutes is one river, but it's for both of us."

His tears fall again on our clasped hands.

"I was so lonely until I met you, baby. That first day, on the Deschutes, with you in your waders and your red hat with the tractor on it, I started falling in love. That river never stops flowing, and I knew my love for you would be the same way. It would never stop. It has never stopped, baby."

Oh. My. Goodness. This is my tough husband! The stud who looks like a gangster.

"We're going to fish the Deschutes again, honey. We will."

He takes a deep breath and holds my hand to his cheek. More tears pour down. "You're going to be safe, Natalie. Everything's taken care of. It's all fixed. I swear nothing like this is going to happen to you again."

I have no idea what he's talking about. What is taken care of? What is *fixed*?

"I am so sorry, honey. I will make this up to you for the rest of my life." His voice lowers to a broken whisper. "I promise you, Natalie. I promise."

What does he mean he will "make this up" to me?

I feel a memory drift in and out of my brain, quick as a lick. I try to catch it, but I can't. It has something to do with me slamming my hands on our granite countertop and yelling at him. Why would I be yelling at Zack?

My dad tells me about the animals he owns, because he believes that I can hear him. Funny that I can. He talks about his four dogs, his two cats, the goat, the cow, the pig, the chickens.

"Bruce Baby and Tarantula Terrier ran off together, Hummingbird. Had to get in the pickup and track them down. Soon as they saw me they waggled their furry little tails and their tongues, I swear they laughed at me, and they ran off down the road. They love when I chase them. Gina the Goat escaped again. I found her in town, right outside the tavern. Richy Morganson, that college professor who likes rocks, called me. He'd wrapped a rope around her neck. I think Richy gave her some beer. He knows she likes beer. . . .

"Can you open your eyes for me, Hummingbird?"

He cries when I don't open my eyes. He sings me Neil Diamond's "Cracklin' Rosie" and Gloria Estefan's "Rhythm Is Gonna Get You." He sings "Hello, Dolly!" too. He has seen all the Broadway shows online.

He starts to read me *Jane Eyre.* "She is my best book friend," he tells me. "Let's begin. Chapter one."

I want to hug my dad. I want to reassure him. I am so worried about him. I have never, ever seen — well, *heard* — him this upset, and there have been many things in

94

his life that he had every right to be upset about.

I can do nothing to help him.

I lie here, in a hospital bed, not moving, bones and skin, as his big ol' tears slide down my hand and my arm as he holds the palm of my hand to his face.

"Please, Hummingbird," he rasps out. "Wake up. Wake up. Wake up." I can hear him sobbing. "Please wake up."

I hear two nurses talking by my bedside when my dad finally goes home to our house to sleep.

"Have you seen her father?" one asks.

"Oh, yes," the other one says. "Gorgeous."

"It's like staring at a mountain man. He's got that earthiness to him."

"Sexy earthiness."

This is not surprising. Women love my dad. To me, he's Dad. To them, he's Sexy Man.

That night I woke up inside my coma after that same, insane nightmare.

The bald, psychopathic, cackling man was after me again. He was chasing me. He had a knife in one hand and the stabbed Barbie in the other, her twisted head flopping. I looked back, and his arms were pumping, trying to catch me. When he had me cornered, he tilted his head to the side. In my panic, I followed his gaze.

And there, running to stand between me and the man who wanted to kill me, was Zack.

He raised the knife over the scar on Zack's ribs, then brought it down. The Barbie screamed, then her head fell off. Then he turned to me and I was cut in half.

Who was the bald man in my nightmares?

A bald man dropped off the bloodied Barbie. Was he also the driver of the van that hit me? Was he the Barbie basher?

I wish I could remember that morning. All of it. Every second. No matter how bad it was.

Rosie Thornton, Jed and Chick's mother, comes to visit. Tall, rangy, lots of makeup, red curling hair, she is a force. Rosie owns an incredibly popular nail salon in Lake Joseph. She has a small, three-bedroom home painted light green with white shutters and a white porch one street off of our Main Street. Every year she plants a magnificent garden out back. It looks like the garden of Eve, but there are no tempting, evil apples or manipulative snakes.

She is unclear who fathered Jed or who

fathered Chick. When Jed asked her she told him, with Chick, Justine, and I sitting at her kitchen table eating chocolate chip cookies. Chick and Justine and I were about six years old, which made Jed thirteen.

"Honey, Jed darling, I had a few wild years, so help me, Jesus. Amidst those wild years, I got knocked up with you. I know, babycakes, that you want to know who your father is. I would like to know who your father is, too. There are only three possibilities." She held up three fingers. "Probably not four possibilities."

She flicked one more finger up, then flicked it back down. "I cannot swear to you, on my grandma's old Bible, Jed, but it's *probably* not four. First possibility. I was following a rodeo circuit around. Man named Hank, met him right here in eastern Oregon, fancy that! He was from Idaho. He had thick brown hair, exactly like yours."

She stopped, cleared her throat, patted her red hair. She was famous for it! That's why she was called Rosie!

"It could have been Hank. He won first place all the time. He could ride those broncos like he could ride . . ." She did not finish that sentence, cleared her throat again. "Hank was going on to another rodeo, and my girlfriends and I decided that we wanted to see California. We wanted to swim in that darn blue ocean, stretches out to heaven, does it not? Saint Peter and Saint Paul, I met a man out there I could not resist. A man named Mott. Dear me. When our Lord and Savior made Adonis, he made Mott. He was so tall, exactly like you. I could not resist him in his swimsuit out in those California waves. In fact, pumpkin, you could have been created right in the Pacific Ocean!"

She stopped, cleared her throat yet again, patted her red hair. Such a blessing she had red hair and her momma had decided to name her Rosie!

"Now the third possibility, sweet child, was a man from Mexico. I met him in Las Vegas. My girlfriends and I wanted to see the lights. He had that luscious Mexican accent, dark eyes. . . ." She squinted her eyes at Jed's. "Exactly like your dark eyes, dearie. Anyhow, this Mexican man, Rafaga, he said his mother was American. I could not step away from him. Even Saint Catherine knows that Spanish is the sexiest language on the Earth, and when Rafaga murmured in my ears, I felt a miracle between my legs —"

"And the fourth possibility?" Jed asked. He has always been quick.

"I don't think so, darling. I was already

upchucking all my breakfast food by the time I met a dull man, a short man, a blond man, named Jerry from Hollywood. You don't look a thing like him."

As for Chick's father? "Only two possibilities," Rosie said. "Probably. Mother Mary, help me. One was a firefighter, one was a police officer. I follow the law. That month I followed two members of it."

"We're never going to know are we, Mom?" Chick asked, reaching for another chocolate chip cookie. Justine and I followed suit.

"No, we aren't, honeycomb. But in the name of the father, the son, and the Holy Spirit, she being a woman, that spirit, I have you and Jed, and I love you both to pieces. And I have the daughters of my own sweet heart, Justine and Natalie! Want me to paint your nails, girls? Jed, do you want another sandwich? I made my special homemade dressing for you."

Jed wanted the special sandwich, and Chick, Justine, and I wanted our nails done. We had built a fort that day and our nails were a ragged mess.

Rosie gives me a special "flower" manicure. The doctors and nurses all come in to admire it. I apparently have ten delicate, intricately drawn flowers on my nails. Rose. Delphinium. Daisy. Daffodil. Tulip. Blazing Star. Dahlia. Sunflower. Crocus. Magnolia.

"I pray to the good Lord for you every day, Natalie," Rosie says, a sob catching in her throat. "You are the daughter of my own sweet heart. I will pray for you right now, in fact, the Lord's Prayer. Are you ready, dear? Our father who is an artist in heaven. Howell be thy name. His kingdom comes, his kingdom goes. On Earth you are to find your own heaven. Give us our daily bread and wine. Not too much wine. And lead us not in to temptation and deliver us from evil men. Amen." She sighs. "Mary, mother of Jesus, get your feminist, woman-empowered self into this hospital and fix my Natalie, I'm tellin' you. If you need help, grab Mother Teresa or grab a woman saint. Heck, grab all of the women saints, Mary, mother of Jesus, but do not grab my great-aunt Milly, as she was clearly the devil's assistant here on Earth. Women unite! Thank you, Jesus."

When I get upset, which isn't more than once or twice, maybe three times a day, I cry inside. It's this wracking, hopeless, shattered crying. Grief and fear and loneliness and devastation all mixed up.

What do I miss the most with the obvious exception of simply being able to walk on my own and see and talk and be a normal human without a catheter and a diaper?

I miss weekend mornings lying in bed with Zack. I miss talking to my dad and watching him work in his shop, turning plain metal into something special. I miss Justine and Chick and Jed. I miss coffee. I miss driving out to eastern Oregon in my truck with the wind blowing my hair around, the city gone, the fields rolling, the sunsets soft. I miss fishing on the Deschutes with Zack.

I miss sunny days and pouring rain. I miss the snow in the mountains. I miss the picnic spot Zack and I have with a view of the coast range, and I miss laughing.

I miss the beach.

I miss love and hugs and deep conversations with the people I adore.

I miss dancing with Zack in the kitchen and talking about the dream home we'll build. *One day.*

Love is free. True friendship is free. Laughter and singing and fishing are free.

I miss all of it. You don't know how desperately you will miss the ordinary, simple joys of life until they are gone altogether.

Today I can see pricks of light inside my head. When I was first laid flat like a pale zombie, I couldn't see any flashes. Zippo. Now those lights are about the size of half a penny. They go off and on. Is my brain healing? Is it fighting its last fight before it shuts down? Is it anything at all?

Maybe, maybe not.

But I choose to see the lights as hope, and I need all the hope I can get.

When one is stuck in a coma, you'll take anything. I mean, it's Desperation City in here. It's "throw me a life ring a hundred yards out in stormy seas and I'll try to swim over and grab it." It's Save My Butt time. If it doesn't look like I'll ever get out of this Coma Coffin in a few months, I'll want to go to the clouds in the sky, but for now, I'll take the lights.

I'll take hope. I'll take the golden miracle.

People come and see me in my Coma Coffin . . . girlfriends from here in Portland, Zack's best friends from college, his pickup basketball buddies, our neighbors. But most of my visitors are from Lake Joseph.

Justine's parents, Chief Knight and Annabelle, come and see me along with six of her seven siblings. One of the brothers doesn't come to see me because he is living with monks in Tibet, or something like that.

I am close to all of them. I've known the twins since they were three and everyone else since they were babies. I rocked them to sleep, put the girls' hair in braids, and held a few of them right after they were born in a pool in their living room, their mother cursing out their father in her white lacy birthing dress for causing her pain *again.* That's bonding that can't be erased.

The chief and Annabelle call me "the daughter of their heart" and tell me they love me. The chief jokes, through tears, that he's looking forward to arresting me again when I'm "up and at 'em."

Some of the people who visit are elderly, one is in a wheelchair, another walks with a cane. A bunch of them are healthy and strong, but still. They have jobs and families and here they are, hours away from Lake Joseph.

They cry, they pray over me, they hold my hand and tell me to wake up.

The minister, Henry Tanner, puts his hand on my forehead and begs for divine intervention. "Jesus, we've got a problem down here," he starts, "and we need your help —"

Gelda Star pushes him away and says I need a dose of "magical healing." Everyone says she's a modern day witch. We do wonder. She puts her hands on my shoulders and chants, "Mighty stars, awaken thee," then claps three times. "Moonshine, sunshine, you are the key." Three more claps. She sprays lavender into my room. Then vanilla. "I implore the powers that be, heal my friend Natalie!"

Gretchen Cho, the pharmacist, reads poems to me in Chinese about healing, then tapes them to the walls. Dr. Angela Steinem talks to me about her latest geological research, and Dr. Jamie Oh talks to me about her latest medical paper titled "Medical Care in Rural America."

They hug me, hug my dad and Zack, and they hug each other.

My dad leads them in song, his voice echoing down the hallways like the Deschutes River, thundering and full. The lyrics might not have exactly matched my situation, but he has them all singing "I Will Survive" by Gloria Gaynor and "Stayin' Alive" by the Bee Gees and "9 to 5" by Dolly Parton. My dad has taken the time to write down the lyrics and make copies so, as he says, "she can hear all of us clearly. Now sing loud, friends."

Oh, they sing loud. Loud enough to wake the dead.

It feels like a family reunion sometimes in my hospital room.

I grew up in eastern Oregon in a small home on a hill with a full ceiling of sparkling stars and views of towering blue mountains and a lake in the distance. I loved boating, hunting, bonfires, canoeing, tractor driving competitions, hiking, and country living.

I left because Lake Joseph was too small. I was the girl whose mother had run off, the "motherless child, poor dear. You know how Jocelyn was. . . ." Cluck, cluck, cluck. My mother left me and that made me feel "not good enough."

I was the girl who had a reputation, along with Chick and Justine, of being wild. Our pranks were famous, as were our arrests by Justine's father, the police chief. My dad and I struggled for years financially in that town when disaster struck.

I wanted to leave that part of my life behind. I wanted to live in the city, I wanted an education, and my own business. I wanted to put my mother behind me.

But maybe I have gotten too far from myself living in the city, working all the time, concrete and traffic and noise. Maybe I need to return to people I've known all my life, who obviously thought I was "good enough," because, look, here they are, in my hospital room, hours away from home.

Some friends here in Portland who I thought would come and see me have not. Where are they? Is it even a friendship if you don't show up when someone's life is in pieces? I don't think it is.

Lake Joseph is a town where your business is their business. Even if you move to the big city, your business is still their business, and right now my business is that I'm in a coma so they come and make it their business.

It's very touching, their company. Inside, I tear up.

And this is what I realize: I have missed them. All of them.

My poems continue, as I cannot hold numbers in my head.

Natalie has a skeleton face.
There is nothing nice about this place.

She lies in bed attached to tubes.
Look out, world, she has no boobs.

Her face is pale, like a ghost.
Her breathing is bad, worse than most.

She's alive in here, to all she screams.
But what she does is have bad dreams.

Oh, heck, no. It's my mother again. She comes a couple of times a week. I call it Mother Monster Time.

She cries a little. Sniffles. She's upset. I feel my heart soften a tiny bit. She is my mother. It would be horrifying to see your daughter in a coma.

"Hello?" She leans in close to me, her voice loud, as if she's trying to wake my brain up with volume. "Hello in there, Natalie? Can you hear me? It's your mother."

Oh, I could hear her. Like a foghorn.

"It's. Your. Mother."

She sighs.

"This is very upsetting for me. Very. Upsetting."

She sighs again. A groan sigh.

"Dell is here, Natalie. Say hello, Dell."

Dell, my mother's fifth husband, says hello. He's older than my mother by ten years. Rich rancher. Working the land his great-grandfather worked. He doesn't deserve my mother, as in, he's a good man and doesn't deserve the hell I'm sure she puts him through and will put him through in the future when she strips him of his money in the divorce.

He says he's so sorry this happened, they'll help me. I can come and live with them, he'll do anything for me —

"That's enough, Dell. Why don't you go to the cafeteria and get me some white wine. Zinfandel. Do you mind?"

No, he didn't mind. I doubt he'll find wine in the cafeteria. I wish they would give me white wine through my IV to get me through this visit, though.

I hear the door shut. My mother dismisses people when they irritate her.

"Dell has a lot of money, Natalie, so I had to overlook a few things. Like his weight and his face."

Dell does not have a bad face. Poor Dell.

"And I had to overlook his obnoxious son, who doesn't like me at all. I mean, his son told his father, in front of me, not to marry me. The nerve of that boy."

Dell's son is not a boy. Dell's son, Ryan, is nearing forty. I met him. He has four kids, one adopted from Africa, and a cool wife, and he runs the ranch with his father. Ryan and Mattie have a home on the property. I can totally understand why Ryan didn't want my mother to marry his father. He knew how this was all going to go down. The marriage would end in divorce. My mother would ask for a lot of money; she might well ask for part of the family's land.

Or, way worse for Ryan, he would work the ranch and my mother would be married to his father when his father died and she would decide to stay in that beautiful home Dell built and he, Ryan, would have to deal with my mother and share with her information about the ranch, the financial statements, employee stuff, etc., as an heir to his father's estate.

I get ya, Ryan. I get ya.

"Ryan said I was only after Dell's money," my mother huffs. "I told him a thing or two. But I do think that Dell is going to buy me a Mercedes. I put a picture of a Mercedes on his desk. I'm hoping he'll get the hint.

"I am mad about something, though, Natalie, and I didn't talk to you about it before because you will rarely return my calls and because I did not need you telling me that I didn't need to get married again. But, here it is: Dell made me sign a prenup!"

She is outraged. Inside, I'm laughing. If laughter could make you wake up from a coma, I'd be awake.

Dell is a smart man then, and not blinded by love or my mother's manipulations. My mother is a multimarried tarantula on the lookout for easy money and he knew he had to protect his great-grandfather's land for his son.

"I get nothing if Dell dies except for one hundred thousand dollars. Nothing! But Dell said if I didn't sign it that we wouldn't get married. He said a whole bunch of lame drivel about this being his great-grandfather's land. It was to go to his son and his son's kids. He said that his son, Ryan, that cow herder, that tractor-driving potato, was instructed in the will to buy me a home *off the ranch* after he died. Honestly, I was so furious I broke up with Dell!"

I laugh again. Breaking up was simply a manipulation tactic.

"I only got back together with him two weeks later because of my love for him," she declares, so irritated. "My love for him. Dell. My husband."

Translation: Dell had called her bluff and she'd crawled back to him.

She sigh-groans again. I hear her sniffle. "Whatever, Natalie. I'm just talking here. The doctors told me to talk to you, that you might be able to hear. But the truth is, I'm filling up the space between us." She sniffles again. "We had space between us before this happened but now the space is so . . . so wide. So awful. Natalie . . ." Her voice cracks. "I have missed you. Every day."

I'm touched. I can't help it. She is my mother.

I feel her lean in and touch my hair. "But, my God, Natalie. Your hair looks awful. I'll tell the nurses to wash it. We're not white trash."

She's appalling, she is.

She makes a small gaspy noise. "And this is hard on your father, too. You know he's still in love with me. Never gotten over my leaving him."

She is dense and clueless.

"I do love you, Natalie, and I want you to wake up. I have yelled at all the doctors to make you wake up. They damn well better do it, too, or I will sue them from here to next Tuesday and they'll end up living in tin trailers or sheds or their rat-trap cars and they'll drive banged-up trucks that don't work and they'll have to raise chickens to eat and they'll freeze in winter and pick berries for money when I'm done with them."

Wow.

I hear the doctors talking later about my parents. "The father is reasonable, rational. The mother . . ."

"Definitely a personality disorder there . . ."

Yes. I would agree.

■ ■ ■ ■

I try to choke back my fear that the man who dropped off the twisted Barbie will come back. I have enough to be worried about right now. But who is after me? And how deranged do you have to be to carve someone's initials into Barbie's too-skinny stomach?

That's the worst part, right there.

I wonder if I will ever go home. I wonder if I will ever return to the home Zack bought and remodeled in the hills above Portland before I married him. I want to hold my grandma's ornate perfume bottles, my china teacups with the pink flowers, and make sure my plants haven't died. I want to see the hummingbirds my dad made me out of metal hanging in a corner of our family room and all my embroidered pillows and my books and the oak tree in our backyard.

I don't miss the neighborhood — it was too ritzy for me — and I do not want to see one neighbor, Melinda, who hit on Zack, ever again, but I miss the love in our home between Zack and me. I miss our bed, soft and warm and piled with comforters and pillows.

Suddenly I have a vision of lying naked on top of Zack and smiling at him. I smiled at the memory and then . . . what? That couldn't be. Zack wasn't smiling back and he said something . . . upsetting. Was it upsetting? What was it?

I can feel myself being pulled into sleep inside my coma. Either that or I'm being pulled into death. I never know which one until I wake up again.

It's rather unnerving.

"Mr. Shelton, Mr. Fox, I know this is very painful for you." It's Dr. Tarasawa talking.

" 'Painful' is not the word for it, doctor." That's my dad talking. Dr. Tarasawa, Dr. Hopeless, and Dr. Doom tell my husband and my dad what I have heard before when they are not in the room: They don't know why I haven't woken up. There may be irreversible damage. They can't guarantee I'll wake up. Something is wrong and they don't know what it is.

"We need to talk to you about Mrs. Shelton's prognosis now and what her life will be like in the future if she wakes up."

"You are not to let her die." That implacable statement comes from my husband, Mr. Shelton. No one specifically said, 'Let her die,' but we all hear it spoken implicitly.

"Sir, can we talk to you again about the scans. . . ."

"I said no."

My sexy husband again!

"Mr. Shelton —"

"I know my wife. She's a fighter. She will not give up and die. She'll battle this out."

Sexy husband has a lot of confidence in me. I wish I had it in myself.

"Hell no," my dad says. "Double hell no. You are not to pull any plugs anywhere at any time or do anything with your fancy-dancy medicine that will bring on the death of my daughter. I will get some donkey-kicking, bone-crunching attorney in here to sue your asses. If I have to stand next to my daughter with my .45 every hour of every day to protect her life, I will. Do ya get what I'm sayin'?"

I hear the silence from Dr. Tarasawa, Dr. Doom, and Dr. Hopeless. I know what the silence says: The husband and father are in denial about this situation. We see it all the time. No one wants someone they love to die. They gently throw out some more medical information, and Zack says, his voice ringing with fury, "That's enough. Get out."

The doctors get out.

So, my life has been spared. At least for a little while.

■ ■ ■ ■

My poems continue:

Natalie cannot walk.
She cannot talk.

She cannot sing.
She cannot ding.

Natalie cannot dance.
She cannot prance.

She cannot fart.
She cannot throw darts.

The fart part of the poem ended up being untrue. I did fart that night. I heard it. Inside, I laughed at my own fart. This is how pathetic my life is. I waited to see if I farted again. When it didn't happen, I found that sad.

Sad, about my farts.

■ ■ ■ ■

PART II

■ ■ ■ ■

CHAPTER 6

I opened my eyes early the next morning.

No one was in my hospital room. I studied the place I had lived in during my Coma Coffin. How long exactly, I didn't know. The days and nights ran together, confusing and blending, a spiral of fear and loneliness.

It was a typical hospital room with light mellow-yellow walls. I studied the machines I was hooked up to.

I didn't want to see a mirror, so it was fortunate that they didn't have one near me. I was afraid that if I caught a glimpse at my undoubtedly pasty and deathly face I might fall back into a coma.

But then I laughed. It was raspy, hoarse. It sounded like a frog's screech. But I heard it. I could hear and I could see. I was not blind, as I'd feared.

I was awake. I was no longer in my Coma Coffin.

I breathed in, then out, then in again. I

blinked. I moved my mouth open and shut. I tried to wiggle my nose, and I did it. I told my fingers to move, and they did. I told my toes to move, and they did, too; then I gave the same orders to my legs and arms.

I could move and wiggle.

I paused on that for one immensely grateful moment.

I was alive. *I am alive.* And I could move.

I laughed again. It sounded more croaky than before. But, to me, I sounded like a symphony.

The door opened, and Zack walked in. I was stunned. He was a muscled, tight, tall man. Not fat, but the man was built like an oak tree. He had lost a ton of weight, his clothes hanging on him. His face was grayish, his light green eyes sporting bluish circles underneath them, his mouth drawn. He looked as if he'd aged ten years.

I was a semi-corpse/coma-stricken woman who had come back to life, and my husband had beat Father Time by aging rapidly. We were quite a pair.

He came and sat down heavily beside my bed in a chair and took my hand. "Hello, baby," he said, his voice rife with hopelessness and grief. I watched him check the machines, check me, then those green exhausted eyes caught mine.

I blinked at him through a film of hot tears. I tried to smile. My lips worked a tiny bit, but they became stuck on my dry teeth. I tried to talk, but I couldn't. There was something wrong with my throat; it felt stricken and clogged with tears.

Zack was completely, utterly shocked. His face froze, and I blinked again. I tried to smile more, a real smile, less like an odd reptile and more like a woman, like a wife.

"Natalie?" His voice broke, and a desperate, raw sound emanated from him. "Baby."

His face crumbled in relief, a ragged moan left his lips, and the tears rolled out. I wanted to say, "Zack, I love you. Thank you for being with me every day, during every horrible moment. You are my life, you are my heart," but there was no way I could talk that much.

"Oh, my God. Natalie, honey." And he cried, my tough husband cried as he leaned in and gathered me to him. He was so warm. I leaned my cheek against his and tried to lift my arms to hug him. Surprisingly, as my brain had clearly been on a long nap, they worked somewhat. My hands rested on his back.

"I can't believe this. Finally. I have missed you so much, Natalie. So much."

I swallowed hard but was determined to

say what I needed to say, "I love you, Zack." My voice sounded rough, the words coming out slow, as if they were stuck in my brain and only one word would be let out at a time with space between.

He pulled back, and I saw all of his love in those shimmering green eyes. He did not bother to hide a broken sob, and rocked me close to him. I laughed, that frog screech, which made me laugh again.

What happened in this hospital was Zack's love for me in action. He was there for me during the fun times before the accident, and he was there for me when things were relentlessly, hopelessly awful. He fought for me, for my life, for us.

"I love you, too, Natalie."

Zack and I kissed and hugged and laughed.

Our laughter became the second symphony of the day.

My dad rushed in. Zack had called him straight away. I heard his feet thundering down the corridor. I heard him bellowing in that deep voice, "Clear the way, clear the way, my hummingbird's awake!" The door flew open and banged against the wall.

He saw me in bed, eyes open, propped up on pillows, and I smiled at him, my heart growing in my chest, like the Grinch's. He stood and stared, panting, for long seconds, the tears streaming down his face. He, too, had aged, but I say that with all my love. What a toll this had taken on all of us.

"Hi, Dad," I said, my voice gravelly, each syllable slowly uttered, and then I started to cry. I love my big dad. He was wearing his University of Oregon green pajama bottoms with the yellow ducks that I gave him years ago and a white T-shirt. Yes, my dad was so excited that his daughter was awake and talking, he rushed to the hospital in his pajamas.

He leaned against the wall for support, and Zack moved toward him, as did Dr. Doom and Dr. Hopeless, both smiling, their faces lit up because I was awake and they were so relieved. We'd already said hello to each other.

"Is this real?" my dad asked, in disbelief, in hope. "Is this real? Is she awake, or am I dead?"

"Yes, Scott," Zack said, grinning. "It's real. Natalie opened her eyes. She can even talk."

"Dad," I said again. I put my hand toward him.

My dad's face scrunched up, and he put his hands on his knees and leaned over, breathing heavily. The doctors leaned over with him, concerned, until he flipped himself back up, as if a spring had sprung. Both doctors stumbled off as my dad shouted, his face wet with a hundred tears, "My hummingbird, my cupcake, my heart! I knew you would wake up! *I knew it.* You're my fighting cowgirl!" He hobbled into the room, sobbing loudly. He hugged me close, as if he would never let go, and rocked me back and forth.

I was his beloved daughter, his life, and he had lived with the knowledge that I might never wake up, that I would die, that he would bury me in our family graveyard in Lake Joseph and he would be alone. That insidious fear, that grief, had wrapped around him tight. *He thought his daughter might die.* But now here I was, alive, smiling, holding him.

I hugged him and he said to me, his voice high-pitched and cracking, a complete departure from his low rumble, "I love you, Hummingbird. My life is not worth living without you. I am so dang glad you're back."

"I love you, too, Dad." I choked out the words, my brain not working quickly enough. "Love you, too."

"It's you and me and Zack, Natalie. We're going to the Deschutes!"

I put my forehead to his.

We were all crying in that room, Zack and me and my dad in his duck pajamas. Even the doctors became all sniffly.

I was grateful to be here. Endlessly, eternally grateful.

Later, I turned to the doctors, to Dr. Doom and Dr. Hopeless and Dr. Tarasawa, and the nurses, particularly Bettina and Darrell. I knew them. I knew how much they did for me, the time they spent with me, in consultation with each other and with doctors outside of this hospital. I knew the care they gave me.

Dr. Doom and Dr. Hopeless had advocated for my father and husband to let me go, but I can't fault them. That doesn't seem right, as I am now alive, but I heard the results of my scans. I heard the percentages of people who woke up after being in a coma this long and the damage that was done. I heard all the scary, depressing stuff they said about what my miserable life would be like if I lived. They were doing what they thought was right, given the length of my coma, which was, apparently, almost four weeks long.

I had been granted the golden miracle.

"Thank you," I said. "Thank you."

They beamed at me. "You're welcome and welcome back."

My mother arrived. She was wearing a green dress and heels and emeralds. Today was — wait for it — Emeralds Day. She liked her designer clothing and her jewels to match. She marched right in, elbowed a doctor and a nurse aside, and gave me a long hug. She kissed my cheek. She was crying. I patted her back.

"I'm so glad you're okay, Natalie."

"Me too, Mom." I remembered her visits, her tears, and her surprising, sometimes touching, honesty.

She held my face, cried some more, her voice wobbly. "How are you?"

"Better than I was."

She smiled, her eyes crinkling in the corners, her makeup perfection.

We chatted, she told me she loved me, missed me, she cried; this was very hard on her, it was stressful, it was tiring for her. She had come to see me many times, often all by herself from eastern Oregon. That was true, she had.

Finally, "We'll get your hair highlighted soon," she whispered in my ear. "It won't always look this bad. Don't worry."

The depths of my mother's worry and anguish were apparent to me that day. When she arrived, that impeccably dressed woman had on one beige four-inch heel and one black.

For my mother, that said everything.

Justine came flying in. I mean, flying. She burst through the door, saw me sitting up with my eyes open like a normal human being and not a closed-eyed corpse, let out a "whoop," jumped in the air, did a hippie dance, and hugged me. Her tears flew all over my face. "I knew it. I knew you'd pull your dimpled butt through this. I knew you'd come out of it. You wouldn't leave me."

"Hi, Justine." My voice was rough as if I hadn't spoken in, well, weeks. My words were slow, stiff, but at least I had words.

"Natalie. This is the best day of my life."

I knew she meant it, so we both cried.

"Look at you, gorgeous. How are you, Nat?"

"Still alive." I smiled, then put my arms in the air in victory. "Alive and kickin'."

"Yes, indeed, you are!"

Justine put her forehead on mine. "I missed you so much. I had to go to my shrink and get more antianxiety medications. I've had panic attacks. I had to stick my head out the window at work every day so I could breathe. I thought I was having multiple heart attacks, so I kept going to the ER. All because of you. Natalie, I love you. Don't do this again." Then she sobbed as if her heart was going to burst.

Chick and Braxton came. Chick stumbled in and said, leaning against the doorway, pale as a sheet, "Hi, friend." Her voice was soft for once, her chin trembling. Chick is a tough woman. She can run a business, six kids, and a husband all at the same time. She hunts. She fishes. She drives tractors. She won all sorts of awards in 4-H.

She stood and inhaled, ragged, her face flushed and smeared with her tears, Braxton supporting her as if she couldn't stand. Then she teetered over to my bed, Braxton's arm clamped around her as she was not steady.

I was propped up in bed, and I held my arms out.

She leaned in on a choked sob and didn't say another word, which is so not like her. Braxton held her.

She wouldn't let me go for a long, long time, her red hair a veil around us.

It was like being hugged by a bear. A warm and friendly best friend bear who cried into your neck and moaned.

In second grade Justine, Chick, and I named ourselves the Moonshine and Milky Way Maverick Girls. We had heard the term *moonshine* in a song that my dad sang to us about making tequila: "In the back woods, next to those 'coons, we know how to make the moonshine right, because we got the bad boy might. . . ."

We loved Milky Ways. And we heard that *maverick* meant that you were a rebel. We learned what *rebel* meant and that appealed to us. We could be rebels . . . after we did our math and studied spelling and went to music class to sing "The Star-Spangled Banner."

Justine invited us over to play the day we named ourselves, but when we saw Mrs. Knight in the bathtub with the blue whales in the living room, her husband beside her, along with the midwife, Mrs. Zeebach, we knew the next Knight baby was coming.

Mrs. Knight was wearing her pretty, white lace "birthing dress." This baby would be number five. She had her knees up and her head back, her black hair wound into a ball. She was panting, gritting her teeth, and moaning.

Chief Knight was pale, his hand in his wife's, soaked with water. He saw us that day and put us to work watching the younger kids.

I gasped as Mrs. Knight screamed and said a bad word that started with an F. She never said bad words!

Chick wet her pants and said, "That scream scared me. I wet my pants."

Mrs. Knight let out a moan from the bottom of her toes. It scared the devil out of me. She said something like, "Damn you, getting me pregnant again. You just sit there, holding my hand, making me go through this pain. You take five minutes making the kid and I spend hours in agony. . . ."

"Honey," Chief Knight said, his voice pained. "I told you we should go to the hospital and get the drugs. Every time I tell you that, but you insist on it being natural. We can go right now —"

"Shut up! Nothing's natural about this pain!" She screamed again. "Get it out! Get it out right now!"

We hurriedly took the kids outside, me carrying Melody. The Knights had five acres and we headed to the end of it, by the fence, under the oak tree. We could hear Mrs. Knight's screams now and then, but the crows overhead cawed and the stream behind us gurgled, so that blunted it out.

Later, when we couldn't hear any more screaming, we went back in the house.

I have no idea how it happened, but I ended up holding the new baby, Savannah, while Mrs. Knight was fixed up by the midwife on the floor of the living room. Chief Knight lay down for a while, being so tired from the birth and all.

I think that's why Savannah and I have always been close. I was the first person she saw. But she's always been nervous, too. She writes scary scripts for Hollywood thrillers, and whenever she sells another one she has a nervous breakdown because she doesn't think she's "good enough." You would think the opposite would happen, but it doesn't.

I think it's because she was positioned wrong and Mrs. Knight was screaming a lot during that birth, so it started things off badly for Savannah in the nerves department.

We ate pickles and peppermint ice cream for a snack, Savannah in my arms. We decided then and there that this would always be the Moonshine and Milky Way Maverick Girls' favorite meal.

■ ■ ■ ■

Zack did not leave my side for two days. He hardly slept. He kept smiling, though. He hugged me, held my hand.

"It really bothers me that I can't remember anything about the morning of my accident, Zack." My words were still so slow, plodding. I was thinking much faster than I could talk. "The last thing I remember is going to bed with you and then waking up here. But I feel like there's something important I've missed. Something I don't know, I don't get . . . I can't explain it. Nothing happened that morning that was odd? Or different? Or bad? Are you sure?"

"I think that the accident, and losing that morning, is traumatic, Natalie. You can't remember one of the most important days, the worst day of your life. You want to know what happened, I get it."

"But is there anything else besides what you've already told me? It was a normal morning, right? Whenever I try to remember that morning, I get this lost, scared feeling."

I saw a vein throb in his temple. Not a reassuring sign.

"We got up. We got ready for work. We had breakfast. You had too much coffee, as usual. You went to work and you were hit by a van."

There was more. My mind had a memory about that day and it kept slipping in and out and I couldn't grab it. "There was nothing different at all?"

"It was a normal morning, honey." That vein throbbed again.

No, it wasn't a normal morning. He kissed my cheek, and I momentarily became distracted. Zack was so handsome. Cowboy handsome. How did I ever get such a handsome husband? A little voice in my head said, *A handsome, lying husband.*

"Thanks for listening to your crazy wife." He wasn't going to tell me anything, but he was hiding something, I knew it. Maybe we'd had a fight? But what was the fight about?

"You are not crazy, Natalie." He cupped my face with his hands and kissed me. "You are the most sane person I've ever met."

"I insanely love you."

"And I insanely love you, too."

I knew Zack loved me. I did not doubt it for a second.

But behind that love there was something else going on here.

I tried to put my squished and battered brain on it.

What was it?
What was it?

A memory pushed itself out after he left. I was in the bathroom of our home. I was staring at myself in the mirror. I looked shocked. The door was locked and Zack kicked it open.

Did that really happen? Zack would never break down a door. Why on earth would he do that?

I did not tell anyone that I was awake, in and out, when I was in my coma. I would tell the doctors, later, because they needed to know for other patients who are locked inside their skeletons in the future.

Maybe it's because I simply can't process it myself. Maybe it's because I don't want my family and friends to know. It would simply cause them more pain to know that I was trapped inside a nonmoving body. I mean, how would you feel if a person you loved awoke from a coma and told you about the horrors of believing that they would live forever like a vegetable or how claustrophobic and panicked they constantly felt, how utterly trapped? How would it feel to hear about their crushing fear of death, and yet their even stronger crushing fear of living like that forever?

Not pleasant.

I might tell them later. Not now. They have had more than enough to deal with and don't need anything else.

But I had another reason for not telling anyone. It's not a warmhearted reason. Something is up with Zack, and I need to figure out what that is. If I tell him I heard him apologizing to me when I was in my coma, taking calls, calling someone a son of a bitch, if I tell him I felt his fury, if I tell him I know that he knows who sent that cut-up Barbie, I won't be able to. He's hiding something, and I want to know what it is.

My gut level is that he'll lie to me. Again.

If I could remember the morning of the accident, it would shed some light, but I can't, so I'll wait this out. It is devastating to know that Zack has a secret.

I am having health issues, some more difficult than others. You don't simply boing out of a coma and everything is fine and dandy. My brain had time to do some healing when I was in my Coma Coffin, but it didn't become a gray mass of intellect and understanding all of a sudden. I'm having memory issues, light to moderate headaches, dizziness, speaking issues, thinking issues. Lights bother me sometimes, and though I am trying to add numbers in my head for practice, they're still spinning.

I have lost nearly all my strength, my balance is off, and I basically feel confused, lost, and off-kilter. I continue to think way better in my head than I speak. My words sound almost slurred, as if they're surrounded by mud. Sometimes I'm hit with an exhaustion so deep, so fast, it's like some naughty sleep fairy cast a spell over me.

"I walk like a drunk, old penguin," I told Zack.

He laughed. Those light green eyes are so warm for me, sweet, indulging, loving. "I will take a drunk, old penguin for the rest of my life, baby."

"Good to know, Zack. I have always liked penguins. We can incorporate my penguinness into our love life. Here, hold my flipper." I held out my hand and he kissed it. "Thanks. You're my apple pie."

"Always."

Recovering was going to take a long time. I tried not to let that discouraging realization drown me.

The nurses washed my hair and brushed my curls back into a ponytail after my sponge baths, and I appreciated it, but on day four of being gratefully alive I rasped out that I wanted to take a shower. Dr. Tarasawa said I could. Two female nurses, one of whom was in special shower-wearing clothes, got in with me.

They untied my hospital gown, and I made the mistake of looking at my face, at my body, in the bathroom mirror.

"Oh no . . ." I cried out, harsh and shocked. "Oh no . . ."

"Honey," my nurse, Latisha, said, "Now, don't you worry." She flipped her long black braids under her shower cap. "You've had a bad time of it. After your shower we'll get your hair brushed and dried. I'll go and find you some lipstick and mascara and you'll feel much better —"

"I'm a hundred years old." My words came out slow, as usual, wobbly. My blond hair was a wreck. It looked as if I'd had a swarm of bees land on my curls. Part of my head had been shaved for the operation, and that part wasn't much more than stubble, my jagged scar visible.

My face was pale, with a yellowish hue. My lips were invisible, my eyes were dull, and my *boobs*. Oh, my gosh. No perk. No lush. No oomph. I was too thin. I had always liked my curves, feeling healthy and solid, and this mess of skinny bones was not me.

"I look like a skeleton. A creepy skeleton." I started to cry. "I look like I'm dead."

"No, no . . . you look fine," they reassured me. "Here, take a shower, we'll get your hair done . . . we'll fatten you up, don't you worry, dear . . . high-caloric drinks . . . dessert after dinner . . . we'll get you some cake. Do you like cake?"

My shoulders sagged, I saw it. My face sagged. My mouth sagged. "I am Cruella de Vil. I am dead clay."

The nurses gently turned me away and I took a shower. I cried, all my tears mixing with the hot water sluicing down. Latisha washed my hair. I used the washcloth. I had trouble standing, so they propped me up on the shower bench, then they dried me off and put a fresh hospital gown on me. I climbed back into bed. The whole thing exhausted me.

Luckily, Latisha knew what to do. She put a dollop of cream rinse and a squirt of mousse in her hand and worked it in. I didn't ask where she came up with both. She brushed my hair out and then gave me lotion to put on my scraggly face and my prunelike hands. I caked it on. I could feel it soaking in. I put more on.

"You're a beautiful lady." She wagged a finger at me. "Don't you forget it." She dug into her pocket and pulled out a lipstick. "I'm not supposed to do this, but . . ." She handed me the lipstick and I put it on.

She dried my hair with a hair dryer, then handed me a mirror.

"I don't think I can look at myself again. It's like looking at a human Godzilla. All I need is pointy teeth and no one could tell the difference." I felt self-pitying tears rise in my eyes again.

"Trust me, Natalie." Her voice was soft, her braids falling over her shoulder. "Trust me."

I trusted her.

She held up the mirror. "You see?"

I saw.

Now that was better. The bees were gone out of my hair, at least. She had arranged my curls so that part of the shaved spot was covered. I did not look like a living skeleton so much. The lipstick gave my mouth a smile. The lotion somehow magically softened the lines.

"Thank you."

She gave me a hug. "Mrs. Shelton, things will get better."

"They already have," I told her. "I'm not stuck in a Coma Coffin and I got to hang out with you in the shower."

She laughed.

When Zack came I was sitting up in bed, my curls all fluffed up. I had even brushed my own teeth and put on more lipstick.

He stopped when he saw me and stared.

Zack has proven a hundred times over during this disaster that he is loyal to me, to us. When I could not move, he held my hand. When I could not see, I heard him crying beside me. When I could not talk, he talked to me anyhow. When all seemed hopeless, he retained hope. When the doctors told him my prognosis was poor and they should let me go, he refused to give in.

He may have a secret, but he is all man and I love him.

"Natalie," he said, tears rushing into his eyes.

I pulled back the sheet. "I think I'm ready for a quickie. Take your clothes off."

We laughed until we cried.

I later lied and told Zack I overheard the nurses talking about the Barbie incident and I knew why there was a guard at my door. I told him that it scared me to think of someone out to get me, especially since I did not have my gun under my hospital pillow.

He studied his clasped hands, and I saw different emotions cross his face. Fury. Fear. And . . . was it guilt? Yes. It was guilt.

"I'm sorry that happened, Natalie."

"Who did it?"

"I don't know."

"Do you think it was someone who used to work for you?"

"I don't know. Maybe."

But he did. *He knew.*

"Zack?"

"What?"

"Do you know?" I watched him closely.

"I don't."

"Do you think the person who hit me with the van is the same person who sent the Barbie?"

"I don't know, baby. Maybe."

"What did you tell the police?"

I could tell he was angry at the questions, agitated. Too bad. I was angry, too — at whomever had rammed me with his van and nearly killed me and who had left me the Barbie present.

"I told them I didn't know who did it, Natalie."

He lied. Again.

■ ■ ■ ■

I met Zack over six years ago on the Deschutes River where I was fly-fishing and camping for the weekend.

Zack was walking up the river in his green waders, dark glasses, and a fishing hat. We were dressed almost alike, except that I had a pink shirt on underneath my waders — why not be feminine while fishing? — and I was wearing my red baseball hat with a tractor on it. We were out in the middle of nowhere and he was a tall man and I was a woman alone, but my grandma had taught me how to fight and I had my fishing knife on me, so I wasn't worried. Plus, no one had ever bothered me on the river. Fly-fishermen and women are a peaceful sort.

The sky was blue with a few lazy, white clouds casting shadows here and there on the smoothness of the water.

"Hello," he called out, and waved. With his glasses, I couldn't see much, but he had a nice smile, lines on either side of his mouth.

"Hi. How's the fishing?"

"Two. You?"

"None yet. I live in hope." The goal was always to catch and release steelhead. But being out on the river, at dusk, under the open sky, the sunset hovering like a painting, was what I wanted most. Being alone on the Deschutes is my Zen. Nature, for me, takes away some of the lurking loneliness I feel. I think when my mother left, a place in my soul gaped wide open and loneliness crept in. The Deschutes fills the hole for a while.

Plus, my continual crush of work as an accountant, the endless hours during tax season, had my nerves stressed out.

"Perfect day on the river," I called out.

"Yes, it is. Much better than working." He walked toward me, smiling.

"Where are you from?" I made another cast.

"Portland. You?"

"Same. I come out here for peace and quiet." He was taller than I thought, both of us standing in the river as it veered around us. A hawk flew overhead, and a fish jumped down river.

"That's why I'm here, too. I think I could live out here." He smiled. Sexy smile.

"I could, too. A house overlooking the river would be awesome. You could fish out your back deck." The sunrises would be incredible. "I could watch the water, the eagles, the bighorn sheep, the deer, the otters, and the osprey all day."

"I think you have described my perfect life."

I laughed. "Mine too."

"I'm Zack Shelton."

"Natalie Deschutes Fox. Named after this very river by my dad. I was in a backpack as a baby as he fished right here."

"Smart man."

We shook hands, then fished together in quiet, the golden sun dropping down behind the cliffs, the pinks and yellows and purples beginning their show, spreading across the horizon, turning the day off and the night on.

"Are you leaving tonight?" he asked.

"I'm staying until Sunday."

"Me too. I have a camper down the road. I used to tent camp, but a few years ago I decided I was tired of getting soaked in the rain and having my tent fall on top of me when it was windy. Plus, twice I found rattlesnakes in my tent down here, and that was it." He chuckled. He had a deep and low chuckle. "Now I feel a little spoiled, but when I have a real bed to sleep in and when it rains and I'm not wringing out a sleeping bag, I have to say I like it."

"I'm still tenting. I have not had rattle-snakes in my tent, but I've had to shoot a few around it. I have to admit that a camper is sounding more and more appealing." I cast again. *Come on, fish, bite.* "A camper with heat for the cold nights. And a refrigerator, maybe a hot tub, a chef who would come along . . ."

"Sounds like you need to sit down and design the perfect camper."

"Do you think I could get it to pop out to about five hundred square feet? Then I could have a library in there, too, for my books."

"I'd need an extra room for my fly-tying stuff."

"I tie flies, too. A long table for fly tying would fit well."

"And a big-screen TV for football games."

"A big-screen TV while you're out on the river? Seriously? Surely you can live without football for a few days?"

He thought about that. "What about a little big-screen TV?"

"No TV. But." I pointed a finger skyward. "There should be a nice deck on top of the camper for a telescope to watch the stars."

"And locate the planets . . . Yep. I'm on board."

We fished through dusk together. We talked as if we'd known each other forever. We both liked fishing and hiking and had fished and hiked in many of the same places. We both liked books. I liked cross-words; he hadn't tried them but vowed to do so. He liked architecture. He built houses, he told me. I liked numbers. I told him I was an accountant. We were surprised to find we'd both gone to the University of Oregon at the same time. He majored in construction engineering. He was also a licensed electrician.

He invited me for dinner at his camper. It was new, the type you haul. Full bed, table, a couch area. He made steaks over the campfire. He had brought salad with toma-toes and French bread.

"This is absolutely gourmet," I said. "I brought hamburgers for both nights to cook over a campfire."

"I love hamburgers on the river."

I pulled out the apple pie I baked. "Would you like some? My grandma Dixie's recipe."

Oh, he did.

We talked and laughed, a lantern on, the stars above mini-lanterns. I told him I had grown up in eastern Oregon fishing and hunting. I asked him where he grew up and he paused, then said South Carolina.

"But no southern accent."

He smiled. "No accent. I think I've been in Alaska and Oregon too long. Tell me more about living with all those animals and your dad."

The campfire crackled as I told him about our horses, the lambs, the goats, the dogs, the cat. The pet pig, Martha. We laughed and talked late into the night, the moon a bright white ball.

I told him about my work as an accountant. I told him I had always loved numbers because numbers never lied.

"Have you been lied to?"

"My mother had a few issues with lying." More than a few.

"I'm sorry about that."

"I don't know why I'm telling you this."

"It's the Deschutes."

"Maybe."

"Makes us all honest. Plus, it's easier to talk to a stranger sometimes."

"Yes. It is."

"I'm sorry about your mom."

"It's okay. I love that British saying, 'Into every life a little rain shall fall.' It reminds me not to whine. What about you? Your childhood?"

"My childhood was . . ." His face darkened and he stared through the night at the river with his cool green eyes. "It was perfect and then it was a disaster. My parents were killed" — he stopped for a second, studied the dark river — "in a car accident when I was seventeen."

"I'm so sorry. What a terrible tragedy."

"It was. They were loving, kind people. My father built homes, my mother was a nurse."

"What were their names?"

Again, he didn't answer for long seconds, which was odd, but I thought maybe he was overcome with grief. "Randall and Cora Shelton."

"What did you do after they died? Who did you live with?"

"I lived in our home. I was seventeen, and about this size. No one thought I needed protection. Our neighbors came by, our friends. I finished my senior year, played sports. I took out all my anger on the playing fields, on the basketball court. I tried to hide my grief and be strong. I worked in construction after high school for about a year, then I became a fisherman in Alaska for five years before coming down to Oregon and working in construction while I was in college. I've had my own construction company for nine years."

I understood why he changed the subject away from his late parents, I could tell it was still painful for him. He talked about fishing in Alaska, the storms, the catches, working with the men. His fishing stories were both fascinating and frightening.

We sat and stared at the stars and had more apple pie, then he said, "Natalie, how about if you stay here in the camper tonight and I'll sleep in your tent?"

"No, but thank you." Very nice. Very sweet.

"I would feel better if you did. Then I won't have to worry about you alone in a tent. It's deserted out here, as you know."

"I'm fine. I've been camping on the Deschutes by myself for a long time."

"But you could have the camper, lock the door, be off the ground."

"It's a tempting offer, but I like my tent."

I could tell he was worried.

"Don't worry. I'm fine. I have a gun. A rattlesnake gun, I call it. But it'll work."

He walked me back to my tent and checked for rattlesnakes. I am quite capable of checking for rattlesnakes, but I liked him doing it. My tent was near the river, by a slope. He could not have brought his camper down here, even if I'd invited him to protect this damsel in distress.

"Here's my phone number. Can you put it in your phone? Call me tonight if you need anything."

As he walked away through the shadows, the Deschutes rolling by, I thought, *Zack*

Shelton, I think I need you. His green eyes were with me all night long. They smiled at me.

Zack's cell phone rang later that night. He looked at the caller ID. I saw it. It said Number Blocked. He gritted his teeth.

"Everything okay?"

"Yes. It's work." He looked as if he wanted to kill someone.

"Is there a problem at work?"

"Nothing to worry about. I'm handling it. Hang on. I have to take this one."

"Alrighty." He gave me a kiss and left.

My brain is slow, but I know this: When I was in my coma Zack lied, and he's lying now.

I was glad there was always a guard outside my door. Nothing like knowing someone is out to get you to set your nerves on fire.

Chapter 7

Detective Zadora and the head of security, Shea Zogg, came and saw me. I was in my room with only Dr. Doom, who had been informed of the meeting and was there to make sure that I was not medically or emotionally compromised, I supposed. They were kind, and gentle, but they asked me a lot of direct questions, including whether I knew about the Barbie that had been nearly decapitated by my bedside, and I said yes.

They showed me a photo. I assumed it was the same one they showed Zack. It was a picture of a heavy white guy, in scrubs, in a doctor's coat, with glasses, head tilted to the side, away from the camera.

"Who is this person, Mrs. Shelton?" Detective Zadora asked me.

"I don't know. I've been having nightmares, and he looks a little like the man in my nightmares, but I've never seen him before."

You can't remember the morning of the accident, right? You can't remember what the driver of the van looked like? Did I know anyone who was angry at me? What about at work? An employee or ex-employee? A client? I couldn't think of anyone. Was there a neighbor dispute? An ex-boyfriend from years ago? Anyone holding a grudge against me? What was my relationship with Zack like? Had he ever hit me? Was he abusive in any way? Did he swear at me? Did I feel threatened by him?

At first I was ticked at that line of questions, but I understood. It's almost always the husband or the boyfriend who goes after the woman. I told them the truth: I loved Zack, we had a great marriage, he was an awesome husband.

Was I having an affair? I could be honest with them, they wouldn't tell Zack. Was I being stalked? Was Zack having an affair?

No. We were not.

Did I know anyone who was angry at Zack? Who might want revenge on him and would hurt me to do it? Had he had any arguments with anyone? Tell us about his business, Natalie: Does he owe anyone a lot of money? Do you? Have there been bankruptcies? Failed business dealings? It went on and on.

I didn't even know what to do. Should I tell them about the phone calls that I'd overheard when I was in the coma? Zack swearing at someone over the phone? I wanted to protect Zack. I loved him. I knew he would never hurt me. But anything I said could be twisted around with the police. They would see something there that shouldn't be there. They would hold it against Zack. Zack might find out and believe that I thought he'd hurt me through someone else. "No," I said. "I don't know of anyone who is angry with him. No one."

They were both incredibly bright, competent, experienced women. I don't know if they believed me when I answered that question.

"I was awake during much of my coma."

Dr. Tarasawa, Dr. Doom, and Dr. Hopeless stared at me, stunned.

I told them what I remembered, and the things they had said about me, and to me, when they thought I couldn't hear. I was specific in my examples, naming them when I quoted what they said.

Dr. Tarasawa was leaning against a wall when I was done, looking quite pale. Dr. Doom had collapsed into a chair. Dr. Hopeless had pushed my legs aside — I don't even think he realized he did it — and was sitting on my bed, holding his head.

They would do with the information what they needed to do to help patients in the future.

"We'll want to talk to you more about this," Dr. Tarasawa said. "Later."

"I know. But don't tell my family. I can't stand the thought of them knowing. It'll hurt them."

They nodded.

It was time to move on.

I was going to the Traumatic Brain Injuries Unit for rehabilitation. I called it the Brain Bang Unit. I was told that I would not be there for long — four to six weeks. I did not want to go. I wanted to go home, but I knew I needed to go. I am a banged-up mess, that is for sure.

Inside the Brain Bang Unit were people like me who had had head injuries/comas/medical issues in the head. They were caused by accidents of all kinds, sports, crime, falls, etc. We were all at different levels. My brain is not moving right, my speech is slow, I have memory issues, I walk like a drunk penguin, but I am telling you, this could have been a heck of a lot worse. I had only to look around to see that I was lucky.

Some people were in wheelchairs and appeared to be barely functioning. Others were functioning and walking around but clearly confused. Some were being helped as they moved around. Some talked well, others didn't.

There were two gyms for therapy with overhead lifts to help people move from wheelchairs to an exercise mat/bed, and a larger gym with a treadmill and some weights. There was a harness system to pull people up and down so they could stand and exercise. There were treatment areas and offices for doctors. There was a practice kitchen and a practice laundry area so people could relearn how to cook and do laundry, an activities room with art supplies and games and a piano, an inside gardening room with lots of plants and an outdoor garden, a lounge for visitors, and separate bedrooms for the patients.

Zack and I went to my bedroom, which was the expected hospital room with a bed with rails around it. This time I had a window, because I wasn't in the ICU. The shower had bars in it to hold on to and a chair I could sit on while showering. My toilet had two handles that came down on either side. The toilet was a tad depressing because I knew I would need those bars because my balance is poor.

At the Brain Bang Unit I would meet with doctors and therapists, including speech, physical, recreational, cognitive, and occupational therapists. I would have a social worker and a neuropsychologist. I would have a full schedule, every day. I would get better. I had to.

I would try to remember the morning of my accident, because it was right there, at the tip of my mind, and I hated that I didn't know my own reality.

I would have my guard with me for a couple of days, but he would leave after that. I was officially "anonymous," in the hospital, a member of the security team told me. That meant that if someone called looking for me, they would be told I wasn't there. There had been no other incidences. I would be fine. Right. Yes. Probably. I took a deep breath and told myself to be brave and buck up.

At least I was in normal clothes. Zack had brought me clothes. I was in my favorite jeans, a loose white shirt with blue embroidery around the V neckline, and two necklaces I'd made myself — one made with five crystals, and another with red beads and a peace sign. Plus he brought me a handful of my gold bangle bracelets. Definite improvement over my hospital gown.

Zack hugged and kissed me. I tried not to cling pathetically to him before he left.

"I'm going to miss you." My speech was still muffled, my mouth and brain not co-ordinating well with each other, but he knew what I was saying.

"I'm going to miss you, too." Those green eyes filled. Zack and I, before my accident, we were not big criers. Now we cry all the time. "Don't be a baby," I said to him, and he laughed. It was hard to see him go.

A friendly doctor came in and chatted with me for a few minutes after Zack left, then another doctor, and a nurse. The nurse later led me to the activities room and showed me around. When she left I sat down on a sofa. I tried to be invisible while I figured things out.

A soldier came up to chat with me. I knew he was a soldier because he was wearing army pants and a green ARMY T-shirt and his dog tags. He was also walking ramrod straight. I would have thought he would be at the VA, but he was here.

The soldier had a head injury from a grenade in Afghanistan, he told me. "Boom!

Blew me off my feet. Boom!" He was wearing a helmet, like several other people here. "You can call me Soldier." I wobbled as I stood up to shake his hand. He politely helped me stand, then he saluted. He spoke slowly. "We're a broken bunch of sons of cats and knitters."

I laughed. That was probably inappropriate, but sometimes, lately, I seem to display the wrong emotions. "Broken but fighting. I need a cat."

He fist-bumped me, the scar on his forehead about four inches long, disappearing into the helmet. "I have not yet begun to fight. Have you seen any purple yarn? I'm learning to knit. The therapists say it will help me hold on to my memories."

"I haven't seen it. But if I do, I'll give it to you. I'm hoping to get my brain back together." I could hear my words. Still slurry, slow. Like Soldier's.

We sat down on the couch because, he said, "You can't stand straight. You're like a Gumby doll. All rubbery and twisty."

We both leaned back.

"I'm fighting for my buddies who did not come home."

"I'm sorry, Soldier." We sat in that deep grief for a while and then I started sobbing for all of his buddies who did not come home. My emotions are unhinged, uncontrollable. What I feel, I show. "That's so sad," I wailed. "That's so sad."

Soldier put an arm around me and said, "It's okay. They're up in heaven now with the angels. They're hangin'. Maybe they're learning to knit, like me."

A woman walked over, about forty-five, thick reddish hair, chocolate brown eyes, carrying something made from clay. She said, "Is this crying session?" She sat on the couch with us and burst into a round of tears. The clay project was a pink frog, and she stroked it. I put my arm around her.

"I like crying session," she said when she stopped. She smiled. "I need to cry or everything that happened to me gets stuck in my heart like the Amazon rain forest and I can't breathe through the rain."

"Have you seen my purple yarn, Frog Lady?"

"Yes, Soldier. I did. It's under the chair in the lounge, by the window."

"Thanks."

"What are you knitting?" I asked.

"Purple socks for my grandma."

"I want my grandma!" Frog Lady said, and then she suddenly picked up a book and threw it across the room. It hit a bookcase. Books fell out of the bookcase.

"Dang it! I am so mad in here today. So mad!"

"Nice arm," I said.

Her face crumpled when she heard the bang, then she perked up. "Thanks! I use it to catch frogs." Then she said, "Are you two brother and sister?"

We said no.

"Huh." She stared at us suspiciously as if we might be lying. "You don't look alike because one is white and one is brown, but you both talk the same. Slow. Like a slow jumping frog."

I'm a wreck, my emotions whacked out.

My anger flares out of control, and all of a sudden I'm in a rage. It can happen when I can't put a puzzle together or answer memory questions my therapists ask me or line cards up or work with flash cards or calculate easy arithmetic.

Numbers, my old friends, keep flipping and flopping in my head. I can't read, the letters jump around. I can't write, same thing. A couple days ago a therapist gave me a pen, and it was as if he'd handed me a wet poodle. Or a river. Or thunder. I could hardly hold the pen. I could hardly write; the words were a mish and a mash, some letters flipped, others missing. For some reason, every time I wrote the letter "m" I wrote it three times. Same with the letter "k."

I was asked to draw a clock with the numbers on it, and I could only do half.

Ten cards were placed upside down in front of me. I picked up one and was supposed to try to remember where it was when I found its pair. I couldn't do it. I tried for almost an hour.

A therapist gave me a list of five items to remember, then we talked about something else and I was supposed to recite the five items about ten minutes later. I could remember only one.

My anger comes in waves, as does a searing frustration and acute anxiety.

My walk is off, and I keep swaying to the left. I keep crashing into walls and tables.

The other day I ran into a little table in the activities room and ended up throwing it. I was in the activities room because there were beads for making necklaces and I wanted to make a necklace. The smashed table made a lot of noise.

Two people's heads whipped up, and both started crying. One man jumped up and yelled, "Where the hell is he, I'll kill him!" and an older woman called out, a worried note in her voice, "Is my husband here again? The police are supposed to be called if he comes."

I was so ashamed. I picked up the table then told everyone, "I'm so sorry. I don't know why I did that. I won't throw tables again."

Soldier said, "I threw that table before, too. It may be the table."

"It probably is a bad table," Frog Lady said to me, nodding. "They have those here. I saw your pink yarn, Soldier. It's in the pantry in the kitchen."

I think much better than I speak, and I think much better than what my actions show. It's like a whole bunch of fuses have blown between thinking and doing. I am one person in my head and a whole different, confused, damaged, emotional person on the outside.

I used to be someone who could get things done, and now I have to use handle bars to sit on a toilet. I can't follow simple recipes in the practice kitchen.

My vision blurs sometimes. I still have headaches, although they are way better.

I am not who I was. Everything is hard. Sometimes I feel as if I'm not getting any better, that I will never be the same, never be me again, and that is so frustrating and depressing. Who am I if I am not me?

On the other hand, I laugh in here, too. Soldier made a funny pink hat out of paper flowers and wore it all day on top of his helmet to make everyone happy.

Other times I laugh, but the humor is unintentional. We're not really laughing at the person, more at the situation that we are all in. One patient, a fifty-year-old woman named Ebony, forgets to get dressed and comes out of her room in only her bra and underwear sometimes. Yesterday she peered down at herself and said, "What the hell? Where are my boobs?"

Another patient, a sixty-year-old college professor named Eddie who was in a rickshaw accident when he was exploring India, gets stuck on the same two sentences sometimes. They are, "I was hit by a rickshaw in India. Do you like saffron?" One time he kept saying them again and again, and Soldier put his arm around him and said, "We got it, man."

And Eddie said, "Thank you, Soldier." And he stopped saying the sentences for about twenty-four hours.

We Brain Bang Unit people have activities together, but when you have a bunch of people with head injuries in one room, who knows how it's going to go. We had to quit playing pool one day because two people had a serious duel with the pool sticks. One had been an Olympic fencer, so it didn't go well for the other guy.

Many people wear helmets because their heads cannot take another hit. One helmeted man told me, "They cut my head out with a saw and now they have it in a toolbox in a freezer. When do you think I'm going to get my head back?"

On the flip side, I tell myself that I'll get better and I need to put aside my type A freakoid personality, born from odd neuroses and old hurts, and be patient.

Every day, though, I am grateful to be alive. To be walking, even though I sway; to be talking, even though it sounds like I'm talking slowly through sludge; to be using a toilet and not a catheter.

Yes, I am grateful.

I kept having the same bone-tingling nightmare. The bald man with the black pig eyes, laughing and leering at me, kept creeping through my sleep. I ran from him when I saw him. I ran as fast as I could, but often my body would freeze or he would simply catch up to me. Last night he bit me then wrapped a rope around my neck and hung me from the ceiling. He pushed me back and forth, and I swayed like a pendulum while he ate a Barbie with his fang teeth and spat out her head.

Who is he? Why do I keep seeing him?

Was he the driver of the van that hit me?

I told Zack about my nightmares. "I don't have them every night, but enough. This man is coming after me. He's bald. Heavy. Small eyes. He's smiling, but the smile is sick."

His face had gone entirely still. "What does he do in your nightmares?"

"He chases me down and kills me. Every time." I swear his face lost color. "Are you okay? Are you sick, Zack?"

He didn't speak for long seconds.

"Zack?"

"I'm sorry you're having nightmares, honey."

"It's okay. When I get to shack up with you again, I'm sure they'll go away."

"I'm sure they will, too."

I smiled; he did not smile back. He looked away, his mind somewhere else entirely.

In the activities room there are art supplies, books, games, cards, and jewelry-making supplies: chains, charms, beads, wires for wrapping rocks and faux stones, and even pliers. Nothing fancy, but there's a lot of it.

Apparently one of the people on the board makes jewelry and donates what she doesn't want to this unit because her nephew used to be here.

I started making necklaces. I would give them to Zack, my dad, and Justine and Chick and their families.

I continued working on the necklaces even when I heard a patient tell one of the nurses that she was going out to garden and was going to "break a rake in half over my own bad damn head."

Another patient, who hardly ever spoke, his head lolling about, announced, "I have not had sex in ten years." A third patient hobbled by with a walker. He stopped for a second and said to me, "Tennessee." I said hello.

I first started making necklaces with Chick and Justine when we were fourteen.

The three of us often felt poor. Chick's mother was a single mother with two kids and a nail salon. Justine's father was the police chief, but there were eight kids and there was no way their mother could work an outside job.

My dad was a roofer. He did well, and he worked from March, as soon as the sun was out, through October, even November if the weather held. He traveled to different towns to construct roofs, on homes and businesses, as our small town couldn't support all the work he needed. He was also a metalsmith. He liked making birdbaths and fountains, which he sold at a local nursery, and he liked making wind chimes. Everything he made was exquisite, so well done, and it flew off the shelves, but he fit in that work around his roofing business.

But my dad had expenses. My mother paid no child support at all. I asked him later why he didn't take my mother to court, and he said it was because he thought she might take him to court to get full custody of me. The chance was small, as I rarely saw her, but my mother was beautiful and she knew how to cry on command. A sappy judge might believe her sob story and give her custody. My dad did not trust the judicial system enough to risk it.

So he was supporting me, with no help, and trying to save for my college education, but he was also supporting my beloved grandma Dixie who had been diagnosed with emphysema. Her smoking a pack and a half a day had caught up to her, and he had had to move her into a medical care home. It was a top-of-the-line care home. She was willing to go; she knew with her labored breathing she needed help. We moved her in and brought all of her precious antique perfume bottles.

I later learned that she paid for the care at first, but when she ran out of money after selling her auto shop, my dad paid for it. She had handed over her finances to my dad because she was so sick, so she never knew what the care home cost or what my dad did for her. "It would kill her pride," my dad told me. "She was an independent woman. If she knew I was paying for her, she would have driven her truck off a cliff to save me the money."

Chick, Justine, and I were in that stage where we wanted money for clothes, ice cream, and music. Even then I was into a hippie/bohemian/country girl chic style. I was pairing cowgirl boots and embroidered shirts, skirts and brightly colored tights, silver studded belts and vintage coats and dresses. And I started making myself simple necklaces out of beads to go with my outfits.

We started making necklaces out of pretty rocks we found near the lake. We polished them up with a solution that Chick's mother found for us and wrapped them in wire using pliers. We sometimes added beads — bought at Goodwill, garage sales, and at a big-box store that my dad took us to.

My dad bought us, in bulk, leather string

we could use instead of chains, and we were in business. We sold our Rockin' It Necklaces, as we'd dubbed them, at a farmers' market each Saturday in town. The rock necklaces sold surprisingly well, especially during summer and fall when tourists came in for camping and hiking and playing on the lake.

My dad made us a booth out of plywood for the farmers' market. With wood from our property he made us stands to display the jewelry. We had wooden tables, and over them we threw white, lacy antique tablecloths that Chick found in the attic of her home. The cloths were stained here and there, but we covered the stains with our displays. My dad made us a sign with the name of our company: ROCK JEWELRY.

My dad said I could keep half the money for fun, 10 percent I had to give away to help others, and the rest went into my college account.

With some of that 50 percent, I bought clothes at Goodwill with Chick and Justine in another town. We didn't want to buy clothes our friends had previously owned. It was our secret, buying used clothes, and we giggled over the prices. I bought some music and a weekly ice-cream cone, and I bought my grandma gifts. A china teacup. A crystal perfume bottle I found at an antique store. A fluffy blanket.

She wheezed out her thanks, attached to her oxygen tank, and I hugged her. "Never spend any money on cigarettes," she admonished me.

I saved the rest of the money. My dad had always told me, "It's not *if* you'll be hit with bad times financially, it's *when.* Always be ready for it, Natalie. Always have savings."

Most families cannot save enough for a true tragedy. It's impossible.

Who knew, though, that the necklaces I made would help us to save our home when a true tragedy struck us.

Soldier came and sat down by me in the activities room as I threaded some white and silver beads onto a chain, my fingers working slowly as they remembered how to make a necklace. "Want to sign my helmet? I can't remember your name."

That made me a little upset, and I put my necklace down as my chin trembled. He couldn't remember my name! Am I invisible? Am I nothing? Then I remembered that this head injury makes me get upset way too quick about ridiculous stuff, and I breathed. "My name is Natalie Deschutes Fox Shelton. I'll sign my name on your helmet and then you'll remember." I wrote *Natliae.* There was something wrong with it but I couldn't figure out what. "There. Now when you need to know my name you can take off your helmet and look at it."

His helmet was still on his head. "That'll work. But I think I'm going to call you Jewelry Maker." He grabbed some pencils and paper. "I'm going to sit here and draw a picture of the three bears and Goldilocks for my grandma. She likes my pictures, says I should draw whatever I want."

The red-haired woman sat down with me and Soldier at the table. She had another ceramic frog with her.

"Hi, Frog Lady," Soldier said.

"Hello, Soldier."

"That's your second frog, right?" I asked. I was pleased I could remember.

"No. This is my twentieth frog. I make one every day. They're for my family and my friends. Everybody in the Amazon likes frogs. Monkeys. Lizards. Species. Subspecies. Genus. Endangered. Field research."

She gave me the frog to hold.

"Be careful! He's sleeping. The nice nurse, Roberto, you know him? He takes all my clay frogs home with him with a hop and puts them in an oven and cooks them for me so they come out all painted and shiny like this. The cooking doesn't kill the frogs. He makes art, too. Not frog art."

I knew the nice nurse, Roberto. He sang me a song in Spanish yesterday when I was having a bad day. It was about music and dancing.

"I like your Mexican shirt," she said to me. *"Adios! Hola!"*

A man hobbled over using a cane. He had black hair under his helmet and dark eyes, like brown ink. "Hi," he said to me. "Everybody calls me Architect. That's not my real name. There were shelves high in the sky, and I fell off and knocked my knocker." He tapped the side of his helmet.

"Hi. I'm Natalie Deschutes Fox Shelton. I'm making a necklace."

"I can't remember names. But that'll be pretty," he said. "Anyone want to play Build a Building?"

We told him we did.

He hobbled over to another area to get a few cardboard boxes, construction paper, scissors, and glue and started making a building on a Styrofoam platform. I was happy I could remember that word: Styrofoam.

"That's Architect." Frog Lady pointed at him. "He builds buildings."

It was a cool building. "Cool building," I

told him.

"Thanks."

"Want to sign your name on my helmet?" Soldier asked him.

"Sure!" Architect's face lit up happily. "Thank you for asking me!" Architect drew a building on Soldier's helmet. It took a long time. It was a sprawling building with a bridge in the center, trees, glass, a tower. Modern and slick. On top of the building he drew a long cow.

Frog Lady grabbed a hunk of clay and started making another frog.

After I made my necklace, I tried to make my mind do math.

Thirty-four plus twenty-six. I wrote the numbers down. I wrote the plus sign. I wrote the line underneath. I wrote an equal sign.

The numbers swam and tilted.

The number four was . . . to the side. The two was upside down . . . and what number was that? Was that a number? Was it a snake? Had I drawn a snake? Maybe it was a six? I kept trying to do math. It was so frustrating. It was frightening. *It ticked me off.* I couldn't do it, so I scrunched up the paper, threw it, and yelled, "Bad and stupid math."

"Stupid math," Frog Lady hissed out. She made her clay frog jump upside down on his head.

"Math and guns are both bad," Soldier said.

"I do math to make buildings. I stack the numbers up," Architect said.

I tried to get un-mad.

Soldier was drawing a graphic picture of men at war. I thought he said he was drawing Goldilocks and the three bears for his grandma. The scene he was drawing, on white paper with pencil, was of three soldiers on the ground behind a mound of sand. One had his arm half off and was screaming, blood spurting. The other two were shooting huge guns, rounds around their chests. A tank had black smoke billowing out of it in the distance, and there were two bodies on the ground. He had drawn an American flag as a background, but it was ripped and bloodied.

"Grandma's going to like my picture of Goldilocks and the three bears," he said, in complete seriousness.

It's confusing in here sometimes.

Frog Lady molded two frog eyeballs in her hands. "Frog's eyes are googly."

What was I trying to do again?

Math.

Bad and stupid math.

I cried.

"Uh-oh. Jewelry Maker is crying again," Soldier said. "I think I'll knit her a hat. Has anyone seen my yellow yarn?"

"It's in the gym by the bikes," Architect said.

"Is this crying session?" Frog Lady asked. "I'll do it!" She burst into tears.

Architect whispered, "I don't think she likes me." He pointed at me with one finger, his hand held close to his chest. "That's why she's crying. She doesn't want to sit by me." He put his helmeted head in his hands, his shoulders shaking. "No one likes me."

"Hey, man," Soldier said, putting an arm around his shoulders. "I like you. You like my fairy-tale drawings and you wrote your name on my helmet."

"I like you, Architect," Frog Lady said, her head wavering side to side. "You drew my frogs in your last building. Thank you."

I was surprised, but not much. We are all a wreck in here. I'm irrational, too. "I like you, Architect."

His head whipped up, his face wet, those dark eyes swimming. "You do?"

"Yes." I wiped the tears off my face. "You're keeping me company and you're nice, but I don't like math."

He sniffled. "Okay. Thanks. I'll build you a building, girl. I don't know your name."

"Her name is Jewelry Maker," Soldier said, grinning. "Because see? She likes making necklaces."

"I like jewelry, Jewelry Maker," Architect said. "When I'm done with this building I'll give it to you. What's your favorite color? Red? Okay. A red building with jewelry."

I abandoned math and made up a poem in my head as I made another necklace:

Natalie has a bad brain.
It is full of dirty rain.
She can't do math.
She needs a bath.
Go home real soon.
Or you'll be a dumb goon.

In the morning, in front of my door, was a red cardboard/ construction paper building. It was three stories, all angles, jewels cut out and pasted on the construction paper. The jewels were origami-like, intricately folded and popping out from the sides of the building. Architect had also cut out dozens of white construction paper circles to drape a long pearl necklace around the whole thing. A line of what looked like blue topazes wrapped the bottom edge of the red building. Rubies rimmed the corners.

It was magnificent.

It was one of the kindest gifts I have ever received.

I cried again because of Architect's kindness.

I found Architect and gave him a hug after one of my therapy sessions.

He hugged me back, his helmet knocking gently into my head.

"I liked my building."

"Good! I'm happy you liked it. It cost forty million."

"I'll pay you later."

"It's okay. It's free for you because we're friends. Want to have breakfast? They're serving cement pancakes. I used cement for the design of your building, too."

"Sure." He helped me walk into the cafeteria because I was wobbling, and he carried my tray for me. I adjusted his helmet when it tilted. He wasn't walking straight, either.

We had "cement" pancakes together. They were pretty delicious.

I made a necklace later. I found a silver car charm. Made me think of my grandma. Then it made me think of that red 1967 Chevy vision, and that made me think of her apple pies and how she loved her perfume bottles and her guns, which made me all weepy because I miss her.

I made Architect a choker necklace with colorful beads.

I made Frog Lady a necklace using two chains with silver charms and silver beads.

I made Soldier a necklace with black beads and a gold peace sign.

The one nice thing about being in rehab was that I had time to make necklaces again.

They all loved them. Architect said, "So you do like me? You're my friend?"

Frog Lady said, "This is the hopping best necklace I've ever had from a frog friend."

Soldier said, "Peace, Jewelry Maker, and thank you."

They all wore them, every day.

Chapter 8

Zack was exhausted I could tell. The lines were deep in the corners of his eyes, and his hair was coming in gray here and there. His phone rang when he sat down with me in my room. His face darkened. He turned it off.

"What's going wrong?"

"What?"

"Is it work? You're getting a lot of calls that seem to make you mad."

"It's all okay. It's . . . a plumbing issue. Electrical. Details. Boring stuff."

"Ah." I studied him. "I'm sorry, Zack."

"What I'm sorry about is that this happened to you. But you're being so strong. I always knew you were a strong woman, but how you've handled everything, how you don't complain, how positive you are, how determined you are to get better, baby, you're a miracle."

"Not a miracle, Zack. If I thought whining would get me someplace, trust me, I'd do it. I'm not happy this happened to me. I'm not happy I can't walk right or talk right, and sometimes I'm so ticked off I want to scream. I mean, listen to my voice. I'm talking slow. But in the meantime I figure I might as well try to get better. There's nothing else to do here."

"And there you are again, sweetheart. Determined."

"Want to see if we can get a milkshake?"

He smiled. Soft, indulgent, loving.

"Chocolate, vanilla, or strawberry?"

"I'll take chocolate."

We had a milkshake together.

"I like your outfit, honey."

"Thanks." I was in my red jeans, a sparkly belt, and a purple cotton shirt with poofy sleeves. I'd added a necklace with an old-fashioned key, the type that you think you'd need to open a treasure chest. "Go home. Go sleep. I'm fine. And thank you for the daisies."

His face was in hard lines. If I saw him in an alley, I would assume he was a marauding criminal and I would hope that I would not be his next victim. "Really, Zack. I know you're exhausted." His shoulders slumped, and he gave in. He kissed me, long and loving, and left.

I thought about that call he received when he arrived. He said it was work.

He was not telling the truth.

I want to talk to him about it. My gut instinct is that he'll lie to me again. If I could remember what happened the morning of my accident I'd get some clarity. . . . It was all there, I knew it.

My head started to bang. This intense fatigue swooped down on me like bricks. It does that all the time. I'm awake and all of a sudden . . . I have to go to sleep.

After we met on the Deschutes River, Zack and I started dating in Portland, where we both lived. I had a studio downtown; he had bought a dated, run-down, dark home in an expensive neighborhood in the hills above Portland as an investment and remodeled it when he had time. When it was done it was bright and airy, lots of windows, a modern interior.

There was a kink in the dating, though.

I held back because I have problems with fears of abandonment, or FOA, as I labeled it. That's a fancy way of saying that since my own mother deserted me, I believe that there's a high chance that other people will abandon me, too. I knew my dad, Justine, and Chick wouldn't, but a man, a husband, that was a huge risk to me.

After all, if my mother didn't love me enough to stick around, why would a man?

My FOA accounted for a number of "quickie relationships" that I'd had. I liked the men. Didn't love them. And when they pushed for more, I pulled back and took off. I did feel bad for hurting them, but I couldn't take that jump. Surely they would leave me, too.

Justine called me "No, no, oh no, Natalie."

Chick called me "Wiley Coyote. Speeding off into the canyon, leaving dust and weeping men in her wake."

But with Zack, something happened. I didn't *want* to hold back. I wanted to be normal. I started falling for him on the river.

But *Zack* held back.

We went mountain biking. We went fishing again. We went to the beach and had clam chowder. We went to the movies and met for lunch.

We never ran out of things to say. Books. Politics. Social issues. Movies. Funny shows on TV. He and his construction business donated to a Boys & Girls Club, and my firm and I donated to a college scholarship program for disadvantaged kids, so we had that in common also. But we started being able to be quiet together, too, which was a relief, because I can't be "on" all the time. I can't be cheerful and upbeat all the time. I find it exhausting.

He liked his work, and I liked mine.

"I love building homes because I know a family is going to live there," he told me. "I know they'll make memories there. I know they'll have family dinners there. I know the kids will run around in the family room and out in the backyard. They'll read books in their bedrooms and, maybe when they're teenagers, they'll sneak out the back door by the kitchen. If I can build something that will make people happy, make families happy, then I've done my job."

His homes were open and light. They averaged around 2,400 square feet — "enough space for everyone, but not too much space" — and had high ceilings, exposed wood beams, stacked rock fireplaces, wood floors, always at least one window seat, and a lot of lighting.

He took me to his job sites after hours and started asking me for my opinions about the homes and what to do to make them special.

I love home decorating and design. The love of it comes, oddly enough, from deep sadness and loneliness in my childhood, but I've studied home décor magazines and books since I was a girl, so to help Zack was a ton of fun for me.

I told him my thoughts, how he should add strips of colored glass or artistic tiles to kitchen backsplashes, and pendant lighting. I suggested different textures and materials; for example, the island should be painted blue and have a different counter than the rest of the kitchen. I showed him how to add armoires for storage and copper hood vents and use repurposed dressers for sideboards and bathroom vanities.

He asked questions about accounting and my business and about my childhood; growing up with my mother, until she left; my dad and his past roofing and metal businesses; our animals; and the pranks that Justine, Chick, and I played when we were young. I told him about the necklaces we used to make and sell at the farmers' market.

I told him about the Big Penis joke. There was a row of tall, thick shrubs in front of our high school. Late on a Sunday night, with my dad's electric saw, the Moonshine and Milky Way Maverick Girls carved out the words BIG PENIS SCHOOL. It was crooked, but we were still proud of our horticulture art work.

Another time we changed the lettering of

the reader board in front of the school late at night. We spelled out GIVE SENIORS FREE BEER.

We had a Friday night Senior Sleepover at the school. The teachers never got wind of it. After the janitors cleaned the school, we all snuck in with sleeping bags, changed into our pajamas, made popcorn, drank beer, turned on music, danced, and had a great time, all night. The girls told their parents they were going to Justine's or my house to spend the night. The boys told their parents they were going to a couple of the guys' houses to spend the night. None of the parents checked on their kids.

Zack thought our pranks were hilarious.

I longed for that man.

I lusted for that man.

I thought I saw passion in his eyes for me, that same lust I was feeling, but he never acted on it. Zack didn't kiss me. Didn't even hold my hand. I was stunned and hurt and started doubting myself and us.

The whole thing started to depress me. I managed to keep my smile on through the dates, then I went home. Alone. What was wrong? Was he not attracted to me? Quite possible. And why did I think he would be interested in me as a girlfriend, or a wife? Like my mother said, I was a gawky thing.

An awkward thing. I really needed to "do something" with my unruly mess of curly hair. My eyes were too big, and I had a hippie style with my flowing shirts and boots and bangles and necklaces.

I had darker thoughts, too: Was he married and had he lied to me? Was he gay? Was he asexual? Was he grieving for someone else, a broken relationship? Was he incapable of a commitment? Was he hiding something? Was he sterile or impotent?

I came back to the same answer: He simply wasn't attracted *to me.*

One night I went home alone after he took me to a fancy restaurant after three months of dating. Clearly I was the only one who was "dating." I loved the man. I was crushed. I asked myself that question that's been asked a zillion times by both men and women: Is it more painful to stay in a relationship, knowing the person doesn't want what you want, doesn't want a future, a marriage, than it is to leave?

Should I break this off now, before I fall more deeply in love with Zack and am then abandoned again?

Or is it better to have him in my life as a friend and lust for him on the sidelines while crying at night all by myself?

Already I couldn't imagine my life without

Zack. On one hand, he had quickly become my best friend, along with Chick and Justine. He was so smart, but he was self-aware, too. He was thoughtful. He was considerate. The man was evolved in a way that so many men never are; they just stumble their way through life, dense and clueless, arrogant and needy, selfish and scared, not ever really getting emotions, getting themselves, getting other people. Stumble, bumble, blah.

On the other hand, I felt his resistance, as if he wanted to be with me and was trying not to get too close but couldn't help himself. I'd feel him relax into our relationship, laugh and smile, but then I'd feel him pulling away again.

There was a watchfulness, a wariness to him. He always noticed who was around us. There was a suspiciousness to him. I'd see it behind his eyes and I could tell he was lost in his thoughts, and those thoughts were closed to me.

I opened the door to my apartment after the fancy dinner date, kept the lights off, and splayed flat out on my bed and cried. I decided I was done. I did not need more pain in my life.

I didn't take his call for three days. I could feel my heart throbbing when I finally picked up.

"Hi, Zack."

"Natalie. How are you? Is everything okay?"

I heard the worry in his voice.

"Everything's fine. It's fine."

We did the surface talk that we all know how to do. We both knew there was something off.

"What are you doing tonight, Natalie?"

"I'm home. I might have a wild night watching a home decorating show."

"Do you want company?"

Oh, I did. I wanted his naked company. But I didn't. I didn't want to end up crying again. So, naturally, I said, "Sure."

"I'll bring dinner."

"It's okay. I made lasagna. Let's have that."

"You are after my heart."

I hoped so. But we were going to talk about that.

He came over and looked delicious in his black shirt and blue jeans. He picked his clothes out well. He was tall and rangy and built, that man. I like men who have something to grip, and he was grippable.

I smiled and gave him a hug and resisted pulling his jeans off because clearly that was not what he wanted. Still, I'd taken time to do myself up. I was in a red cotton dress that stopped midthigh, my usual chains and charms, and half an armful of bracelets made from beads and leather.

My studio loft was about two blocks off a main street downtown with restaurants and shops. It was large for a studio, with near floor-to-ceiling windows. It used to be a factory. My kitchen had white cabinets and an island with white marble and wood floors. My bed was in the corner next to the windows because I loved looking out across the buildings to the river.

My bedspread was white with painted red poppies, and I had a stack of flowered, lace, and striped pillows on it. I'd found three cool branches that had fallen on our property in Lake Joseph, and I nailed them to a wall next to dried flowers I picked on our back acre. I had a blue shelving unit filled with flowering plants and my books. On one wall I'd hung an old saddle from when I was a kid, my cowgirl hat, and two fishing poles.

I have a hummingbird collection. They are made of wood, ceramic, faux gold or silver, origami, or glass. My dad has made a bunch for me with metal. I hung six ceramic hummingbirds over my red couch and another three from my dad near the windows. The rest were on a red table.

I'd asked the owner if I could hang two chandeliers, and he'd said yes, so I hung one over my kitchen table and one over my bed. I also hung up white Christmas lights around the entire studio.

I cannot live in drab and plain, because it triggers soul-sapping memories, and so I don't. In a drawer of my dresser I had a pile of new lingerie, all from Lace, Satin, and Baubles. I wanted to wear it for him.

After Zack hugged me, I turned away quick because my eyes filled up and went to the island and started making a salad.

"Natalie." He was right behind me.

Why am I so emotional? Why can't I control my tears better?

"Natalie, turn around, honey."

Honey? *Honey?*

I sniffled and wiped my tears.

"What's wrong?" He gently turned me around.

I could make something up, but Zack has bright green eyes that stare right through me, and I couldn't lie. "I think we want different things."

"What do you think I want?"

"I think you want to be friends with me."

"I do." He nodded.

"Daaannng." I turned around to attack the salad again, but he curved an arm around my waist and pulled me back around.

"And more, Natalie."

"You do?"

"Yes. I want a lot more than friendship, Natalie. I knew it the day I met you on the Deschutes."

"But . . . but you haven't even tried to kiss me."

He bent his head and went to that place that Zack goes sometimes. It's the place he goes alone. "Natalie, I didn't want to rush you. I didn't want to be too forward. I respect you. I have never met a woman like you. You run circles around me with that brain of yours. You're fast thinking. You're funny. I love how you live. You work hard, your career is important, but then you have this other side where you're a total outdoorswoman. You're honest. You're sincere. I trust you."

"But, Zack, something's off here. We've been together more than three months. . . ."

"I want us. I want you."

He did? "You do?"

"Yes."

Double dang! My tears came again and rolled down my cheeks. "Thanks."

"Thanks?" He smiled.

I laughed. He laughed.

"Yes, thanks, Zack. I want the same. I want you. I want us."

And ol' Zack took things from there. He reached behind me and turned off the stove, and those muscled arms pulled me close, and he gave me a kiss that swooped all through my body and lit me on fire, and we stumbled off to my bed with all the pillows.

After the second time, the moonshine glinting through my windows between the hummingbirds, the city quiet, he said, his eyes filling with tears, "I love you, Natalie," and I said, "I love you, too, Zack."

We smiled and kissed, and I knew it was a miracle, our love. That we would meet on the Deschutes River, the river of my life, that we would find each other, reach out, hand to hand, take a dare and a jump, and fall in love was nature giving me a gift. I did not believe in soul mates until I met Zack.

We both called in sick the next day and spent our time in bed together, my new, lacy lingerie appreciated and enjoyed. I was wiped out by the end of it, but it was the best kind of wiped out to be.

In the middle of the night, though, on the third night, Zack sleeping beside me, I knew

I had missed something. There was a reason that Zack, an American male, awesome in bed, did not kiss me for three months. I didn't buy the explanation that he didn't want to rush me.

There was another explanation as to why he waited. It was a gut-level, instinctual knowledge. He wasn't telling me everything. And the answer to why he didn't kiss me for three months lay in that mystery.

But as I peered over at that sleeping he-man, I decided to let it go. I brushed a hand over his hair, touched the scar on his cheekbone, ran a hand down his chest and over the scar on his ribs.

I loved him. He loved me.

And when thoughts entered my head that Zack was hiding something, I pushed them out as hard as I could and went back to kissing him, laughing with him.

Now I know this: It is never, ever a smart idea to push warning signs out of your head when you're dating someone.

The warning signs will come back later and bash you in the face.

I tried to put the stabbed Barbie incident and the hit-and-run out of my mind as much as I could. There was nothing I could do about it. Zack said he was handling it, and I assumed he was talking to the police. The police were handling it, and security here knew about it.

I was trying to get my brain together, and I had no room for the fear that the stabbed Barbie with my initials engraved in her stomach brought in.

"Mom."

"You don't have to sound so surprised, Natalie," my mother snapped as she sat down across from me at the table in the activities room. She was wearing a light blue pantsuit and pearl earrings, necklace, and bracelets. It was Pearls Day. She patted her blond hair. Every hair in place! She did not bother to hug me.

She plopped her red designer purse on the table, right on a pile of beads I was using. The beads scattered, and she sighed impatiently but did not try to pick them up. The purse was expensive and new. Must be from Dell. My mother does not work.

"I didn't know you were coming."

"I have to make an appointment to see my own daughter in the hospital?" She raised her perfectly plucked and drawn-in eyebrows at me.

Yes, I think you should have made an appointment with me so I could prepare myself for this Maternal Onslaught. You should have made, and kept, your "appointments" with me when I was a kid, too. "How are you, Mom?"

I saw her eyes skitter around the room. There were people in wheelchairs and helmets. Nurses and doctors. Some people engaged in activities like trying to line up magnetic cards on a dry-erase board. Others trying to hold pencils to write. One woman was trying to put the alphabet together with flash cards. Crafts. Puzzles. Ping-pong. Varying levels of success with all of us.

"I'm exhausted." Her eyes skidded back to mine. So much unpleasantness here! She had not driven all this way to see *this*! "I see you are still indulging your hippie style, despite your age."

"It's hippie bohemian." I was in my purple jeans, a white T-shirt, and a beige buttoned blouse with a sequined and embroidered guitar on the left side. I was wearing dangly gold earrings with purple beads. "I like to wear what you don't like."

"Manners, please. Respect your mother." She waved a hand. "I have a lot going on right now, Natalie. A lot."

Gee. So did I. "What's going on, Mom?"

She narrowed her eyes. Her makeup

looked as if it was done by a professional. Full foundation. Powder. Several shades of eye shadow expertly blending into one another. "What is wrong with your hair?"

"What do you mean?" I patted my hair, self-conscious, especially about the area that had been shaved, but it was growing in pretty well. . . . But, shoot! Dang it! Why did I still let her get me all riled up? I was a grown woman. I did not need her approval.

"It's not brushed. Your curls are all over the place. And it's long. Really, Natalie, you're pushing forty, you should cut your hair. It would give a lift to your face."

"I'm thirty-five."

"Old enough not to go around thinking you're a teenager. Your hair is halfway down your back."

"I like my hair."

She raised an eyebrow as in, "Well. I don't like it and you *shouldn't* like it."

"Mom. I don't care whether you like my hair or not. I am not here to fix my hair."

"There's never a time when a woman shouldn't attend to her appearance, even when she's recovering from an accident and working on her speech and how to think and control her emotions, particularly her rudeness." This time she raised two eyebrows at me. "Your speech does sound better, dear. Not so much as if you're talking very slowly through algae water."

Reading this, one might think I am making it up. What mother comes to visit her daughter in rehab and criticizes her hair? My mother. She's like Godzilla, human form. "I am trying to think again, Mom. Like right now I am thinking that you are difficult to be around."

Her eyes widened. "Don't speak to me like that, Natalie. Aren't you relearning manners and social etiquette in your therapy classes?"

"There is no manners class in the Brain Bang Unit, Mom."

"I drove all the way out after a long week to see you."

"What did you do during your long week?" Oh, do tell, Mother.

She groaned. Life was so hard! "Dell and I are having an enormous party next weekend and I am exhausted from the planning. Exhausted." She plucked at her two pearl bracelets.

I felt that familiar stab of pain in my chest. My own mother was having a party and I was not invited. Now, I wouldn't go. I obviously *couldn't* go. But it would have been nice for her to invite me anyhow.

She is an insensitive thing, but she caught

the expression on my face. "Oh, for God's sakes, Natalie. Don't get all sulky with me. We *can't* invite you. It's for Dell's family — his four kids from his previous wife, the dead one; everyone thinks she's perfect, she died an angel. If I have to hear one more story about Saint Marisa I think I'll puke. Anyhow, we're also inviting all of our employees and their families and our suppliers. It's over two hundred people and we simply can't add more."

I felt a second stab of pain. The stab was for the little girl I used to be, how she deserted me and I was not invited to the rest of her life. She rarely even came to my birthday parties. I would see her a few days before Christmas, not *on* Christmas Day, and I might see her a few days before Thanksgiving, but not *on* Thanksgiving Day, because she was always busy with her new husband and his family.

I was not even in the top two hundred people she would invite to a party, though Dell's kids, her "new family," were invited.

It was ridiculous for me to let her hurt me again, but obviously it was a huge party. She didn't decline to invite me because I'm in the hospital, she declined because she has never invited me to her life, so why start now?

I glanced longingly at my beads, the crystals, a few charms that I was using to make a necklace for a twenty-eight-year-old patient here who crashed her motorcycle, and I wanted her to leave.

"This party has taken up all my spare time. All of it."

I tried to put the pain aside. I'd been doing it all my life, after all. "Isn't Dell hiring people to handle the party?"

"Yes. Glenda. She's the director of . . . what do you call it? Human something. She directs humans. No, that's not it." Her Botoxed brow furrowed a tiny bit, as much as the injection would allow. "She's a human director. Ah!" She snapped her fingers. "She's the human director of people resources for Dell. What a name. Glenda. Like Glenda the witch? The woman even has red hair. I don't like her, and I have informed Dell of my opinion."

"Why don't you like her?" But I already knew. Glenda was probably pretty, smart, friendly, normal, or all of the above, and that my mother could not have. Women like that were a direct threat, especially if the woman was anywhere near one of her husbands.

"She's always smiling. When she sees me she'll fake a smile. But with everyone else, she's always smiling and laughing. Everyone loves her, friendly Glenda the witch! Dell say she's one of his best employees. She's been on the ranch for fifteen years. He says she's one of the smartest people he's ever known. And he employs her husband, too, and two of their teenagers. Personally" — she leaned toward me — "Glenda needs a makeover."

"You think everyone needs a makeover."

"Except me!" She chuckled, but she meant it. "I don't. But I have told Glenda, and I've tried to be gentle, that she needs a makeover, and I offered to help her."

"You didn't. Please say you didn't."

She was irritated. "I said it one second ago, Natalie. You need to work on your memory problems. I noticed when you were in the other hospital that you forgot a lot. All the time! So I said to Glenda, 'Have you ever thought of becoming a brunette?' and she said no, and that fake smile of hers dropped off her face. And I said, 'I think that brunette hair would complement your, *interesting,* coloring. And her coloring *is* interesting, Natalie, if you know what I mean."

"No, I don't." I did. I so did. I can't stand this part of my mother.

She waved her hand. "Glenda asked me

what I meant by that comment, and I told her that brunette would simply make her face match better with her hair. That the red color did not seem to be organic to her heritage."

"Oh no." I felt sick for poor Glenda. "I hope you said those words only in your head."

"I have been clear, Natalie." My mother's voice was impatient. "I said them *out loud.* I am getting frustrated with this conversation. I know you've had a head injury, but please listen."

"That was incredibly rude, Mom."

Her mouth twisted, her blue eyes narrowing. "No. It wasn't. I was trying to help her. Help her appearance."

"Mom, why do you think people want to know what you think about their appearance? And why do you think that you're qualified to offer an opinion?"

"Because I have understood fashion and style my whole life. I learned from the cradle. My mother knew how to dress, and so did her mother. Fashion is practically in the DNA of our family ancestral line." She sat up ramrod straight. "I wasn't born white trash. I learned about elegance and proper social normalities and how it's important to present your full beauty to the people of this earth every day as a gift to them."

I wanted to smash my head with my fist, but I wouldn't. Head injury! "What did Glenda do?"

My mother's mouth tightened, despite the Botox. "She said to me, 'Jocelyn, when I want your opinion on my hair color, and whether or not it should match with my skin color, I will ask for it. As I will never need your opinion about how I look, please refrain from telling me your opinion again.' Honestly, Natalie. She talks to her employer's wife like that?"

"I think you had it coming."

"I did not!" She huffed. "I told her that I would be informing Dell about her rudeness, and do you know what she said?"

"I can hardly wait to hear." My head was beginning to pound. I wanted to go to bed. I wanted to make my necklace. I had speech therapy in half an hour, and after that physical therapy, then a meeting with my neuropsychologist, and I needed a break from Mother Monster before then.

"She told me, 'Go ahead, Jocelyn. Tell your husband.' " She glared at me as if I were Glenda. "And I went and told Dell, and do you know what he said?" She was so angry she twitched under her designer pantsuit.

"He told you never to talk to Glenda like that again, to be kind and respectful to his employees, especially Glenda, as she is supersmart and competent and friendly and he didn't want to lose her or her husband, who have been around longer than you. And he was angry with you, which surprised you. He should have been mad at Glenda, right?"

Her blue eyes flew open. "This is unacceptable! Did Dell tell you that? He did, didn't he?"

"No, Mom. But I know Dell and I know that's what he would have said."

She twitched again, her manicured nails flying. "Whatever! Anyhow! Well!"

"Mom, I have therapy, so I have to go."

"I'm so busy right now, Natalie. So stressed out. Dealing with you and your condition has been extremely hard on me."

She took out her mirror and studied her face, fluffed her hair, dabbed on more lipstick. "You see, Natalie, you're not wearing lipstick and you look ghostly. Put on lipstick. I am your mother. If I have time for lipstick and blush and mascara, with my busy schedule, then you do, too."

"You can't be serious."

"And, Natalie." She stared at my chest. "Get a push-up bra. You are too young to sag like that. Look at mine." She shoved her chest out. "As upright as a teenager's!"

She neglected to mention that they are fake. "They're fake, Mom."

"Now. Before I have to run off, tell me how your father is doing. Is he single or still dating that woman with the unfortunately enormous nose, Rhonda? He compares all the women he has dated to me, and they fall short. That's why he's never remarried, the poor man still loves me."

I groaned, dropped my clanging head to the table, and covered it with my arms.

I heard Soldier's voice. "Are you hiding from the enemy, Jewelry Maker?"

"That woman looks like a mean frog," Frog Lady said.

"I don't think I like her," Architect said. "And it would be okay if she didn't like me."

Frog Lady, Architect, and Soldier helped me pick up my beads after Mother Mayhem left. They are true friends. I made Frog Lady a necklace with silver and green beads and a leaf charm in the center. She said, "I'll wear it today when we begin our research in the tropical forest. Genus. Species."

I used three strings of leather, braided together at the top, for Soldier. I attached a four-leaf clover, a heart, and a peace sign.

"I feel more lucky and more loving and more peaceful already," he said, and saluted.

I used black leather for Architect's choker necklace. I found a charm in the shape of a house and lined it with black beads. He said, pointing at me, his hand close to his chest, "I didn't even think you liked me, Jewelry Maker," and burst into tears. "I'm so glad you do."

CHAPTER 9

I continued to work on my addition skills.

Twenty plus twenty equals . . . two twenties.

Fourteen plus sixteen is twenty-nine.

Thirty-four plus six is forty-one.

Twelve plus twelve is twenty-four.

I will get better at arithmetic.

I will get better at adding and subtracting.

I will be an accountant again.

My hand shook around my pencil.

My love of numbers, math, and story problems came about because of my mother and dad's cyclone of a marriage and, later, the pain she caused when she abandoned me.

When my mother snapped and became enraged at my dad for some tiny thing when I was a kid, I headed outside to visit the animals. Our horses, Bryan A, Mrs. Gretchen, and CQ Coyote; our cats, Lady Macy, Goofy, and Corn; our two dogs, Horse and

Captain Angelique; and our goat, Mrs. Quimby. But if it was late or raining or snowing and I couldn't go out, I reached for my math workbook. Math drowned out my mother's harsh words and her screaming at my dad. I loved the story problems and the equations. I loved long addition and subtraction.

I thought my mother's unhappiness and anger was my fault. Sometimes I would catch her staring at me, this shattered expression on her face, and she'd tear up, or turn away and mutter something like, "I can't believe they did that." I'd ask her what she meant by that and she'd snap, "I don't want to talk about it, Natalie!"

She said she couldn't stand living in this "flea-bitten town, this shack, this deserted piece of backwash Oregon," saying "not even the bugs want to be here."

She called my dad Hillbilly Scott and Scotty the Roofer Boy. She told me she had grown up in much better circumstances, a better house, better cars, and she had had no idea she was going to have to live like white trash when she married my dad. She couldn't stand this! This was a disgrace! She was used to a better standard!

When my dad would sing to me, he asked her a couple of times to join us and she would say, her face rigid in sudden anger, "No. I am not singing, *ever,*" and would leave the room and slam their bedroom door.

When I was seven, she packed up her suitcases on a Saturday when my dad was working and set them by the front door. I was instantly nervous. She made me nervous. This made me nervous.

"Where are you going, Mommy?"

"I'm leaving, Natalie." She pulled on the new red coat she had recently bought.

"Am I coming? Is Dad coming?" I went from nervous to scared.

"No." She flipped up the collar and examined her face in the mirror, tilting it this way and that.

"Why? Why not?"

"Because you need to stay with your dad. He would be lonely without you." She fluffed her hair.

I thought my mother was gorgeous. She always wore pretty dresses and had thick blond hair, no messy curls like mine. She wore jewelry and lipstick and lacy bras. Men always came up to her in town to talk and flirt with her. She smiled back, winked, swayed her hips. I didn't like it.

She put on red lipstick, then smoothed her lips together.

"You'll be fine, Natalie."

I started to cry as I understood what was going on. My mother was leaving with her suitcases. I was not going with her. I had always worried about this. I had always known, even as a child, that my mother wanted out. It was probably why I was such a nervous, insecure kid.

I hugged her and begged her not to leave. She disentangled herself from me as if I were a barnacle. She straightened her pink dress. "Stop that right now. I have to go. I'll call you and I'll see you soon." She grabbed her suitcases and turned to leave.

"Mom!" I cried. "Don't go, Mom! Don't go!"

"Stop crying, Natalie. Just stop. I have enough stress right now. I can't take a temper tantrum."

"But why are you leaving? Where are you going? When are you coming back? I'm sorry, Mom! I'm sorry!" I grabbed her around the waist again. "Mom! Mom! Please don't go." I was shaking, begging.

"Get ahold of yourself," she snapped. *"Let go of me, Natalie."*

She detached my hands from around her waist. I wrapped my arms around her again, choking on my sobs. She pulled my hands apart and told me to stop it *this instant.*

"Please, Mommy! Wait. Don't go. Can I come?" Instantly I thought of my dad. I didn't want to leave my dad!

"No, you may not. Not now."

She climbed into her car, the new car my dad bought her, and reversed out of our driveway. She threw me a cheery wave out the window. I chased the car as far as I could down the street, screaming at her to please come back, please, I would be good, I love you, Mom, I love you, come home, I'm sorry, Mom! I'm sorry!

I wet my pants I was so upset. She did not stop. She didn't even slow. When I couldn't run through my sobs any longer, I lay in the middle of the road, crying. A truck almost hit me. It was Mrs. Spanley, a teacher at our school. I remember her kindness to this day.

She held me in her arms, the dust from my mother's car settling around us. I told her my mother had left me. She didn't want me anymore. She didn't love me. "Natalie," she said, "she loves you. I don't know what's going on, but I know she loves you. It's all right, dear. Let's get you home to your dad."

But it wasn't all right. It never would be.

Mrs. Spanley drove me home, and we waited for my dad to get back from his roofing job. She made me oatmeal cookies.

When I told my dad what happened, crying and choking, he held his arms out and hugged me. I think I cried myself to sleep every night for a month. Then I cried every other day, at least, for months on end. Then once a week, a couple of times a month, and all holidays and my birthday when she did not show up.

I drowned myself in math. What kid drowns out pain by doing math problems? Me. Nerdy me. My dad bought me math workbooks and textbooks, and I worked my way through them. Numbers made sense.

They took me away from my tears and my hurt and this uncontrollable longing for my mother. She had often been critical, crazy, and screeching, but she was my mother. The answers to math problems were right or wrong, but there was no emotion. No yelling. No anger. No one abandoned me.

Numbers didn't lie, as my mother did when she promised to see me the next weekend, or on a Wednesday to take me to ice cream or to meet her "new family" and then she didn't show up.

I still do math and arithmetic problems in my head, and on paper, and in an online math group that I'm a part of, and I enjoy it all. It is amazing that a traumatic part of my childhood engendered a love of math.

And my love of math turned me into an accountant, which is a huge part of my identity.

I would have to work hard to get my accounting skills back.

Thirty-two plus twenty-six is sixty. Wasn't it? Was that right?

I started to shake.

It is difficult to forgive my mother. She deserted a seven-year-old, vulnerable, innocent little girl who loved her mommy.

Hard to get past that.

It is also hard to get past who she still is, today.

The next day Frog Lady sat down beside me in the activities room and gave me a ceramic frog. The frog was pink with blue googly eyes. She had painted numbers all over it.

"I put numbers on it because you keep writing numbers down." Frog Lady is a caring person. Her smile is somewhat vacant, and she will sometimes get lost on our floor and wander around. A couple of times she's escaped from the Brain Bang Unit. They found her in the outside garden "looking for monkeys in their native habitat."

She talks about obscure insects and rare,

dangerous snakes and species in the Amazon rain forest, but then she interjects things about fairies or hopping or multiple magical monkey husbands. It's interesting.

Architect came and sat down, too. "Today I'm building a glass tower. I have a contract to complete." He used cardboard, straws, glue sticks, and construction paper to make a six-story building. Someone had given him Saran wrap, so he used that for the windows. He used sticks from outside to create trees inside the building. "I can't remember what it's called when you have trees inside a building, but it's a forest in a building with bears and hawks."

Soldier came by in the middle of it and said, "I hope I don't have to bomb that place."

"You won't," Architect said. "Because there's trees in the middle of it."

"Are there any enemies?"

Architect took the question seriously. "I don't think so, but I'll check behind the doors. Do you like me today, Soldier?" His eyes rounded with hope.

"Yes."

Architect's shoulders sagged with relief and his eyes filled with tears. "I'm so glad I'm not your enemy."

"Okay. Mission accomplished." Soldier

looked at me. "Are you going to cry today?" He asked it nicely. I told him maybe. Maybe not.

He nodded, his helmet moving slightly forward. "Yes, ma'am."

"What time is crying session?" Frog Lady asked. "I'll do it. Hey, Soldier. Want a frog?"

"Yes. I do. I won't shoot it."

"Preserve all animals," Frog Lady said, "especially the endangered ones. This will be a friendly frog."

For some reason that made Architect sad, and he put his hands in his lap, his helmet tilting to the side.

"What's wrong, Architect?" I asked.

At first he didn't answer. He shook his head, his shoulders shaking.

"What is it?" I tried to be gentle.

He tilted his head back, his helmet tilting, too, as he stared at the ceiling. He wiped his dark eyes.

"Architect?"

"I am not going to get another frog from Frog Lady," he whispered. He held his hand close to his chest and pointed at Frog Lady. "Why doesn't she like me? Do you know, Jewelry Maker?"

"I think she likes you." Why would Frog Lady not like Architect?

"I like you," Frog Lady said, nodding her

head vigorously. Then she grabbed her head, as if it hurt her to nod that quick. She has a long scar under her hair. She showed me. "Don't cry, Architect. It's not crying session yet, right, Jewelry Maker? It's not until midnight. We'll climb up in the trees to do it."

"It's not officially on the schedule," I told her. I try to be helpful here.

"Oh," Frog Lady said, confused. She turned to Architect. "I sit with you all the time and talk about frogs. That's how I show people I like them. I'll make you a frog."

His head shot up as fast as a helmeted head can shoot up. "You will?"

"Yes!" She croaked like a frog. "I'm happy you want one."

"I do. I do want a frog." His smile lit up his face.

"It'll be special. For sure. Because you're an architect."

"When do I get my frog?"

That was a little pushy. But, okay.

"Soon. Really soon."

He smiled and wiggled in his seat and held up two straws in his hands, as if in victory.

"Hey. I lost my pink yarn. Have you seen it?" Soldier asked.

"It's in the basket by the elevators," I told him. I was proud of myself for remembering. I still talked like sludge, my balance was bad, I had dizziness and headaches, and numbers and letters bopped around in my brain, but I remembered where Soldier's yarn was!

"Thanks, Jewelry Maker."

We went on like this, chatting, having important conversations. Architect built his building. Frog Lady made a frog out of clay for Architect. The frog had a happy smile. She used a toothpick to carve trees and a bear into its body, because Architect had trees and bears in his building.

Soldier made a drawing for his grandma in black pencil. This one was of two dirty, hunched soldiers carrying one injured, limp soldier between them. They were in a bombed-out village. He drew blood and smoke behind them. "I'm going to show my grandma this picture of Aladdin and the Magic Lamp. She likes my fairy-tale drawings."

I thought that Grandma would probably be upset when she saw the drawings.

I went on with my math on paper.

Two plus five. Seven.

Seven plus seven. Thirteen.

Thirteen plus thirteen. Twenty-thirteen.

Twenty plus twenty. Forty-two.

Forty plus twenty. Sixteen.

Twenty minus four. Thirteen. Fourteen.
Fourteen minus sixteen. Four.
Twenty-two plus twenty-two. Forty-four.
Forty-four plus forty-four. Eighty-forty.
I think I'm getting better.
My hand shook.

I do have to use the rails on my bed sometimes to get up and down. Worse is that I
still have to use the bars around the toilet,
too, and in the shower. My goal is to use
them less every day. It is discouraging to
hover your naked bottom over a toilet like a
helicopter and then slowly lower yourself
down as if you're 110 years old.

The next day Justine came to see me after
occupational therapy and time in the practice kitchen, where I'd burned soup. We
talked about the firm, which made me feel
confused. Tax code is too much for me.
Then we laughed about the pranks we
played in high school and chatted. I love
Justine. She left when I had to go to recreational therapy and gave me a long hug. Her
eyes were sad. "What's wrong?"

She shrugged.

"You. But you're doing so much better.
You talk better, you don't need as much
help walking, you aren't forgetting things."

"And something else, right?"

"Same stuff."

So I knew. Jed and the secret had upset her.

I hugged her again.

Justine has always loved Jed. We were seven and in first grade when she first declared her love for him to Chick and me. We were out at recess and we were wearing our reindeer antler hats. We'd made them in art, it being near Christmas and all.

"I know what I want for Christmas," Justine said as Chick and I held two jump ropes and she jumped over both as her reindeer antlers flopped about.

"What?" Chick said.

"I want Jed."

"What?" Chick said, dropping the ropes. "What do you mean you want Jed?"

"I mean, I want to marry him."

"But he's my brother," Chick said, baffled. She adjusted her reindeer antlers. "That's weird. You can't marry my brother."

"Why not?"

"Because he's my brother." Chick looked at Justine like, "duh, that's all the explanation you need."

"He's cute and I'm going to marry him. He's like a prince and he even has a horse."

That was true. Chick and Jed both had horses, Mr. Marshmallow and Mrs. Cracker Box.

"But we're only seven." I was quite confused. Only adults got married. Except for Laina Horleson, who ran off to marry a man named Jeffy Lawson who was thirty-six when she was sixteen and her mother went after them with a shotgun.

They were hiding out in the Lawson family cabin in the mountains, which was "plum donkey-butt stupid," my dad said later. Everyone knew that the Lawsons, an old, wealthy family in Lake Joseph, had a family cabin in the mountains.

Chief Knight raced to the Lawsons' cabin, Mr. Horleson in the car yelling at him to "go faster or my wife will blast Jeffy's head straight off and send it rolling into Idaho."

Now, mind you, Mr. Horleson wanted to kill Jeffy, too, but he loved Mrs. Horleson and he didn't want her to go to jail. It wasn't right. The *father* should take on the role of protecting the daughter with his shotgun, not the *mother.* This was an American tradition that could not be broken.

They sped down back roads. By the time the chief and Mr. Horleson arrived at the cabin, Mrs. Horleson had Jeffy out on the front porch, on his knees, his hands up in the air, her hunting rifle pointed straight at him. Laina was cowering behind the begging Jeffy yelling, "Mama, don't shoot. Don't shoot, Mama!"

"Get the hell out of the way, Laina," Mrs. Horleson ordered. "I'm going to make a new hole through this loser and then you're grounded. You hear me? You are grounded until I know that you know how to think, because what you're doing now doesn't even qualify as thinking."

Mr. Horleson and Chief Knight sprinted out of the car, and Mr. Horleson stood right in front of Mrs. Horleson with his hands up.

There was no way she could shoot Jeffy without taking out her husband. Mr. and Mrs. Horleson had been together since high school, and even last year someone said they were making out behind the drugstore, Mrs. Horleson's bra clean off.

"Babycakes," she told her husband, "now you get out of the way."

"No, sweetie pie, I won't," Mr. Horleson said, panting from exertion and fear of what his wife would do if given a clean shot. "I want Jeffy dead, too, but I can't have you in jail, pumpkin. You warm me up at night, you know you do, and you know I can't sleep without you."

"Move, darling," Mrs. Horleson said. "Six inches to the left and I'll take this sicko clean out so he can't touch anyone else's daughter again."

"Come on, now, honeybunch," Mr. Horleson said, determined, moving closer to his wife. "You don't want to go to jail and then have some other woman making me my pancakes on Sundays."

Well, heck. She didn't want that at all.

"You would do that to me?" She kept her aim steady.

"I don't want to, love bunny, but if you're in jail for twenty years, that's pressing a man too hard against a wall."

The thought of another woman with her husband, that slut, *that tramp,* made Mrs. Horleson pause long enough for Chief Knight and her loving husband to snatch the gun away from her and put her in the back of a police car to cool her jets. She continued to swear colorfully at Jeffy from inside the car. The chief and one of his deputies arrested Jeffy Lawson.

It was the talk of the town!

So if Laina was only sixteen and couldn't get married, then Justine, at seven, couldn't either. "I think you're too young to be a wife."

"I don't mean I'm going to marry him

now, Natalie," Justine said. "Here, you jump. I'm tired."

I went to the center and she and Chick whirled the ropes, and I jumped and jumped, fast as I could. I had to throw off my reindeer antlers. "When are you going to marry him?" I figured it wouldn't be until we were at least seventeen. Laina had been sixteen and Mrs. Horleson almost sent Jeffy's head straight into Idaho!

"I'm going to marry him the day after I graduate from high school. Or maybe sooner."

"Does Jed know?" I asked. "Here, Chick. You jump now." Chick jumped in the middle as Justine and I whirled the ropes.

"I'm going to tell him today what we're going to do."

We didn't know why that day was special enough to announce love — it was December. A little cold. Some wind. Christmas trees up . . . but okay!

"You can come with me," she said.

It was a generous offer.

"Okeydoke," Chick said, puffing, her red hair flying under the reindeer antlers.

"I bet he'll say yes," I said. I thought it was polite to be encouraging.

"Yep," Justine said, still whirling both ropes as Chick jumped and then fell on her rear. "My turn again!"

Chick and I went with Justine after school to the high school's basketball gym where Jed was practicing. He constantly played during the games because he made so many baskets. We sat in the bleachers with our reindeer antler hats on, then we grew bored so we drew pictures of Rudolph the Red-Nosed Reindeer in our notebooks. My Rudolph looked as if he'd been hit in the head, his eyes crossed, his mouth drooping.

"He's done practicing," Justine said, pointing at Jed. He waved to the three of us, and we scrambled off the bleachers, pulling our backpacks onto our backs.

We all headed out together. Jed's teammates called out to him, said good-bye, slapped him on the back, said they'd see him later, and could he help with their math homework, and did you understand chemistry today, and hey, you want to hang out this weekend, Jed? He was a popular guy.

Jed never seemed embarrassed to have us bopping around. He was always kind to everyone, polite, quiet, confident . . . and somewhat shy, which was endearing.

We skipped around Jed as we headed home down the main street of town, snow sprinkling, our reindeer hats falling off now and then. Justine, Chick, and I showed him our Rudolph pictures. He praised my antlers for being "pink-and-white striped" and Chick's drawing for a "perfect red rose for the nose" and Justine's reindeer for having "nice straight teeth."

She said, "I drew it for you, Jed."

"Thank you, Justine. I'll put it up in my room."

She grinned. She was missing two teeth. "You're welcome. See how he's wearing your blue shirt?"

He did! She handed Rudolph to him with ceremony.

We walked past the library, police station, café, and bakery. When we reached the lake near Jed and Chick's house, Justine saw her moment. She stood up tall, squished her antlers down tight on her head, and said, "Jed, you and I are going to get married."

Jed smiled at Justine. "We are?"

"Yes." Justine was sure of this. "I think when I graduate from high school. Or maybe when I'm sixteen."

"I would be twenty-three then, Justine."

"Yep!" Justine said. "I know math. So will you?"

"Will I what?"

"Marry me?"

The three of us with our reindeer hats tilted our heads back to stare up at him, Jed being a tall and lanky sort of kid.

"Justine, I appreciate your offer." His tone was gentle. Protective. "You are smart and brave, but you are way too young for me and I won't be getting married for a long time."

Justine actually stomped her foot. "What are you talking about?"

"Justine, you are seven and I am fourteen."

"Seven years. I already told you I know math." Her face was flushed. This proposal wasn't going well.

"And we're too young to be thinking about getting married."

"No, we're not. What do you know?" Justine had a temper. Being the oldest of a bunch of kids born in a kiddie pool in the living room would wear anyone out.

"I know that you are a special friend to Chick and to Natalie."

"And I'm a special friend to you and I gave you my Rudolph the Reindeer picture!"

He smiled. "And you're a friend to me, too."

"So we're going to get married." She crossed her arms and stuck out her chin. She was so mad. "Aren't we?"

I saw Jed hesitate. I wasn't sure of all the dynamics here, but I had seen *Snow White* and *Cinderella,* and asking someone to marry you didn't go exactly like this.

"Justine." He kneeled down so he was eye to eye with her. "I can't marry you."

"Yes, you can, you stupid head."

He almost laughed, I could tell, but he stopped himself.

"I'm going to marry you and you're making me mad. I'm very, very mad at you!" She pointed at him with both hands.

"I don't want to make you mad."

"You have. You don't know anything." She capped off this pronouncement by moving with lightning speed and smashing her foot over Jed's.

He let her stomp him the first time, then he moved his foot at her second stomp, then moved it again when she tried to stomp him a third time.

"You say yes, Jed Thornton, you brat!"

"I'm sorry, Justine. I don't mean to hurt your feelings."

Tears flooded those golden eyes, and Justine threw her reindeer antlers at him. For the finale, she kicked him in the shin and ran off.

"Wow," Chick said. "You shouldn't have done that, Jed. I'm telling Mom. You made Justine cry."

"Maybe you'll change your mind," I said to Jed. "Justine knows how to climb trees really high, and she also knows how to take care of babies because her mom keeps having them in their pool in the living room. The pool doesn't have a slide."

He blinked at me, and I could tell he almost laughed, yet again, but didn't.

"She is fast at climbing trees and she's nice to her brothers and sisters," Jed agreed. He bent down and rubbed his shin. Justine had a strong kick!

"I think you should say sorry to her, Jed," Chick said. "She asked nicely. Well." Her brow furrowed. "Pretty nice."

"Yes, you should say sorry," I said in all seriousness. "She did give you her Rudolph the Red-Nosed Reindeer picture."

Justine was way too young for Jed for years. Then that one event happened to Justine that ruined her for a long time. In her twenties, she saw Jed, but only now and then, mostly when all the families — mine, Jed and Chick's, and Justine's — were together for holidays or weddings.

It hurt her, but she did it because she couldn't stay away from him. She was too screwed up and scared that if he found out what she did, he would lose all respect for her. He would think she was "a sick, awful, cold person."

From the time Justine graduated from college, which was the only time that Jed would have even thought of dating her, being seven years older, their timing was off.

Jed had a serious relationship with another attorney for years. Justine gave up on ever being together with Jed at that point and had the Ridiculously Stupid Disastrous Sucky Marriage for four years, then a fireworks divorce, handled by our friend, Cherie Poitras, that lasted almost two years because Marco, The Needle Penis Husband, didn't want a divorce, so he tried to ruin her financially.

When that was over and Justine had her head on straight, Jed was in another relationship, then Justine met Xavier, a proctologist, and convinced herself she loved him for a year. She broke up with him one month after they became engaged when she finally faced the fact that she could not marry anyone but Jed and this wasn't fair to the fiancé.

Xavier flipped out, stalked her, and she had to get a restraining order. We had to bar him from the building where our accounting firm is located.

Justine has always loved Jed, and I do think she always will.

Both of them are single now and have

been for a while.

As for Jed, he always asks me how Justine is when I see him. Behind the mind of a successful prosecuting attorney, he is shy. He is still the Jed we knew as kids.

"Zack!" I stood up from the card game Go Fish I was playing with Soldier, Frog Lady, and Architect in the activities room. It's about all we can handle. We still goof it up by not handing over kings or sixes or fours. We're not trying to cheat, but sometimes things blur.

Frog Lady said, "He is hot," and Soldier said, "Ask him if he knows where I put my green yarn. He looks like someone who would know," and Architect said, "I wonder if he lives in a building I built." He frowned, then his face turned sad. "I don't think he likes me."

I hurried over to give Zack a hug.

"Hey, baby." Zack smiled at me, gave me a kiss on the lips, and hugged me close. "How are you?"

"I'm fine." And I was, because he was with me. We sat down on my bed in my room, away from the others. He helped me sit down. I still wobble. Head injuries aren't helpful to balance.

"What did you do today?"

"Therapy. More therapy." I was glad I'd worn my Jimi Hendrix T-shirt and my black jeans. Jimi made me feel rockin'. As much as I can rock at this point, at least.

"I think it's helping, honey."

"I do, too. Torture chamber sometimes, though." Every day the therapists pushed me to do what I couldn't do, but tried, the day before. Sometimes I can do it, sometimes I can't. Sometimes it truly ticks me off and I rage, sometimes I get so frustrated I cry, and sometimes I have a tiny victory.

"I miss you, baby." Zack kissed me. We do have to restrain ourselves in here, which is unfortunate. I would not want to be straddling Zack when a doctor walked in.

"I miss you, too."

"Aw, honey. Don't cry."

"I can't help it. I almost fell in physical therapy today. José caught me."

"I'm sorry, Natalie."

I could tell by those green eyes, shattered, tired, that he was. He was truly sorry.

I smiled. He smiled back. Whew. That man is hot, like Frog Lady said.

"I want to wear my lingerie for you again."

"I can't wait until you do, honey. You and your lingerie haunt me more than you'll ever know."

"Look what I made you." I took off the

necklace I was wearing. It was made of leather string and in the center was a simple silver circle with two tiny silver beads on each side. "The circle reminded me of the moon over the Deschutes River."

That man! He teared up, pulled away, those green eyes growing even brighter. He dropped his head.

"What's wrong?"

He was upset. He didn't answer.

"Zack?" I ran my hand over that bent head.

He put his head up and I saw it then: Anguish. Total anguish.

"Zack, what is it? What's wrong?"

"Natalie," he said, his voice gruff, "if you are all right, everything in life is all right."

"Tell me, Zack, please. I want to know. I was in a hit-and-run. Someone cut up a Barbie and put my initials on it. You're upset. You take phone calls and you're mad. . . ."

"Nothing you need to worry about, honey. I'm having some problems with the business. I think an ex-employee brought the Barbie in, but everything is going to be okay."

"What are the problems? Who was the employee?"

"We're figuring it out."

"With the police?"

"Yes. They're on it. Hey. I love this. I'll wear it every day."

"You're not going to tell me what you know?"

"Natalie, you have enough to worry about. Let me handle it."

"But —"

"Baby, please."

I didn't want tension with Zack. He is delicious and kind and has been there for me every single day during this whole disaster. There was nothing I could do in here anyhow, and even if there was, I can't handle it. I can barely handle myself and my skittery brain. I felt that familiar rush of extreme fatigue. The only way to describe it is to say that it's the worst jet lag you've ever experienced. My brain caves in and *must* sleep.

"Okay, Zack." I kissed him, gave him a hug, and he hugged me back, so tight.

The tightness of that hug worried me even more. It was as if he was afraid to let go of me.

My dad comes to visit every weekend. We talk and laugh. He continues to read *Jane Eyre* to me, and he catches me up on his animals and the townspeople. Afterward, almost every time, someone will say something along the lines of, "That's your *father*? Looks like a movie star . . . was he in a band . . . Is he . . . single?"

I do not see a movie star, I see: Dad.

He had even brushed his hair this last time.

As I was going to sleep that night, stuck in that halfway place between being awake and asleep, a vision shoved its way through. It was me, and Zack, in our house. I was running from him, to my car. He was yelling at me to wait, wait, wait. I jumped in my car and drove and he followed me, fast . . . then the vision ended, and I was wide awake in my hospital bed.

I wish I could remember the morning of my accident. There were answers there, I knew it. Zack was lying when he'd said it was a normal morning. There was nothing normal about it.

I put a hand on my forehead. I think I might be getting better.

CHAPTER 10

I received a box in the mail. Stelly, a CNA, brought it to me. It was wrapped in brown paper. There was no return address. "Here ya go, Mrs. Shelton. A present for you." She smiled. I liked her. She plays trumpet in a jazz band.

"Thanks, Stelly." I opened it up in the activities room where I was making necklaces. Frog Lady was rolling clay around in her hands and humming; Architect was drawing architectural prints of a building, complete with blue dogs and smiling blue whales around the edges; and Soldier was drawing a picture for his grandma of a destroyed city with sand everywhere and one man on top of a building shooting other people in the streets. He called it Peter Pan and Wendy.

"Jewelry Maker has a present," Frog Lady said. "It could be a frog."

"Are you going to cry today?" Soldier

asked me, curious only.

"I don't know. I could."

"Okay. Yes, ma'am." He went back to his drawing, then nodded at my present. "If that's an MRE, I'm not eating it. I've had enough of those."

"When is crying session?" Frog Lady asked. "I think I'll do it today. Hop goes my frog. There are millions of genus and species, dead and alive. You have to explore the whole earth to find the ones who are hiding."

"Is there steel in that box?" Architect asked. "I need steel for the structure of this building. We can buy it from the Chinese, but I'd rather get American-made steel."

"I don't know. I'll check." I pulled off the tape. It took a long time. My fingers couldn't do it. It was frustrating. I finally used scissors. I pulled back the top of the box. There were newspaper pages on top, the comics section, so I lifted them out.

Soldier, Frog Lady, and Architect stood up and peered into the box with me.

There was a dead bird inside.

I sucked in my breath. The dead bird had *no head.*

Soldier started whimpering. "It's dead. It's dead. I didn't kill it. I never wanted to kill anyone in that sandy place." He ran to a corner, leaned his helmeted head against the wall, and started to cry, rocking back and forth. "I didn't want to! I didn't want to do it!"

Architect said, "That dead bird with no head is upsetting. I like animals." He turned around and ripped up his building plans, I don't know why.

"That is not a nice friend who sends you a dead bird," Frog Lady said, her hands shaking around a frog. "You need new friends. I would not send you a dead frog." She burst into tears. "All animals are precious and must be saved."

I heard a scream and then I realized it was me. People started running toward me, doctors and nurses.

One doctor said, "Oh, my God."

A nurse said to someone else, "Get Shea Zogg in Security and tell her what happened to Natalie. Tell her to call the police."

Another nurse ran to be with Soldier, who was now knocking his helmeted head repeatedly against the wall. "I had to do it or he was going to kill me. I had to! He had a knife. A knife! I'm sorry! I'm so sorry!"

Architect patted me on the back, then gave me a hug, his helmet hitting my head. "I don't build cemeteries, Jewelry Maker, or I would bury that bird for you."

My hands started to shake. I would not be making any more necklaces that day.

I had a guard reassigned to me in ten minutes.

Security came immediately, led by Shea Zogg. The police came soon after, including Detective Zadora. Zack came right after the detective arrived. Detective Zadora had one of her officers talk to Zack and lead him away. He was not allowed to talk to me.

A nurse had already removed the headless bird and given it to Security.

Once again my reality stunned me: I was being targeted. I was hit by a van. The driver drove off. I had a stabbed Barbie with her head on backward dropped in my hospital room, and now a headless bird had been delivered to me. It was so sick, so twisted, a demented message sent and received.

Detective Zadora asked me the same questions as she had before, in different ways.

And then, "Natalie, can I see your phone?" Detective Zadora asked.

"What?"

"Can I see your phone?"

"Sure."

"What's the number to unlock it?"

I told her. She looked through it. She listened to voice messages. It felt invasive, but being targeted by a sicko felt invasive, too.

"Someone might be mad at your husband," Shea Zogg said, watching me closely, when the detective and she were done with my phone.

I nodded. I felt dizzy. Ill. I knew it was Zack. Someone was after Zack through me. I am a jumbled mess, but I am not stupid.

"Maybe a former employee?" Detective Zadora also watched me carefully. They were both looking for any clues, said and unsaid. This question had been asked before.

I nodded. That's what Zack had told me. "It could be. He said you all have been working on it."

"We have been," Detective Zadora said.

Should I now, finally, tell them about the phone calls Zack received when I was in my coma that had made him so furious? I wanted to protect Zack. I knew that Zack was not guilty of doing this. He had not paid someone to hit me with a van, he had not sent a scraped-up Barbie to my room, he had not sent the headless bird. It wasn't Zack, and I didn't want the police to think it was.

Detective Zadora and Shea Zogg were still studying me, analyzing me.

"Anything else you want to tell us?" Detective Zadora said to me.

"No," I said.

"Are you sure?" Shea asked.

"No." I paused. "Yes. No, there is nothing else I have to tell you."

Silence.

"Help us help you," Detective Zadora said.

"I will."

"We need to catch this person before you or Zack is hurt."

"Yes. I know."

"Are you sure there's no one you can think of who would do this?"

"No one."

More silence.

They knew I was hiding something.

Detective Zadora, the police, and Shea Zogg talked to Zack alone downstairs. I wobbled back to my room, with the help of a nurse and Soldier, who insisted on "helping my buddy," and lay down on my bed, my head throbbing as if an elf were in there with a sledgehammer. Zack came in later and hugged me close. I was nauseated. He rubbed my temples, nice and slow, like I like it.

"I am so sorry, Natalie."

"Who would send me a dead, headless bird?"

"I don't know, honey."

I pulled back and studied his expression and caught my breath like a cape of truth: *Zack knows exactly who sent the dead bird.* "I think you know." My voice was hesitant.

"I told you, it's probably one of my employees, in the past, who I fired or a supplier who's angry he lost a job with me. The police are going to figure all of this out."

I was freezing cold with fear. Someone was gunning for me, and Zack, and his answers did not add up.

"But —"

"Natalie, I'm taking care of it."

"But —"

"I've got it, Natalie. The police have it. You rest."

My head was slammed with pain. The intense fatigue struck. I would figure this out . . . after I slept.

Before we were married, Zack and I took a drive into the country, coffee in hand. We saw a crumbling red barn. It tilted to the left.

He stopped and we both stared at it.

"I wonder who built that," I said.

"It's got to be a hundred years old."

"I wonder what the family was like who owned it."

"Many families. Ton of history there."

"You could use the wood in your homes."

"How?"

"Wrapped around the kitchen island. Shelving. The mantle. A cool design on the wall where they could hang pictures. Flooring in the den. The barn doors could be doors in a home." I had more ideas. Living with my dad taught me that wood could, and should, be reused.

He turned to stare at me. "You're a smart one, Natalie."

I gave him a kiss. Zack was brilliant. No one becomes a construction engineer unless they're super ridiculous smart.

And that was it. We went to talk to the owner.

The home owner was eighty-five. We had dinner with him. He told us the barn was a hazard and said we could take the wood. Zack had a warehouse, and his crew put it in there.

Now he repurposes all kinds of wood for his homes — old gym floors, demolished bowling alleys, a roller rink once, barns, old homes, old schoolhouses, churches, interesting doors, bleachers, a bread factory, a bar from a saloon — anything that was coming down that had a history, we would collect wood from it.

He left a calling card, so to speak, in all of his houses: old wood, historical wood, special wood that held a story. When he listed his houses, he included the information of where the wood came from. People loved it. The homes were new, but they had personality and history and character.

Zack took the highest bid for his homes — usually. When a widowed single mother of five kids, one with autism, bid on one, he took her offer. When a twenty-six-year-old, stressed-out, and grief-stricken uncle who had adopted his four nephews after their parents died in a car accident didn't come in with the highest bid, Zack still let him buy it. He let two grandparents buy a house when they were raising their three granddaughters because their own daughter was in jail. None of them had the highest bid.

"I couldn't say no," he told me. "I just couldn't."

And that's one of the reasons I love Zack: He does not turn his eyes away from people who are struggling.

Like me.

His homes attracted attention at the state level, then at the national level. He was often asked for interviews. He did only print interviews, no on-camera interviews. He would not allow a photo of himself in any magazine, in a newspaper, or on his website; only the homes were allowed to be photographed or his foremen or employees. He said he was private.

The one time that his face was on the cover of *US Home Building,* he was furious. "I specifically told them that there was to be no photos of me. Only the homes, or my employees."

I was stunned at how angry he was. "But, Zack, you own the company. You build beautiful homes. People want to see the face of the builder."

He wasn't even listening. He stalked to the windows of our home and glared into the night. It was clear he did not want to talk. I didn't understand it, at all. I knew he was private but to be that ticked off?

That night I went to bed alone. I woke up at three and he was still in the family room, in a chair, staring into the night, his jaw tight.

"Zack?"

"Baby, go back to bed."

"Is everything okay?"

"Yes. It's fine."

It wasn't fine. His anger over this was beyond incomprehensible, but he shut down all talk on the subject, and I let it go.

I kept thinking about his simmering anger that day.

Zack told my dad about the dead bird.

My dad insisted on seeing the president of the hospital when he came to see me the next day. Amazingly, the president made time for him. He also insisted on seeing the doctor in charge of my unit. And the second in command. I was to receive no more packages. Security had already told everyone in the Brain Bang Unit that all of my packages were to be opened first, after the Barbie incident, but Stelly, the CNA, had simply not gotten the message. There were a lot of people who worked on the floor; it was a communication issue. The doctors apologized for allowing a package to get to me, and said it would not happen again.

Later, after my dad left, a doctor said to me, patting her hair, "How long has your father been married to your mother? Oh, they're divorced? Is he currently married?"

In my nightmare that night the bald man chased after me, stuck a live bird without a head into my mouth, then duct-taped my mouth shut. I couldn't breathe. The bird clawed my mouth and throat, then it died. Then I died because I choked on the bird. The bald man laughed.

The Moonshine and Milky Way Maverick Girls came to visit me again. Justine snuck in peppermint ice cream and pickles in a cooler.

"We should do the Naked Bike Ride in Portland." Chick pointed at me with a pickle. "It will be a celebration of Natalie getting better and all of us grabbing our inner wild and crazy selves and riding off with them."

"I need to be wild and crazy," Justine said. "To shake things up. To feel young again. To feel free. Geez. I sound like a cliché. I'm pathetic, aren't I? I know I'm pathetic."

"You're talking about getting naked. In Portland. On a bike." My speech was slow still, plodding, but it was coming along. I ate the peppermint ice cream without the pickle. "That means no clothes."

Yes, we have an annual Naked Bike Ride here in Portland. People do ride buck naked. Some paste artificial flowers to their nipples. Some cover up their bottoms with thongs or bikini bottoms. Many don't.

There are funny hats and wigs, no doubt for disguise, and others are riding happily along, not a stitch on.

"We'll get you one of those three-wheeled bikes," Justine said. "So you don't fall over on your naked bottom and bop your head."

"One with a pretty flowered basket in front," Chick said.

"It's like truth or dare, but it'll be a dare," Justine said. She was eating the peppermint ice cream straight out of the carton.

We had done so many daring things when we were younger. We had jumped off The Rocks over the lake holding hands. We had drag raced. We had skied fast and devised creative pranks and teased a bull and strung up the bras of all the girls in our high school on a flag pole to protest that *yet another* principal was a man, and not a woman. The man left, a woman was hired.

Then we all grew up and had to display a modicum of normalness to maintain our reputations and so we did, and it has been dreary in the wild and crazy department ever since.

"It's so boring being boring," Justine said.

"It's so dull being dull," Chick said. "But look at me." She pointed to herself. "I own a hardware store with leaf blowers and pillows and drills and curtains. Who would have thought I'd grow up and do something like that? Hit me in the head with a hammer, I never would have thought it. I have six kids running around." She scrunched her nose up. "They're all so odd, too, totally odd. Oh, my gosh." She smacked her forehead. "Ellie built a huge volcano on the football field and blew it up with a firework for science class. She taped it. She was suspended. Hudson ordered worms in bulk because he wants a worm-selling business. Three boxes of worms. Joshua only wants to wear pink pants and sing Broadway songs. He might as well wear a T-shirt that says, 'I'm Gay.' Ally had a ballet recital with those mongo-sized feet of hers and fell twice, and Timmy and Tessie escaped again on their trikes and made it into town. They were both wearing black capes and black Batman masks."

Justine and I laughed.

"I want to do Portland's Naked Bike Ride because I want to get myself back," Chick said. "I want to be who I used to be before I got married and became a mother and had a herd of odd kids."

"I'll do it," I said. "I could go for some wild and crazy. I have bars on my toilet and I tilt to the left when I walk. I sound like I'm a slow drunk when I talk. I want to be who I was before the accident. Actually, I want to be who I was in Lake Joseph, when we were teenagers."

"I'll do it," Justine said. "I want to add laughs to my life. I'll ride in costume."

"Oh, definitely in costume," I said. "Wigs. Hats. Big glasses. I need to be totally unrecognizable while I'm going wild and crazy."

"I'm covering my butt," Chick said. "With this honkin' thing people will think my butt has swallowed the bike seat when they see me."

"Cheers to that," Justine said.

We grabbed our pickles and whacked them one against the others.

"I'll invite Jed so he can see what he's missing out on with you, Justine," I said.

She grinned. "You're a true pal."

Chick and Justine had known about the Barbie in my hospital room. I told them about the headless bird, which explained the guard. They both leaned back in their seats for once, silent.

"You're being stalked," Chick finally said.

"Someone's trying to take you out," Justine said.

"Seems like it," I said.

"Or Zack," Chick said.

"Yes," I said. "Or Zack, through me."

More silence.

They reached out and held my hands.

When I was younger, while other girls, except for my fearless Moonshine and Milky Way Maverick girlfriends, were poring over fashion and movie star magazines, I was poring over home décor articles in magazines at the library. My dad bought me a subscription to two of them on my eleventh birthday and I jumped up and down. That's how well my dad knew me.

Our house was small, with two bedrooms, on twenty acres outside of town. My grandma's dad built it himself, and she grew up in that house. She insisted on giving it to my dad when I was born and moved to a brand-new double-wide trailer about a half mile away.

Grandma Dixie didn't like my mother any more than she would like a grizzly bear in her kitchen, because she didn't think she was kind to me or her son but, looking back, I realize there was another emotion my grandma held toward my mother . . . pity. I don't understand it, but that's what it was.

Pity or not, Grandma Dixie would not live with "Princess Jocelyn," and her generous heart wanted to provide a home for her young son and his family, so we got the house.

Our kitchen was galley style, with dark brown cabinets, and closed off. We had a family room and dining area. To me it was home, it was what I knew, it was where my parents and I lived and then, after my mother left us, driving away with a cheery wave, it was where my dad and I lived.

But even I knew, because I had been to other kids' houses, that it was dark, cluttered, and depressing, despite the 360-degree view of both sunsets and sunrises.

Some of my mother's stuff was still there, too. Her clothes, her coats, her knickknacks, etc. All stuck in closets. It had been five years, and I knew she was gone. I didn't know why my dad didn't get rid of it. Maybe he was simply overwhelmed by raising a daughter alone, with both a roofing and a metalworks business, and didn't want to deal with it.

I wanted it out.

"We need to get rid of Mom's stuff. She doesn't want it," I told my dad at breakfast one day. We were having buttermilk pancakes. He made the best pancakes.

He paused, pancakes halfway to his mouth. He put his fork down. "You're right, Hummingbird. We do need to get rid of it."

I teared up.

"It's hard, isn't it?"

I nodded, and he ran a hand over my curls, caught up in a ponytail.

"She's not coming back and I know it, but . . ."

"This seems final. Done. Door's shut."

"Yes."

"I'm sorry, Hummingbird."

I wiped my hands over my teary face. "Me too, Daddy."

"I love you."

We grabbed black plastic bags and filled them with her stuff and piled it all into his truck for Goodwill. My dad even lifted up his bed and dumped the mattresses and frame into the back of his truck. I heard him mutter something about "Getting rid of the woman in bed, too."

We then decided to attack the rest of the house. We threw out everything we didn't need or want. We filled one black trash bag after another.

We went through the kitchen and threw out broken dishes and cups, piles of plastic containers, old food in the fridge and pantries, and we ripped broken blinds off the windows. We threw out furniture that didn't work: two wood chairs that wouldn't balance, a lounge chair, a couch, a small table that wobbled.

I looked at some of the pictures on the walls. "They're all ugly."

"They are."

We took them all down and threw them out.

Within a few hours, drawers opened smoothly because they weren't crammed. Nothing fell out of the kitchen cabinets. In fact, some of the cabinets had hardly anything in them. The bathroom cabinet doors closed, too, as we'd cleared out my mother's hoard of shampoos and cream rinses and makeup. My closet shut, and I realized how few clothes I actually had that fit. There was nothing under my bed.

"Now we need to clean, Daddy."

My dad's head dropped. Cleaning? Not so fun. Perfect day out, too, for fishing, steelhead jumping in the river. Clearing out most of the house helped, but it also exposed how dusty and dirty everything was, from the floors to the walls.

"How about if we clean and then we go to the Deschutes tomorrow?" I said.

His head perked up. He held up a hand and I slapped it. "Deal, Hummingbird."

We dusted, we swept, we mopped, we vacuumed. We cleaned the kitchen and the bathroom. We washed all the sheets and blankets and towels and opened all the windows. We took several trips to the dump and Goodwill with our trailer, then fished on the Deschutes the next afternoon when we were finally done.

I caught two steelhead at dusk, and my dad caught three.

When we came home, my mother's ghost was gone.

That night my grandma Dixie brought us her apple pie. She drove it over on her motorcycle. It was even more delicious than usual. When she walked in and saw the house, for once Grandma Dixie was speechless.

Cleaning our small home got rid of the cloying, scraping sadness of my mother leaving, as if we opened the windows and the bad memories of her flew out. For me, an organized, clean, pretty home means that I have control over where I live and my life and my mother's desertion is nowhere near it.

It was why I so carefully decorated my dorm and my apartment in college, it was why I decorated my studio in Portland, it was why I decorated the house I shared with Zack. We painted walls, we bought comfortable furniture, we hung up Grenadine Scotch Wild's paintings and my hummingbirds. I packed our bookshelves with my china teacups; collections of white ceramic vases; and my plants, books, candles, and pictures.

Most important, I created a place on a shelf for Grandma Dixie's antique perfume bottles.

I didn't *want* pretty and clean. I *needed* pretty and clean.

For sanity.

Getting a puzzle together with one of my therapists brought me to tears the next day. It was a kid's puzzle and I couldn't do it. How was I going to be an accountant again if I couldn't even get Humpty-Dumpty back on his wall? How can I work if *I* don't work?

If I couldn't get the numbers to align in my head, if I couldn't remember how to use deductions and credits, financial statements, and tax projections, and couldn't work within the maze of the U.S. tax laws, what would I do?

Sometimes I'm terrified about my new life. Sometimes I'm livid. I'm livid at the driver of the van. He had taken so much of my life from me. Deliberately. Criminally. Sickeningly. And he's still after me.

But then I tell myself to buck up, quit whining, that I'll get better. Then the next day I'm unable to put playing cards in order or I forget to put laundry soap in the washing machine in the practice laundromat and I'm infuriated again.

And what about my marriage, what about Zack? He married the old me, the smart one, the competent one, the worker, the one who could talk about anything. Now I'm physically weaker and mentally a mess. I also cry a lot, often for no reason other than that I'm having a bad day.

But I'm angry at him, too. He won't tell me something I need to know. He is lying. The old me wouldn't let this go on for one second. I'm a fighter, and I would insist he tell me.

But the new me doesn't have enough energy to fight with Zack, even though I know someone's gunning for us, someone dangerous and demented. Not pleasant. Why won't I fight? Because I'm a wreck still. I have prioritized walking over truth. I have prioritized speech therapy over insisting on honesty. I have prioritized putting Humpy-Dumpty back together again over dealing with his evasiveness.

It's depressing to lose yourself. To be the person you had been your whole life and then to change and morph into someone you don't recognize. Someone who needs help, someone who isn't independent, someone who is weak, whose brain and body don't function like they did. You have become the pathetic person you used to feel sorry for.

I am not Natalie anymore, and yet I am.

Natalie can't add.
Natalie can't subtract.

She can dance
And she can clap.

She has a husband.
True love it be.

But he's lying to her.
One, two, three.

On Wednesday Architect got so frustrated with the building he made with popsicle sticks that he smashed the whole thing with his fists and started pelting the sticks at the windows.

Frog Lady grabbed her clay frog and hid under the table. "Come along to my tree, Jewelry Maker," she whispered with a smile.

I left my jewelry and crawled under the table. "He'll stop soon," I said. "He'll run out of sticks."

"At least he's not throwing frogs," she said.

Soldier stood up and said to Architect, "You are not the enemy so I won't kill you, but stop throwing sticks at the civilians. We can't bomb civilians."

I peeked over the top of the table. Architect stopped throwing sticks. He started to cry, and Soldier put his hand on Architect's shoulder, then put his helmet next to Architect's. I stood up, and so did Frog Lady, holding her frog. We had a group hug.

"It's okay, man," Soldier said. "We're all at war here and we gotta stick together. We're buddies. I'll protect you, you protect me."

"Okay," Architect cried. "Okay. But I can't get this building to work. The bridge between the buildings keeps falling down. It's all screwed up. It's broken. It's broken. I'm broken."

"I'll help you," Soldier said.

"You will?" An expression of happy hope crossed Architect's face.

"Yes."

"I'll help you, too," I said.

"Me too," Frog Lady said. "I'll bring my frog and we'll build a building. Hop to it, scientists!"

"Finally," Architect said, wiping his face. "A team. I finally found my team. We can build it together."

And that's what we did. We built a building.

Together.

It's hard to see people all beat up, wearing helmets, sitting in wheelchairs or leaning on canes. Some people I met the first day still don't talk at all. Some mutter. Some go into rages. Some are clearly permanently disabled. Their families are upset, their friends are upset.

Sometimes all you can do is sit by them.

Jed came to see me again. This was his fourth or fifth visit. Under penalty of being ejected from the Moonshine and Milky Way Maverick Girls, I did not say a word to him of Justine's undying love and lust.

"I hear you might be a judge soon."

"Maybe." He smiled. "I hope so. Have you seen Justine lately?"

I had! "I'm glad you asked. She's doing very well, not seeing anyone. We're going to do Portland's Naked Bike Ride. . . ."

I received a letter from Chick. She had drawn the three of us on bicycles, naked.

Our bodies were outlined only. It was hilarious.

I couldn't believe I was doing anything like this. Part of me didn't think I could do it, that my balance would still be so bad that I wouldn't be able to ride a bike, even one with three wheels and a flowered basket. I can hardly walk a straight line and my brain is still popping and cracking and doing its own thing.

The other part of me was scared to death that I would be better and I would *have* to get on a three-wheeled bike naked because I'd promised the Moonshine and Milky Way Maverick Girls that I would try to get my "wild and crazy" back and become who I used to be.

But did I have to get my wild and crazy back buck naked, at night, in a thriving city?

"Hey, sweets."

"Zack." I had been resting in my room between appointments with my neuropsychologist and Dr. Doom and Dr. Hopeless, who were coming to visit me and talk to me again about being awake in my coma. I was feeling nervous, anxious.

"You look beautiful."

"Thanks." I had washed my hair that morning. I had put on makeup. I had put on my light blue jeans, a shirt with a parrot on the back that I'd bought in Mexico, and two necklaces I'd made here: one with faux turquoise I'd wrapped in wire and the other with five silver hearts that I'd made as a choker.

Zack ran his hands through my curls. "Are you okay?"

"Yes."

He tilted his head. "What is it?"

"I was worried about . . ."

"About what?" His eyes narrowed. His body, close to mine, became taut.

"About . . ."

"Natalie?" he prompted. He was worried about my answer, I could tell.

"About my job."

He relaxed. He seemed relieved by my answer, as if he had expected something else. He pulled me in closer. "Babe, don't worry about your job right now. Seriously. You need to worry about continuing to get better."

"I am. But it's so scary, so depressing not to be able to add, to subtract. The numbers run all over, I can't keep them in my head."

"It takes time, Natalie. This whole thing will take time."

"But what if I can't be an accountant anymore?"

He kissed the top of my forehead and then pulled back. "Then you'll do something else."

I sagged against him. On one hand, it was devastating for him not to say, "Natalie, you'll be an accountant again in no time. Wait a month and your mind will clear and you'll go zipping back to work!" On the other, it was a relief for him not to lie to me, not to try to smooth this over or pretend. He was honest.

"I don't know what else to do."

"I know what you can do."

"What?"

"Help me with the designs for my business. Full time. I need help. I don't always ask you for help, because you're running your firm and I don't want to overburden you, but I need help, Natalie."

I thought about that. "Working for the man I sleep with?"

"You wouldn't be working for me, Natalie. We would be working together. Every time you study the plans for the houses I want to build, you add things I hadn't thought of. All the tiles and counters and flooring that you pick out are so much better what I can do. The reclaimed wood has helped to sell my homes more than anything else I've done. Before you came along, well, you saw my houses."

"They were perfect."

"No. They weren't. They were solid. They were well designed. But they weren't original. They weren't creative. From the time you started helping me, I've increased the price for all of my houses because of you."

"But I like numbers."

"I know, honey. I do."

I hugged him and kissed that hard jaw. "You're still my apple pie, Zack."

His eyelids lowered, then he glanced down at my mouth. Well, this ol' girl did not need any more of an invitation. We had a long and hot kiss then and there. . . .

I wrote a poem in my head that afternoon after Zack left.

With Zack I like to kiss.
He makes me feel hot bliss.

He's warm and snuggly.
That is true, that's why I said "I do."

And his hands of magic
Make me groan and moan.

What is he hiding, I don't know.
I only wish he wouldn't go.

Again, I never said my poems were well
written.

CHAPTER 11

Once I put aside my FOA (fear of abandonment) and Zack gave in and put behind him whatever had been preventing him from committing to me, things went quick from there.

He was six years older and ready to move on down the aisle. I met his friends from college, from work, from his pickup basketball team, and two fishing buddies, and I liked them all. He met Chick and her family and was quite comfortable around the chaos.

Chick said, "Marry him. Haul his butt to the altar as soon as you can."

He met Justine, and she declared him "a fine specimen. Speaking in mathematical terms, statistically I'd say you have a one hundred percent chance of this working out happily ever after."

My dad loved him. They had a lot in common: Home construction. Fishing. Hunting. Me.

My dad did say to him, "Zack. There is no one in this world I love even a fraction of how much I love my Natalie. You hurt her and I will get my rifle out."

Zack nodded. "I understand. I swear I will never hurt Natalie. I love her. I will always love your daughter, and I will protect her my whole life."

Zack still didn't talk much about his childhood — he always changed the subject, but that was because of the death of his parents and that terrible grief, wasn't it? Sometimes I still felt as if he was holding back, hiding something, but I was wrong, wasn't I?

We were in love and lust, and we made plans to build our dream home. *One day.*

Zack and I were married on the Deschutes River right where we'd met. I wore a hippie/bohemian/country girl white lace dress with a train, a flowing gauzy veil, and my blue cowgirl boots, given to me by my dad to symbolize "something blue."

There were about 150 people there. His friends, my friends, many from Lake Joseph, including Rosie, Jed, and all of Justine's family. My dad came in a tux, and my mother was there, too, with her latest husband.

"It must hurt your father terribly," my

mother whispered to me in her fancy, pink mother-of-the-bride dress, "to see me with my new husband, Hank. I mean, Ted."

"Get the husbands' names right, Mom." We glanced over at my dad, laughing with Chief Knight and Annabelle and a couple of their kids. "Yes," I drawled, "he looks totally broken up."

Zack and his best friends from college made an altar from wood. Justine and Chick covered it in flowers. We propped up fly-fishing rods. A minister from Lake Joseph, Leesa Arrowsmith, who was two years older than Chick, Justine, and me in high school, married Zack and me. We both cried happy tears, as we had when Zack asked me to marry him in this exact spot, on one knee, ring in hand nine months ago.

We had the meal catered. The wedding cake was four tiered, steelhead painted in icing around the sides. It was delicious. The day was bright and sunny, the river rolled, kids played, the younger ones in life jackets, we danced, and I held on to Zack knowing that I would be happy with him by my side forever.

And I have been.

I have been happy by Zack's side, even though now and then I've felt as if he was hiding something from me, that he had a secret.

As soon as I get better, as soon as I can walk right and get my brain in gear, as soon as I don't exhaust easily, as soon as I trust my own instincts, I will figure out what the heck is going on with a cut-up Barbie, a headless bird, and a hit-and-run accident and how that's all tangled up with my husband.

Oh no, it was my mother. Again. She hadn't called, as usual. When my mother wants to visit, she arrives.

One of the nurses, Olivia, came to get me in the activities room. I was making a necklace for my dad; Architect was building a tower with toothpicks and marshmallows; Frog Lady had drawn a detailed monkey, which was a curious departure for her; and Soldier was drawing his grandma another picture of, in his words, "a playground for Sleeping Beauty." The drawing was of a mess hall where members of the armed forces were eating, two with their heads wrapped in bandages and one with his head in his hands in despair.

"Mom." I patted my hair. My blond curls were a mess. She would tell me that. "What are you doing here?"

"What do you mean, what am I doing here?" She was standing near the doorway of the visiting lounge. I walked over, still unsteady on my feet but coming along. I prepared for a headache after her visit.

She was dressed impeccably, her thick blond hair in its usual bell. She had applied a full spackle of makeup with foundation, powder, blush, three colors of expertly applied eye shadow, and fake eyelashes, not too long. Today was Blue Topaz Day. She was wearing a dark blue dress with a ruffle on the hem. Matching blue topaz earrings, a necklace, and a bracelet completed her ensemble appropriate for a visit to the Brain Bang Unit.

She handed me her coat; it was wet. It was a designer coat. I hung it over a chair. Then she handed me her umbrella, soaking. Mother Monster even had a designer umbrella.

"I'm your mother. I have come to visit you, Natalie." She sat down at a table. I sat down, too, reluctantly, as if I were going to get my head chopped off by an executioner in a black mask.

She eyed me over her clasped, perfectly manicured nails, the blue topaz and the diamond ring flashing. This was what she wanted. This was why she left my dad and went through a series of husbands. She wanted the designer clothing. The coat and the umbrella. The jewelry. She wasn't "social climbing," she was "money climbing." Taking divorce settlements from each new husband.

"I have therapy in about twenty minutes —"

"What are you wearing?" She examined me head to foot, even leaning over the table for a more complete style examination.

I rolled my eyes. I was in a pink T-shirt and jeans. I was wearing tennis shoes because I needed the balance they gave me. "I'm wearing comfortable clothes, Mom. I'm in rehab."

"There's never a time when a woman shouldn't dress, Natalie."

"Not even here?"

"No. Remember, your clothes say who you are, what you are, your social standing, and your financial class."

"As I have told you before, I cannot even imagine worrying about something so shallow and silly."

"My gracious. How can you stand this? You need to go home soon. When I was waiting an interminably long time for the maid to tell me where to find you —"

"Olivia is not a maid, Mom. She's a nurse.

She's one of my nurses."

She waved her hand as in, *Do not bother me with these facts that I do not wish to hear.* "I spent too much time waiting in the entrance for you, waiting to be checked in, and all these people were wandering around with helmets and wheelchairs and walkers, all tottering about. Many of them are having trouble speaking, did you know that, Natalie?"

Was she serious? Yes. She was. "Yes, Mom. I did. I am having trouble speaking, too, as you can tell."

She narrowed her eyes at me. "You speak slowly, Natalie, and it is somewhat irritating, but your words are much, much improved. In the other hospital you sounded like you were gargling a mouse, but now I can understand you. I can hardly stand the thought of you living here, Natalie, with all these sick people in helmets."

She was deranged. No empathy. Zip. "I am living here until I can talk better and walk better and think better."

I thought her eyes might have softened, sympathy lurking. I realized I saw something that wasn't there when she said, while fiddling with her mongo-sized wedding ring, "Anyhow, have I told you that Dell and I had an argument?"

"Not yet." This was my mother, Jocelyn Miller Fox Andretti Moscovitz Chavez Smith, facing a daughter with a brain injury. The conversation *could* focus on the daughter for a few minutes, but no. We were now on to her favorite subject: Herself.

"We had an argument." She wiggled in her seat, then crossed her hosed legs, one expensive heel rocking with angry agitation. "He is giving me a monthly *allowance.* As if I'm a child."

"Why do you need an allowance, Mom?"

"That's what I said!" She was so indignant. "He gave me a credit card to use as I saw fit, and now he's telling me I can't use it as I see fit because, he said, I spent too much. The only things I ever bought were the essentials."

"Essentials" meant new clothing and jewelry, to my mother. "I meant, Mom, why do you need an allowance at all? Why aren't you working? You could make your own money. You could be independent." My mother didn't work. Ever. She leeched from husband to husband. Her rich parents had not instilled a work ethic in her. She told me when I was a girl, "Daddy knew how to take care of the women in his family."

"I don't have time to work, Natalie," she said, aghast at the prospect. "I help out on

Dell's ranch."

That was not remotely true. I was getting tired. I had woken up this morning, had breakfast, gone to my therapy classes, then started working on my necklaces. I loved my art, I did. Making jewelry was soothing to me, creative. And now the Spoiled Devil had arrived, sucking my energy out like a hose.

"He's limiting me. I feel controlled. Condescended to."

"What is the amount that he's limiting you to?"

"Two thousand a month."

I almost choked. "Two thousand? You pay bills with that, too, right? Food?"

She was offended, her lips a straight line. "No. You must be joking. Dell pays the bills. This is my *personal* money."

"And two thousand is not enough?" Was she serious?

She sat up ramrod straight in her chair. "Natalie. Please. I do not dress like you. As a leader in the community, I must dress the part."

"He's a rancher. No one expects you to wear designer clothes out in the fields."

"I don't go out in the fields. That's for the hired hands. Truly, Natalie." She held out her hands, her nails manicured and painted.

"Do these hands look like they could do anything, ever, in a field?"

It was a long morning.

Before my mother left, she hugged me. It was a long hug. Then she cupped my face with her hands and the mask fell, the arrogance and the obnoxiousness. "I love you, Natalie."

"I know, Mom."

"It's hard for me to come here, to see you."

"I know, Mom."

"It's a long drive, too."

"Very long."

"And I have to do it all by myself."

"Difficult."

Yes, coming to see me was hard for her. She's not a wise, compassionate woman who works within the messier parts of life. She doesn't like any upset, any trouble, any stress. Her life must revolve around her. She's not well versed at sticking around when life gets troublesome or difficult. That's why she left her first husband, my dad. It was hard to be the wife of a roofer. He didn't make enough money to indulge her, and his life could not revolve around her bottomless ego and her shallowness.

"I'm glad you're better." She hugged me

again, then whispered, "But wear some makeup, dear. At your age, you need it."

I was trying so hard to remember the morning of my crash. In the middle of occupational therapy, in the practice kitchen, I remembered yelling at Zack in my pink lace robe. It was something about a lie. It was something about a man named . . . Devon.

Then I had that vision of my grandma pushing me again . . . which was just ridiculous.

Grandma Dixie became my mother after my own left. We were always close. I worked with her in her mechanic's shop and learned all about cars. I went to her home regularly to visit, and make pies with her, especially apple pie.

She taught me how to play poker, shoot guns and bows and arrows, and how to defend myself. She taught me about life and compassion and how to change oil and flat tires. She taught me to appreciate the slick speed of a sports car and a dented, reliable truck and how to work hard.

Grandma Dixie loved me and when she died when I was sixteen I was heartbroken.

We buried her in the family plot, right next to her parents, and I planted bulbs on her grave. Sometimes, when I'm home, I'll bake her apple pie, bring it up, and eat it while I talk to her.

I have never stopped missing her, and when I see her antique, ornate, crystal perfume bottles and open the stoppers, I can catch her rose scent . . . and sometimes, I swear, her laugh.

Which made me think of that elusive fight with Zack again and then staring right at Grandma Dixie's perfume bottles in our home and thinking that she would know what to do. . . . What happened that morning?

My dad came to visit again. "I'm still making necklaces, Dad."

His face lit up. "Let's see 'em."

I showed him a few. I had given a bunch away to other patients. "Want to make a few together?" He did. Soldier came over and saluted and asked my dad if he knew how to knit. "I lost my blue yarn, but then Frog Lady said it was under the couch."

My dad asked him to show him how to knit, and Soldier did. It was touching to see Soldier and my dad knitting together.

Architect came over and drew my dad a house with modern lines. "Does she like me?" he whispered to my dad, holding his hand close to his chest as he pointed at me.

"I'm sure of it, son," my dad reassured him. "You seem like a smart fellow, so why wouldn't she?" That pleased Architect. He added smiley faces to the front of my dad's house.

Frog Lady made my dad a clay frog with a beard. "You are handsome," she said to him. "Do you study species?"

It was a nice afternoon with my dad and my new banged-up friends. I had to lie down after that, my head hurting, my words not coming out right, still slurring.

"I love you, Hummingbird."

"Love you, too."

My dad fell off a roof when I was seventeen.

He broke four vertebrae in his back. He was not a risk-taker, and he'd been tied to the chimney, but he fell on a slippery, shingled roof and landed wrong.

He had an operation and was in the hospital for three weeks.

When he came home, he could hardly move, the pain excruciating. He refused to take painkillers after he left the hospital. His best friend had gotten addicted and overdosed. He would not be that man, so my dad took over-the-counter meds only, which did not work.

But my dad's accident soon sent us off

the deep end. He had managed to save about three months of living expenses. My beloved grandma had died the year before from emphysema. My dad made sure she was able to stay in her gracious, elegant (expensive) care home until the end. He refinanced his home to do so.

But with his back injury, he couldn't work. He could barely stand.

I had a part-time job at a bakery in town, but I didn't work for a month because I spent all my time after school with him at the hospital. By his bedside, I made the rock jewelry. Sometimes Chick and Justine would come and make the rock jewelry with me.

The second month, when he was home, I didn't work at the bakery, either, because he needed help when I got home from school. I also took care of the animals and then picked the apples from our orchard to sell at the farmers' market on Saturday along with the rock jewelry. You could buy necklaces at our stand, and apples. His condition worsened. He had an emergency operation and was in the hospital for a week.

I took over the checkbook and paid the bills and knew we couldn't go on forever. The third month, I went back to work at the bakery, part time, as my dad was able to get out of bed. The fourth month he was able to walk around, but getting on a roof would have been impossible. He could no longer climb; he could no longer work that hard. He could stand only for short periods of time. Determined to make money, he worked on his fountains and windchimes and sold them to the nursery in town.

We were in for another blow, though. Premium Health Insurance Company sent a letter saying they would not pay for my dad's hospital stays, operations, or treatment. Hadn't he read the fine print of his contract? They wouldn't cover his injuries because he should have been covered by workman's comp. Or a union. Or a separate policy.

We don't cover falls off roofs. Duh. Sorry. This is on you, buddy.

This, after my dad had been paying monthly premiums since he had me. My dad hired Jilly Tebow, an attorney in town. Jilly used to work in a high-voltage firm in San Francisco. She retired her multimillionaire-self and moved to our town to be closer to outdoor activities. She married a farmer and learned how to drive a tractor. She loved a hot fight. Thrived off of it.

Jilly smothered Premium Health Insurance in legal letters and threats.

But Premium told Jilly that *in addition* to not having the "correct" policy, my dad hadn't gone to an "approved" hospital, when he was carried in to a local hospital after falling off a roof, only semiconscious from the pain, by his employees. They didn't cover medical care at *that* hospital, out in eastern Oregon. He should have instructed his coworkers to take him to St. Mary's, in Portland, five hours away, though, again, he was semiconscious and not speaking. Jilly smothered them in more legal letters and threats.

Then Premium said that, *in addition,* my dad had chosen doctors who were not under his "assigned and agreed-upon 'umbrella' of medical personnel," while in the emergency room after he fell off the roof. The doctors who later did both operations also were not under his "assigned and agreed-upon 'umbrella' of medical personnel." And, please note, they had *never* approved his second operation in the first place, which was clearly unnecessary.

In addition, his follow-up appointments were also "unnecessary," as if after an operation for broken vertebrae, he never should have seen a doctor again. Even so, they would not be paying for any part of his care, as it was "unfortunate" that my dad had not read the full legal contract, which he signed, that their lawyers had written up in a format that is incomprehensible to anyone who is not a long-term lawyer and also brilliant at deciphering code for "We suck as an insurance company and we will make you pay us your monthly premiums and then we will abandon you when you have a medical emergency."

Next, Premium Health Insurance officially dropped him altogether. "*In addition* . . . we regret to inform you that your insurance policy with us is now cancelled. . . ."

Jilly filed a lawsuit.

In the meantime, as that lawsuit ground on, my dad couldn't get on a new health insurance plan because now he had a preexisting condition. I, also, was not covered. We struggled. I worked at the bakery, I went to school, and I sold my rock jewelry and our apples at the Saturday market in town. I paid for our phone, our electricity, our water. I paid as much as I could toward the mortgage. Luckily, we were on the receiving end of endless meals/ deer meat from our friends in town. They didn't know how bad it was for us — my dad would never have shared that — but the meals meant our food bill went way down.

My dad was humiliated, stretched out and

aching in bed, his face white, his body rigid in pain, the second operation a dismal failure. My dad had always provided. He had always bought me school clothes and a new coat each year, and shorts and T-shirts for summer. He made sure I had boots and tennis shoes. He bought me Christmas and birthday presents, a mix of what I needed and what I wanted. Nothing lavish. He took care of me, and now the tables were flipped.

"I'm proud of you, Natalie," he told me, his voice strained with pain. "But I am sorry."

"Don't be sorry, Dad. Please." I hugged him. His head bent in defeat, but only for a minute. The man was a fighter.

On the day we had twelve dollars in our account, the house payment only partially paid, our medical bills completely unpaid, we were hit with a ray of hope. An artist moved into town. Margarita Hammer specialized in outdoor art, the enormous type that graces parks and city squares and libraries and government buildings.

Margarita, "half Mexican, half Dutch, one hundred percent rebel woman," as she told us, was famous, eccentric, kind in a gruff way, and provided health insurance to her six employees. She needed a metalsmith for her artwork. She hired my dad. He would work sitting down most of the time. It wasn't comfortable — his back still felt like a vise was squeezing him — but he could do it. He absolutely loved Margarita, the work, and his coworkers, three of whom had come from San Francisco specifically to work for her.

With the new health insurance he was able to go to a specialist. The specialist ordered an immediate operation and said the second operation had done more damage than help. My dad put it off as he'd just started his new job, but after three months Margarita Hammer found out what was going on and insisted my dad get the operation and threatened to fire him if he didn't go. "Get your butt in there, Scott, or you're out," she told him. I was there when she said it, and I almost cried I was so grateful.

The operation helped immensely; the surgeon was brilliant.

My dad began to get better, stronger each day, and with it his fighting spirit returned. He now had the energy to go after Premium Health Insurance to pay for what they did to him. "Not only for me, Hummingbird," he said, "but for my fellow Oregonians who don't know what a rat's ass of a company this is. They, and their children, are not protected. I would run them over with my tractor if I could."

My dad's case in court received a lot of attention, thanks to a talented young journalist named Draper Yates Hernion at our small town newspaper who was gunning to make a name for himself and move on. Jilly managed to get the trial set in our county, though Premium Health fought it.

Premium Health was arrogant and elitist. They thought they could lean on the fine print in the contract my dad had signed years ago to slither out of their obligations. They thought their slick attorneys could turn the heads of "easily swayed" people, the jury, who lived in eastern Oregon. It did not help that Draper overheard, and recorded, on the first day the attorneys were in town, those slimy city men talking about the "hicks" and "uneducated mice" and "tractor-driving, cow-herding, pig-slaughtering farmers and their fat farmer wives" and "straw-brained idiots" in Lake Joseph, and he printed it in an article here in town.

We have two hotels in Lake Joseph. After that article came out, all of a sudden, one of the hotels was chock-full. No rooms at all, they were booked for six full years. Sorry, Mrs. Golda Reams told the attorneys, "You'll have to go somewhere else, gentlemen. Perhaps a cave, where you belong. Or a swamp. Have you considered the dump?" The attorneys blinked at her. Mrs. Reams has white, curly hair and stands six feet tall. She was in the army. "I can drive you to the dump," she offered.

Avery Lindal, the owner of the second hotel, told the attorneys they were infested with lice and rats at the moment. She thrust her own pet rat, Maxie, in front of their faces and said, "Look what I found in the pantry!" Then she scratched her head hard and said, "Lice are impossible to get rid of." They grabbed their suitcases and turned around. "Don't you want to pet this rat?" she called after them, running with poor Maxie clutched in her hands. "They're members of your own family!"

Our two bed-and-breakfasts had "no room, not one, especially for liars." The attorneys went to the next town and the next town and the next, and by golly, no one had any room. Not one hotel or bed-and-breakfast. The attorneys ended up commuting two hours, each way, each day, to the trial.

They should have known that the "tractor-driving, cow-herding, pig-slaughtering farmers and fat farmers' wives" across county lines would talk to one another.

Jilly walked the jury through all of my dad's bank statements, showing how he'd paid his health-care premiums monthly, then she detailed my dad's accident. His trip, semiconscious, to the hospital. How he was penalized by Premium Health for not protesting his entry into the local hospital because he was, again, semiconscious and in grave pain and not able to speak. How he was supposed to tell his employees to drive five hours to the hospital in the city that was "approved for care." How Premium continually refused to pay because of "absurd and criminal reasons." How he, a single dad, had had to fight Premium Health after breaking four vertebrae in his back.

"This man, Scott Fox, paid premiums, every month, to get care, and when he fell off a roof, where was Premium Health Insurance? Cutting Mr. Fox out and laughing about it."

The jury, filled with "fat farmers' wives" and "cow-herding farmers," took twenty minutes to decide that Premium Health Insurance had done wrong. I'm told it took twenty minutes because the jurors needed to run to the bathroom, lickety-split.

When the decision was announced, that whole courtroom, filled with "hicks and uneducated mice," stood up and cheered, including me, Justine, Chick, and their families. The judge, Zan Millotti, a respectable woman who hated when the big guys tried to eat/cheat the little guys, sat and glared at those lizard-like attorneys over the top of her glasses.

"Arthur Yelsen, Frederick Kennesen, and Maxim Meredith *the third*" — she could barely contain her sneer at "the third" part of his name — "Premium Health Insurance is legally obligated to care for its policyholders. You did not do that. One of your policyholders fell off a roof after years of paying his premiums on time. You declined to meet your responsibility. While this man was suffering, you told him you wouldn't pay his hospital bills. While this man was in pain, you abandoned him. While this man was struggling to walk, you made his life worse. You cut him off when he needed medical care at his most desperate point. As he was suffering, you then took away his, and his daughter's, health insurance.

"You, Arthur Yelsen, Frederick Kennesen, and Maxim Meredith *the third*" — there was that sneer again — "are a disgrace. Premium Health Insurance is a disgrace. You will not only immediately pay all of Scott Fox's medical bills, you will pay his attorney. In addition, you will return all of Scott Fox's monthly premiums to him, as you did not hold up your side of the contract until you were dragged to court." She shot them a deadly stare over those glasses. "Disgraceful," she said again. "You should be ashamed of yourselves and Premium Health Insurance. You should call your company Trash Insurance. Or Nothing Insurance. Or We Will Not Pay Anything Insurance."

I loved how she kept saying "Premium Health Insurance"!

"I'm reporting Premium Health Insurance to the state, as your company should not be allowed to work here in Oregon. I will not have more of my fellow Oregonians, or my fellow Americans, victimized by your" — she paused, heavily — " 'organization.' " She slammed the gavel down after one more glare at the shamed attorneys and a hissed "Court dismissed."

As the attorneys left the courtroom, heads down, townspeople made oinking and mice squeaking sounds at them. Eda Hathaway, a woman who owns thousands of acres, yelled, "Am I a fat enough farmer's wife for you, assholes?" as they passed. And Dick Mason called out, after an especially good oink, "I'd like to feed you to my pigs."

It was too bad that the tires to their car were flat and there were no tow trucks available to help them out. None.

They started walking out of town.

The case had gotten widespread coverage, and Premium Health Insurance was out of business in one year.

My dad still works as a metalsmith for Margarita, but the artist has declared that she is moving to Arizona because that's where her new "lover, my Greek lover" is living. Soon my dad will not have a job. He will find another job. Zack and I would help him immediately, but I know my dad. He will not accept any money. I am worried about him.

He is the hardest working man, besides Zack, that I know.

He is proud. Confident. Tough. Sensitive. Loyal. He has a kind and forgiving heart. I mean, Jane Eyre is his best "book friend." How can you not love a man like that?

I am his hummingbird. He is my hero.

Soldier had a bad day in the activities room. He stood up suddenly and yelled, rage tumbling out. It was impressive. "This is what I want to know!" Soldier demanded, his fists in the air. "This is what I want to know!" He started to cry. He was so furious

288

he was shaking.

"What do you want to know?" Frog Lady asked. "I know all about monkeys."

"If you want to know something," Architect said, "I'll build you a thinking building."

I put my arm around his shoulder. It was hard to balance because he was flailing around. "What do you want to know?"

"Why do people have to kill each other? Why? Why did that war happen?"

We didn't know that answer.

"Here's a frog." Frog Lady gave Soldier a pink clay frog with blue eyes she'd tucked into her pocket. "Maybe she'll know."

"Your thinking building will help you figure this out," Architect said. "I'll get it done tonight, Soldier."

"How about having chocolate cake with me?" I said. "I saw some."

Soldier was trying to breathe, panting, tears streaming from his eyes, his helmet wobbling. I patted his arms, and he seemed to get control. He exhaled, the fight draining from his body. "Okay, Jewelry Maker. Let's go and get cake."

"Can I come?" Frog Lady asked. "I can hop on in."

"Yes. Come," Soldier said, straightening up. "I'll keep you safe. There are no AK-47s or grenades allowed here."

Architect started to cry.

"What's wrong, Architect?" I asked. There was a lot of stuff going on today.

"Why don't they like me?" he whispered, tears filling his eyes. He held his hand close to his chest and pointed at Soldier and Frog Lady. "Why didn't they invite me? I want to get chocolate cake."

Soldier put a shaking arm around Architect, who was sniffling. "Man, I like you. Come on."

"Hop to it, Architect," Frog Lady said, hopping. "I like you as much as I like my monkeys."

We went to get chocolate cake and we all felt a lot better when we were done.

We are emotional basket cases but I am telling you, the four of us are true friends.

Finally, I was going home.

I was leaving the Brain Bang Unit. I was leaving my doctors, nurses, and therapists. I was leaving Soldier, Frog Lady, and Architect.

I wasn't all better. I wasn't close to it. I still walked at a slight tilt to the left, and my brain had been scrambled. My adding and subtracting skills weren't as disastrous as they'd been, but the numbers still flipped and flopped, often, and I couldn't get them to stay in rows. Reading was going poorly, as the letters did the same thing as the numbers, as if they were in cahoots together. Saying what I was thinking at a normal speed was still a problem, but there was, thankfully, progress. I had had endless therapy and would continue to receive therapy. Dizziness and headaches came much less frequently, for which I was grateful.

I was sad to leave, in a way. I was leaving my new best friends: Frog Lady, whose real name is Dr. Rose Bingham, from Stanford University and who is a noted zoologist. She fell out of a tree studying apes in Africa. Her husband, Dr. Leonardo Bingham, was with her at the top, and she was flown out first by helicopter, then by private plane. He had been a constant visitor.

Architect, whose real name is Sanjay Kapoor, designed three buildings on the West Coast that all won prestigious awards. He came to the Brain Bang Unit after he fell off scaffolding. He is married with three children. His entire extended family had come often to see him.

Soldier, real name Jefferson Titus, is the recipient of a Purple Heart from his service in Iraq. He was the student body president of Howard University. The grandma he draws his fairy-tale pictures for, depicting war, owns Grandma's Cupcakes, a chain of cupcake stores.

I had found an honesty in my relationships with them that had been endearing and refreshing. We came into the Brain Bang Unit at the bottom, and we all had to work ourselves up. There were no pretensions here. There were no cover-ups, no bragging, no trying to present a certain image. We were struggling, open, sympathetic, and compassionate.

I hugged all of them before I left.

Architect said, "You found your happiness building, Jewelry Maker?"

"Right here." I held it up. He had made me a one-story building, using pink paper and cardboard, with cut-out flowers sticking out of it in 3-D form. "Thank you, Architect. You're a true friend. Everyone likes you."

He started to sniffle, those dark eyes swimming. "Do you think so?"

"I do. I know it."

He gave me a hug again and said, "I like you, too, Jewelry Maker. Thank you for my necklaces."

"You're welcome." I had made him another necklace with a heart on it. Because, I told him, people love him.

Frog Lady handed me a purple frog. It must have weighed seven or eight pounds. It had red lipstick lips, yellow daisies, and numbers painted on it. "I will miss you, Jewelry Maker." I had made her another necklace, too, with a frog on it. I had had to specifically ask Zack to order a frog charm for it.

Soldier handed me a picture of him fighting in a war, pointing a menacing gun toward a village. "This is a picture to give you a smile. It's so you can remember Robin Hood and Maid Marian."

"Thank you, Soldier." I hugged him, too. He was wearing the necklace I recently made him out of small silver tubes.

Zack shook hands with everyone and thanked them for taking care of me.

"No problem, sir," Soldier said, saluting. "I protected her with my guns."

"She's nice," Architect said. "She made me necklaces. See?"

"I like her poems," Frog Lady said. "But you should make more poems about monkeys. Hey! Thanks for my frog necklace!"

I still could not remember the morning of my accident, or the accident itself; there were only odd fragments, and the doctors told me there was a high chance I would never remember.

"Let it go, Natalie," Dr. Ugande said. "You lost one morning. Yes, it was a traumatic moment in your life. We all want to remember our own lives. But maybe, in this case, not remembering the crash, it's better."

"Let your mind relax on it," Dr. Eeko said. "Don't try to remember, that will simply lock it in place more tightly. Focus on healing your mind and body. Take it easy."

I was excited to be going home and I was scared to death, already overwhelmed, confused, insecure, and worried. I had been in the hospital and in the Brain Bang Unit for almost three months. It was a different world out there, and that world was fast paced. I could not keep up.

Plus there was the hit-and-run and the Barbie with the twisted head and the headless bird, which were direct threats to me. The police clearly had no leads. Zack and I had talked, and he had promised me I would be safe and secure. "This will all go away. Trust me. Please. I will protect you."

I wanted to believe him.

I was grateful to be alive. I am a different person than who I used to be. If there was any shallowness left in me, I believe that's been blasted out. I am more serious than I used to be, more thoughtful, more introspective. I know I need to make changes in my life in the future in terms of how much I work and the stress I'll allow myself to be under.

On the other hand, I laugh more, and I laugh over the smallest things. I cry more often, too. It's like the steel walls I put around my emotions are down and I let myself *feel* more now. I think I am more a part of life now. I know who my true friends are.

I had almost died. My life would not be the same again.

In almost dying I saw my life ever so clearly.

I glanced across the car seat at Zack, holding his hand. He had given me a bear hug and a kiss in the parking lot of the hospital and swung me around. We both laughed.

He smiled at me. Gentle. Sexy. Encouraging. I was dressed in new jeans. I'd lost weight, and Zack had bought me a couple of pairs. My shirt was burgundy, long sleeves, with burgundy lace. I was wearing my black cowgirl boots and two chokers I'd made in the hospital, one with silver triangles, one with silver flowers.

I wanted to look like a woman and not a patient for Zack, which is why I had Justine buy me a red bra and matching panties from Lace, Satin, and Baubles. He would get "red romance" when we got home.

As we pulled away I noticed there was something in Zack's eyes, in the way he was holding himself. What was it? Wasn't he happy I was coming home? He seemed . . . worried. Was he worried about my health and how I would do, or was he worried about the man who mangled Barbies and birds?

He turned those light green eyes to me. *Man.* He is all stud. Total ex-Alaskan fisherman, house-building, construction stud. After five years of marriage he still gives me the sizzles.

"Ready, honey?"

"Yes." Ready for Zack, that is. We would talk about the rest of this stuff later; it was making my mind swirl. I could not handle it right now. All I could handle was going home. I wanted to sleep in our bed, I wanted to touch my grandma's antique perfume bottles, my china teacups with the pink flowers, and make sure my plants hadn't died. I wanted to see the hummingbirds my dad made me hanging in a corner of our family room and all my embroidered pillows and books and the oak tree in our backyard. "Totally ready."

"Natalie, honey," Zack said, pulling me over to him when he stopped his truck.

"Yep?" I leaned over and kissed him. Zack had driven, without my asking him, out to the country, to our special place, with a view of farmland and fields, and beyond that, pine-tree-covered hills and the coast mountain range. It was cool so he had brought my jacket. We held hands as we sat on the blanket and enjoyed the scenery, no one around.

I had missed most of fall, but there were still some orange and yellow leaves on the trees, they weren't completely bare, and the sun shone in the cool blue sky. To me, being outside in nature was a sweet balm to my soul. I had made it out of the hospital and was sitting underneath a tree. How cool was that?

"There have been changes since your accident." His jaw was clenched.

"Yes. I know." I decided to explore his chest with my hand. I felt the long scar on his ribs. "I have a jagged scar underneath my hair that looks like a snake. I've lost boob and much of my butt, but don't you worry, I'm going to build those suckers back up. I'm going as soon as I can to get my hair highlighted, because I look like a skunk. I had no idea my hair was so dark underneath the blond."

He didn't smile. "Baby, that's not what I need to talk to you about."

"What else changed?" I ran my hand over his brown hair, now shot through with a little gray, brought on by my vacation in the hospital. He is tall and broad and kissable. "I missed you, baby." I straddled him and kissed his mouth.

He pulled away.

Zack, my Zack, never pulled away from me. He was always eager for a romp. My fingers froze on his buttons.

"What is it, Zack?" I pushed my lust aside. "Zack, honey? What happened?"

His hands were on my hips, and he stared off for a second and his face was so . . . so . . . *defeated* it took my breath away.

"We don't have the house anymore."

"What?" Our house was gone?

"I sold our house."

"What? Why?" Zack had bought and remodeled the house years before we met. He had offered to put my name on the deed, but I declined. He'd bought it, it was his house; I wasn't worried about the future. The man didn't even let me pay him rent.

"You are the love of my life. I am not taking any money from you, Natalie," he'd said.

He stared back at me, bleak, hopeless sadness in every inch of his face. "I'm building six homes right now, and I took a loan out on our house because I had an issue with the bank. I had problems with a couple of the homes, and they didn't sell when they should have."

I didn't even know what to say. I was thunderstruck.

"This is completely my fault, Natalie. I leveraged the money wrong. I took a risk and it was a bad one."

I tried to talk, but I couldn't.

"I am so sorry, Natalie. I really am."

"Zack." I took a breath. Okay. We'd lost the house. We could get another house. I leaned down and kissed him. He was devastated, I could tell. "I'm sorry you had to sell the house." I kissed him again and smiled, though I felt like I'd been sucker punched. "We'll get another house."

"We will, honey. I promise. I will have you in another house as soon as I can."

My brain started to work after that blow, and the truth surfaced. I rolled off of him. "Zack, you were with me all the time. That was the problem, wasn't it? You didn't even work for weeks."

"No." He shook his head, emphatic. "That was not the problem. I overextended. I made a bad decision with the loan I had with the bank. This was not you at all."

"It had to be." It was. I knew it.

"Hon, you know the men I have working for me. They don't need me looking over their shoulders."

"I'm sorry, Zack." He had bought and remodeled every inch of that house. The work was exquisite. It was a showplace. It had been photographed for a couple of home magazines.

"I'm the one who's sorry, honey. So sorry. You're in the hospital, you're in rehab" — his voice cracked — "and you finally get out and find you don't have a home."

"It'll be fine." I grabbed his hand. I was shocked. I was shaking. I felt like I'd been run over again. This was a terrible loss. We had no home. But I was struck by another thought. "Why didn't you use our savings, though?"

"Because that was *our* money. Yours and mine. I had caused this problem, I was not going to use your money to get us out of it. And I wasn't going into our retirement accounts for the same reason. Plus, they tax and penalize the heck out of you when you take money out early, and we're going to get old one day and we'll need it."

He and I always thought the same about money. The tax accountant in me said, "Nice choice. Can I be honest with you, Zack?"

"Please." His voice was ragged. He had hated telling me we'd lost the house, hated it. "Always."

"Honestly, I didn't like the neighborhood much with our fancy, rich neighbors. They always bragged. They bragged about their kids, their boats, their businesses, that club they go to downtown that is so snooty, and their snooty golf clubs. I grew up riding horses and tractors and jumping off rocks into a lake. I'm a small-town eastern Oregon lady, and I never felt like I fit in there. You did a gorgeous job on the house, and I loved living there with you, Zack, but I didn't fit into that neighborhood."

He closed his eyes for a second, I think it was in relief. "You should have told me."

"I loved the house. You turned it into house art, and I loved being with you. But now that we're out, we'll find a better neighborhood."

"When I bought the house, all I saw was an awesome investment, and it was. I'm a former Alaskan fisherman. I build homes. I'm an electrician. And the neighborhood didn't fit me, either."

I grinned at him. "Then we're in agreement, once again, sweets. Where are we living now?"

He was not happy. "We have an apartment. It's a two bedroom. It's in the Rockford neighborhood."

I could feel my eyes widening. The Rockford neighborhood? Rough. Poor. Gangs. Geez.

"I'm sorry, Natalie. A contractor of mine moved out of this place, told me about it, and I took it. Our house sold in a day, multiple offers. I took the cash offer, and they offered ten thousand above list if I moved in two weeks. I was seeing you, working, trying to get the houses done, and this was just easiest."

It was not surprising that the house sold that quickly.

"My business is struggling, but it won't be for long. I'll sell the houses soon, and we'll take the money and buy a new house. Justine has continued to send your check, too. I didn't want to buy another house until we could make the decision together. You also need to sign the papers, too, so it's a jointly owned home."

There was something very wrong here, something amiss. I couldn't catch it. It had to do with the money, the loan, the bank, overextending. . . . It wasn't making sense. . . . Zack was excellent with handling money . . . but it drifted away again, as my memory of the morning of my accident kept drifting away.

"We'll be at the apartment for only a few months. You're in no shape to hunt for a house now anyhow, and I'm swamped at work."

Zack was crushed. He takes being a man seriously, and in his mind he should provide and he felt like he wasn't providing. His pain stuck in my heart like a sword.

"Zack?"

"Yes."

"We do have one problem."

"What?"

"You still have your jeans on."

He laughed, that booming, attractive laugh that I loved hearing. "I think I can fix that."

"Good," I said, unbuttoning his shirt. "Do it quick."

Nature sex is awesome.

■ ■ ■ ■

PART III

■ ■ ■ ■

CHAPTER 12

We were in an apartment. The house was gone. It was an earthshaker for me. Once more my world had spun, tipped, and careened me off of it and into a wall. But this would be fine. I'd get used to it, I told myself. I would. *Buck up, Natalie.*

The kitchen was at least thirty years old, the gray Formica cracked, the white refrigerator dented, the windows not so clean, the beige carpets gross. We were also in a near-to-falling-apart neighborhood. A few blocks over, there was a gang problem.

There were four two-story apartment buildings that circled a courtyard. In each building there were four apartments. The apartments were all old, probably built in the 1950s. The courtyard had dead grass and a large concrete fountain, but the fountain had obviously been turned off for years. Maybe decades, judging by the weeds.

We were on the bottom floor. Zack had

installed three locks on our door, and all of the windows had metal bars in the grooved area that could be locked for security.

In the first bedroom was our bed. I loved that bed. Zack bought it before we met. It was king-sized and took up most of the room. My clothes were in the bedroom closet, and he had his in the second bedroom. The second bedroom also held a bunch of our stuff, in boxes and bags, as if everything had been hastily packed, which it had, by Zack and his employees. More of our furniture was in Zack's warehouse.

Our L-shaped blue couch took up much of the family room, on top of our blue and white rug. In front of the couch was our ottoman that my dad had made us out of wood from an old church in Lake Joseph that had blown down in a windstorm. Our white wood kitchen table was in the small kitchen nook with our white chairs. He had a vase of white daisies waiting for me.

Zack hadn't decorated. I looked around. This was a place owned by a man who clearly had no time. Plus, Zack was not a decorator type. He left that to me.

I took a deep breath, standing in the middle of the family room after our mini-tour, Zack leaning a shoulder against a wall as if he was having a hard time standing up.

We had fallen from one home to the next about as much as you can fall and still have indoor plumbing.

Everything was gone. My books; my grandma's perfume bottles; my china tea-cups with the pink flowers; and my plants, pillows, and paintings by Grenadine Scotch Wild. Where was our Scrabble board? Where was our chess set? Where was my collection of white ceramic vases?

Then, remarkably, I laughed. I couldn't help it. Maybe it was tinged with a bit of hysteria, of loss, of feeling I'd once again been flung off the planet.

But the truth is that nothing seems that bad after you've been in a coma. A coma where you're alive and trapped and you're screaming, terrorized that you're going to die and terrorized even more that you won't and you'll be stuck in that body prison forever. Then you wake up from the Coma Coffin and your brain is scrambled and you can't walk right or think right and you have to live in a hospital and then a Brain Bang rehab center.

Honestly, when you almost die and you get a second chance at life again, "prob-lems" are no longer problems. Most every-thing is an "irritant," or a "minor blip," or a "hurdle." Problems are critical illnesses, injury, death, grief, that kind of thing. We had fallen down the economic ladder. We'd taken a tumble. We would climb back up the ladder, that I was sure of.

"I like it." It was bright. There were three huge windows in front. The rooms were medium-sized. The family room opened to the nook and kitchen. The walls had recently been sprayed bright white, as had the kitchen cabinets.

Zack's head was down, his broad shoulders slumped.

"Zack." I put my hands on his face. I could tell he was humiliated. Defeated. "Don't have a heart attack over this. Listen." I leaned heavily against him. I kissed him. "I'm alive and so are you. I can walk, and I'm swaying less to the left. I have scars, but I can breathe. My emotions are roller-coastering, but I'm going to get ahold of them. I can talk and you can hear me, even though I still sound like I'm talking way too slow. I'm not trapped in a Coma Coffin." I kissed him again. "So, we've lost the house. But you are still sexy, and we're here and safe and I'm not in the hospital."

He closed his eyes, and I saw that flash again. I couldn't place it. Couldn't put my finger on it . . . Was it a flash of fear when I used the word *safe*? What did I not know?

"What, Zack? What is it?" Tell me. Tell me what you know.

"I'm just sorry, baby. I am."

That apology was from his gut. "I don't know why you keep telling me you're sorry. There's nothing to be sorry for." Even when I said that, I knew something was missing, a detail that I couldn't grip in my befuddled head, but I let it go. "Stud man, this is temporary. It's fine. You are magic with home building, and we'll get out of here soon." He was. He was a magic home-builder.

"You are my magic, Natalie."

"Homes are nice, but working brains are better. Eating is heaven, and I am craving your spaghetti Bolognese. Can you make that for me?"

He could. We ate it in bed, the bed I had missed so much.

I had missed the man so much more.

I woke up in the middle of the night, hugging Zack, his voice, his apology, ringing in my ears like a warning, a premonition.

But I loved him. I loved Zack so much and I had missed him. I went back to sleep on his chest.

Zack stayed with me the next six days for

about half the day. We did drive out to his work sites, he talked to his employees, who were so welcoming to me, asked me how I was doing, and then we went home. Later, when I was settled, he would go back out to his homes for a few hours and he would work on paperwork at night, after I was asleep.

Despite the loss of our home, it was a romantic, emotional time for us. We did not talk about the morning of the accident, or the headless bird, or the stabbed Barbie, which might seem strange, but I couldn't handle any more stress. We both knew what was out there: a demented monster.

But we needed to be us, without a coma or a Brain Bang Unit between us. We needed to be Zack and Natalie. I needed time to enjoy, and get used to, being in the world again. A world without doctors and therapists, hurting people all around me, and the stress of living in a hospital.

We drove out to the Deschutes and fished off the bank, exactly where we'd met, the air chill but crisp, the hawks diving.

We went on a drive to the country holding coffee. We watched movies, and he read me a book as we restarted the Deschutes Family Book Club.

I couldn't do crosswords or play chess,

but we took walks in a park each day so I could regain my strength, and we watched the sunsets, the magic of a kaleidoscope of colors spreading over the horizon.

I was already in love with that husband of mine, more even after my accident, as he was always by my side, fighting for me, fighting for us. But in this new phase, the love grew yet again, like wild flowers and Italian dinners and Beethoven's Fifth all mixed together. We laughed more, it seemed, maybe because we were both so grateful that I was up and with the program again. There were tears, too. We talked about everything we used to talk about — his work, my work and how I missed it, the places we wanted to travel to, things we wanted to see and do, the dream house we would build. *One day.*

The passion that had always been there between us fired up again, hotter than before even, because of what we almost lost. I was thinner, weaker, with odd balance issues, but love and lust prevailed.

We started healing from the trauma of what happened.

We were, once again, Zack and Natalie.

I was able to start showing off my collection of lace negligees again to Zack. Some have my hippie/bohemian vibe, others are classic, and still others are . . . naughty.

Zack seemed to like them all. And, for me, wearing the lingerie made me feel like a woman again. A wife. Someone who could be sexy for her husband.

I wanted that. I had missed it.

On the seventh morning, seeing I was quite capable of taking care of myself, Zack left, the sun barely over the horizon. The night before, he had showed me where two guns were. One was in the kitchen on a shelf, the other in a side table near the door. It made me feel better given the fact that a psycho was after us.

He kissed me and I went back to sleep, then I sat back in bed drinking coffee, grateful I could do so. I needed a minute to get my head together.

The house was gone and we were in a rather dreary, but bright, apartment. I was a little nervous to be alone, especially with that bird killer running around, but the door was locked, I had my phone on, there were two guns, and I refused to live in fear. I'd had enough fear.

I decided I needed to fix the place up. It was making me nervous and anxious. I needed to unpack what we needed and make this apartment pretty. I could not live in ugly. I could not live with clutter. Clutter and ugly in a home make me nervous because of my mother, and it brings me back to a place I don't want to be. The clutter and ugly had to go.

I started working.

Our apartment was about one-fourth the size of our home, plain and dull, so my first job was to add color and life.

Zack had saved my beloved plants. They were all in the second bedroom on one of our dressers near the window. I dragged out a skinny, long glass table and put the plants in front of a window. I said hello to all of them and gave them water and a trim.

I opened boxes and bags until I found our pillows for our blue couch. The pillows were in bright colors, embroidered, beaded, sequined. They had all been made by Ellie Kozlovsky in Portland, my favorite pillow designer on the planet.

In another box I found my collection of white ceramic vases, candles, stacks of books, my grandma's precious perfume bottles, and my china teacups with the pink flowers. Everything went on windowsills and in two bookcases Zack had brought in. I put our chess set and Scrabble board on a side table. I found our tablecloths and put one with red poppies over our kitchen table. Then I put an eighteen-inch-high red vase in the middle.

I found a hammer and nails in the third drawer in the kitchen, which is where they were in our previous home, and started nailing up our pictures and framed photos. I decided not to care if we weren't supposed to put nails in the walls. Zack could fix it. On our family room walls I hung collage paintings we'd collected over the years, all by Grenadine Scotch Wild, our favorite artist who lives out in central Oregon.

We'd commissioned work from her three times. One painting/collage was of the Deschutes River, exactly where we'd met. We had sent her, at her request, branches found on the side of the river, three fishing flies, fishing line, and material from an old, ripped flannel shirt of Zack's. She had incorporated all of it into the collage. We were wearing matching flannel shirts, our back to the viewer, our lines in the water, our drift boat nearby.

Another painting/collage was of us on our wedding day. We sent her a photo of us standing under the arch that Zack and his friends made on the Deschutes River covered in flowers, and she made that day come alive. I sent her some of my favorite lace for the wedding dress she created, complete with a gauzy white veil drifting in the wind. She used dried flowers, tiny pinecones, and small wood sticks for the arch and the trees nearby.

The third painting was commissioned by Zack. It was a picture of the yellow home I grew up in. Zack had sent Grenadine a photo. She used wood to form part of the wraparound deck, chips of brick for the chimney, a rectangular piece of wood for my swing hanging from my favorite tree, and red fabric for the door. She'd also used real black rubber to create the wheels on my favorite pink bike my dad bought me when I was young, and she added my dad's old blue truck. The license plate said FOX.

Right there, the apartment was transformed by Grenadine's art.

The gray, cracked Formica was particularly ugly, so I put our wide, wooden butcher block cutting board down, made by Zack, to cover it. I put my red teakettle and red teacups in a corner to add cheer. I put a plant in another corner and a stack of cookbooks along a wall, a number of which were my grandma's mother's, which my grandma never used. I checked to make sure her apple pie recipe was still tucked into her mother's favorite cookbook, and it was. I would make it soon, I told myself.

In our bedroom I washed the sheets, then hung up three pictures of the Deschutes River that Zack had taken, right in the spot where we'd met. I had enlarged them to twelve by eighteen and had them framed. They showed a sunrise, midday, and sunset.

Our bedspread is white, but Zack hadn't put out any of Ellie Kozlovsky's pretty yellow and white pillows we used, so I found those, too, stuffed in black garbage bags in the second bedroom, and threw those on the bed.

I dragged out a couple of our wooden chairs, with tall, curving backs, and put them between two of our large windows. On the seats of the chairs I stacked up a collection of old books my grandma had given me from her relatives.

I found our red and yellow flowered rug and wrangled it under the kitchen table. I put a smaller yellow and blue rug in the entry. The more of the yucky carpet that was covered up, the better. I grabbed four of our lights with white shades and funky crystal balls on the stems and put them on two side tables in the family room and on our nightstands in the bedroom.

The last thing I did? I hung some of my

ceramic/metal/glass/ metal hummingbird collection in a corner of the family room and three in front of the windows.

I felt better already. There was pretty around me and there wasn't clutter. Clutter meant pain. I needed no more.

Then I took a nap for three hours, my head swimming, my body aching.

Before my eyes shut I thought, *Now this is looking more like home.*

Zack's eyes widened when he came in the door that night. He gave me a long hug and kiss after he looked around, three candles burning, lights on. "It looks like home, Natalie." His voice was gruff. Unexpectedly emotional. "I left a boring, plain apartment and I come home to this. It's . . . it's . . ." He choked up. "It's us again, isn't it?"

Aw! That was so touching. "Yes, Zack, it's us again." I kissed him. "I made a dinner, but then I forgot that the lasagna was in the oven and it burned. So I made another dinner."

"What is it?"

"Scrambled eggs. Have a seat. I'll try not to burn them."

He laughed, pulled me close again, and gave me a long smackeroo. My clothes ended up on the kitchen floor. The scrambled eggs had to wait.

That night I had the same nightmare.

I sat straight up and sucked in air. That bald, pig-faced man was chasing me again. In a van.

He was coming after me, faster and faster. I turned to run, but I couldn't outrun him.

He was laughing.

He was trying to kill me.

Then he was going to kill Zack.

He crashed right into me.

I woke up gasping for breath, Zack holding me.

Life was feeling overwhelming: a deliberate hit-and-run, a mangled Barbie, and a dead bird continued to haunt me, especially because I had a gut-level feeling that it wasn't over yet.

I sat down at our kitchen table and made jewelry the next morning, a light rain falling. I lit a couple candles, put on country music for the country girl in me, then played my favorite, Beethoven's Fifth, and opened a box of chocolates that Zack had bought me.

The Brain Bang Unit let me bring some supplies home, which was very generous. I also found, after talking to Zack, my own jewelry-making supplies inside black bags in boxes in the corner of the second bedroom. It was like seeing old, inanimate friends I hadn't seen in too long: my wire cutters and pliers; my memory wire and beading needle; my headpins and eyepins; my measuring tape; and all my beads, gems, broaches, chains, lockets, turquoise, cut glass, and the necklaces I had been working on before I'd been smashed. Under the constant weight of running our accounting firm, my favorite hobby, jewelry making, had definitely been left at the wayside of my too busy life. I would need to change that, too.

I began to work.

I used colorful beads, crystals, charms, and even a few rocks I found outside near the dead fountain. Hours flew by. My anxiety over my future, my zinged brain, my career, and the sudden loss of our home disappeared.

When I was done, I was delighted with the necklaces I'd made. I slept for three hours. I do not have the energy I used to at all.

"This is not where I pictured you living, Natalie. I must tell you that."

My mother had "dropped in for a quick

visit" the next afternoon. She had not called, as usual. She had arrived. When she saw me, she put her hand to her chest, right over her blue silk flowered dress, and said, "Oh my. Have you been ill?"

"Yes, Mom, I have. I was in a coma up until recently." I was in jeans and a white blouse. Plain and simple for a rainy day. "How are you?"

She raised her perfectly plucked eyebrows at me. "I meant have you been ill *recently.* Have you had the flu?" She didn't wait for an answer, simply let herself in and handed me her black designer coat. It was — wait for it — Sapphires Day. Sapphire earrings, necklace, bracelets. Beige four-inch heels.

"No." A blast of rain hit the windows. The timing was almost funny.

"I'm exhausted from the drive." She stood in my family room and slowly turned around, those critical blue eyes taking everything in. "I'm going to be honest with you, Natalie. Someone has to do it. This is not the right place. Not the right neighborhood. This is not a home, Natalie. Why, this is almost a shack."

I sank into the couch. I had to. I can endure my Mother Monster only while sitting. Our apartment wasn't a shack. It was actually starting to grow on me. It was small and cozy, and I'd continued to decorate it. "I think it would be best if you weren't insulting, Mom."

"I'm not being insulting." She sat on the edge of Zack's leather chair, her knees and ankles tight together, as if she were afraid bugs would jump from our carpets up her legs and into her crotch. "I'm being truthful. This is a dangerous neighborhood. Beneath you. Beneath our family ancestry line."

Our family ancestry line? "It is not beneath our family, Mom."

"All I can say is that I'm glad I have my gun in my purse." She patted it.

I had noticed her designer purse. It cost at least a thousand dollars.

"I hope the safety is on."

"No. It's not. A lady must be ready to shoot, especially in this neighborhood."

"Please put the safety on."

"Don't nag. You know my daddy taught me how to shoot, starting when I was eight years old." She mimed shooting.

"I know, Mother, you've told me a zillion times." The sky outside darkened as the rain poured.

"It's unfortunate that Zack cannot provide better for you. You're living my life when I lived with your father, and this saddens me.

This makes me very angry. I did not raise you to live my life of poverty, the life of deprivation, that I endured with your father."

I was instantly filled with rage. "You did not live a life of deprivation with us, Mom. Dad worked six days a week and he provided. He would come home and make dinner and sing me to sleep at night."

"I'm sorry if I didn't *sing* to you, Natalie." Her eyes flashed. I'd hit a nerve.

"If we lived a life of poverty, Mom, why didn't you work? If it was a life of poverty, why did you leave me there? Our home was fine, the land was beautiful, but it wasn't enough for you."

She threw her manicured hands up. "You were a child. All you needed were shorts and sneakers. You did not need what I needed. I want what's best for you, and this neighborhood is not anywhere near the best. It's like you've gone backward, Natalie. You're poor again, as we were when you were a child."

"I was not poor as a child, but it would have been nice if you had sent child support for the child you gave birth to. That would be me."

"Please, Natalie. Let's not get into past history. We disagree, let it go."

And there was Mother Manipulator. Whenever I said something she didn't want to hear, she would shut the conversation down, change the topic with a dismissive wave of her hand, make a critical comment to me about something else, minimize what I was saying with a dose of condescension, tell me how I felt was wrong, or dispute the truth. She would never accept responsibility, admit she had done something hurtful, or make any effort to see my point of view. Hard to get along with people like that.

"I don't understand what happened with Zack and why he had to sell your home."

"It's not your business, Mom, and I don't want to discuss it."

"Men provide." She tapped her sapphire necklace.

And there was that tone. Patronizing. Superior. "Stop, Mom. Now."

"Don't say I didn't warn you." She pointed at me. "I'd like some coffee. Always offer a beverage to your guests, Natalie. Black. One tablespoon cream. Half a teaspoon of sugar, no more. A thick mug, preferably white, not a thin mug."

"I know how you like your coffee." I wobbled to the kitchen. "I'm already wiped out from your visit, Mom."

"Don't be rude." She followed me to the

kitchen. "Do you have tea biscuits? A lady should always have those around for a nibble. I'll take a glass of ice water. Three cubes."

Would I live through this? Maybe I should go back to my coma. Unbelievably I heard thunder crash in the distance, and ten seconds later saw a flash of lightning.

She shook her finger at me. "Don't marry a farmer. Dell is getting so persnickety."

I endured my mother's talk about Dell and his "persnicketiness," life on the ranch, their upcoming cruise, her neighbors who didn't like her, Glenda who especially didn't like her, but she was always so "cheerful. It's so annoying."

Cheerful people are annoying to my mother.

"I don't like the allowance thingy."

I rolled my eyes.

"Don't roll your eyes at me, Natalie. It's offensive. I brought you up better than that."

"Dad brought me up, Mom." The rage boiled again. Why do I let her do this to me? Why do I even let her in the door?

"Nonsense. I was always there for you." She touched her sapphire earrings.

"No, Mom. You weren't. You were hardly there at all."

"How is your father, by the way?"

"Dad is doing very well."

"And?"

"And what?" More thunder. More lightning.

"Is he seeing anyone?"

"I don't talk about him with you, Mom. You know that. You can call him yourself and ask."

"I don't think so. It's hard for him to hear my voice."

I laughed out loud. "Not for the reason you think."

"Between you and me, he's never gotten over me leaving him."

"I have heard you say that a hundred times. Mom, once again, he was over you leaving him years before you ever walked out the door."

She sucked in her breath. "That is not true."

I said, in all seriousness, "It is."

She made a *humph* sound.

She missed him, I knew it.

My mother yammered on. She never once asked me how I was doing. She did say to me, "Are you getting some white hairs? I can't tell. Don't let your hair go white, or you'll lose Zack. But, perhaps, that would be preferable, if he can't provide you with a better life."

That was it for me. I stood up. "Okay, Mom. That's it. I have to go and so do you. I'm not going to tolerate you criticizing my husband, and I have a therapy appointment." I did not have a therapy appointment. I'd been to two that morning. But if she stayed any longer I would have to go see a therapist who specialized in how to stay sane with insane mothers.

She muttered to me, "Your manners are appalling," when she hugged me good-bye, then said, "You still need to put on some weight, Natalie. Too thin. Men do not like thin. They like curves." She pointed to her curves, two of which were enhanced through implants. "I am naturally busty. By the way, I have a gift for you." She handed me a box. "Open it after I leave."

There was something in her eyes when she cupped my face with her hands, then kissed both my cheeks and hugged me close. Could it be kindness? "Bye, darling. I'll come by again soon."

Affection! What a surprise. "Good-bye, Mom."

A few minutes later, the skies cleared. I laughed.

After she left, I opened the box. Inside was a necklace with a heart-shaped locket. It was not cheap, I could tell by the box. There were a few diamonds on one side of the heart.

Inside she had engraved, "I love you, Natalie. Love, Your Mother."

I had to lie down for three hours after she left.

Do other people have mothers like this? Critical. Selfish. Concerned about social status and other shallow trivia. Then they throw something deeply kind your way, like an emotional curve ball, and you don't know what to do with the whipsaw of emotions.

I was not impressed by the cost of the jewelry. That she had thought to give me a heart, and tell me that she loved me, that was what made me catch my breath.

The next day, Saturday, the Moonshine and Milky Way Maverick Girls knocked at my door. I was making jewelry at the kitchen table.

"Surprise! Spa day, Maverick Lady," Justine told me.

"And we're getting our hair done. Look at my hair." Chick pulled her thick red waves away from her head. "I need it cut and I need it dyed so I don't resemble an estrogen-infused rooster."

"We're getting manicures and pedicures, too, for the fingers and the toesies," Justine said.

I about clicked my heels together. "Really?" My voice squeaked.

"Really!" the Maverick Girls said.

I raced off to my bedroom to get dressed. I pulled on my army-green jeans and a blue cotton shirt with a lace ruffle and dumped a few of my homemade crystal and rock necklaces over my head. I shoved my feet into my red boots. I was ready!

"Love you, Natalie. Have a great time." Zack smiled and hugged me.

I kissed him, hugged him, and sailed on out, almost giggling. "I think I'll feel like a new woman when this is over."

"We all will," Chick said. "I look like I've been brushing my hair with a hammer."

I stared at my face in the long mirror at the spa.

Better. So much better.

Chick and Justine put their faces next to mine, all sorts of hair products on the counter in front of us. We'd started with massages. We progressed to our manicures and pedicures. I chose pink with white daisies for my ring fingers. Next came lunch of salads and French bread and coffee and chocolates.

Then we had our hair cut and highlighted. I am not biased when I say this: Justine and Chick looked gorgeous. Justine's dark hair was thick and shiny, as were Chick's red waves.

"My face doesn't look so ghastly," I said.

"My face, magically, isn't so fat," Chick said. "I don't look like an exhausted mommy. My God. Braxton wanted to have sex twice last night. Wait 'til he sees me now."

"Did you say yes or no?" I asked.

She turned to me. "Are you kidding? I said yes. I'm not going to turn down a twofer. I've got a lot of backed-up orgasms that need to come out."

"Backed-up orgasms?" Justine said. "What a way to put it. Although I completely understand what you mean. Maybe you should get a vibrator. I call my vibrator Jed."

"That's a surprise," I drawled. "I never would have guessed that."

"Braxton is a man with a high sex drive," Chick shared, "and I meet those needs like a tractor meets the needs of our land."

My. I loved my hair now. It was blond with gold highlights, as it had been before I'd checked out of life and into my Coma Coffin. My stylist, Kelly, had cut off about four inches so the curls were lighter, curlier. The spot that the surgeons shaved was covered up better now.

"I talked to Jed the other day, Justine," Chick said.

"You did?" Justine's face lit up. "What did he say?"

"We talked about the Ducks and the Beavers and football."

"What? Football? I don't care. Did he say anything about me?"

"I didn't tell him that you're madly in love with him and start to salivate when you think of him. I have kept the Moonshine and Milky Way Maverick Girls promise all these long and stupid years."

"Thank you."

"I told him that you're dating someone named Lawrence."

"Lawrence?" Justine's brow furrowed. "Who dates men named Lawrence?"

"You do. I lied to my own brother for you."

"What did he say?"

"Did invisible Lawrence make Jed ragingly jealous mad?" I asked.

"I think he did," Chick said. "Just like he was when you were married to Marco, the Needle Penis Husband."

"This could be your time, Justine." I tried

to be gentle. "You're not attached, he isn't, either."

She stared down at the counter.

"Let that guilt go," Chick said. "Like you would let go of lice."

"You're ashamed of something you shouldn't be ashamed of," I said.

"It's this grief inside of me," she choked out. "This loss."

We gave her a hug. "But you don't have to be lost from Jed anymore," I said.

"I'd snag him," Chick said. "Snag and drag."

"Make some reindeer antlers again like we did when we were seven," I said. "Draw him a picture of Rudolph with straight teeth to seal the deal and re-ask him to marry you. Maybe this time he'll say yes and you won't have to stomp on his foot and kick him in the shin."

"I could wear a red Santa negligee and the antler hat," Justine mused.

"That would work," I said.

We put on our makeup and had more champagne. "To the Moonshine and Milky Way Maverick Girls," I said.

"To us!" We clinked our glasses.

"And mostly to you, Natalie," Chick said. "You've got that brain back."

"Yes," Justine said. "To you, friend."

"And," Chick yelled — I don't know why she yelled, but she did — "to the Moonshine and Milky Way Maverick Girls' upcoming Naked Bike Ride!"

We clinked our glasses to that one, too.

Gall. Was I, an accountant, even though I'm a bad accountant currently, really going to do that? "Naked. On a bike. At night. In a parade."

"You're doing it," Justine told me. "You are so doing it, Natalie. Don't you dare back out."

"Can't back out now, girl," Chick said. "We're getting our wild and crazy back one step at a time."

"Or," Justine said, "one naked bike ride at a time."

Afterward we went to a bar and had too much to drink. They had karaoke. Justine, Chick, and I love karaoke. We sang. We busted loose. We danced. People cheered. Chick fell off the stage. Justine turned around and wiggled her butt at the audience. I sang a solo with as much passion as I could while holding two wineglasses, one in each hand.

Zack had to come and get us. He dropped Justine and Chick off at Justine's place downtown. Justine warbled on and on in front of her high-rise apartment complex, trying to hit that high C. I laughed so hard I sounded as if I was shrieking. Chick trailed along, her legs crossed. "Too much laughing, Justine," she protested. "Stop singing, dang it all. Stop now or I'm going to wet my pants."

Chick has never had a good bladder.

Justine threw her arms out and sang full force, super high-pitched. She held one note a long time. People turned to stare. A few clapped. I cracked up, and so did Zack.

Poor Chick.

She crossed those legs tight, but it didn't work because she was laughing too hard. Seeing a puddle on the sidewalk at Chick's feet had Zack and me crying with laughter.

I love the Moonshine and Milky Way Maverick Girls. They are true friends, through the laughter and through the tears.

CHAPTER 13

Justine became pregnant our senior year of high school.

The father was her boyfriend at the time, Taye. Justine still loved Jed. But it seemed hopeless to her. It was hopeless. She was seventeen, Jed was twenty-four. That relationship was not going to happen. It wasn't even in Jed's head. He saw Justine as a teenager, barely past childhood, like a little sister, and he was not remotely interested.

So Justine momentarily tried to let go of Jed and started dating Taye.

Taye was a nice young man. He treated Justine well. They were both loud, outgoing, perfectly matched. We all ran around together, and Justine and Taye's hormones got the best of them . . . and the birth control did not.

When Justine found out she was pregnant, she was holding a pee stick over a toilet at my house with a plus sign. She was terrified, her face like white oatmeal. Chick and I were terrified for her.

"Oh, my God." She sank onto the toilet and cried like I'd never heard her cry. The next week was worse. She stayed home from school and threw up most of the day, morning sickness and stress kicking in. Her parents thought she had the flu. I went over and climbed in bed with her as she choked on her sobs.

Justine told Taye. Taye did not tell his family. His mother believed herself to be a devoutly religious and pious person and did not approve of Justine. She called Justine, to her face, "a disgrace," because she and Taye were brought home after curfew by Chief Knight when they snuck out to the lake one Saturday night to drink beer.

She disapproved of the relationship because the Knights did not attend a Christian church, and she thought that Justine was "corrupting my God-fearing, Christian son. When it is time, he will look for a God-fearing Christian wife, not you, Justine!"

Justine said to her, with remarkable maturity, "No, you are the disgrace, Maeve. You go to church every week. You teach Sunday school. And yet you are the most judgmental, unkind woman I have ever met. How do the two mesh together? How can you call yourself a Christian? Aren't you a walking, talking hypocrite?"

St. Peter must have caught Maeve's tongue and given it a twist, because she didn't know what to say. No one talked to her like that, especially her husband, who drank himself into a stupor each night after dinner so he could drown out her nagging.

Justine skipped school and took a bus to a clinic in a town four hours away. She said that as soon as she put her feet in the stirrups she became nauseated and sick and started to cry. The doctor was very kind and waited. Justine ran out of the clinic, buttoning her pants up on the way out.

Justine told Taye what happened. Taye, also seventeen, told Justine they should get married. "Let's do it, Justine," he said eagerly. "We can still go to school and party at the lake while we raise the kid. I've taken care of goats and horses and puppies and kittens my whole life. It can't be that much harder to take care of a baby. They're tiny. We can do it. Plus, I love you, Justine, I do."

But Taye's love was a problem, too. Justine loved Taye as a . . . close friend. A childhood friend. She had tried to be in love with him and it hadn't worked. She was in love with Jed. "We're seventeen, Taye," she said. "We can't get married."

"Why not?"

"Because we're seventeen."

"So what do you want to do? Hey! Can we talk about this after basketball practice? Want to get root beer floats?"

She couldn't abort. She didn't want a baby.

"I think you have to tell your parents, Justine," I said to her later, at my house, as we made necklaces, Justine's hands shaking. "They're going to find out. You're going to get as big as a cow and your mom's been pregnant eight times. They'll know soon."

She sobbed again, head down on the table.

Justine told her parents a week later. Taye, once again to his credit as a seventeen-year-old boy, insisted on going with her.

It was one of those closed-door meetings. Her father couldn't even speak. Then he glared at Taye as if he wanted to throttle him. Justine's mother was calmer, but shocked, her face flushed, then pale, and back to flushed. Taye apologized. Said he was sorry.

Justine told them she couldn't abort.

"I should say not, young woman," Chief Knight said.

"That is out of the question," Annabelle said.

"What do I do?"

"We'll raise the baby," her mother said.

"That's right," her father said. "Together."

But that wasn't what Justine wanted. She didn't want to be a mother. There were already eight kids in the house. Her mother had recently been diagnosed with arthritis and was not responding well to the medications. One of her younger siblings, Savannah, who I had ended up holding right after she was born, needed a heart operation. She would be fine, but a heart operation is not something that is a "minor inconvenience" in a family. She would need extensive care and medical help. Chief Knight and Annabelle were already exhausted from having eight kids.

Justine had always said she didn't want kids. She had helped raise her seven siblings. She was still raising them. To all of her younger siblings she was the second mother, and they still came to her for everything, from hugs to advice and help on homework. She did not want a baby. She did not want to marry Taye.

Justine told them she wanted to give the baby up, and Taye and her parents, with heartbreak, agreed. Taye did have basketball practice every night, he said, and he thought he could win state in the 400-meter dash in track if he had time to practice. "Plus, now that I think about it, my mom will kill me if I bring home a baby. She wasn't happy when I brought home two stray kittens last week."

The chief suggested Justine move to his sister's house in North Dakota when she started to show. The sister, Jerrilynn, the oldest of nine, was 67. She happily agreed to host Justine. "These things happen to nice girls from nice families all the time. Come on up, Justine!"

Everyone knows when you go "visit an aunt in the country" for an extended time, it's code for: The girl's pregnant. We lived in a small town. Justine was seventeen. She didn't need town gossip adding to her spiraling depression.

So when Justine barely started to show, and we knew the "visiting her aunt" announcement would have to come soon, Justine, Chick, and I thought of a solution to that growing problem.

We thought of a prank. It was a perfect prank. A perfectly preposterous precocious prank. It would do the trick.

We created a chicken/goat farm using my chickens and goats. In the school library. When the librarians walked in on Tuesday morning, the place was a-cluckin' and a-bleetin'. The students loved the clucks and the flying feathers, the chickens on the bookshelves and the goats on the tables, but the librarians were not amused. Justine, Chick, and I were suspended for three days, plus we had to clean up the library and round up the animals.

Justine's parents pretended that Justine "needed a new environment where she could mature and make better decisions," and off she went. Taye kept his mouth shut, and so did Chick and I. My dad knew why we created the chicken/goat farm, I could tell. Chief Knight and he were fishing buddies, after all.

He and I didn't talk about Justine's pregnancy because that would have made me break my promise to Justine about keeping it secret. He did say to me, "You are a true friend, Hummingbird," and I was not in any trouble for borrowing our feathered and horned friends.

In North Dakota Justine met with the adoptive parents, with whom her aunt had been close friends for years. They were in their thirties. They did not have children. The father, a high school teacher and coach, had lost a testicle in a diving accident when he was a teenager and could not get his wife, a nurse, pregnant.

Justine said they were two of the kindest

people she had ever met. She met with them three times and told them she had chosen them to be the baby's parents.

They cried. Justine cried. Her aunt cried.

Taye agreed and signed the paperwork that was sent to Justine's home. Taye, according to Annabelle, cried, too. He was so upset that he didn't even stay for Annabelle's steak tacos, and he loved her steak tacos.

After Justine left for her aunt's, Taye calmed way down in terms of partying. I don't think he laughed for months, until Justine came home. Taye and Justine did not get back together. They were children who had had a child. They had given their baby to another couple. They had aged and they were heartbroken.

Though Justine has always said she didn't want children, she has never stopped mourning the loss of her daughter, whom she named Natalie Chick. She has not contacted her daughter; she told the parents she wouldn't. She doesn't even know if her daughter knows she was adopted. Every year Justine flies to North Dakota. She says she feels "compelled. I can't stop myself."

She drives past the home where her daughter lives. Each time she has seen a black-haired girl playing in the yard, or getting into a car, or laughing with friends, laughing with her parents. It tears her up like razor blades on her soul, but she has to know that her daughter is alive and well.

Every year Justine, Chick, and I get together on Natalie Chick's birthday and go for a long hike in the woods in a state park. There are ten waterfalls, a river, steep canyon walls, lush trees, and an abundance of ferns, squirrels, and chipmunks. You can walk on the trail behind one waterfall that shoots off a cliff. There are double waterfalls and a waterfall that plunges into a blue-green pool. If heaven has a waterfall, you will find its counterpart here.

It is a magical place where Justine tries to find peace. But to find peace, she has to open herself up and go through her worst worries and deepest fears.

"Do you think my daughter likes the woods? Do you think she likes sunsets like I do? Do you think she wants to be an accountant? Do you think she's healthy? Do you think she's happy? Do you think she has an ache inside of her for me and she doesn't even know why? Do you think she's lonely for me? Is there something in her soul that says she was rejected, and hurt, and betrayed? Will I ever meet her? When she's eighteen, do you think I should contact her parents and ask if I can contact her?"

And then the guilt, the pain, the shame. "I shouldn't have given her up. . . . No, I made the right choice. . . . No, I didn't. My mom had arthritis, Savannah needed heart surgery, I was seventeen and I never wanted kids. . . . What about college? I probably wouldn't have even gone . . . but I am so ashamed. What mother gives her kid up? What would Jed think? He'd think I'm a sorry excuse for a mother. That I'm cold and have no heart."

We hug her, console her. "Everything you think Jed would think is what you think of yourself, and you shouldn't," I said. "You made the right choice, Justine. You were only a teenager."

Giving up her daughter has caused an avalanche of pain for Justine that has never ended. She desperately wants to see Natalie Chick, to talk to her. "Just once," she says. "I want to know she's okay, that she's happy."

We always end up crying together on that hike, sitting on a log, in front of a waterfall, wishing Justine's daughter a life filled with peace and health, love and laughter.

We hold hands.

Afterward, Justine goes home to her high-rise condo in Portland and stays drunk for a weekend. It takes another week for her to pull herself together. She goes on with her life, the two people she loves with all her heart, Jed and Natalie Chick, not with her.

I tried making Zack my grandma Dixie's apple pie. I had made it so many times with her, in her white and yellow kitchen. We'd roll the dough together, add the nutmeg, the cinnamon, the brown sugar, and handfuls of chopped apples from our orchard. We made crisscross crusts. We baked it, we invited my dad over, we ate it. In between, my grandma and I would read or hike or she'd talk to me about being a mechanic or what being a feminist meant. I loved that time with her.

That day, I burned the apple pie. I also forgot to put in the cinnamon. It was frustrating. I threw it out before Zack returned home but greeted him in my red negligee with the see-through flouncy skirt, so he didn't seem to mind.

"Dad, can you help me with something?"

"I will do anything to help my hummingbird." My dad sat across from me at our kitchen table, my jewelry supplies between us. He had brought lunch all the way from eastern Oregon for us. He'd killed a chicken so we could have chicken sandwiches. He brought us an apple pie, too, Grandma Dixie's recipe. Delicious. Certainly better than my burned one.

"I'm making jewelry, as you can see, and I need metal pieces. So, for example, this necklace. I want to have a bird as the centerpiece, maybe a blue heron, in full flight. I'll line it with these red and silver beads, and these tiny silver hoops. I also need two birds, the same design, but about a third the size, for right here. Can you make them for me?"

"Hummingbird, it would be my pleasure. Anything else?"

"Well . . ." I flipped through my drawing notebook. "What about . . ."

We had a fun time studying the necklaces I'd drawn in my notebook. I could tell he was thrilled to be making things for me for my necklaces. He wanted to help. He wanted to do something, anything, to help his hummingbird.

I love my dad with my whole heart.

Just as I love my lying husband, Zack.

This is what I've learned: Sometimes you have to let people help you because you love them and they love you and they want to help you. They will feel better if they help you. They will feel useful and needed. They will be grateful that you let them help.

Let them help you, then they will let you help them when their life falls into hell.

My mother was dating my dad for about two months before she found out she was pregnant. They met at a state fair. She told my dad she broke up with her previous boyfriend to date him. My mother has always looked for "new and improved" in her life. My dad could have been the "new and improved" at that moment. I am sure my dad married her because she was pregnant. He was twenty years old. Few twenty-year-old men want to get married then.

Anyhow.

My dad is six four, 230 pounds.

I am five three and small boned.

My dad has black hair shot through with white, and dark eyes, and his skin is slightly dark. His grandmother on Grandma Dixie's side was half Cherokee, half French Canadian, with black hair. His granddad was Italian. Black hair, dark eyes.

I have fair skin, like my mother.

I have blond hair. I have blue eyes, like my mother.

I have no features that are the same as my

dad's. I do not resemble Grandma Dixie, either.

I know my grandma's brother and sister. I know their children. I know their children, too. Everybody has black hair, olive-colored skin, dark eyes. They are gorgeous. They are tall.

There is no resemblance between me and them.

I know my dad and I could take one of those DNA tests.

But we won't.

We don't need to. He is my real dad. I am his real daughter.

And that's all we need to know.

The window in our bedroom, right above our bed, shattered.

The earsplitting crash and falling glass yanked me out of sleep, my heart instantly pounding. The gunshot echoed through the quiet night, and I found myself on the floor, on the side of the bed near the wall, Zack on top of me. "Stay down, Nat!" he insisted. "Stay down."

He reached over my head, underneath the dresser, and pulled out a gun.

"Oh, my God," I breathed out, shocked. Not only because of the bullet through the window but because Zack had a gun under the dresser.

"Don't move."

Zack crept toward the window, holding the gun with both hands. I heard laughter. It was familiar to me, that giggly laughter, but I couldn't figure out where I'd heard it before. It made my blood freeze in my body. I reached up and grabbed my phone on the nightstand and hit 911. As the operator answered, I heard tires screeching through the parking lot. The car gunned down the street.

"We need the police!" I shouted at the 911 operator.

"Address?"

I couldn't remember our address. "Zack, what is our address?" He didn't answer, his face grim as he stared out the window, gun still pointed out. "Zack? Zack? What's our address? I can't remember."

In the darkness of our room, the shadows slanting over his hard jaw, the streetlight glinting off the scar on his cheekbone, our window gone, I saw an emotion I could not understand: Defeat.

"I have already told you, Detective," Zack said to Detective Zadora, "I don't know anyone who would do this to us. I've given you the names and numbers of everyone

350

who has worked for me, even the few I've had to fire over the years."

"Are you sure?" Detective Zadora asked.

"Yes."

I looked from Detective Zadora back to Zack. There were two other police officers with her, but their names didn't even register. It was five in the morning. The detective was called in because this was her case. *We* were her case, Zack and I, because of the hit-and-run, the stabbed Barbie, the headless bird, and now a bullet. We were being stalked. I had been attacked. So, ta-da! You get your own detective.

"We can't help you if you don't help us," she said.

Why would she say that to us in that *tone*? What did she know? Why was she implying that we weren't helping?

"I can't help you if I don't know who would do this." Zack's voice . . . it was lower. His hand was gripping mine fairly tightly. He never held my hand that tight. Our hand holding was a reflection of our marriage: a loose, warm grip.

"Business is okay?"

Zack paused. "It's getting better."

"I have a previous address listed for you."

"Yes. I sold that house."

"Why?"

Now that was odd. Why was the detective asking about our previous home sale? Shouldn't we be talking about the bullet blasting through our window?

"So I could pay the bank off and finish the houses I'm building and sell them. I was overextended. I thought the market would keep up with the homes I was building, and it didn't."

"In this market, homes have been selling quickly," the detective said.

"My homes weren't ready in time, I had a cash problem."

"And we had a lot of expenses," I said. "Our deductible for my health care and expenses for rehab." I was trying to help Zack, as I heard the suspicion in the detective's voice.

Both my husband and the detective ignored me. The police officers sat quietly, watching Zack.

"Anything else you want to share with us, Mr. Shelton?"

"No."

They all stared hard at him again, and Zack returned their gazes. I watched with my mouth hanging open. Gall. I was right. They knew something. They believed Zack knew something.

"Mrs. Shelton," said Detective Zadora,

"may I speak with you alone?"

I nodded. We went to our bedroom. She shut the door.

"Mrs. Shelton, is there anything else you want to tell me?"

"What are you looking for? What do you think I know that I'm not sharing?" Somewhere amidst my fear from the bullet zinging through our window and my fear at the cryptic conversation Zack was having with the detective, I was surprised at myself. I had actually came up with prying questions through the fog of my broken brain.

"I don't know, Mrs. Shelton. We're trying to figure out what's going on here. Clearly you and/or your husband are being threatened. Someone is after you, and they are not giving up."

"I know. He's sick. The whole thing scares the heck out of me. I don't know what he wants. I don't know what Zack or I have done to bring this on. I have no idea who it is."

"Do you have life insurance?"

She was implying my husband wanted me killed. "My husband is not trying to have someone kill me for my life insurance. And no, I don't have any."

"Okay." She smiled. It softened the interview as she continued her questioning, which contained more financial questions about Zack's houses and business, to which I said, "What do you think his finances have to do with this?" and she was vague in her answer.

I knew she was doing her job, but I didn't like that she was implying that Zack was behind this, as if he had planned it all for some devious reason, because he wasn't. I knew that, and I told her so.

The officers and Detective Zadora said they'd check the security cameras at our apartment complex, although I knew they probably weren't working given the overall decay of this place, and they would check security cameras from businesses down the street to see if they could pick up a license plate number, etc.

"That was pretty scary," I said to Zack after they left. I wrapped my arms around him and put my head on his chest.

"Yes," Zack agreed, his jaw tight. He was furious. Barely contained fury.

"Obviously someone is still after me, or you, or both of us, and I'm freaking scared."

He closed his eyes for a second. "Natalie, everything will be okay. It will."

"But who's doing this? Who hates us? And why?"

He pulled me closer.

I was so tired. Tired to my bones. I couldn't even think through my tiredness anymore.

"Let's go back to bed for a while, Natalie, then come to work with me. We'll bring a card table and a chair, and you can bring your books and your jewelry supplies."

"I can stay at the apartment, Zack. I'll be in your way." I wanted to go with him, though. I was flat-out scared.

"I insist you come with me." There was Zack's steel again. He hugged me. "You are never in my way, honey."

"Okay, then." I smiled. I willed myself not to cry. I was scared about what was going on, but I was no wimp. I would buck up and figure this out. In the meantime, Zack could work on the house. I could work on my jewelry. Jewelry was the one thing I seemed to be able to do. It was art. I was using my hands.

"I'll bring my gun," I semi-joked.

"I have one in the truck."

He did?

His face grew more serious than before. "Listen, Natalie. I will do all I can to protect you. But if I'm not home, and a man comes in, you are to shoot. You saw the gun under the dresser. Remember, there's also one in the drawer of the side table by the door, in addition to the one on the shelf in the kitchen."

"Three guns in this house."

"Yes. You are not to hesitate. Not at all. No man should be in our apartment, so if one is here, shoot him."

"Makes me sick to think of it."

He put a hand to my face. "It makes me sick to think of you doing it, too. It makes me a hundred times more sick thinking of something happening to you. So promise me you'll do it. No matter what he says, no matter if he seems friendly, or pretends that he and I are friends, you will shoot if some strange man enters our apartment."

"I will." I would, wouldn't I?

"Natalie."

Those light green eyes held mine. He knew I was thinking it through. "Yes."

"Thank you." He kissed me, and that kiss became deeper and more passionate. Who would have thought that a bullet would have created this kind of heat? "Honey, let's go to bed and take off your clothes." He picked me up and swung me into his arms.

I smiled through my own ravaged sanity. Nothing like a little lovemaking to make you feel alive again after having the window above your bed shot out.

■ ■ ■ ■

Zack's new home was going to be a work of home art, so to speak, as usual. There were two other employees working upstairs. He would work downstairs. I had suggested to him before my accident that he use wood from a former barn like wainscoting around the dining room, and he had. He had also used it on the downstairs windowsills to add a rustic flavor to the house and as a mantle. It would help to sell the home, I knew it.

He set up my card table in the breakfast nook with built-in seating, and I was soon absorbed in making a necklace. I had gone to two Goodwills and several secondhand stores to buy unique pieces, just like I'd done as a kid with Chick and Justine. I was especially interested in using old brooches in new ways. I found an old-fashioned brooch with a picture of a woman carrying a blue parasol with a frilly, tilted blue hat. I paired that with two strands of blue beads, and it ended up looking cool.

At a secondhand shop I found an eclectic collection of old buttons in a jar. Anchors, hearts, birds, suns, moons, all colors, all shapes, some quite old. I couldn't believe it. Who would throw a jar full of old buttons out that were this unique?

My dad was also sending me a box of metal treasures. I would combine those with the treasures from Goodwill and the second-hand stores and the fantastic buttons, beads, and charms, and my necklaces would be ready to go . . . somewhere.

I didn't know what I'd do with all of them at the moment. Maybe I would sell them at a farmers' market again in the future, but for now it was therapy. I tried not to think about anything stressful as I worked: not my injured brain, not a bullet splitting my bedroom window, not my husband who knew something that I did not.

My hands still trembled.

When we got home, our window was fixed. Zack had called in a couple of employees and they'd gotten it done. Whew.

That night Zack received a call at one in the morning. He went outside to take it. I followed and tried to listen through the closed door, but he was talking near the dead fountain. He wasn't shouting, and I couldn't make out all the words, but I know that man's body language and he was livid. I could tell he was arguing. I could tell, when he turned in profile, that he was threatening someone.

I didn't say anything when he came back to bed. He hugged me close and whispered, "Love you, baby."

I didn't answer because I wanted to pretend I was asleep. I wanted to say, "Who were you talking to outside at one in the morning?" I wanted to say, "What the hell, Zack?" I wanted to say, "You know what's going on. You get it. Tell me."

But I didn't. I would wait. I would try to figure this out myself if I could get my brain in gear long enough. I knew, as messed up as I am, that Zack would lie to me, as he'd been lying to me, and the police, from the start.

I was devastated: My husband had lied to me in the past, he was lying to me now, and he would continue to lie to me.

Until I figured things out myself, I would play along.

I blinked at my own thought processes. That I was even able to have these thoughts, to have a rational and reasonable opinion, to have a plan, to be able to see what was going on . . . well, that was encouraging! I could think on my own! My brain was chugging along again. . . .

On Friday evening, three nights after the

call, I made manicotti. I forgot to put in the ricotta cheese. It was awful. So frustrating. And the other night I thought my brain was improving.

Part of the reason I messed up was because my nerves were shot and shriveling. I could not get the recent shooting out of my mind, the piercing sound of the glass breaking, the creepy peals of the man's laughter, or the squealing of the tires as that maniac raced out of the parking lot. I kept replaying that whole night in my head. It was like a circle of anxiety with a headless bird, a carved-up Barbie, and a stalker thrown in. I was trying to be brave, and fake being calm, but it was affecting my sleep, and it was affecting my days.

"Should we leave, Zack?" I put my fork down and pushed the manicotti away. "Should we go to my dad's until this maniac is caught?"

"No," he said quickly. "You don't need to. You'll be okay. We'll be okay."

That was telling. How did he know I was going to be okay? Wouldn't a loving husband send his wife out of the city and out to the country to be safe?

Maybe I should leave for my dad's. Just because Zack told me no, that didn't mean it *was* no. I did what I wanted to do. He had no hold over me, he never had. He was not a controlling person at all, and I would not have taken that crap to begin with.

My brain said, *Get the hell out of town,* and my heart said, *I cannot leave Zack. I know he's lying to me. But I love him and I trust him.*

Lies and trust do not go together, so I could only surmise that the rational part of my brain was completely, utterly damaged.

"How do you know, Zack? This is all getting worse."

"Natalie, I just talked to the police. They're on it. They're close to finding who did it."

"They are?"

"Yes." His tone was impatient.

"Who is it?"

"They won't tell me, but they're almost there."

"I'm not buying it."

"There's nothing to buy, Natalie," he said, anger riding through his words. "You have to be patient. Wait. Concentrate on getting better and I'll concentrate on this."

"But —"

"Natalie, I've had a long day."

"Me too, Zack."

There was tension there between us as we glared at each other across the table. It was looming like an angry elephant in the room.

Zack and I rarely had tension between us, and I didn't like it. I didn't need it right now, either. It felt negative and fraught. I wanted to concentrate on speaking and thinking like a fully functioning human again. I didn't want to get into this confusing feud with my husband.

I wouldn't let it go forever, but I had to let it go now. That's not a smart life or marriage strategy, burying what I don't want to think about, not questioning when I know there's something he's hiding, but right then I couldn't take on one more thing.

"Sorry about the manicotti." How strange. I was afraid we were going to have bullets shattering our windows again and there I was, apologizing about the manicotti.

"It's delicious," Zack said. He stood and hugged me for a long time.

Even though I was suspicious of my husband, I still put on my purple negligee with the ruffles that night. Our sex was hot and rollicking. Nothing like being chased down by a human monster to put some passion into naked wrestling, I suppose.

Chick mailed Justine and me another picture.

She had cut out pictures of our faces from photographs, all three of us. She glued them on paper. Then she drew us naked — not too many details — on bikes. She wrote, "Moonshine and Milky Way Maverick Girls First Annual Naked Bike Ride."

Had I truly agreed to this? Had I signed a contract? Could I get out of it?

Naked? In Portland? At night?

My dad came back the next week with a box. "Hummingbird, you tell me if your old man did what you wanted him to do."

He poured out the contents of the box.

I could hardly speak.

"I didn't do it right now, did I, Hummingbird? Let me try again. We'll get these suckers pounded out exactly how you want 'em so you can make your jewelry. I like that necklace you have on today, by the way. . . ."

"Dad . . ."

"Size wrong? Color wrong? I think you call it a learning process and I gotta lot to learn. No hurt feelings here, Hummingbird. You let me know how I can fix these doo-dads."

"Dad . . ."

"Learning keeps the brain young." He tapped his head. I almost laughed. My dad hides it sometime, but he is super smart.

"They're perfect, Dad."

"What?"

"They're perfect. I love them." I so did. He had made the birds I requested. He had made, in different sizes: butterflies, the moon, stars, swirling designs, humming-birds, hearts, birds, and leaves. He is a talented, creative metalsmith. I gave him a hug. "Thank you so much, Dad. Thank you."

He became all misty eyed, poor guy. "Anything I can do to bring a smile to my hummingbird's face, I'll do." He sniffled. "When I didn't think I was going to see that smile again . . ." He choked up and wrapped me in a bear hug. It still killed me to think of the pain he went through, a father watching his daughter, in a coma, for any sign of life, grief and fear hanging like doom around you. . . .

I showed him what I was making, and he sat down and watched me. I used a leather strip for a chain and I attached a silver bar, about a half inch wide and three inches long. I put it around my dad's neck, and we stared into a mirror together.

"I think it makes me look like a motorcycle gang member," he said, pleased.

"I think it does, too. It's tough guy jewelry,

isn't it?"

"Real men wear jewelry," he said.

And there wasn't a lot of jewelry out there for men, was there?

That got me to thinking.

"Dad . . ."

I gave him a list of things I needed for my "stud man necklaces." I was so excited to see what he could do, and I think he was excited, too.

Later, I turned on country music, we sang along together, and I made chocolate chip cookies. The first batch didn't work because I forgot the flour. My dad and I added flour to the remaining batter, and that worked out fine. He read part of a chapter out of *Jane Eyre* to me when they were baking.

The cookies were delicious, warm and melty. I was proud of myself. I had made chocolate chip cookies in only two tries!

CHAPTER 14

Detective Macy Zadora called. The police had the license plate of the car that the person who shot a bullet through our window was driving. They obtained the camera footage from two convenience stores down the street. It was late, there was hardly anyone out, and the car went through the view of those cameras less than a minute after I'd made the first call.

The car had been stolen. Whoever was driving was wearing a full black mask.

"Do you think you'll be able to catch this person?"

"We're trying."

"Zack said he talked to you the other day and you said you're getting close to finding this person."

There was a silence. To my ears, a *loud* silence.

"Zack said we were close to finding out who it is?" the detective asked.

"Yes, he did." I did not miss the surprise in her tone. "That's why we're not moving out to eastern Oregon, where I'm from."

"You should consider moving temporarily, Mrs. Shelton."

"But you're close to figuring this out, right?"

"We're trying. It's more complicated than I initially thought. What is clear, however, is that these crimes are continuing to escalate against you both. I'm going to ask you again: Is there anything about Zack that you think we should know? Anything about his business? Anything he's doing that would bring this on? Anything about his past, his history, relationships, finances? How does he seem to you? Is he acting as he normally does? Any changes?"

What should I say? That my husband was lying to me about what was going on and clearly had not spoken to the detective recently? That he was often angry and detached lately? That he continued to get phone calls that infuriated him? That I couldn't remember the morning of my accident, but I think the answers lie there?

If I said all that I would be implicating Zack. It would be like pointing my finger at my husband and saying he was a partner in all of this, that maybe he'd paid someone to do it all. My husband would not do that and he would not pay to have someone do that to me.

"No, there's nothing else. He's a home-builder. He's my best friend. He's always been a wonderful husband." All true. But wonderful husbands don't lie.

I could almost hear her frustration in the long silence. "Okay. We'll keep you posted."

"Detective, wait. You know something." I might have an injured brain, but I could sense this.

There was a silence. "We're still investigating."

"Investigating the person who did this? You have a suspect? What else have you found out? You said it was more complicated than you initially thought."

More silence. Then, "We have people working on this at the moment, Mrs. Shelton. We'll get back in touch."

I felt numb.

The detective knew something she was not sharing.

This whole horrible thing was not near to being over, I knew it.

Justine came by and saw me at lunch.

"We miss you at the firm."

"Thanks. I miss you all, too." I did.

"How are you?"

"Confused. Baffled. Trying to get my brain to work. I can't add, Justine. I can't subtract."

"That's what calculators and computers are for." I saw the worry in her eyes. She is concerned about my ability to be an accountant again. She should be. I'm concerned.

"You look fantastic, Natalie. I love that shirt."

"Thanks." I called it my "artist shirt." It had been painted with a swirling design, as if a rainbow had been smooshed onto the fabric.

"And you sound better. Your words are faster."

"I'm trying." I tried to get my emotions together. Head injuries strip the ability to control emotions right out of your brain. "It's . . ." I didn't want to whine. "It's, uh . . ." I didn't want to complain. Zillions of people in the world have it worse than me. "Trying to . . . sometimes it's . . ."

"The whole thing sucks."

"Yes. That's it. It does."

We held hands.

Sometimes that's all you can do.

"Looking forward to the Naked Bike

Ride?" she asked.

I groaned.

Justine and I started our own accounting firm nine years ago in downtown Portland after we partied for four years at the University of Oregon and had a splendid time. She started college one term late but took extra classes and double majored in accounting and marketing, I double majored in accounting and finance. I took jewelry-making classes, too, and sold my necklaces in the student store and in Eugene's Saturday Market.

We knew in our freshman year that owning our own firm "Knight and Fox" would be the goal.

The reason her name, Knight, came first was because she beat me at poker one evening, despite my grandma Dixie teaching me all she knew. I had had too much beer.

When we graduated from the University of Oregon, we both rented studios in the same building in the middle of Portland. We went to work at different prestigious accounting firms in Portland to pay off student loans and save money for our own firm, and we basically hated it. The work was long, the environment competitive.

One of Justine's coworkers, whose name was, no kidding, Destiny, slept with Justine's boyfriend at the time, Torvin Sakavea. They all worked at the same firm. Justine didn't mind that the married Destiny slept with her boyfriend, who we named Ping-Pong Balls because of a small problem with his balls, in that they were — wait for it — totally tiny.

She minded that Ping-Pong Balls and Destiny slept together because it was flat-out wrong. She thought she was in a committed relationship with Ping-Pong Balls. She didn't love him, she loved Jed, but she was *trying* to love Ping-Pong Balls.

In retaliation Justine had a private investigator follow Ping-Pong Balls and Destiny. "It's their destiny," she told me as we cackled over their fate while clinking our margarita glasses together in a Mexican bar in Portland.

Justine cackled over all the photos the private investigator took and, late one night, taped them to the door of the staff refrigerator, in the conference rooms, the foyer, and Destiny and Ping-Pong Balls's offices.

The next morning everyone was transfixed by the photos, especially the one where Destiny was straddling Ping-Pong Balls in the front seat of his car, naked as a newborn hyena, head back. Ping-Pong Balls's face was screwed up tight with desire. It did not appear that they were discussing the tax code.

The photo behind the building at night was especially popular! Everyone knew where they were because you could see the alley behind the coffee shop right behind them. My goodness, it was impressive how limber Destiny was with her leg up so high and all that!

And the photo of Destiny and Ping-Pong Balls having sex in the conference room, at night, was also intriguing. The table should be wiped down and disinfected, certainly. Good to know it was made out of strong wood, though, and could hold the weight of two. They'd paid a fortune for that table! (Justine took that photo herself. She was proud of how the composition and the shadows worked so well together.)

Justine threw an impressive fit when she saw the photographs, saying, loudly, "Destiny, have him. He's all yours. How do you like his Ping-Pong balls?" Torvin grew red at that. I mean, it was what it was. He knew his balls were Ping-Pong ball size.

Destiny could hardly argue, either. By the expression on her face, she confirmed that Torvin had Ping-Pong balls.

It was widely assumed that Destiny's husband took the photos and somehow stole her key card to the office to make the photo display. He was, after all, a famous photographer, with a long history of taking photos in war zones.

Destiny quit, Torvin quit. Justine stayed on for a few months, then quit, everyone assuming she was simply too humiliated to go on.

At the same time, one of the married partners at my firm was hitting on me. His name was Leonard Speight. I called him Mr. Fat Gut and started recording what he said to me, how he asked me out and made sickening comments about my body; how he said he could be an asset to my career and he liked sex; how he asked if I watched porn, if I was lonely, if I needed company after work, etc. He was a rich, old, entitled, and disgusting man who for some bizarre reason thought that I would be attracted to him.

I had told Mr. Fat Gut, with his fleshy face, pregnant stomach, and sweaty hands, to stop. I said to him, "Your comments disgust me. I don't want to go out with you. I'm just staggered at your arrogance. You are old enough to be my grandfather." He laughed. It never occurred to him I was telling the truth. He thought I was playing "hard to get." He winked. He relished his power over me, his dominance.

I managed to record a number of our conversations with my cell phone between my boobs.

I figured I would go out with fireworks.

As one of the account managers, I had been asked to make a brief presentation to the executive board about how to maintain and attain new clients. Essentially: How to keep everyone happy.

My presentation involved a PowerPoint presentation with special pictures and the recordings of Mr. Fat Gut coming on to me. The firm's top dogs were at the meeting, including Mr. Fat Gut.

I had taken a photo of Mr. Fat Gut in front of our firm. He had smiled at me, tried to be sexy. He thought I wanted it so I could gaze at him as I wished. Late one night I snuck into his office and took photos of framed pictures on his desk where he was with his wife, kids, and grandkids. I also took pictures of him shaking the hands of "important people." The picture in his office I liked best, though, was one of him as a deacon in his church, a Bible in his hand, standing sanctimoniously next to a minister.

In my presentation, these photos were all

juxtaposed against him saying things to me like, "Natalie, you have a tight ass. . . . I can be a help to you in your career, if you and I can agree on a few things. If not, if we don't have an understanding, don't be expecting much in terms of a promotion or advancement. . . . Natalie, you should wear your shirts unbuttoned more. . . . Lean over me, right over the desk, would you? Why don't you smile at me more? I have never seen an accountant who looks like you. Delicious. Mmmm mmmm! Every morning I walk in and see you and think, 'Yum.' Do you think that when you see me? I think you and I could make each other happy. Turn around. Let's see that ass again. You make me want to groan, honey. Baby . . . Sweetheart . . . I'm getting impatient with you, Natalie. I need to see you be friendly to me. I can help you, but don't make me mad. Don't alienate me. I know everyone in this town, and I can make sure you never work again."

When the presentation was finished, with a final photo of Mr. Speight in a Speedo suit, which he had sent me via his cell phone of him on the beach, his gut hanging out, apparently thinking I would lose my cookies over him, *and* a picture of his private pistol, there was silence. Yes, a shocked silence surrounded that private pistol up on the big screen.

Mr. Fat Gut, who had tried to intervene several times during my presentation but was sharply told to "Sit down, Speight," by the owner, Bob Giovanni, said, weakly, "That's not mine," in reference to his private pistol.

"Yes, it is," I said.

Bob Giovanni glared at Mr. Fat Gut in the stunned silence, turned to me, and said, "Natalie, I am sorry. You should have told me, because I would have taken Speight out."

I told Bob exactly why I didn't tell him.

Why didn't I tell? Because I was trying to do my job. I was twenty-six. I was building a career. I was worried about what Mr. Fat Gut would say about me to people in this firm and to people in other firms if I left. I was afraid he would lie about me. I didn't know if anyone would believe me if I told the truth. I was afraid of the firestorm and the attorneys who would be hired, by him, if I told the truth. He would have denied it. He would have threatened to sue me for defamation. I would have been ground through the court system. I would lose my job or it would be so uncomfortable here I would have to leave. So I recorded him for proof.

Mr. Speight was fired by unanimous vote that minute, his face red, sweaty. He stalked out, Security met him, and he was on the sidewalk in less than ten minutes.

I took the settlement money, and Justine and I opened up a firm in downtown Portland called Knight and Fox, as we'd agreed to during the poker game. We were going to name it Maverick Accounting, but since Chick wasn't in on it, we thought it might make her feel left out.

We had a loft downtown for our offices in what used to be a warehouse two blocks from our studios. It was modern and cool. There was a steel knight at the front door to greet people, and next to it a five-foot-tall fox that my dad made out of metal. Knight and Fox.

We hustled for business. Many of our clients from our previous firms came with us. We went after companies to do their taxes, and we went after individuals. We gave talks at retirement homes, too. Many of the seniors had high net worths. Who knew that Mrs. Candace, who brought her cat in in a cat stroller, was worth almost four million dollars? Who knew that Mr. DeShawn had all those apartment buildings? He had holes in his shoes.

We were in business. Individual and business accounting, that was our jive. Our groove. Our music. We never took clients with shady backgrounds. Our goal has always, always been honest and fair service.

We now have four employees, all women, and a male receptionist. He is very kind. He adopted a brother and sister out of foster care, so we gave him parental leave.

If my brain didn't start to work, I would never be able to provide honest accounting services, in my life, again.

I love numbers.

I want to work with numbers again.

The question is: Can I?

Chick stayed over at Justine's on Friday night, and the next morning Chick, Justine, and I left for our annual hike in the woods. It was Justine's daughter's birthday. We parked where we always do, at the trailhead, quiet and peaceful. Winter was definitely swooping in; it was cool, windy, the skies heavy and gray.

Chick and I always take Justine's lead. If she wants to talk, we do. If she wants to be quiet, we are. Today she didn't want to talk much. We hiked through the woods, along the tumbling river, passing one thundering waterfall after another, as we watched squirrels climb and birds swoop in and out of the branches. We would not do the full hike today because of me. I am not up to it. I am slow, so we would do part of it.

We sat down on a rock together, a waterfall crashing twenty feet away into a pool.

"Natalie Chick is seventeen today," she said.

"Yes, she is."

"I hope she's happy," Justine said.

"I'm sure she is," I said.

"She's probably thinking about college," Chick said.

"Yes. I wonder what she'll study. I wonder if she likes math. Maybe she hates it. Maybe it's frustrating. I could help her with it. I hope she has friends. I hope she likes high school. What if she's lonely? I worry about that a lot. What if my daughter is lonely or bullied or left out?"

That was a repeated worry for Justine. She had grown up with seven brothers and sisters, a mother, and a father. She had Chick and me and Jed. She was close to my father and Chick's mother. It was a small town. Everyone knew her. Justine never got lonely as a kid, only frustrated that Jed didn't love her as she loved him. But after she gave up Natalie Chick, she was deeply lonely for her daughter. It never went away. She didn't want loneliness for her daughter.

Justine pulled her knees up and put her head on them. We wrapped our arms around her as the waterfall continued to thunder, the river rumbled nearby, and our best friend quietly mourned for the daughter she had never stopped missing.

"You really should sell your necklaces again," Justine said.

Chick, Justine, and I studied the necklaces I had made using my dad's metal art while we ate peppermint ice cream with a pickle on the side. The combination isn't tasty, but traditions like this one don't die.

Both of them had already been to my apartment and had been as classy and kind as I knew them to be. Classy and kind as in, they didn't look at me with pity, which would have been infuriating and condescending.

We have been through too much together already. I knew they were upset I'd lost my home. That's a no-brainer. But why make it worse by getting all mushy about it, by pointing out the obvious, that Zack and I had tumbled down and out?

"I agree," Chick said. She took a bite of the peppermint ice cream. On the plate beneath the bowl of ice cream was the pickle. "Chicks like us will love these. Cool chicks. Hot chicks. You have talent, Natalie." She peered down at her chest, then pointed at her necklace. "Yep. I'm wearing the one you made me in the rehab center right now."

She was. I had wrapped a piece of turquoise in wire, then added a silver chain. Along the silver chain were silver beads, interspersed with four silver stars. It was simple, but the turquoise was a unique piece. Justine had on one of the necklaces I'd made her, too. Leather rope, a large faux pearl in the center, other faux pearls on either side, three strands.

"These are for men, right?" Justine picked up a few of the "men pieces."

"Yes. These necklaces are for studs. Motorcycle riders. Surfers. Adventurers. Mountain climbers. Sexy men. And men who *want* to be studly, sexy motorcycle riders, surfers, adventurers, and mountain climbers."

"If Braxton wore one of these I'd want to take his clothes off in the morning, and morning is not my time for sex. I like to get my body up and moving first, my teeth brushed, and I want to be fresh as a daisy down there. But geez. I'd rethink it if he wore these."

"Men will wear jewelry if it makes them feel more manly," Justine said. "Not floppy, if you know what I mean." She wiggled the pickle. "They're sensitive about floppiness."

"Look at these things my dad made for men: A replica of a shark's tooth. A cross. A knife. A little violent, but okay. A snake. A hatchet. Men will like this stuff. They don't want to wear hearts and flowers."

Chick picked up the necklace with the faux silver shark tooth. "Oh yeah. Bitey. Very bitey."

"These are manly man pieces. I mean it, Natalie," Justine said. "This jewelry, and I don't even think I'd call it jewelry, this man-wear, these necklaces are for studs. I like the chains you chose for the men, and I like the leather. Plus, they're simple. No frou-frou."

I could make jewelry all day and be happy. It was so entertaining. The designs, the beading, the colors . . .

"Come back to pickle land, Natalie," Justine said. She hit me on the shoulder with her pickle.

"Pickles shouldn't be weapons," I told her.

"I'm selling these at the hardware store," Chick said. "Pack up a bunch of them. I'm taking them with me and we are going to rock this, Maverick Girl."

"Really? You think they would sell?" I picked up a necklace with three silver chains. On each chain I'd put a different bird. A bluebird, a blue heron, and an owl. All made by my dad with hammered silver.

"Uh, yeah. Duh."

I grinned. Okay! "Thanks, Chick."

"I want to go back to work."

Zack's silence was noisy. "Your silence is noisy, Zack."

He turned toward me on the couch and I studied those light green eyes, shadowed now. Light green sea eyes, intense. When Zack looks at you, you know he truly sees you. He hears you.

"I don't think you're ready yet, Natalie. You took a hit. You still sleep a lot, you take naps, your head hurts sometimes, you're working on walking."

"I know I'm not ready. The numbers are still swimming for me sometimes. I can work for only a short period of time. But I need to go back. Justine and I already talked. Remember, a calculator is my friend. That's what's almost attached to my hand at my desk. Like another appendage. A third hand." He didn't think my joke was funny.

He pulled me onto his lap. "I think you need to rest. I think you need to sleep in, take walks. Make your jewelry. Your jewelry is incredible. I've never seen anything like it. It's original."

"Thank you. But making jewelry is a hobby."

"Does it have to stay a hobby? Why don't you make and sell jewelry as your full-time job?"

I entertained the thought. I'd done it before as a teen and in college. It would be fun. I would love it. No commute, no clients . . . I let my mind drift on that thought, then reality slammed on in. I wouldn't make enough money if I sold my jewelry. Nowhere near what I made now.

Plus, I'm an accountant. I went to school to become an accountant. I worked hard to build our firm. Justine and I are Knight and Fox, and I am the Fox. I'm supposed to give that up without a fight? And what about Justine?

I felt precarious financially. My dad worked so hard as a roofer. He saved as much as he could but spent most of it when he took care of my grandma in the care home. And one accident, one fall off a roof, and our security went out the window. I will never forget the notice I saw from the bank telling us we could lose our little home on the hill because he'd refinanced it to pay for my grandma's care. And look what happened to Zack's home construction business. A problem with the bank, overextending, and our house was gone, gone, gone. My anxiety level was high. I was triggering back to my childhood.

"I've been resting, and I'm bored. I feel out of sorts. I've worked forever, Zack. It's hard for me not to work."

"I don't want you to work, Natalie." He rubbed a hand over his face. "I don't. I want you to recover. It makes me feel sick to think of you going downtown, working, getting stressed, getting tired, working all the hours you used to work. I have a house that's almost done, and we'll sell it soon. We'll combine that money with our savings and get a house when you're up to looking for one, until we have the time and land and money to build our dream home."

The *One Day* house. "I have to go back to my firm. It's for me, Zack. My brain. I can't become someone I don't want to be. I have to fight this. I can't let that man destroy my life. He put me in a coma. He put me in rehab. He put me in therapy. I've had to fight my way back, and I'm still fighting." I felt myself getting choked up as I talked. "I can't let him take *me.* Take my job. My profession, my business, who I am. I can't let my fear of him take me, either."

"I understand, Natalie, hon, I do. You've had to work so hard. I've watched you working on your speech, your balance, doing all the work with your therapists, doing work here at home. I've seen your courage and your determination and your humor. You are the strongest person I know, baby. But the most important thing is for you to get better, to heal all the way. We're a team. You can help me with designs for the houses, choosing materials, but please stay here and rest."

"Zack, helping you with designs is only sporadic and you know it. It's hard to be home all day. It's lonely. I'm isolated. I'm stuck with my thoughts and my fears. I'll get better if I'm not home all the time worrying about my brain or worrying that this sicko will shoot another bullet through our window."

His eyes were worried. He finally sighed. Then groaned. "I wish you wouldn't. But I know I can't stop you. Why don't you go in for a few hours? That's it. Then come home?"

"I think I'll do that." I smiled at him. That had been my plan. I just let him say it. I let him think of it. I knew he would.

He nodded.

I smiled and straddled him. "Want to get naked?"

He did.

■ ■ ■ ■

After a hot romp in bed, Zack sleeping while I hugged him, I studied his face. Hard and chiseled. Not a soft spot on it. Except for that mouth. That mouth was soft and sweet and lusty and daring, that it was.

Who would have guessed that a man who looked like a gangster could be so gentle and caring? I would never, in my life, forget that Zack was there for me every day, hours every day, when I was in that coma. I would never forget him begging me to wake up, his tears, how he fought for my life.

He was my soul mate.

He was the life of my heart even if he has secrets that he is not sharing with me. The police were suspicious of him. They knew something I didn't. They thought he had something to do with this dangerous debacle we were in.

But I knew this: Zack loved me. I loved him. I would protect my husband. I would be loyal to him, and to us, as he has always been to me. He would never do anything to hurt me. I don't know what's going on, but he's my man.

Sleep grabbed me, pulled me over and, hugging Zack, my tired brain shut off for the night.

I went to work on Monday at ten o'clock. For the first time in what seemed like forever I was wearing business attire, a blue skirt and blazer. There was black piping on it, which I liked, and I was wearing knee-high black boots, but it did feel constricting to be without my flowing cotton shirts and jeans. Justine greeted me with a hug, as did our employees, who clapped and cheered and rushed out of their offices to greet me. They smiled, they laughed, they hugged me again and welcomed me back. I thanked them for coming to see me, for the cards and flowers. I got teary eyed and said, "One thing you all should know. I cry all the time now, I'm a total baby." They laughed. "Just ignore it."

I was overwhelmed, I was nervous about my abilities, and it felt absolutely surreal to be standing in our offices after being gone for so long. It was as if I went to another planet where a lot of bad things happened, then returned to civilization.

It was great to be back at Knight and Fox, where I am the Fox.

Justine and I went to my office. She shut the door. Her hair wasn't its usual neat, black silky mass, and she'd buttoned a blouse button wrong. She was clearly stressed and anxious. "We have way too much work here. I feel as if I've fallen off a cliff and I'm still falling," she said. "Hope you're here to catch my butt."

I buttoned her up right as we laughed.

"I didn't know you were going to come back to work and try to take off my clothes," she said.

"Had to check which bra you're wearing."

When she was all buttoned up correctly, our jokes over, we had a business meeting. It took two hours. I could see why she was overwhelmed. I was overwhelmed thirty minutes into the meeting and had trouble tracking everything. At one point she stopped and said, "Are you okay?"

"Yes. No. I'm trying to be a competent accountant, but it's not working so well."

"Let me tell you about the Andreskys, then I'm out."

She gave me a few files. I shut the door when she left and lay down on my couch to breathe. I have a corner office, as does Justine, two windows. The front of my office is all glass, so I can see out. I have a long, wide desk. I have a table in the corner with four chairs and red pillows on my couch. I have two metal hummingbirds in one corner from my dad and a picture of Zack and myself in our drift boat.

Our offices aren't typical. We're accountants, but we're cool. We have an open work area and a conference room, with offices surrounding it. We have a collection of guitars hanging on one wall and framed posters of rock stars on another.

Everyone was encouraged to decorate their offices in a way that resembled them. Abigail is a surfer, so she hung two of her old surfboards on a wall. Maggie plays drums in a rock band. When she's stressed, she bangs on the set in her office. The rule: No longer than ten minutes.

Monique is getting a master's in literature. One of her walls is lined with the classics, and she has a life-sized cutout of Jane Austen. Terry likes knitting so she has baskets of yarn. She knits when she's nervous.

In the open area of our offices we have a table that people often work at together. The table is long and painted blue. A mural we all painted one afternoon stretches across one wall. Each person painted something/someone they loved. We had people and pets and childhood homes and a lake.

We have plants on bookshelves. Ten colorful umbrellas hang from our high ceiling. We have wine in the fridge and coffee and tea all day. First Friday of the month is Pasta Day. Fourth Friday of the month is Chinese Food Day.

I loved our firm.

I was there for four hours.

At the end of those four hours I knew I would not be working as a competent accountant anytime soon. The numbers swam. I couldn't concentrate. My head started to hurt.

I was not competent.

I put my head down on my desk.

Not. Competent.

The next afternoon Jed came in to our offices. Justine does his taxes.

She was nervous. She always became nervous around Jed. She tried on three different outfits in front of me to find "the best one."

"Hard to figure out what to wear for the man you're in love with," she said. "Who would hate you if he knew the real you." Her voice cracked.

"He would never hate you." I knew where the hate came from, and it wasn't from Jed.

"I hate myself." She covered her face with her hands.

"Justine." I gave her a hug. "Please don't."

"I can't help it."

"Tell him. You'll see. He won't react the way you think."

"No, I can't tell him. I don't want to see his reaction. He'll never look at me the same again."

What a mess. In some ways I was surprised that Chick never told Jed. But we'd made a promise years ago, the Moonshine and Milky Way Maverick Girls, and we'd all kept it. What's a friendship if you can't keep the secrets?

"Hi, Jed."

He gave me a hug, ambled into my office, and sat down at my table to visit. "Natalie, seeing you here, it makes my day. I am so glad." Those eyes teared on up. Jed is so successful in his career, but all I see is a brother who is not officially related to me. I see the brother who saved my life in the lake and who we followed around when we were kids. I see someone I can trust.

"Thanks for coming to see me in the hospital and the rehab center."

"Of course."

"I really appreciated it." Jed had sat with Zack and my dad many times, and he'd been a friendly visitor at the Brain Bang Unit. We'd even made a necklace together.

Architect didn't think he liked him, Soldier saluted and said, "I've cleared out the enemy for your visit," and Frog Lady gave him a frog. It had been the usual. He'd also visited me at our apartment, bringing flowers and chocolates.

"I'm glad I'm here, but I can't get much done, Jed." I took a deep breath. "This isn't working. My brain is broken for complex numbers, tax laws, tax codes. . . ."

His eyes grew serious. "I would think that being an accountant this soon after that head injury would be difficult."

"It's more than difficult." I leaned forward. "I wanted to talk to you about something." We talked about the hit-and-run, the mangled Barbie, the dead bird, and the bullet through our window.

"What do you think?"

"I think someone is after you or Zack. Probably Zack."

I swallowed hard. "He said he thought it was an employee he'd had a falling out with. I asked him who it could be, and he was vague then said he didn't know."

"It sounds like much more than what an angry employee would do."

I sagged. "Yes. It does."

He spoke aloud what I already knew: "It's dangerous. The whole situation is dangerous. You should move out and go live with your dad."

"I don't want to leave Zack."

"He should force you to move."

"He told me he doesn't want me going to my dad's."

"That doesn't make sense. He should want to protect you."

"I know. I don't understand his reaction."

There was a long silence between us and in that silence hundreds of words and questions and worries flew back and forth.

"So you're sitting down with Justine to talk about your taxes," I said, because I had no answers.

Jed smiled, he flushed, he twitched in his seat. "Yes."

"Have a lovely time."

"Thank you. I will. I'm sure of it."

"Maybe you should take Justine to dinner soon, old friends and all."

"I'd like that." His smile grew wider. "Do you think she would say yes?"

"I absolutely do. You need to stop being shy around her."

"I'm trying."

"Try harder."

"I will. And think about moving home, Natalie."

"I will." Maybe. Maybe not.

■ ■ ■ ■

After Jed left, Justine and I left early. First we went to our favorite lingerie store, Lace, Satin, and Baubles, so I could add to my collection. I bought a sweet little black lace number with garters and a seafoam-green slip. Justine bought a pink one, backless. "A woman has to hope. Today I thought Jed was going to ask me out, but then he didn't. Whatever. Maybe I was dreaming that up in my head."

Then we went for drinks in the city. I bemoaned the loss of my brain, she bemoaned not being able to be with Jed because of "the secret," but she said, after a few drinks in a candlelit bar near the river, "Look at me, Natalie." She waved a hand over her curves. "I want to give these lusty curves to Jed. I will say it again, loudly. I want to give these curves to Jed."

That time she said it on high volume, and many people turned to see what the sappy commotion was about. One woman raised her glass and said, "Go for it, girl," and a man said, "I'll take those curves, honey."

I clinked glasses with Justine, the guilt-ridden goddess. I was a CPA who couldn't add numbers; someone was trying to kill me; and Zack, my yummy husband, had secrets and lied to me.

It was a therapeutic, if semi-drunken night. As we left the bar, we stopped on a corner and sang Neil Diamond's "Sweet Caroline," and were delighted when other people joined in, with gusto: one group of men, in their fifties, who were obviously going to an event, all dressed in suits; a homeless man, who sang the best; and a couple who looked to be in their eighties, the woman holding a cane.

We all then tootled our way over to "Cracklin' Rosie" and a couple more of Neil's songs.

There is something about singing that is healing.

My mother never sang to me.

CHAPTER 15

"I may have to leave Dell."

I brought my wineglass to my mouth. I was grateful the waitress had kept it filled. I needed it to help me get through this Mother Monster torture lunch. "Why do you have to leave Dell?" At the same time, I thought, *We've had this conversation before. Here comes Divorce Number Five.*

"I am having a difficult time with his attitude."

I'd heard that line before, too.

She flicked a hand through her blond hair. It was Amethyst Day. Light purple dress. The neckline was plunging. You could peek at her lavender lace bra. That's what she wanted. When one marriage was going sour, she started hunting for a new husband, thus a plunging neckline.

She was wearing amethyst earrings, necklace, and bracelet. She had driven from eastern Oregon, gone to a high-end salon in

Portland, then arrived unannounced on my doorstep, as always.

My mother simply appears. Like a vulture with a manicure. Like a shark with earrings. I had heard her high heels tapping outside my door before the ominous knock.

Mrs. Godzilla insisted on going to lunch so she could "take you out of this hovel. My goodness. This is not how you were supposed to live, Natalie! This is not how the women in my family lived and it's certainly not what I wanted for you. We're not white trash!"

White trash. Oh, geez.

It was Saturday but Zack was at work. I had looked forward to a day of making necklaces as I shut out how wretched I felt about my fading accounting career.

"You mean, Mother, you're having a difficult time being married to Dell because he is limiting you to two thousand dollars a month in spending money?" I took a long gulp of wine.

"No," she snapped. "That is not it."

But it was, I knew it, she knew it.

It was his lack of generosity, she said. His tight-fisted spirit. His excessive frugalness and selfishness. She took a swallow of her wine, her pinky up in the air.

I tried not to laugh. We were in an expensive restaurant by a lake. My mother had ordered a salad. I had ordered steak, French bread, and a salad. I was eyeing a piece of caramel dulce de leche cheesecake.

She said to me, after we'd sat down, "Now what kind of shirt is that to wear to a restaurant? Surely you could have dressed for our lunch?"

"It's a picture of one of Monet's paintings, of his Giverny garden." I loved this shirt. Every inch was covered with water lilies, the Japanese bridge, and shimmering water.

She snorted through her nose. "Whose?"

"Monet. I like wearing art."

"It's a garden. Not art."

She surprises me sometimes with what she doesn't know. I knew I would need a lot of wine.

"Dell is simply not who he used to be when we were dating and at the beginning of our marriage."

"That's because you were different when you were dating him and at the beginning of your marriage. You were flirty. You were kind. You listened to him. You didn't take all his money. You didn't make demands. You knew how to reel him in.

"Dell had been married for forty-one years. His wife died two years before you met. You knew he was vulnerable and lonely. You comforted him, made him laugh. Then you slowly started to change after the wedding. He now believes he's your bank and that you want him only for his money and for what he can provide. You're not making him laugh. You're not listening to him. You're causing problems with his long-term employees, especially Glenda, and his neighbors, whom he has been friends with for years, if not decades. They don't like you because you haven't been nice to them and, more important, they see how you treat Dell."

She gasped. She put her hand to her chest, right over her light purple dress and the amethyst necklace that she'd told Dell to buy her. "You talked to Dell. How dare you! I am furious with both of you, and I will tell Dell that I will not tolerate him sharing our marriage problems with my daughter. My daughter, of all people!"

"Dell didn't talk to me, Mom. You did. And I know your pattern with husbands."

"I have no pattern, I am patternless." She pointed at me. "You didn't talk to Dell?"

"No, Mother. It wasn't on my list of things to do postcoma."

She signaled the waitress, who came over smiling, but I could tell her teeth were clenched. I clenched my teeth, too. My mother had ordered her salad, extra this, none of that, dressing on the side. Heat the bread to medium heat, no further. Bring my coffee, black, one tablespoon cream, half a teaspoon of sugar, a thick white mug. This time she said to the waitress, "Please take my plate away. I am through."

I rolled my eyes at the waitress so she would know we were in cahoots. I asked the waitress if she could bring me another glass of wine, and I ordered the dulce de leche cheesecake. I needed alcohol and dessert.

"I have always been a perfect wife to my husbands." She folded her napkin carefully, but I could tell she was rattled.

"Have you?" No, she hadn't. I felt that familiar wave of frustrated anger at her and her selfishness. She had been a lousy wife to my dad. I remember their arguments. I remember her screaming and throwing a plate now and then, a chair once, a side table, his books, and his chess set and checker board.

"Yes. I am a perfect wife." Her tone was edged this time, anger simmering. "I cater to their egos. I listen to their drivel. I perform in bed with passion and exuberance and lie and tell them I've never had better sex. I clean their homes."

"You hire maids."

"I hand them drinks when they walk in the door. I smile as sweet as I can. I tell them how wonderful they are. I compliment them and laugh at their inane jokes." She stopped, her eyes suddenly tired and cynical. "It's exhausting."

"It sounds like it."

"I earn my money."

"Don't say that. Please. You make it sound like a job you hate performing."

"Maybe I do."

I saw the sadness in her eyes and I should have felt pity, but I couldn't. Hard to feel sorry for someone who repeatedly digs herself into the same problem and hurts other people doing it.

Her voice lowered, trembled a tiny bit. "Dell used to like my cowgirl porn outfit."

"When did you dress up in that for him?"

"When we were dating."

"Maybe you need to dress up in the cowgirl porn outfit."

She dismissed that thought with a swoosh of her manicured nails. "That was for dating only."

"That's my point, Mother." I might need three glasses of wine. "You did all kinds of things for Dell when you were dating. I remember seeing you date Dell. You were loving and cheerful and hugging him all the time. You smiled. You bought him little gifts. Then you got married, and you changed on him. It was bait and switch."

"Nonsense."

"Think about it." The waitress came by and gave me my goodies, and I thanked her.

"Maybe I could try on the cowgirl porn outfit again," my mother said. "If it will make him be more generous."

The waitress almost dropped the wine. I steadied it.

"Don't do it so you can syphon off more money. Here's the thing, Mom. You do this every time to your husbands. You lie to them. You lie about who you are and who you're going to be as a wife." I held my hand up as she tried to interrupt. "You know you do it. Maybe one time, Mom, this one time, you shouldn't hurt your husband. You shouldn't crush him. You shouldn't get another divorce. Dell is your fifth husband, Mom."

"Natalie, I will not tolerate —"

"Please. I've been in a coma. My brain is funny and I have no time for this anymore. I do not want to listen to you as you drag another innocent man through a divorce and take half his money. Why don't you try to love Dell, Mom?"

"I do . . . I do . . . love Dell." Her lips tightened. There might have been a sheen in her eyes.

"He's an honest, hardworking man, Mom. He's always been kind to you. He took a chance on you, being your fifth husband. He's incredibly generous. He's smart. He loves his kids and he loves you."

"I don't know if he loves me anymore."

She blinked. Twice. Holy moly. Were those tears? "Mom, do you act in a way that makes it easy for Dell to stay in love with you?"

Her mouth opened, shut, opened, shut.

"People are not required to stay in love with each other. If Dell is falling out of love with you, maybe it's because you're argumentative, demanding, selfish, and a leech. Maybe it's because you require two thousand a month. He's seeing you clearly and why you married him. You're hurting him, can you not see that? I know that Dell loved you when he married you. I saw the hope and adoration in his eyes."

"You did?"

"Yes."

"Is your father seeing anyone?"

"Mom." I took her hand. "Dad is not in love with you, he doesn't pine for you, he would never get back together with you."

"And I don't want to get back together with him."

I stared at her.

Her eyes filled up, and I finally saw the mask come down. "I ruined our marriage," she whispered. "I was angry and immature. I didn't know how to be a wife or a mother, and everything seemed hard. I didn't like being poor. I had had enough of that when I was younger. Poverty is like a stench over you and your whole life."

"What do you mean? You said you grew up wealthy."

She dismissed my comment.

"Mom?" What in the world? She had always talked about her parents' money.

"I made a mistake leaving your father."

Yes. Those were tears.

"I loved him very much." She sniffled, not graciously at all. "I still do."

"I know you do." I was trying to feel sorry for her and her long-lost love, but I couldn't. It was impossible. "You said no to Dad decades ago and left. You can say yes to Dell and stay happily married for the rest of your life. Another husband is not going to fix the problem here. You're the problem. You need to go home and put on that cowgirl porn outfit and be kind and loving to Dell like when you were dating and remind him why he fell in love with you in the first place."

She sat in that thought, her hands crossed, her rings from Dell glittering. "Perhaps I do."

We sat at that expensive restaurant by the lake quietly for a minute, then she eyed my dessert. "Keep eating, dear. Remember what I said about bosoms. You need them. Two full ones. You're too thin. Men like curves. Don't forget you're pushing forty."

My mother did not ask me how I was doing.

She didn't ask me how I was feeling.

She didn't ask me about my work.

She didn't ask what I was doing during the day, so she didn't know about my jewelry.

But she hugged me and kissed my cheek when she left and said, "I do love you, Natalie. Very much."

Later that week flowers arrived from her. There was a note:

Cowgirl porn outfit worked. Hee-haw!

I would ask her about her comment about growing up poor the next time I saw her.

Not long after my dad and I cleared out all

the junk from our home, when I was twelve years old, and I felt I could breathe without the harsh glimpses of my mother's chain-rattling ghost, I settled back in with my home décor magazines. I wanted a pretty home, like in the magazines, where normal families lived. I wanted to be normal.

I didn't feel normal. My mother had left me in a town where almost every single kid had a mother. The parents might be divorced, but the mom was there. The pity of being "poor Natalie, her mother left. You know, *Jocelyn . . .*" was nauseating.

I wanted a home that felt like a home, not dull and dark and motherless. I wanted a home like Chick and Jed's, who had a mother who loved to decorate with tons of clashing, bright fabrics.

I wanted a home like Justine's, filled with eight kids and two parents, comfy furniture, books stacked up everywhere, plants and pillows.

I read an article about how a family took walls down in their home to open it up. I showed my dad the before-and-after photos after he'd spent the day on a roof. I told him that we should do this, too. "When walls come down," I quoted the magazine, "the sunshine comes in."

Kind, encouraging, and deeply saddened

because my mother kept hurting my feelings by not showing up in my life when she should, he said, "Let's do it, Hummingbird."

He called in favors from friends, and that weekend they took down two walls in our home, opening up the whole living and dining area and kitchen. It didn't seem so small and dark anymore. They added a long beam to keep the roof from falling in. Our shabby, dated cave of a kitchen was gutted.

A friend of my dad's was a contractor. He remodeled kitchens. Herman had pulled white cabinets out of a client's house. They apparently were not fancy enough for her. They were only fifteen years old, in perfect condition, and they were definitely fancy enough for us. My dad and Herman hung those up in a weekend. "White cabinets signal cleanliness and freshness," I quoted again. My dad blinked at me.

The woman had also thrown out her stove, sink, fridge, and oven. All too old! All too dated! Not fancy enough! When I saw them, I danced.

I told him we had to paint all the walls and ceilings white.

"White?" my dad said. "Everything?"

"Yes. If a space is small," I said proudly, quoting an article again, "paint it white. It will add dimension and the appearance of roominess."

He raised his eyebrows at his young, geeky daughter's declaration but borrowed equipment from a painter friend of his and started spraying. He sprayed the impossibly ugly faux gray rock on our fireplace when I said, "For a simple fix of an old hearth, paint the whole thing white and add a natural wood mantle for candles, pictures, and other treasures."

"My treasures?" my dad said. "Like my beer?"

"No, Dad, not your beer!"

He winked at me.

The next weekend I showed my dad a picture of a kitchen island I liked. He stopped his tired sigh halfway out of his mouth and forced a smile at his eager daughter. "I can build this in a day, Hummingbird."

He built the island from old wood stored in our garage. He put shelves on two sides of it for storage. He grabbed an old door that my grandma had saved from a burned-down church, sanded and stained it, and dropped it on top.

I showed my dad how other people in the magazines had a long coffee table in front of the couch. "A coffee table is both useful and decorative," I said to him, again quoting from my home décor magazines. "You can display your personal belongings."

"My what?" my dad asked.

"Your personal belongings."

"Like my tool belt?"

I sighed. "Dad . . ."

He grinned at me.

He made a table out of wood from our red barn that had fallen down years ago. He sanded it down but left some of the red paint. Then he made us two side tables with the same wood. "For our new lamps," I told him. "Lamps bring light to dark corners and set the mood of the home." His eyes widened once again at his odd little daughter.

We needed curtains. I knew this because my home décor magazines said, "Add color to your home with brightly colored curtains."

I went to Goodwill and bought a sewing machine. I had no idea how to use it, so I grabbed a book from the library and my dad and I figured it out together. There was a hoarder down the street named Bo. He didn't sew, but he had stacks of fabric from his mother who died fifteen years ago. My dad had done his roof. He offered Bo money for some fabric, but Bo declined. "You did right by me with my roof, Scott, so I'll do right by you. Take all the fabric you want." That comment made me screech with glee to the fragile Bo's alarm. Bo screeched back.

We walked out with a trunk full of fabrics and threads, even lace, and I made the curtains. I had to start over three times and three times Chick's mother came over to help me, but soon we had light-yellow flowered curtains up.

I made a slip cover out of blue jean material for our old gray and pink couch. It wasn't perfect, but it was better, and then I made pillows, just like in the magazines.

We went garage sale hunting and I saw two chandeliers I fell in love with. My masculine dad is not a chandelier kind of guy, but he bought them for cheap and hung them over our kitchen table and in our family room because he knew his daughter loved them. We also found a pink tulip light to hang over my bed.

It took months.

But we had a remodeled home with colorful pillows and curtains, chandeliers, and a modern island. We had white kitchen cabinets and coffee tables like everyone else.

We were proud of our home.

We were what I always wanted to be: normal.

My dad and I later painted our house yellow with white trim. We painted the door blue because that's my dad's favorite color. We tore down the broken-down deck and built a new one, all the way around, extra wide in front and back.

My dad still lives there. The view is spectacular, an ever-changing painting.

We've made some décor changes. Five years ago I bought him brand-new furniture, a comfortable couch and two leather chairs. We kept everything he built, though, which still looks so rustically stylish. I paid to have all his windows replaced and to have two sets of French doors installed to let in more light. I did this as a surprise when he was on a fishing trip with Zack. I feigned getting a cold so I could be home when the window people arrived. He would never have let me do it if I had asked, but he loved it.

We almost lost that house because of the medical bills that came after he broke his back and the loss of his livelihood. We never should have been put in that position. No one should. But now that his home and the land is paid for, it will always be his.

I am happy knowing that my dad is happy,

in his home, out in the country.

I never thought I'd say it when I lived there, but I missed Lake Joseph.

Work kept getting worse.

I was so tired, my bones felt as if they were cracking. My brain wanted to leap out of my head and take its own nap.

I couldn't do my job. The numbers, even with a calculator, even with computer programs, weren't working for me; they twisted and turned. I was lost within the maze of the tax code, words swirling. I stared at my computer, at files, and nothing made sense.

I made calls to clients, they made calls to me, and I was able to answer them in a general way, but I struggled with the specifics. I told them I'd get an e-mail to them immediately, but I needed help from Justine or from Maggie, who let me bang on her drums.

I was failing.

On a rainy Tuesday I stared out my office window and watched the raindrops slide down the glass.

The question was, Would I get better in time? Would I ever be able to work at the high level of competency that I needed to be successful in this firm?

I doubted it.

But not be an accountant anymore?

How could that be?

How could that be *me*?

I'm a numbers woman. A math woman. Numbers don't lie. Numbers are honest. Numbers are right or wrong. Numbers don't abandon you, hurt you. I'm a CPA. I had wanted to be a CPA since high school. Having my own firm was what I had worked for.

And yet.

The commute was tiring. The work was relentless. The clients were often difficult, the tax forms complicated, particularly for our larger business clients, the hours long for many months each year. Most of our clients had a lot of money, and there was no redeeming value for my work.

Zack had asked me to quit. He was worried about me, worried I wouldn't heal. My ghostly pallor and my headaches, which were galloping back since I started working, after they had gone completely, mercifully away, weren't helping.

"Please, baby," he begged. "I sold one house, and the money's coming in. I'll sell the others soon. We'll be fine. Quit. Rest. Get all the way better."

I knew we would move when he wasn't so

busy and when we had time to figure out where we wanted to live. We would use our savings, too, to buy a house.

All I wanted to do was sleep, my head so filled with confusion and pain and blurring numbers I was surprised it didn't crumble. The office was busy, clients in and out, meetings and conferences. . . .

I used to love it.

Did I still love it?

I stared out the window and continued to watch the raindrops slide.

I made my grandma Dixie's apple pie again.

I remember how, while the pie was baking, my grandma and I always did something fun, something interesting. Sometimes we went outside and she had me shoot cans off a log. Sometimes she pointed out different birds and had me memorize their names. We drove her tractor. She taught me how to drive her truck when I was fourteen. She taught me how to be a "bull-crackin' poker player," and how to shoot darts.

She taught me about perfumes, too, and we smelled all of hers in their antique, ornate, or crystal bottles with the stoppers. "A woman can wear perfume, fix cars, drive tractors, and beat the men, all at the same time. Don't you forget I told you that." And

"Don't let anyone silence you, Natalie. Always speak up for yourself." And "Never forget that I love you, kid. You and your dad are the people I love best."

I sure missed her. She used to talk about her favorite car: a red 1967 Chevy. I don't know why that image kept popping up in my head. . . . I could see her in her blue mechanic's overalls. . . .

This time I didn't burn my grandma Dixie's apple pie.

I forgot the nutmeg and didn't use enough brown sugar, but it was better than last time.

"It's delicious," Zack said.

My dad brought me another package on a windy, rainy day, and we sat down at my kitchen table and worked. We'd already discussed what I needed.

The man was a genius with metal.

He made blue herons in flight. Flamingos. Cranes. Owls. Robins.

He made circles, which I had requested. Plain, simple silver circles to hang on leather strips for men. I'd also had him make plain rectangles, ovals, and triangles with the centers cut out. Men want plain, I think. Masculine.

I strung the leather through them, tied the knots, added the silver clasps.

Now I needed men who wanted to wear them. I would call this the Stud Man Line.

My jewelry gave me hope.

"Why does Mom still hurt me, Dad?" I put down my mug of hot chocolate after we were done making jewelry. With my mother I needed wine; with my dad, hot chocolate. "It's been years since she left us, but she'll say something mean and it'll drag me right back to being that lonely kid. Or she'll say something rude, and I'll let it get to me."

"She can still hurt you because she's your mom, Hummingbird."

"I was a kid. A little girl. And she walked out. I barely saw her during my childhood, you know that. But I'm an adult. This pain, the anger, it should have stopped by now."

My eyes filled up, so his did, too. When I was growing up, every time I cried, my dad cried, too. I'd feel bad because I was crying, then worse because I made my dad cry. We were a mess.

"I try to forgive her, but how do you forgive someone who walks out on a seven-year-old child, who does not feel bad about it, who will not take responsibility for it, who can't see your side of things, or feel apologetic or compassionate, and still says awful things sometimes?"

"Listen, Pumpkin Pie." He drummed his fingers on the table. "For some reason we've got this fad going on about forgiveness in this country. You know how I feel about chicken-squawking fads."

I laughed through a couple of tears. "Yes, Dad, I do."

He tapped his head. "Common sense. Now, see here. There are some things that people do to us that are unforgivable. Your mom not being in your life, that could be one of them. Our society says, 'Forgive her. Don't forgive her for *her,* forgive her for *you.*' "

I nodded.

"That is the biggest bunch of bull I've ever heard." He brought a fist down on the table. It did not alarm me. "What that requires you to do, my hummingbird, is to sit with your mother in your head and think about what she did to you until you can forgive her. That means she's in your life, the old hurts recirculating, the anger bubbling up like hot tar, the loneliness gutting you, causing you stress. You get stuck like a truck in the muck with that. Then this chicken-squawking fad makes you feel bad if you can't forgive, as if it's your fault or you're not trying hard enough or praying enough or you're not a forgiving person."

I nodded my head.

"That is junk. Psychobabble junk, I call it. She was not a mother to you, and it's impossible to reason, rationalize, or forgive that one. It would be easier to break a horse in your living room."

"Then how do I handle her? How do I handle that relationship?"

"You choose to live in the sunshine instead."

"What does that mean?"

"It means you don't try to forgive her anymore. Let it go. All the negative, bad emotions she brings up in you? You shut 'em down like you'd shut a barn door. You don't allow her to cause you more pain. You accept that what she did wasn't acceptable. Like it's not acceptable to treat your farm animals badly even if you are going to eat them on Sunday."

"Okay."

"Accept what happened. Accept that she did you wrong. Accept that she did not have the personal integrity to do the right thing. Accept that she is not willing or able to apologize, and not willing or able to take responsibility. She never will be. That's your mother. But don't dwell on it for one more minute, because it only brings you down. Don't allow her to do that to you. Don't allow her to take one more minute of your life and make it negative, or painful. Then decide how much a part of your life you want her to be."

I thought about that.

He took a deep breath. "Maybe it's time I break a promise for the first time in my life and tell you something about your mom that will help this situation."

I could not even speak when my dad was done with his story.

I drove by my and Zack's old home up in the hills, above Portland, about a week later, after six days of "work" where every day I felt as if I were falling down an anti-accounting rabbit hole of doom.

I finally acknowledged that I felt as if I was in mourning. I was grieving. I have been running from a lot of feelings, trying to simply function normally, but I finally realized it.

I had lost my memory of the morning of my accident, which kept darting through my mind, a shadow here, a shadow there, something tapping me, begging me to remember what I couldn't remember.

I had lost time in a suffocating, traumatizing coma.

I had lost time in rehab.

I had lost my ability to be an accountant.

I had lost my ability to walk without a wobble, but that was getting better.

I had lost my feeling of safety with the hit-and-run, the Barbie, the bird, and the bullet. I was scared, often.

I had lost my trust in Zack, as I knew he wasn't telling me something.

We had lost the house.

I didn't pity myself. I didn't ask: Why me?

That's stupid. Why *not* me? I am no better than anyone else. There was no reason I should be inured from tragedy or injury or anything else crappy life threw.

So I decided to do a full dive into what I'd lost in hopes of coming to terms with my life. I drove up into the hills of Portland, around the curves, to our old house, to help me move on.

I stopped in front of our house and I got out of my car. I made sure I had my balance, then I leaned against the hood as I studied our former home and the towering oak in the backyard. Zack had showed me the pictures of how it had looked when he'd first bought it, and I marveled again at his skills in transforming an older, traditional home into something special. It was gray-blue with black shutters. Two sprawling stories. He had bought it for an investment, and it had worked.

The house was impressive. The neighborhood was impressive.

I didn't belong here.

I liked some of the neighbors. Others I didn't, and I avoided. Overriding the neighborhood was this wealthy, elitist feel. A tone of entitlement. Designer this and that, vacations people bragged over, shiny new cars. I was from eastern Oregon. I had little in common with the people here who chased wealth and stuff and were rather snobby about their educations.

Although, not all of them. There were a few I liked. They were wealthy because they worked hard, all the time. Like Shaundra, who was an anesthesiologist, and Debbie, who was an artist, and Alejandria, who ran a nonprofit for homeless kids while her husband was a VP at a tech company.

"Oh, my gawd!"

I turned at the voice. *Oh no.* Melinda Lordman. Snobby trophy wife. Did not work. Obnoxious. Platinum hair, her heavy makeup a hard mask. About five women, exactly like Melinda, ran in a gang. A spoiled and privileged wife gang who went to the same exclusive downtown club and belonged to the same expensive private golf club. They were deadly.

"Natalie!" She flung her arms around me. She was in heels and a silk blouse and skirt, diamonds in her ears.

I was in my cowboy boots, black tights, a black skirt, and a leather jacket. Around my neck I'd thrown a scarf I'd bought in Alaska. My hair was down, and my home-made earrings were long and gold. We could not have been dressed more differently.

"I am so happy to see you! I am so glad you're okay!" She gushed. "I couldn't believe what happened to you. I was *so* upset. I cried *all* the time. I told the moms at school, I told my book club." She started to smile, it had all been so exciting! "I told the women at the Axel Club downtown and the golf club and —"

"Hello, Melinda," I interrupted when I'd had enough. She had told *everyone* about my accident? I know why she told them. Because it was *so much fun* to tell people about her friend in a coma! She, Melinda, could be the center of attention. She could fake that one of her "best friends" was in a coma, oh woe is her, you poor thing, wor-ried about your dear friend. I'll bet Melinda cried, too, appropriately misty eyed. She was going to be strong for her coma friend!

She borrowed my tragedy so she would have something to say. But Melinda never came to see me at the hospital. She never came to the rehab center. She never sent a card or called. She did do one thing, though.

"How are you, Natalie? I know you were in a coma. Can you think? Can you talk?"

"No, I can't think and I can't talk."

"Oh, my gawd! You can't?" Hand to her enhanced chest, gaudy rings glittering. "I am so sorry. Do you understand what I'm saying? Should I talk slowly?" She started talking slowly. "I can do that. Here. How. Are. You —"

"It was a joke, Melinda. I can think and talk. You might be seeing me doing both right now."

"Oh. Ah. A joke." First her shifty eyes showed her confusion, followed quickly by resentment as she knew I was making fun of her and she hadn't caught it the first time.

"But what are you doing here? Oh. I know." She swung her gaze to my old home. "You miss your house. You and Zack." She false pouted. "You lost everything, didn't you? Everything. Your whole lives." One more false pout came out, collagen-filled lips turned down.

"No. I didn't lose my life. I'm still here on the planet. Zack is alive, too."

She was unsure what to do with that. Was Natalie being sarcastic? Maybe her brain *wasn't* working?

"I have missed you so much!"

No, she hadn't. We had never been close. She used to flirt with Zack. He always walked away from her. "Are you sure it's me you missed? Maybe it's Zack."

"Zack? I miss him, too. How is he?"

She could not hide the eager lust in her eyes. She still wanted my husband. "He's doing well."

She twitched. Her lips tightened. She batted her false eyelashes.

"Are you still married to Albert, Melinda?"

"Yes. Yes. Absolutely. Married." She turned the false pout into a false smile. "We would never divorce. We have a wondrous marriage. So happy. We're always happy. Albert." She said his name as if she had to remember who he was. "Being a vice president at a bank takes up so much time. He has so much responsibility. So many people under him. But then" — she giggled — "that's what bought us our vacation house in Maui and our most recent trip. Did I tell you about it? My daughter and I — you remember Crystal, right? We went to Thailand for two weeks, then we cut down to New Zealand and Australia, took a cruise, whoee! We shouldn't have, but we couldn't resist! Then we cut back up to Maui to our vacation home. Albert wasn't with us; he had to work, poor man."

Unbelievably, she then began to tell me about her vacation, in depth. I got the days she stayed at this or that hotel, the friends she saw, the places they went, the wedding they attended, the expensive side trips. . . .

In the middle of yet another monologue of Our-Lives-Are-Perfect, I said, "I think I'm going to go now, Melinda."

"But let me show you a few of my photos from my vacation!" She grabbed her phone. "Have you ever seen pictures of our vacation home in Maui?"

"No, thank you."

"What?"

"Melinda, I'm trying to recover from a head injury. And you are too much for me to handle."

She sucked in her breath. "What do you mean?"

"I mean, Melinda, that I didn't like you when I lived here, and I don't like you now."

"I . . . I . . . well! Oh, my gawd!" She was befuddled! But mad. Why didn't I like her? "I don't like you, either, Natalie."

"I know. It's why you didn't come and see me in the hospital, but told all your friends about what happened to me so you could be the center of attention. You did come over and try to see Zack, though, didn't you?"

I knew that to be true. Zack told me. We laughed. He never let her in. Even when she tried to come in with dinner. Three times.

"I was trying to help him." She swung her blond hair. She avoided my eyes. Bad liar.

"I was in a coma and you were hitting on my husband."

"I was not." She flushed. Bright red.

We both knew she was. She couldn't stand her husband. He couldn't stand her, either. It didn't take a genius to know that Albert sent his wife and stepdaughter out on a long vacation so he could get a break. Her eyes skittered away.

"Good-bye, Melinda. I don't think you'll be Mrs. Zack Shelton in the future. Sorry."

"I don't want to be Mrs. Zack Shelton." She put her hands on her hips. "He doesn't even have a home."

I laughed. "But he's Zack, and that beats a Maui vacation home any day."

Her face got all scrunched up. This was not part of her perfect, monied world.

As I drove off, I laughed. I felt better. I went to the neighborhood to get rid of some of my grief from the losses, and it had worked spectacularly well. Good-bye, old life!

I did glance in my rearview window. Melinda was standing in the middle of the street flipping me off.

I stuck my hand out the window and flipped her off, too.

I should not take delight in flipping anyone off, but I did. I cackled.

My trip had been worth it!

As I drove down our street, and came to the intersection where I'd been hit, a crystal-clear image of me lying on Zack in bed and listening to him talk entered my head. He was upset. He was so angry . . . then he was telling me to get dressed. He kept saying, "Hurry."

What happened? Did that happen?

"Did you ask me to hurry on the morning of my accident?" I asked Zack.

I swear he grew a little white around the edges. "I may have. I think you were going to be late to work."

I didn't think that. I was never late to work. I didn't like being late. Zack would never have told me to hurry, either.

"Is that it?"

"Yes."

"Was there anything else?"

"No, baby." He looked away.

Why does he keep lying to me?

CHAPTER 16

On another rainy evening, chilly and dark, before Zack got home, I thought about Lake Joseph.

Living in Lake Joseph was like living in a postcard. The blue-tinted mountains were close, the tranquil lake was closer. The fields rolled with farms and orchards. I loved my dad's property, which used to be Grandma Dixie's property, which used to be her parents' property, and how our home had panoramic views and peace in all directions. I loved how the moon shone down, the stars were numbered in the zillions, the sunrises clear and pink and soft.

I didn't appreciate it enough when I was a kid, because it was always there. I wanted out. It was small and I wanted the action of the city. I wanted to fly off and explore, I wanted to go to college, I wanted to live in the city and build a career and make money and never worry about losing my home again.

But now I missed it.

Lake Joseph had changed since I left for college at eighteen.

It had suffered over the years as a factory closed and the timber industry collapsed. But in the last ten or so years, new businesses had moved in. A cheese factory started up and not only employed a ton of people but also built the factory to attract tourists. You can watch the cheese being made and then you can get an ice-cream cone. People came from all over to see it.

A beer distillery set up shop, the owner three years ahead of me in school. Two other graduates of my high school, Janice and Tokai, set up a woolen mill and started making thick sweaters, and another woman came in and started a soap business and employed ten people.

The beauty of the area continued to attract artists — painters, sculptors, and ceramicists. It was cheap living where you could live on land. The artists needed some place to sell their art, so art galleries popped up. In the last three years the town had sponsored an art fair for a week in summer. Grenadine Scotch Wild came. They sold all of Grenadine's paintings/collages and her husband, Kade's, carved tables.

Stevie Barrett brought in ten of her fantastical, Alice in Wonderland type chairs and they were put in the middle of the town square. They had to hire a full-time officer at night to make sure they weren't stolen, but all of the chairs sold the first day.

The Bommarito sisters, from Trillium River, brought in their famous oversized cupcakes and sold those in a booth. The line was over an hour long, but people waited patiently because their cupcakes are heaven.

Ellie Kozlovsky, who made my pillows, came, too. We called her "the pillow artist." She set up a booth and sold her pillows. She was supposed to stay three days but sold out in one, so she went fishing instead with her sisters, Toni and Valerie.

Other businesses have popped up. Stores. Cafes. Restaurants. Gift shops. Bakeries.

Chick and Braxton's LaSalle Hardware store has thrived. The lumber they sold flew out the door for new homes and businesses. Chick's housewares section was like walking into home décor heaven, and I am picky about home décor. She said, "We sell the hard stuff and the soft stuff."

The town passed a school, fire, and library bond. The library was rebuilt and a new high school constructed.

Lake Joseph is now this quirky, artsy, eastern Oregon town, a gateway to nature and mountains, the lake, fishing, and fun. But it was still small. Small and homey and people knew each other. There were homes right off Main Street, and kids and families were always outside, walking up and down, chatting and visiting. When I was in the hospital, so many of my friends had made the long drive, leaned over my near-corpse in my hospital bed, and cried/prayed/cast a healing spell/chanted Hindu verses/talked/read to me.

One of the quilting groups made me a quilt. They asked everyone to donate an old shirt or fabric, and they sewed them all into one gorgeous piece of quilting art. I received baskets of fruit; treats; and, from Eddie Tsako, steaks. He is proud of his cows. So many bouquets were delivered when I was in my Coma Coffin from friends in Lake Joseph, Zack told me it was like going home to a florist shop.

I have loved living in Portland. There is no city like it. There is serious business going on here but it's funky, too. People ride bikes wearing feathered hats. It is not unusual to see demonstrations and protestors in Pioneer Square. People wear pink tights and business suits, dreadlocks and heels, high fashion and grunge. You can eat in fancy restaurants or head to a food cart. Coffee shops and breweries are everywhere. The sloppy person on the corner could be homeless, he could also be a millionaire tech geek. It's close to the mountains and the beach. You can literally ski in the morning and catch the sunset at the beach in the same day.

It's a thriving, quirky, live-as-you-are kind of city. I would always love it.

But I was finding it overwhelming and too busy. The cars, the buses, the noise. It was as if my head had crashed and my ability to be in a city every day had crashed, too.

I thought of those shining stars over my dad's house.

I thought of the blue mountains and the lake.

I thought of the people who had made me a quilt.

I thought of Lake Joseph.

He was shooting me. I was standing in front of our old house holding two headless birds upside down, a Barbie attached to my chest, as the rain poured down like a wave. The bullets kept coming, again and again, blasting through my body. Finally, he put the gun down and giggled, his teeth a picket fence in his mouth, his tiny eyes evil.

I fell to the ground and Barbie died.

I woke up not being able to breathe, Zack soothing me. I told him the nightmare and he groaned.

A few days later, I decided to quit. I had to leave Knight and Fox, even though I am the Fox.

"I'm quitting," I told Zack.

"How do you feel about that?" His eyes were gentle and sympathetic.

"Utter sadness." I flung an arm around his waist, the rays of the moon tunneling into our bedroom. We'd had a nice naked roll after I'd sauntered into the living room wearing a light pink negligee. An hour later, after all that passion, we were discussing life. Zack is awesome in bed, and awesome as my best friend. "But I feel relieved, too. It's a loss. Everything I worked for, *pfft*. Gone. He took that from me."

I hated that creep for doing so. I took a deep breath. "But I can't do it anymore. I know I'll continue to get better, Zack, but I will never get better to the point where I can do what I was doing as a CPA and the co-owner of our firm. The numbers swim, I can't concentrate for that long, I can't grasp the complexities of tax law anymore."

He kissed my forehead, then he kissed the tears on my cheeks.

"Justine will buy me out, and we'll use that money toward a down payment for a house."

"You need to take it easy, Natalie, and this is the right decision."

"I can't not work."

"Make your jewelry. Sell it."

"I won't make enough money." I wiped the tears off my face.

"I don't care how much money you make. My other houses are almost ready to sell, and we'll be fine. But I think you will sell far more necklaces than you think you will when this becomes your full-time business." His voice brooked no argument. "Natalie, I am not a woman. But even I look at your necklaces and think they're like nothing I've ever seen before. You've got stones, metal-work, birds, a bunch of colorful beads, everything. I wear the necklaces you've made me and I've had men ask me about them. It feels kind of weird to be talking to other men about my necklaces, but I do it."

He was wearing a simple leather necklace, one silver bar in the middle.

"You don't have to work at all if you don't want to. Ever. But I also know you and I know you can't stop working, so I'll just say that I think you'll love selling jewelry."

"Maybe I will." I could. It was fun. I had always loved making jewelry. And I loved running a business, too.

"You're a talented jewelry designer."

I took a deep, shuddering breath. "So one career ends and another begins?"

"I think so, babe." His voice was low, and it cracked with emotion. "I almost lost you. My life would be worth nothing to me without you. My primary goal is to make sure that you're happy and safe and healthy. Make the jewelry. Sell it if you want. I will do anything you want me to do to help."

"I love you, Zack."

"I love you, too, Natalie. You're my life."

"And you are mine." I leaned over and kissed him again, on his mouth, the scar on his cheek, and his forehead, then rested on his chest, his heartbeat a reassuring thump beneath mine.

Accounting was me, and yet it wasn't me anymore.

Accounting was the old me, this was the new me.

I knew I'd cry about this loss again in the coming weeks and months. I knew I'd miss it. Well, not everything. Not our obnoxious or pampered clients or the ones who said, in one way or another, that they wanted us to help them cheat the IRS, which we never did.

But I would miss the numbers. And the firm. And working with Justine.

I thought about a necklace I was working on. . . . It was going to be so pretty. I was using clear red beads. . . .

I asked Justine to go to lunch on Monday. We were both in our proper accounting suits, but I had swirling designs on my black tights and she had turquoise bracelets up her arm. At least we maintained some semblance of non-boringness in our work attire.

She cried when I told her what I wanted to do.

"But this firm," she said, "it's Natalie and Justine. It's Knight and Fox. We named ourselves after a poker game. It's our dream. It's what we worked for."

"I can't work here anymore, Justine. I can't do the work."

She argued, told me I could do something else at the firm. I could solely focus on getting more clients. I could be the human resources manager. I could be a figurehead and come in when I wanted. "Don't leave me, Natalie."

"Nice line. I'll never leave you, but I need

to leave the firm."

She refused to accept my resignation for days.

"Okay, Natalie. I will buy you out, but I hate you for leaving me and I will make you ride first on our naked bike ride."

"I know."

We later had a professional, analytical discussion about the value of the firm, the future value, etc., and came up with an amount we were both happy with.

She handed me the check. We announced, together, that I was leaving. I was honest with the staff about my abilities, and how I simply couldn't perform anymore at the level I needed to. Our employees hugged me, told me how much they would miss me. They asked if I was sure. Maybe take more time off? Work half days only? We can help you, Natalie!

No, that wouldn't work. Justine cried in front of everyone, that baby.

Zack came by and helped me pack. He hauled out the carved metal fox my dad had made.

Leaving my own firm, Knight and Fox, was a wrenchingly sad day for me.

Until I got home and looked at all my jewelry supplies. My dad had mailed me another box. Oh, wow! Yes! Everything was perfect. I wanted to do a flower line, so he'd made me roses, tulips, and daffodils, but they were all so unique, each had a different flair. . . .

I sat down and hours passed.

When I was done working I stopped in front of my grandma's perfume bottles on the bookshelf. I took out the stopper on the crystal bottle and smelled it. Roses. I thought I heard her laugh.

I loved her. I still missed her. You don't stop missing the people you love, you just deal with it, that's what I believe.

We used to ride horses together into the woods. She taught me to love nature on those rides. We used to hike along the lake. She taught me to love wild animals on those treks. We used to watch the sun go down from her back deck. She taught me to love the miracle of a sunset.

Why did I keep envisioning her pushing me?

I was wiped out the next morning and slept in. My speech was almost back to normal, my walk was almost back to normal, and thinking and getting my thoughts/actions out more quickly was almost normal again, but I still tire easily. So I lay in bed in my long, black rock star T-shirt, drank coffee, and thought about the surprising, sad conversation I'd had with my dad about my mother.

"Your mother told you that she came from a wealthy family."

"Yes. Sounds like she grew up rich, obnoxious, and spoiled."

My dad's dark eyes were sad. "Your mom's parents weren't wealthy. They were about as poor as you could get. They lived in Idaho."

"What?" I was totally confused, but I remembered the conversation I'd had with my mom the last time I'd seen her. She had shut down my questions about her being poor as a child as fast as she could. "She said they lived in Portland."

"No." He shook his head. "They had nothing. I don't know what was wrong exactly, why they didn't work. It sounded like her father may have had bipolar disorder. He could be productive for a while, then he'd sink into a depression so bad he couldn't move. It trapped him. He drank too much, too. Slugged 'em down. Alcoholic. Her mother was a beast."

"What do you mean?"

"She was mean. Mean as a snake. They were homeless. Your mom grew up squatting in different abandoned homes outside of small towns in Idaho. They didn't have electricity, they didn't have water. Often they'd sleep in the back of their truck. To earn money her parents put her on street corners on a plastic crate and told her to sing."

I knew my mouth had dropped open as I tried to grasp the enormity of what he was telling me. "That's why she's always refused to sing, isn't it?"

"Yes. Singing triggered her back to her days of homeless poverty, like a slingshot. She started when she was four. Her parents would leave her on that crate and come back later for the money. One time they came back and instead of singing she was leaning against a wall. She was starving and couldn't sing another note, poor thing. And they smacked her and had her get right back up on her crate."

"I thought she had money. An expensive home in Portland. She always talked about her clothing and all her pretty dresses when she was younger. Fancy cars, fancy vacations. She said her father was in construction, that he built businesses and apartment buildings."

"Her father was in construction now and then, when he got his hide up to work. He would construct sheds."

"Sheds?"

"That's what he knew how to do when he wasn't drunk. She told me that sometimes he'd build them a shed out of scrap lumber, and that's where they'd live until some farmer came and kicked them off his land. Or the police would come and they'd move on in the truck."

"She had nothing then." I felt as if I'd been kicked in the gut by my mother's misery.

"Nothing. She remembers being scared. Hungry. Frozen. She raised chickens one year to eat. She picked berries for money. She would wear the same coat for years. It would be too short, too tight, but she had to wear it because she had nothing else. Her shoes, same thing. Sometimes her shoes were too big, sometimes too small. She was dirty. The kids at school, when her parents settled down long enough for her to be in school, would make fun of her. They called her Dirty Girl, and Mud Face, and Lice Hair.

"She got lice one time and was sent home with lice shampoo from the nurse. She said she followed the instructions and rinsed the shampoo out in a river, but that did it for her at that school. The kids wouldn't sit by her at lunch, and if they accidentally touched her they would race to the bathroom sink and yell, 'I have lice from Jocelyn!' They called her ugly and stupid. She felt stupid. The worst was when she was called white trash. She hated being called white trash. Hated it."

"That's why she always told me, 'We're not white trash,' with such vehemence." I hurt for her, I did.

"Yes. Your mom won the lead role in a musical one time when she was fifteen. She had been in that school for eighteen months, the longest they had ever stayed anywhere. Her parents found an abandoned trailer in the woods. She said she finally started to make friends because she could sing and that gave her a small step up at school. Her parents yanked her out of school a week before the performance and drove her up north because her father thought there might be a job for him up there. The night of the musical they had her out on a street corner singing to make money. It was drizzly and cold, and she cried while she sang all the songs she was supposed to sing for the musical."

"That's pathetically sad." I pictured my mother standing in the rain on a crate crying and singing at the same time.

"It was, Hummingbird. For once in her life she had friends, had acceptance, and had a starring role, but she couldn't stay long enough to be on that stage. She went to another town, her father built a shed for them to live in, and she went to another school where the kids called her poor and stupid and white trash."

"Poor Mom." And I meant it. Poor Mom . . .

"She remembers being alone all the time as a kid and being scared. Her parents would sometimes leave for days or weeks or drop her off at a distant relative's house or at the home of someone they just met in a bar. She often thought they would never come back."

"They dropped her off with people they met in a bar? That's criminal."

"She told me once that sometimes bad things happened to her when that happened. In fact there was one time she said that she had to leave a house where she was dropped off because, and these are her words, 'I had to defend myself.' "

"What did she do? Where did she live?"

"She hid out around the house in the woods. It was summer, she was used to helping her dad make shelters, and she made a crude one for herself and sang on street corners. When her parents came back about a week later, she ran to their truck and told her parents what happened. This may be the only protective thing they did in their lives, but her father got out his shotgun and started shooting at the man. He ran off, didn't get hit, but she told me her dad was livid. For a while they didn't drop her off with strangers. Then they started doing it again, but she told me they only dropped her off with women."

"So she was repeatedly abandoned."

"Yes."

"Then why did she abandon me?" It still hurt. Still. "She knew how it felt."

He shook his head. "Because she's damaged inside, Hummingbird. Your mom had a breakdown, of sorts, after she had you. She cried a lot. She spent days in bed. Sometimes I'd catch her staring at you, sadder than all get out, and she'd whisper something like, 'I can't believe they did that to me. I was a child. *A child.* Like Natalie.' I don't even think she knew I heard her.

"I know they have a fancy name for it now, but I'd call it the severe blues. She had had a traumatic childhood, and I think after she had you her childhood was harder to forget. She would look at you as you grew up and remember what she'd been through when she was at your exact age. It kept hauling her back to her past. She grieved, and was furious at her parents, for their neglect and abuse. That stuff doesn't leave you. It's stuck in your head like a bullet. She never felt good enough. She never felt like she was equal to anyone else. She always felt like white trash."

That was how I felt for years: Not good enough. Not equal. My own mother hadn't even loved me enough to stay in my life.

He tilted his head. "Jocelyn wanted more than I could give her, too. More money. More status. An expensive home and cars. Most of all, expensive clothes. She never forgot being called Mud Face and Lice Hair and ugly and poor. It's why she always dresses up. She is still running from her days of poverty, dressed in rags with shoes that didn't fit.

"I think, too, that she had a problem with being close to anyone. Her parents, whom she should have been close to, never filled the role. She didn't learn to trust. She didn't learn what healthy love looked like. She didn't know how to be in a happy marriage. Her parents fought all the time, threw things, got drunk, screamed at each other, hit each other, hit her now and then, and both were arrested for it. That does something here." He tapped his head. "And it's permanent."

"So she made up being wealthy . . ."

"Because she didn't want anyone to know she came from nothing."

"How did you know?"

"One day we were in Grande City and an older gentleman came up to her and hugged her. He was her mother's great uncle. He asked about her parents. You were about four then. She stuttered, she got all red, she tried to pretend she didn't know him, then she took off with you in the stroller like the devil himself was on her heels. I stayed behind. The man was very sorry he caused her to get upset. He was upset that he upset her. I asked him to explain himself and he did, and later on I talked with Jocelyn and found out the truth."

"Did you believe that she came from money, that she had grown up wealthy?"

He hesitated. Sighed. "Not really. There were holes the size of a tractor in her story. She talked about having money, but she didn't have a formal education. She told me where she graduated from high school, but she'd made up the name of the high school. She never graduated. Your mom couldn't do math at all. She hadn't read many books. She was confused about history, couldn't write well. I don't say this in an unkind manner, just as a fact. Her education was not what you would see in someone who was wealthy, or even someone who had graduated from high school. And if she came from wealth and her parents died, she would have had money. She would have inherited. She said she had no siblings, but she had no money at all when I met her at the state fair. She made up some story about how her parents had been sick at the end and the illnesses used up all the money, but it didn't ring in this old head as truth."

"Are her parents alive?"

"I don't know. They could be. They would be in their seventies, eighties. She left them and that was it."

"When did she leave them?"

"Your mom was on her own, by her own choice, at sixteen."

"Sixteen?" How scary. How lonely. How dangerous.

He nodded.

"Why didn't you tell me this before?"

He rubbed his face. "Your mother made me promise that I wouldn't tell anyone, especially you. She didn't want you, her own daughter, to think of her as white trash. As she told me, 'Uneducated, low class, and poverty stricken. I am the ugly and stupid daughter of two child-abusing drunks.' She wanted to hide it."

I swallowed hard. "And why are you telling me now?"

"Because, my poppy, I think that your mom needs you."

"Needs me?"

"Yes. She loves you and needs you."

"I think she loves and needs *you.*"

My dad knew it was the truth. "I wish Jocelyn the best, but inviting that woman back into my life would be like inviting a tornado in."

Finally, we laughed.

Then he said, "I think you need her, too, on a limited basis. You need to know she loves you and, my sweets, she does. Your mother is a complicated, difficult, critical woman with a past she has tried to outrun and keep secret her whole life. She has failed as a wife and a mother. But she does love you, and maybe knowing her past will give you some peace and help you to deal with her. I don't like that I broke my promise of secrecy. My word means something to me. Without your word, you're nothing. But this one time, Natalie, you needed me to break a promise more than I needed to keep it."

"Thank you for telling me."

I thought about my mom's depressing story. Her wretched childhood. It all made sense now. Now I understood why Grandma Dixie pitied her. I wish my dad had told me sooner. I wish my mother had told me. But I understood why neither of them did. My dad because of a promise he made, my mother because in her heart she still felt like white trash.

"I love you, Dad." I reached for his hand.

"I love you, too, my hummingbird."

Detective Zadora called me, but this interview felt different. She had questions about Zack.

Where did you and he meet?

Fishing on the Deschutes.

Where did he grow up?

South Carolina.

Where were his parents?

Deceased.

How did they die?

Car accident.

When did they die?

When Zack was seventeen.

What did they do for a living?

Home builder and nurse.

Siblings?

Only child.

How long was he in Alaska for?

Five years.

What did he do before that?

Construction.

Where did he graduate from high school?

I don't remember. It was in South Carolina.

"I don't understand why you're asking these questions, Detective."

"We're running a complete investigation, and we like to know everything."

"But what does his childhood and his parents and their jobs have to do with anything?"

"We'll get back to you, Mrs. Shelton, when we have more information."

I told Zack that night what Detective Zadora asked me.

I swear the blood drained from his face.

"What's wrong? What is it?"

"It's nothing, Natalie," he rasped out. "I'm upset about what's happened. The hit-and-run. The Barbie, the bird . . . and when she calls and talks to you it reminds me yet again of what we're dealing with."

"You mean *who* we're dealing with."

"Yes."

"But why would she ask about your parents?"

"I don't know. She's a detective. They ask

about everything."

"It's an odd detail. There's no reason for it."

"They're trying to see if there are holes in our stories."

"Are there? Are there holes?" I heard the sharpness of my words.

"No. Natalie, I'm the husband. In cases like this, they always suspect the husband, we've talked about this already. They're wondering if I did this to you. If I paid someone to hit you with a van, bring in a Barbie, send in a dead bird, and shoot through a window. They're looking at me."

"But why are they asking these kinds of questions now? Why weren't they asking about your family, which is still bizarre to me, at the beginning of the investigation?"

"I don't know, honey."

He looked exhausted. I was exhausted. My brain still feels like it blows circuits sometimes and I have to sleep.

"I made spaghetti. I tried to make meatballs, but they fell apart. I don't know what I did wrong."

We ate dinner together.

"It's delicious, Natalie."

That night I woke up about four, the rain lashing at the windows, the wind howling around the corner of our apartment. My arms were around Zack, as usual.

Something was going to happen in this investigation. I could feel it. It would be soon. I heard it in the detective's tone. Zack wouldn't tell me what it was, I knew that for sure.

I didn't want to wait and find out, but I didn't have a choice.

I tilted my head to look at my husband. He was wide awake, his face somber, intense.

Chick called. All of my necklaces had sold. "I put them on a rack right by Ellie Koz-lovsky's pillows. I also put them by each checkout stand. They are gone, baby. Gone. I had Zeddy send you a check. Send more."

"Did they really sell?" I asked. "Or are you pretending that they sold and buying them yourself?"

"Look, Natalie. I love you. You and Justine are my best friends for life. We're the Moonshine and Milky Way Maverick Girls, capable of getting arrested for putting dish soap in the town's fountain and riding our horses into the school's hallways to protest racial injustice. But I am a businesswoman, I own a hardware store that sells pillows and curtains, and I have six extremely odd kids. Not a normal one in the bunch. My food bill alone is well over a thousand a month for the rebels and rug rats.

"Ellie was doing a science experiment in her room. She caught her bed on fire. I had to use the fire extinguisher and toss the mattress out the window. Hudson found three baby mice and brought them home. Now I am raising mice because he wants to start a mice breeding company. Who would buy them? A lab? A snake farm? Joshua wants me to buy him burgundy-colored pants. Burgundy. In Lake Joseph. I might as well put a sign on him that says 'Beat Me Up.'

"Ally is determined to be a ballet dancer. She tripped over her own feet the other day at school and smashed her head. She should swim with those feet flippers, not dance. This is not a dancer. This is a klutz. I'm sorry to say that about my own child.

"Timmy and Tessie escaped again. They brought their wagons with them and took off when I was taking a bath. It was naptime. They were asleep. The next thing I know my phone is ringing and Gail Shurgood is calling me telling me the twins are at her house chasing the cats.

"I don't know how I got sidetracked onto my strange offspring. Oh yeah. They're frickin' expensive. All of them. So I'm not buying the necklaces. I don't have the money for that, Natalie. Do you know what college is going to cost me? I'm going to have to take on a second job as a stripper to pay tuition.

"Anyhow, the women are buying your necklaces. One woman bought eight. Christmas presents. And a few men. I had a separate rack for the men, for your Stud Man Line. I had all the cashiers wearing them. I had them leave the price tags on. They have flown out the door, Natalie. Send more. We're raising the prices."

"Okay. But you're taking a cut. We have to have a business discussion. . . ."

And we did. It was like Justine and I when I sold my business to her. It was calm, it was fair. We both felt like we got a fair shake.

By that afternoon, I had another box full of necklaces to send to Chick ready to go. They were a combination: Some I made with rocks, others with beads and crystals, and my dad's metal art, and others were made with the fun brooches, faux jewels, etc., that I found at garage sales and Goodwill and took apart from their original necklaces.

I giggled. Yes, I, a grown woman, giggled. It would have been an embarrassment except that I was so happy. I missed being an accountant. It was like a part of who I wanted to be from the time I was a kid to now had been ripped out of my gut by a maniac.

But I had something else now. I sold jewelry. I was an official jewelry maker. I put a few of my creations over my head and giggled yet again.

I sent my dad yet another check for all the work he did for my jewelry business. He didn't want to take money from his daughter, I knew that, but I also knew he needed it. The artist he worked for had moved; he could not ever roof again. I knew he was a saver, but the savings would not last forever.

He sent it back.

I called him and told him to cash the blankety-blank check.

He refused. "My hummingbird, I am doing this for you."

"Cash the check."

He laughed. "Tell me about your day, butterfly."

"No."

"No?"

"I will not tell you about my day ever again unless you cash the checks I keep sending you."

"I could not do that, my lightning bug."

"Then, good-bye." And, for the first time in my life, I hung up on my dad.

He called back. "Now, honey."

"Are you going to cash the checks?"

"My sweet wiggle worm, I can't do that. . . ."

I hung up again.

He called back.

"Dear Rainbow, don't do that to your dad, you're hurting my feelings."

"Will you cash the checks?"

It was a long series of hang-ups.

Finally, he agreed.

"Love you, Dad."

"Love you, too. You stubborn old goat."

I laughed. Never in my life had he called me a stubborn old goat. I had an idea. "Dad, can you make me some goats for my necklaces? I think there are some quirky buyers out there. . . ."

He could.

I did not tell him about my husband sneaking off in the middle of the night like a sneaky Billy Goat Gruff to take phone calls he refused to talk about or about Detective Zadora asking about Zack's dead parents.

CHAPTER 17

I glanced outside my apartment window on a soggy, blustery Friday afternoon, the trees bare, their branches sharp and tangled. I was hoping that Zack would come home early. About six feet away from the door was a man with a baseball hat on. He was about forty-five, white, small-eyed, fleshy-faced, and heavy like a tank.

Where had I seen him before?

He stared right at me. Intent. Still. Watching.

A cold shiver danced up my back, wrapping around my spine.

He smiled. His teeth were crooked, like a picket fence. He was missing a few.

I did not smile back.

He waved, slow, deliberate. Like a predator playing with his prey.

I did not wave back.

He scowled, but he kept staring at me, as if in challenge.

I did not back down.

He turned to leave. When he was almost to the street he turned and met my eyes again. This time, he laughed, dark and rumbling. The laugh was familiar to me.

He mimicked shooting me with a rifle.

I was frozen with fear. It rattled down my body until I couldn't move, could hardly breathe. It was as if fear was a living thing within me, paralyzing my every cell.

He was the man from my recurring nightmare. He was the man who brought the twisted Barbie to my hospital room.

He was the man driving the van that hit me.

As my brain opened up, as if a concrete wall broke around it, as if the terror I felt brought all the iron curtains down around my lost memories, I remembered.

I remembered everything.

I remembered that morning.

I remembered my fight with Zack.

I remembered the accident.

I remembered the lies the man I married told me.

"Don't lie to me anymore, Zack. Not one more lie."

We sat at the kitchen table that evening, the blinds closed. He had brought me white

460

daisies, which I angrily tossed on the counter.

He studied his clasped hands, then stared at me, those green eyes bright. "You remembered."

"Yes. Maybe not everything about the morning of the crash, but most of it. I know your name is not Zack. It's Devon Walton. I know you lied to me. I know you said you killed a man."

"That's right, honey."

I took a deep breath, shaky, but so angry at him. Lies, all of it. And he had killed a man. Why? *Why?* "Why did you lie about your name and your life, and why did you kill a man?"

He took a deep breath, too. "I killed a man named Willie Hotchkiss, who was beating a woman up outside of a restaurant one night in a parking lot. I didn't mean to kill him, but I did." He ran his hands over his face, as if he were trying to wipe away the memory. "He was slamming her head against the hood of a truck, presumably his truck, and I thought he was going to kill her. She was almost limp, hardly fighting."

I exhaled. And there it was. That's why he killed a man. He was defending a woman. Zack would do that. But was he telling the truth? Could I trust him amidst all the other lies?

"I pulled Willie off of her, and we fought. I knocked him to the ground, and his brother, Ronnie, came at me. I knocked him to the ground, too. Willie charged at me again and pulled a knife. The scars on my face and on my ribs that I told you I got on the fishing boat in Alaska are from his knife. I knocked the knife away, pummeled him, and he fell straight back on my last punch, his head hitting the edge of the truck on the way down.

"Willie was passed out, I thought, but Ronnie was on the ground, glaring at me, moaning, blood pouring out of his head. I told him if he got up I'd lay him out, too, and I went to help the woman. She was slumped on the ground, leaning against the tire. She could hardly move. Her face was all bashed up, nose broken, jaw broken, one eye swelled up, blood all over. I wanted to take her to the hospital, but she told me not to move her. She was holding her neck with both hands, and I knew her neck might be broken. She was crying hysterically.

"We could hear the sirens. Someone had obviously called the police. She told me to go, she told me to run. She said that the guys on the ground were brothers and their

462

father was the police chief and their uncle was the district attorney and they were really rich and they would put me in jail for years for beating those two up.

"I told her I wouldn't leave her, and I tried to steady her head with my hands. She told me that the police were coming, an ambulance would come and she'd be okay. She told me again that I would go to jail if they caught me, and to run.

"I was nineteen years old. I was scared. My parents were dead. I had been working in construction about an hour up the road because the pay was better up there, and I was headed home for the weekend. I had stopped in that restaurant for a hamburger. One of the guys on my shift said that a lot of construction workers stopped there because they made the best burgers.

"I was planning on going to college. My mother had a small life insurance policy for me, but it wasn't enough for college. My father had not been able to get a policy because he'd had a heart problem in high school, which was fixed, but it excluded him from any policy in the future. I wasn't ready to go to college, anyhow. I was trying to get through life, I was trying to survive. The grief still came at me in waves. I still couldn't believe they were gone."

"Zack." I reached for his hand.

"I waited until I saw the lights of the police car so I knew she would get help, then I ran back through an alley, around the block, and got in my truck and took off. I didn't know I'd killed Willie then. I thought I'd knocked him out. It was only the next morning, on the news, at home, that I heard about it, and I heard that the police were looking for me. There was a manhunt, and I was the man.

"I couldn't believe that I'd killed him. I had never meant to kill Willie. I wanted to protect the woman, and myself, when he came at me with a knife. I didn't want to die. I panicked. I didn't trust the legal system in Tallie Springs, Arkansas."

"Tallie Springs?"

"Yes. I'm not from South Carolina."

"Okay." I shook my head. "Keep going."

"The legal system in Arkansas then, especially for people like me, with no money, no family, up against powerful police chiefs and district attorneys, two of whom were the father and uncle of Willie and Ronnie, wouldn't have worked in my favor. I suspected that the chiefs and attorneys were all friends with one another. Hell, their grandparents were probably friends. It was all rigged. I figured I had no chance, even if the woman told everyone that I was protecting her.

"When I was younger, in our small town, a man was falsely accused of raping the mayor's daughter. He was developmentally disabled. He admitted to raping her when he was grilled by three detectives. He didn't even know what the word *rape* meant. He was jailed for ten years. Another man, an African American man whom my parents were friends with, was also falsely accused of attacking a white woman. He went to jail for five years until they found the real criminal. Even then it took a year to get him out. A woman went to jail for shooting and killing her husband. Everyone knew he beat her and the kids all the time. But she went to jail. For protecting herself. I had no reason to believe, in that circumstance, that I would get anywhere near a fair trial. And remember, I was nineteen years old. A kid. I was scared to death I was going to prison forever.

"Ronnie, beat up, was interviewed on TV. I saw the interview. He said that I had interfered in a little spat his brother was having with his girlfriend and I had continued to beat his brother even after his brother was laid out on the ground not moving. He said that he jumped in to save his brother from being killed by me and then I beat him up and wouldn't stop punching him, either. He said I was vicious, a murderer, that I had almost killed him, too, and that I should get the death penalty. He said he thought I was on drugs.

"He lied about everything. Obviously the woman wouldn't have been interviewed at that time. She was probably in surgery. Or knocked out from medication. I've never seen anyone that beat up before. I thought that she would tell the police what really happened. That she would tell the truth. But maybe she wouldn't. I didn't know her. Maybe she loved Willie and would lie to defend her dead boyfriend and back up what Ronnie said. Maybe she would be too scared to testify at all. Maybe she would take off when she was better and disappear. But the lies that Ronnie was already telling on TV, along with his father and uncle, were what I was up against."

"What did you do after that?"

"I packed up and left Tallie Springs. I left the home that we moved to when I was seven. We moved there from Connecticut because my mother, a nurse, had a calling to help people who were poor in rural Arkansas. My father wanted to help build them homes. It's why I don't have a southern accent, which you asked about when we met.

"I didn't take my truck. I took my mom's car in case someone had my license plate. I knew that when I didn't show up to work that it would look suspicious, so I called my boss and told him that I was moving home to work with my uncles. I had no uncles. He believed me, said he was sorry to see me go. I wanted to get as far away as I could."

"And that's when you went to Alaska?" I was awed by his courage.

"Yes. I withdrew all my money from the bank, took a few things from home, and headed out."

"You took off across the country and headed to Alaska. At nineteen." That poor, scared kid.

"Yes. I snuck in by boat. Paid a man. I did not go through the Canadian border patrol because I didn't want them to have a record of my being there. I went to a small fishing village and started asking around for work, and I ran into Captain Drake Knutson.

"He asked me my name. I had one in mind already: Zack Shelton. My mother used to talk to me about her grandfather whose first name was Shelton. He was from Scotland. And I chose the name Zack because I had a football coach named Zack. The captain asked me for ID so he could report my income to the IRS, but I told him I lost it. He asked me a few more questions. I was shaking, desperate, and he stared at me, evaluating the situation.

"He knew I was running, I could tell. It must have been blatantly obvious. But he needed an extra pair of hands, the ship was leaving soon, and I think he felt sorry for me. I climbed aboard. I had no idea what I was in for, on a fishing boat in Alaska. The relentless work, the danger, the storms, the waves. It was sometimes terrifying. But nothing was as terrifying to me as believing I'd go to jail. Then I got used to it. I liked working on the boat.

"The other fishermen watched over me, made sure I didn't fall over, didn't give me the most dangerous jobs. I was a kid to them. A kid on his own. The captain told me one night, after a storm that we weren't sure we'd survive, that he had a past he wasn't proud of, either. He eluded to making mistakes as a young man and coming up to Alaska. When I knew him he'd been married for twenty years and had three kids.

"One day the captain said to me, 'Son, do you need some help with some new ID? Hard to get a new license sometimes.'

"I knew what he was talking about. And I said yes, thank you, and he got the license and a social security card for me. I don't know how. He knew a lot of people, though. There were some tough men on that ship, and maybe they helped. But I had the right paperwork. I worked for the captain for five years, rented a studio above a grocery store, saved my money, then came down to Oregon to work in construction again and to go to college. I wanted to build homes, like my father."

"You weren't afraid to come down to Oregon?"

"Yes. And no. I'd done some research on the case. They couldn't find the man, me, who had killed Willie Hotchkiss. They didn't have a name. They didn't have a picture of me. It was a cold case. It happened in Arkansas. I was headed to Oregon, and I was five years older.

"The man who was at the door today, who ran into my van, is Ronnie."

"Yes."

Vengeful, sick, angry man. "How did Ronnie find you?"

"By total coincidence. It's one of those coincidences that you simply can't believe. Ronnie works in construction, too. He owns his own drywall business. He's the only employee. Remember that article on me and my homes in *US Home Building* magazine? I insisted that they not take my photo, we agreed to it, but they did it anyhow. I don't even remember the photographer taking a picture of me. Then they put the damn thing on their cover."

"I remember you were furious. I've rarely seen you that mad. You were up all night. That's why you never wanted your photo on your website, either."

"I'm older now, I look different, but obviously not different enough. And Ronnie obviously got a solid look at me that night. Anyhow, he saw the magazine. The odds of that happening are so small, but they weren't small enough."

"He didn't call the police, though?"

"No. He wanted revenge. He wanted to make my life hell. He knew I had money, and first he wanted to strip me of that money. He thought I would start paying him off when he came by one of the houses I was working on. He told me to pay up or he was going to the police about me and he would tell them I was a murderer and had been on the run for years."

"What did you say?"

"I said I would not pay him. I told him to get the hell off my property. I was not going to be blackmailed. I couldn't live with him, with that threat, hanging over my head. And logically I knew that it would never stop. Ronnie would ask for money here, more later, then in the end he would tell you, tell the police, anyhow. There was no way to win here.

"Ronnie called me early that morning before the accident and told me if I didn't pay him that he would come after you, that morning, that day. My goal was to get you to your dad's, where you would be safe, and then I was going to the police to turn myself in. I would work with the police and arrange to meet with Ronnie, hopefully have him arrested for blackmail or extortion, and jailed, so you would be safe from him, at least for a while. My expectation was that after that I would go to jail, probably in Arkansas, to await trial. I would employ the best attorney I could get to help me prove it was self-defense.

"After he hit you with the van, he won, Natalie. I think he knew, based on our meeting the day before, that when I said I wasn't going to pay, I meant it. But he wanted his revenge. After the accident I could not go to the police, because I knew I would be taken into custody and couldn't take care of you, couldn't be with you in the hospital. I was scared to death you were going to die in that coma, honey. I couldn't risk it. And I couldn't risk being away from you when you were in rehab, either. I could not leave you. Your health was so fragile, and I wanted to help you, I wanted to be with you. I had to make sure you were better and you could live on your own before I went to jail."

"So you paid him."

"Yes. I paid him after your accident to prevent him from going to the police as he threatened to do."

"How much?"

"Two hundred thousand, out of my company."

"Oh, my God."

"I knew he'd be back. And he was, but I had no way out. After the Barbie incident, I paid him another hundred thousand to stay away from you. He put the Barbie in your room to show me that he could get to you anytime. After the dead bird, another hundred thousand. After the bullet, another hundred thousand."

"He threatened, you paid, he gave you more time, and then he came back, right?"

"Exactly. He'd call and I'd be screwed, and I'd know it."

"You sold your house to pay him after the first payment." This made sense now. Zack had said he was overextended, he had problems with the bank, that's why he sold his house, but he was excellent with handling money and he had never had a problem with the bank.

"I did. I didn't have a choice. I knew he would come for more and more money. He knew I was caught. He wanted to make my life hell because I killed his brother. That I did it in self-defense meant nothing to Ronnie. He's insane. He has been obsessed with finding me."

"What are we going to do now, then? He's coming after us again."

He closed his eyes for a second. "There's not a 'we' here, baby. It's me. I'm going to the police. You're better now. You can live on your own again. You can live with your dad if you need to. You'll be safe. I am so sorry about the money. But after I go to the police and tell them the truth, I'm hoping that I can make an arrangement to meet Ronnie and he will be arrested for the hit-and-run, attempted murder, firing a gun into our house and harassing us, blackmail, and extortion. There will be a trial and he'll go to jail. At least when I'm in jail I'll know that he's in jail, too. He will be locked up and you'll be safe."

"But Zack." I was feeling desperate, a cold

knot of fear in my stomach. "The woman who saw what happened. The girlfriend of Willie. She could testify for you."

"She could. If she's still alive, if they can find her, if she would be willing to testify, if she's a reliable witness, if she hasn't changed her mind over these twenty years about what happened, if the prosecutor doesn't twist up her story in front of a jury. I don't know any of those answers. What I do know is that though it's a cold case, there is no statute of limitations on murder. The case will be thrown back to Arkansas. The police here will work with them, but I will be in Arkansas as I await trial.

"I don't trust the system there now any more than I did then. That's why I didn't turn myself in years later. I built a new life. Why upend it, why destroy it? I knew I was defending that woman's life. I knew that Willie came at me with a knife and what I did was in self-defense. I knew, later, as a grown man, that I was not guilty of a crime.

"What I didn't know is if a jury would believe my story, especially if they couldn't find the girlfriend. For sure, Ronnie would get on the stand and lie about the whole thing. I don't think there were any other witnesses who could back me up, with the exception of the woman. They would have her medical reports, which would work in my favor, if they hadn't been deliberately destroyed or lost in the last twenty years, and they would have police interviews from her, but who knows if those reports would have been tampered with or shredded by Ronnie and Willie's father, the police chief, or their uncle, the district attorney? They would have my word against Ronnie's. Plus, I looked guilty for running in the first place. Even with an outstanding attorney, it was too much to risk."

I tried not to cry. I tried to be brave as I thought of losing Zack to jail, for years. I had more faith in the legal system than he did, but he could still go to jail simply for evading the law, even if he wasn't prosecuted for murder. My hands shook.

"I never thought I could kill anyone, Natalie. Guilt has stalked me my whole life. I think of the pain that Willie's parents went through at his death." He ran his hands through his hair. "Who am I to take a life? I only wanted him to stop bashing that woman's head against the hood of the truck. When I saw that knife, though, all I could think about was surviving. Not being stabbed to death."

"You have nothing to feel guilty over. Nothing."

"It is easier to know that logically, intellectually, than emotionally."

"Oh, Zack, honey . . ."

"Do you remember how I held back when we were dating? How I didn't kiss you for months?"

"Yes."

"I was struggling. I was trying not to fall in love with you. I knew that my whole life might explode and then you would get caught in the crossfire. You would find out that I had lied, that I wasn't who you thought. I could go to jail. We might have kids by then, and what would it do to them? But Natalie, I fell in love with you that day on the river. I couldn't stay away from you. And it was selfish. Complete selfishness on my part. I loved you, I wanted you, I wanted us. So I gave in."

He reached out and wiped the tears from my cheeks. "Zack, I'm so sorry you went through this. I'm sorry this happened to you."

"I'm sorry it happened, too." He took a deep breath. "Ronnie could send an anonymous letter to the police at any time. Once he thinks I have no more money, why not? He would be glad to see me in jail, even if only awaiting trial. Then he'll take off with our money. He'll go to Mexico or Central

476

America. He's sick in the head. He's an angry, violent man. But this is why, now, I'm going to the police. I will tell them everything. It's better for me to go to the police first, Natalie, before he does, as I planned to do before he rammed you with that van."

"We could leave." I couldn't believe I said that, but I meant it. "We could go to Canada or Mexico or wherever people go who want to hide."

"No. That, for sure, is not going to happen, babe. I will not make you live your life looking over your shoulder like I've lived mine. I won't do that to you."

I sagged. I knew he wouldn't do it. "*You* could leave. You could disappear again." The words killed me. Zack gone, me alone, never seeing him.

"No, I'm done running. I'm sick of hiding. I am sick of worrying about someone coming after me, someone finding me. I had hoped my old life was gone forever. It had been twenty years. But I was wrong, and you paid for it." His voice cracked. "You were critically hurt, you were in a coma, you've had to fight every day since then to get your life back. You lost the job you love. You lost accounting. I feel so guilty, Natalie, every day, every minute. I hate myself for letting this happen to you. It never leaves me. I cannot tell you how sorry I am." I saw the anguished, broken sheen in his eyes. "What happened to you is completely my fault."

"No, it's Ronnie's. It's all on him."

"I would understand if you left me." His face was drawn and exhausted. "In fact, you should leave me. Look what happened to you because of me."

"I will never leave you, Zack. I love you. I fell in love with you on the Deschutes, and I'm still in love with you. I have always sensed something, sensed that you were holding back even before this happened. I couldn't figure out what it was, and it made me feel like a suspicious wife. I always tried to push it down. I told myself that I was imagining it, but my gut told me I wasn't. And Zack, these last few months, I've known you were lying to me, but I kept pressing and you wouldn't tell me the truth." He shook his head, and I saw his pain again, his guilt. "But Zack, I . . ." My voice faltered. "Why didn't you tell me? From the start? After we fell in love?"

"How could I do that, sweetheart? You would then know the truth. If the police ever came and arrested me and asked you what you knew about me, about my past, you would know nothing. You're a bad liar, Natalie, because you don't lie. The police would believe you. A lie detector would back up what you were saying. You would not be an accessory to my crime. Also, if you knew my past you would start looking over your shoulder, too. You would be worried all the time that my past would come back to haunt me, haunt us. It's no way to live, trust me on that one."

Zack is my soul mate, even with all the lies he told me. I can't help loving him. "I remember being so furious with you, Zack, the morning of the accident, because you lied to me about your name and your past, and it triggered all the times my mother lied. I didn't know why you killed a man and I didn't even give you time to explain it to me. My fury blinded me. I am sorry, Zack, for not listening to you that morning. If I had stopped for two minutes —"

"You have nothing to be sorry about, Natalie. Nothing. Out of the blue I told you I wasn't who you thought I was, I told you I killed someone, that someone was threatening to kill you, and we had to leave immediately. This is all on me, and you took the full brunt of it. I am sorry."

I started to cry for what he went through as a kid, for what we went through in the hospital, for what was ahead of us, and he stood up and hugged me close, my heart this tight, throbbing mass of pain in my chest. I now knew the truth, and the truth felt hopeless and bone chilling.

"We need an attorney," I gasped out. "The best we can get."

I had the same nightmare that night.

Ronnie was hunting me down. He was wielding a knife as long as his arm, and I was running away from him, down the street in the hills where we used to live. He threw the knife at me, but at the last second Zack jumped between us and it plunged through the scar on Zack's ribs. Then Ronnie banged my head into the hood of my totaled truck until I died.

The next morning Zack and I talked again about the disaster looming before us. He left for work. He would call Ronnie, put him off, tell him he was getting more money together, as Ronnie had requested yet again.

Zack would turn himself in as soon as the money cleared for the three houses he recently sold. We would use that money for the attorney. Ronnie had $500,000 of our money. Would the police let us have our money back for legal fees, or would it be held? I had no idea. I didn't learn this type of thing when I was becoming a CPA.

I felt sick and scared, but I was bucking up and getting myself together. Being a wimp would not help here, only strength would. I couldn't predict what would happen. For sure, Zack would be initially arrested. The police wouldn't let him out of jail before trial. He had run once, he could run again. Waiting for a trial, which would undoubtedly take place in Arkansas, would take months, probably well over a year.

Zack could spend the rest of his life in jail if the jury believed he killed Willie without provocation. The optimist in me said, "Of course the jury will believe Zack over Ronnie, who would be arrested for hit-and-run, attempted murder, extortion, and blackmail, and that would be brought up in trial. Wouldn't it? Zack is a law-abiding business owner. Ronnie probably has an existing criminal record. Zack has the scars to prove what happened that night. The woman he saved would probably be found and she would probably testify for Zack. There are probably still police and medical reports. Doctors, nurses, other police officers could testify, too. Ronnie's testimony would probably easily break down under intense questioning."

Probably.

The pessimist in me said, "I'm scared wit-less."

"I want you to go to your dad's, Natalie, until this is over," Zack said. "It's only for a few more days. I'll get an attorney and tell Detective Zadora everything. Based on her recent questions, she's obviously right on my trail."

"No. I won't leave you." I would stand with Zack.

"Yes. I'll call your dad and tell him every-thing. I didn't want you at your dad's before because I didn't want you isolated out there in the country without knowing what was going on. I wanted to take care of you, and I knew that the payments to Ronnie would keep him away from you here. But we're going into something different now. I think the police will arrest him immediately once I tell them what happened. He'll be jailed and everything will be okay, but I'd like you out of here during that time just to be safe."

"I won't go. I'm staying here with you."

"You're going."

"Don't tell me what to do."

"I just did."

Zack is not the sort of husband who orders me around at all, but we had a roar-ing fight about me going to my dad's. It wasn't pretty. Zack actually yelled at me and I yelled back and he yelled and I yelled again.

"No. I will not leave you any more than you would leave me." I kissed him when we'd settled down. "Plus, there are so many guns around this apartment."

"If he comes here, if he comes in and I'm not here, shoot him, baby. Aim for the chest, the widest spot. He rammed that van into you, he hurt you, and he will do it again if he thinks I'm not paying up again. He has nothing to lose."

He hugged me tight. I love that man.

There was something else. Something about that morning. I kept seeing my grandma, felt her pushing me in her mechanic's overalls. . . . What in the world was all that about? And why did I think that Beethoven's Fifth had something to do with it?

I worked on my jewelry that morning, my hands shaking.

I listened to music, from rock to Bach.

I dressed in my favorite blue jean skirt with an embroidered turtle on it, my blue tights with the swirls, a white sweater, and my blue cowgirl boots. I went to a coffee shop and had two brownies.

I should be cowering at home, but then that would mean that he won. That Ronnie won.

I had fought my way out of a coma.

I had fought my way back to thinking like a normal person.

I had fought my way back to walking in a straight line.

I had fought my way back to talking normally.

I had even remembered the morning of my accident.

I was not going to let Ronnie change my life for me again.

I was going to be strong and smart and figure this out.

I stopped working on the necklaces I was making because my hands were shaking too hard.

I knew what I had to do.

I picked up my phone and called Jed. "I need to come and see you."

"Of course. Anytime."

"I'll be there within the hour."

I heard his pause, loud and clear, and then he said, "See you then," even though he is so busy, and might soon be a judge, because he is a true friend, the brother of my heart, and he knew I would not be coming in unless it was serious.

It was very serious.

"Darling. I'm going to come and see you soon." I gripped my phone as my mother's voice shrilled down the line. I could tell she was driving as she was semi-shouting.

Why had I even answered? I had so much in my head I could almost feel my brain cells popping. I was in Portland, on the sidewalk in front of Jed's building downtown, after our meeting. "Mom, it's not a convenient time for a visit. Not right now."

"What? You're breaking up. By the way," she shouted into her phone, blowing my ears out, "I did what you said. I've been wearing the trampy cowgirl porn outfit for Dell. He loves it. Then, I thought to myself, why stop there? I bought a sexy waitress outfit and a sexy monster outfit and a sexy Tinker Bell outfit."

Sexy monster? Sexy Tinker Bell? "Excellent news, Mom. I am not going to let myself get a vision of that scene, but I'm proud of you, but about you coming to see me —"

"Let's say that Dell and I are getting along better. In fact, he was so nice to me I told him that he was right and I didn't need two thousand dollars a month anymore for my personal expenditures, and I don't. Why, you ask? Because I've bought a women's clothing boutique in town from a woman named Evelyn!"

What? She bought a clothing boutique?

"This is how it happened: I went shopping in town one day at Evelyn's — that's the name of the shop but I'm going to change it to Jocelyn's Fashion Boutique. There was a Help Wanted sign and I went in to apply because you told me I should get a job to be independent. After I shopped around I told Evelyn that she should hire me because most of what she had was poorly chosen and not fashion forward. She seemed offended and all huffy puffy at first, but then she smiled and said, 'Have you ever thought of owning your own clothing store, Jocelyn? You're so fashionable! Everyone admires you and your clothes. Why, you're the most in-style, hip person here in town!'

"I thought to myself, 'Well, I am that!' Why be falsely modest? I *could* own a clothing boutique! The women need help out here. All these ranchers and farmers, they look like ranchers and farmers, Natalie! Can you imagine? Dusty. Boring. Not how women should look at all. They never wear heels. They rarely wear dresses. And where is their makeup? I could sell makeup, too, and do makeovers so these women won't look like pig farmers. Every woman needs makeup. You're remembering to put on lipstick, aren't you? Your lips are pale without it.

"Anyhow, I said to Evelyn, 'I've never thought of owning a clothing boutique, but I do know a thing or two about fashion.' And then Evelyn said, 'It would be so hard for me to give my boutique up because it has been such a money maker for me, but I might think about selling it. I am seventy-two, after all. But I would only sell it to someone who appreciates modern style and design, as you do, Jocelyn. Your glamorous outfits are impeccable. You look like a movie star. You never miss a step!'

"Evelyn has never been so nice to me. I think her snootiness was because she was jealous of me, because she is frumpy dumpy. Anyhow, I immediately thought of Dell giving me a teeny, tiny loan for my new boutique and I said, 'Evelyn, I'll buy your Evelyn's!' We shook on it, Evelyn and I, like real businesswomen! She said that she trusted my, and I quote, 'financial solvency.' "

Despite the disaster I was dealing with, I tried not to laugh as I saw the wheels in Evelyn's head turning. She wanted to retire. She was selling clothes in a small, eastern

Oregon town and wasn't making much money, but if she could sell it . . . When my mother showed up she saw her prize chicken. She knew my egotistical mother, with a heavy dose of flattery, could be convinced to buy it.

Jocelyn was married to Dell, a wealthy rancher, whom Evelyn had probably known for decades. Dell could supply the money. It was a newer marriage. Wouldn't Dell be indulgent? Wouldn't he want my mother, a spoiled and obnoxious woman, off the ranch every day? Poor Dell. He hadn't understood what he was marrying, had he? A fluffed-up doll. A selfish gold digger. Here in town, they'd all tried to warn him!

Evelyn was already searching for a condo in Florida, I was sure of it. She would head out for warmer weather, laughing in the plane and tossing back straight shots in celebration, toasting my shallow, silly mother who needed only a bit of fake flattery to make her buy a downtrodden shop, whose clothes she didn't even like.

"I wore my princess porn outfit," my mother shouted, "and then I asked Dell for the loan, and he said yes. I'm going to earn all of my own money with my clothing boutique! Everyone will come from miles around to get my fashion advice and buy

488

my clothes. Only designer clothes, though. These small-town mice need a lesson in how to dress. First thing I'll buy for them: high heels."

"I'm not sure that farmers and ranchers need heels, Mom, but I think this sounds like an exciting project."

"I'll help women look their best. Dressing well says something about your character and social class. When you're dressed in rags and appear poor and your shoes don't fit right and your coat is too small, people treat you like you are less than others. Like you're nothing. Like you're a disease, or have lice, or you're stupid. They'll treat you like you're poor white trash. I can help women to not appear poor and trashy."

"You could. But don't tell your customers that you can help them to avoid appearing poor and trashy. About the visit. I don't know when you're planning to come, Mom, but not this week —"

"You're cutting in and out again, dear. Ta-ta. I'll be coming to visit you very soon. It will be a surprise! I'll show up and we'll go and get our nails done. My treat. Last time I saw your nails . . . all I can say is that this is what mothers are for! Making our daughters prettier when they need help. Bye now."

Bye now, Mother Monster. You're like sandpaper.

Jed called me two hours later with the answers I needed. He was fast. He was sizzling smart. I would tell Zack what he said as soon as he walked in the door that night. Now I knew exactly what Zack should do. It scared me to pieces, but we'd fight this one out together.

Chapter 18

I never heard him come in.

I had taken a walk. Not a long walk, but a short walk. That I could walk at all and not resemble a drunk penguin was an accomplishment. I had to clear my head. It was crammed with everything that Jed told me.

I was drenched in rain when I got back to the apartment. I slammed the door and hurriedly hopped in the shower because I was freezing. When I was done, I wrapped a towel around myself and headed toward the bedroom, and there he was. In my family room. *In my home.* How had he gotten in? But I knew. In my race to get warmed up, I had forgotten to lock the door.

Ronnie Hotchkiss. The brother of Willie Hotchkiss, whom Zack killed in self-defense.

Ronnie was even larger up close, like a bull, his bald head shiny, his beady eyes dark, skittering, and dangerous. His eyes had an odd light to them, but even scarier was the way his fingers were wriggling at his side. As if they couldn't help themselves from moving, as if they couldn't wait to touch me. He had pulled the drapes shut and turned off the lights. It was dark and shadowy, only a sliver of light coming through the middle of the two curtains in my family room.

"Hello, Natalie." He grinned at me, as if he was glad to see me, as if we were friends. As if I would smile back and say hello.

"Get out." My voice was strong. I held tight to my towel.

"No, thank you. I believe I'll stay here."

His small eyes stared straight at mine, then they traveled down my body.

I was terrified, my breath stuck in my throat.

"I've wanted to be alone with you for a long time." He laughed, dark and rumbling.

"We're not alone. I have neighbors." I tried to make my voice brave. It wavered. "They'll hear me yelling and they'll come."

"Nah. They won't." He giggled then. High-pitched. "It's the middle of the day. Most of them aren't home. Plus. This neighborhood." He giggled again. "It's a bad one. For poor people. Like you and Devon. You're poor now, aren't you, Natalie? No one's coming."

I thought about the guns. One under the dresser in our bedroom. One in the kitchen, top shelf. One by the front door in the drawer of the side table. I couldn't get the one in the kitchen or the side table, as he would block me, but I could make a run for the bedroom.

"You're so sexy, Natalie. All those blond curls. Big lips. Big boobs. Devon doesn't deserve you."

"If you don't get out of here now, I'm going to scream."

"Scream," he said, his voice soft. "And I will have my hands wrapped around your neck so quick, your neck will snap."

"What do you want? Zack has already paid you. As you can see, we have no other money."

"It's not money I want anymore, Natalie. I'm getting out of town." He took a few steps forward, slow, almost jaunty. "It's you I want. I want what Devon wants most. I want Devon to know I had you. He doesn't deserve a pretty bitch like you in bed every night. But I do."

I thought I might collapse. My whole throat dried out. At the same time, I thought, *I will fight. I will fight him with all I have.*

"You're looking much better than you

were when you were knocked out cold in the hospital, although seeing you lying down, defenseless, that was exciting for me. If I wasn't worried about people coming in I would have enjoyed myself on you. I went home that night and all I thought about was you. You, you, you." There was that giggle again. "You've been in my head for months now. Delicious and sexy. All I could do then was leave you the Barbie. She reminded me of you. Busty. Skinny. I could hardly breathe thinking of you as I carved her up. Especially when I put the knife between her legs. Did anyone tell you about the Barbie?"

"You're sick." I felt as if I were liquefying from fear, but I also wanted to kill him.

"Ah, I can see they did. You, Natalie, are my Barbie." He smiled at me and took a couple steps closer, stalking his prey. "You're sexier now than you were before the accident, and I thought you were a fine slut then. Your hair is so curly. I want to wrap your curls around my fingers. I want to yank your head back when you're on your knees.

"Your body has grown lush again. I like my women to have something to hold. Something to bite and squeeze." His eyes stared right at my chest. "You have no idea how much time I've spent thinking about that ass of yours and how it will look when you're facedown on the mattress."

He was repulsive. Demented. I would not give in to this sick beast. I did not want to be facedown on a mattress with that pig rutting above me.

"You're disgusted, aren't you?" His face suddenly twisted, and he raised his voice. "You're disgusted even thinking about me being naked on top of you, inside of you. Making a baby with you. You bitch. I know women exactly like you. They think they're better than me. You're as bad as Devon.

"I searched for that son of a bitch for years." He started yelling, his fingers moving faster. "I even hired a private detective. Devon killed my brother. Willie didn't deserve that. Devon intervened in a fight between him and his stupid girlfriend, Stephanie, that whore. My brother wouldn't have killed her. He knew how much a woman could take before she died."

I tried not to sway when I felt my blood rush out of my head.

"We started practicing on animals when we were kids. Our mom would wail on us. She'd use a rope, a belt, her fists, and we'd go out and do the same thing to the animals we caught in our traps. Our momma taught us a thing or two." He sniffled then, his face falling. His chin trembled, then stopped as he snapped his head back up. "Hey, you know what happened to Stephanie after she betrayed my brother and he died because of it?"

I shook my head. I would keep him talking.

"I beat her up for my brother." Ronnie clapped his hands, fingers moving like snakes. "Later. After she was out of the hospital. And you know what she did after that?" He picked up one of my china teacups with the pink flowers and threw it. It shattered over the couch. He picked up one of my white ceramic vases and threw that, too. "She left. In the middle of the night. Poof. Gone. If I ever find that bitch, I'll go after her, too. She was trying to break up with my brother. Who does she think she is? Who do you women think you are? You think you can walk off whenever you want, climb into bed with some other man?

"My dad and my uncle, they knew how to treat women. Knew how to treat all of their wives. The man is the head of the house, he's the boss, and sometimes you have to treat a woman like a rebellious horse. Smack 'em. Show 'em who is in charge. Break 'em. I saw my dad do it with my own mother."

He took a deep breath, then, unbelievably, he started to cry, his shoulders hunched.

When he spoke, even his voice was different, as if he were a child. "I miss my brother. I miss Willie. He was my best friend. Always tried to protect me from our parents when we were little. From the belts. The wooden spoons. The branches. Always tried to take the blame so I wouldn't get hit. He always made sure I ate before him. When kids picked on me, he beat them up. We slept together in the same bed, and he used to read me fairy tales. Yep. We read fairy tales." He wiped his wet face with his sleeve. "But we knew they were all lies, lies, lies because of what we were living in at home. I miss him. I have always missed him. Every single day I miss my brother."

The tears suddenly turned off, his face returned to hard stone, and he picked up one of my Grandma's antique perfume bottles and pelted it across the room.

"I have wanted revenge on Devon for twenty years. I vowed on my brother's grave that I would get him, and I have. I got Devon. I got his money and I got his woman. I can't wait until that towel comes off of you. I can't wait to see you naked. I'll have you all to myself. You'll like it. You like the rough stuff, right? I know you do. When Devon walks in, he'll know that you cheated

497

on him. I'll tell him everything we did together."

He yanked one of my hanging hummingbirds from the ceiling and threw that against the wall, too. Then another one. And a third. "I'm killing your birds, Natalie," he whispered. "One by one." He smirked.

I would run to the bedroom. I would jump the bed and fly to the dresser and grab the gun. He would be right behind me, but it was all I had. I would die fighting. I would die punching and hitting and screaming.

"Natalie. I like the way your name sounds on my tongue. Natalie, Natalie." He ran his tongue over his lips, then stuck it straight out at me. "Tasty. You know how I found Devon? Did he tell you? *US Home Building* magazine. He was on the cover. Famous homebuilder, Zack Shelton. I saw it when I was on a job site. What a coincidence. How does that happen? Everyone thinks we Arkansas boys are stupid, but we ain't. I remember everything." He tapped his head. "Photographic memory."

"I'm one of the smartest men you'll ever meet, and I have never forgotten Devon's face. When I saw his face on the cover, I looked him up, found out where his company was, his home, you. I found out everything. All by myself."

He took a couple more threatening steps closer to me, slowly, as if he wanted to tease me. "Smart me. I am so smart."

I thought I might be sick. Sick with fear. I understood that saying now.

"You know, Barbie, I'll tell you a story." He leaned toward me and started whispering, that odd light in his eyes back. "This is funny. Devon ran off, right, so he wouldn't go to jail. Changed his name. Never came back home to Arkansas again that I know of. Anyhow, Stephanie went to the hospital in the ambulance. She was hardly moving and she was covered in blood when they put her on the stretcher, and I was glad of it, seeing my brother dead on the ground like that. I hoped she would die. She was the one who started all of it, thinking she could break up with my brother and shack up with some other man.

"But my uncle and my dad, they can't go to the hospital and tell her to shut the hell up because they're crying over my brother. That whore Stephanie." He slammed a fist into his hand, three times, his face scrunched and red. "She told the doctors and the county police that your husband saved her life. She couldn't talk right at first because of the lesson my brother taught her on his truck and her jaw and nose were broken, and she had to go in for a bunch of surgeries, but that's what she said. Devon saved her life. That bitch didn't even show up for my brother's funeral, can you believe it?

"So because my dad and my uncle were personally involved, my dad being the police chief and his brother the DA, and it was my brother killed, the whole case had to leave our county. So another district attorney, a stupid woman named Delle Lindberg, interviewed Stephanie and she talked about all the times my brother had to teach her a lesson, and how she'd broken up with him months ago, and how he was stalking her, and how she'd already called the police for the stalking twice.

"Stephanie, that slut, told Delle that my dad and my uncle squashed the stalking investigations. Then Delle started investigating the night Devon murdered my brother and talking to a whole bunch of people who knew us, and do you know what, Natalie? Do you know," he yelled, "do you know, do you know?"

"No, I don't know."

"The DA named Dumb Delle quietly called off the chase for your husband." He put one finger to his lips. "*Shhh!* That DA hated my father and my uncle. She later took both of their jobs. Said they were corrupt. Liars. Unfit. We found out how many people were against us after that. It's an open case still, who killed my brother, but no one was working it anymore because of Stephanie and what she said. My dad and my uncle were told that it was clearly a case of defense for another, or some stupid phrase like that, and self-defense for Devon."

That was what I'd learned, too. From Jed. It was ironic, it was grossly, horribly ironic, that this violent man, today, was telling me what I already knew. The case wasn't officially closed. It had never been announced as closed. But Jed found out that the authorities in Arkansas were not actively pursuing the case at all and hadn't since shortly after it happened. It was self-defense. There had not even been an indictment.

"Yep. They called off the case and the chase. Ain't it funny? Devon didn't need to run and hide. Didn't need to become someone new. Isn't that funny?"

No, it wasn't funny, you lunatic. And if you touch me I will beat you and kick you and scream. . . .

"Doesn't matter, though. I now have five hundred thousand dollars, and look where you two are living. A dump. I'm taking off.

But first I'll take from him what was taken from me. He took my brother away from me, and I'm taking you. First we're gonna have some fun in that bedroom, and when Devon comes home, he'll find you tucked away in bed dead." He laughed, this was so funny. "He'll try to wake you up, and you know what? He won't be able to wake you up. You will be deader than you were in that coma. Like my brother was dead and I couldn't wake him up."

I saw a shadow between the curtains of the window. Was it Zack? Was he home early?

"Get naked, Natalie." Ronnie took three menacing steps toward me, his face screwed up in an ugly mask, and I turned to run toward the gun in the bedroom. The towel fell and I stumbled because I still have balance issues. Ronnie giggle and grabbed me, spinning me around and pulling my naked body up tight to his. I leaned my head back and screamed, and his fist came pounding into my cheek. I crumbled to the ground.

"Dumb bitch. You didn't have to make this hard. You know that. Stand up."

I couldn't stand up. I was dizzy. Blood dripped down my face. He had a ring on and it had sliced my cheek.

He took a deep breath, and his tone

changed. "Come on, now. Don't be a cat. When we did that to cats they died just like that." He snapped his fingers. "Meow for me." His voice sounded reasonable. That was the scariest part of all. "Meow, meow. Look at those boobs. So big, but the rest of you is small. Except that butt. How do you and Devon have sex? Tell me. Tell me, tell me, tell me."

He reached down and grabbed my hair and yanked me up. I pushed at his chest, reeling, but it did nothing. "I like a feisty woman. Fight me all you want." He put his greasy, sweaty hand on my ass and pulled me up tight against him, then his other hand came around my throat, and he squeezed. I couldn't breathe. My throat was being crushed, the edges of my vision darkening, his red face blurring and drifting away. I struggled, I fought as hard as I could, but soon I couldn't move and everything went black.

Suddenly the pressure was gone from my neck and I felt myself floating. I looked down and I saw myself, Ronnie's hands around my neck, my face red and purple, my eyes closing. I felt myself being pulled into a soft tunnel, safe and warm. I felt someone with me, holding my hands. I felt love. Peace.

I flew through the ceiling of my apartment, watching Ronnie and myself grow smaller and smaller, and into the sky. I saw light blue and dark blue and puffy white clouds. I heard Beethoven's Fifth, my favorite, then I heard my father singing to me: Johnny Cash's "Ring of Fire." "Old McDonald Had a Farm." The Beatles' "Let It Be."

It all came back to me at once as the musical tunnel pulled me through, my hands held: *I've been here before.* After the car accident. I remember drifting away from my truck and seeing my own head on the air bag, the splattered blood.

I was dying. I looked for my grandma and there she was, sitting at a table with three other people, including the love of her life, Howard MacIntosh, who grinned at me and waved.

She was playing poker. She had stacks of chips in front of her. She saw me and her face lit up with love and joy, then it was filled with fear and anguish. She ran to me, as did Howard, who now looked equally concerned.

"For God's sakes," she said. "This is the second time. What the hell is going on down there? You and Zack aren't supposed to be up here for fifty-five years. You come together."

"Grandma, help me, please, I love you —"

"I love you, too, darlin'." I could smell her rose perfume. "Hang on." She ran back a few feet, palms up, and I braced myself for the hit. I fell back down the soft, musical tunnel, through the light and dark blue and the puffy white clouds and back into my apartment, my neck held in a vice by a giggling Ronnie. . . .

It was at that exact moment that my front door exploded.

The noise was deafening. Wood flew into the room, and I was dropped, gasping, to the floor. I heard another blast, then a third. A fourth. Gunshots.

"What the hell —" Ronnie screamed.

I didn't know what was going on, but I tried to crawl toward my bedroom and my gun, the room tilting, rocking back and forth, as I struggled to inhale, to breathe.

It wasn't necessary to get my gun, though. As soon as I moved, I heard two more blasts. I turned and saw Ronnie crumble to the floor, onto his back. There was a bullet hole in his head and one in his chest, where he was bleeding profusely. He did not move.

I turned my shocked eyes to the front

door, my hand against the wall to balance myself.

And there was my mother. Both hands extended, clasping her gun. She was wearing a red dress and matching red heels. It was Ruby Day! Her hair was perfectly coiffed, the nails that held the gun painted red.

"Hello, honey," she called out, as if we were meeting at a tea party. "Hope you're okay."

"Mother," I croaked, holding my bleeding face with one hand, the pain banging through my head.

"I did tell you that I was going to surprise you, Natalie. Surprise!"

"Nice to see you, Mother," I whispered, stunned.

"I wanted to tell you, darling, that you were right about another divorce. I cannot go through it a fifth time. I decided that Dell is the right man for me."

She tottered in on her four-inch red heels and stood over Ronnie lying on the ground. Her gun was still pointed at him, her red designer purse on her arm. I heard sirens in the distance.

"I am an excellent shot," she said. "That is the one thing my miserable father taught me."

"You do have talent." I could hardly breathe through my bruised, crushed neck. Blinding pain, residual white hot fear, and relief all mixed together.

"I don't miss. A woman always has to have a gun, you never know. You told me to keep the safety on. Now do you understand why I don't?"

"Yes, I believe I do." My face hurt. There was blood all over. I slumped over, leaning against the wall.

"Now, who was that, dear? And why did he hit you in the face, and why are you naked?"

"He's been stalking us. Stalking Zack." My voice was a rough croak. "He was the one who rammed my truck and put me in a coma. He threatened to kill me today."

She kicked him in the head. "Asshole. No one hurts my girl. That's why I killed him." She grabbed a dish towel from the kitchen, crouched beside me, and held it to my face to staunch the blood. "Why was he after the two of you?"

"Because Mother . . ." I tried to breathe. "Zack is not who he says he is. He had a different name when he was younger. He killed this man's brother when the brother came at him with a knife. Zack was defending a woman. Zack went on the run and disappeared because he thought he would go to jail forever. This man's father was the chief of police and his uncle was the DA. Zack was nineteen. His parents were dead. He was scared. But I talked to Jed, and everything's okay."

"Oh. I understand. That makes sense." And amazingly, she did. My mother's education was severely limited, due to her abusive parents, but she is sharper than an ax about some things. She checked her nails. "Darn it. Just had these done and now two are chipped. You'll have to go with me to the manicurist. I'm sure you need your nails done, you always do. You should take better care of them."

"Looking forward to it," I wheezed.

"Are you hurt badly?" She still held the towel to my bleeding head. "Obviously, you're bleeding like a stuck pig, but how bad is the pain?"

She pressed a kiss to my cheek, the one that wasn't covered in blood. I was touched. I was further touched when she sniffled and her blue eyes filled with tears. Next, she kissed my forehead. Honestly, I was shocked to have been attacked, but having this much affection from my mother was quite shocking, too.

"Not too bad, Mom." It hurt like the devil.

"Glad to hear it, dear." We heard the police outside. She smiled, raised her eyebrows. "I'll go and greet the police, say hello, welcome them in, play the hostess role. You go and get dressed. A lady knows to always look her best, and she knows she should get naked only in front of her husband." She paused, then winked, the tears clearing. "All five of them."

I could not move, as my brain was throbbing and would undoubtedly fall out of my skull if I did, so the police were going to see my naked self. Right by the dead body. It was the least of my concerns, this nakedness.

I had one thought as I watched my mother gracefully step over Ronnie's dead body in her four-inch red heels so she could go "greet" the police and "welcome" them in: I have never been so glad to see her.

"I saw that the drapes were drawn and I thought to myself, 'My. Isn't that strange?'" My mother's voice reached me. She had lowered it for best story-telling effect for the police officers, serious men and women in suits and uniforms, and Detective Zadora. "Natalie doesn't shut her drapes unless it's nighttime. I taught her to always let the sunshine in. I know a lot about home décor."

I was on a stretcher. I was covered with a blanket. My face had stopped bleeding, but it was still throbbing. There were police, firefighters, and paramedics crammed into my apartment.

"So I peeked through the curtains." My mother mimicked peeking through the curtains, raising her perfectly plucked eyebrows. This was her chance to show Important People that she was a super sleuth. "And I saw this man advancing on my daughter. Natalie turned to run and he caught her and hit her in the face with his fist. Well, I'm telling you. I am her mother, and no one hits my girl. When I saw that, I got my gun out of my purse." She mimed holding her gun, both hands, feet spread apart in her red designer dress. "I shot through the locks, all three of them, then the door itself, then I kicked the door open like you see women police officers do in the movies." She mimed the kick in her red high heels. "Hiya!" she yelled, quite loudly.

"When the door opened, that rancid piece of white trash whipped around and started to move toward me. He dropped my beat-up daughter right to the floor, and that's when I decided to defend my and my daughter's virtue, dignity, and honor." Her voice rose with indignation and pride. "I shot twice. Clean shots. Head and chest. Down he went."

I laughed. It hurt my face. I tried not to laugh again. What an odd person I am. I had been attacked, but there I was, laughing at my mother.

"I always carry my gun with me," she said proudly. She patted her blond hair. "Safety off. You never know when you'll need it, and you must be prepared to shoot. A woman can be both beautiful and an excellent shot, don't you think?"

I glanced at the officers. They blinked at my mother, not sure what to make of her. I wasn't sure, either.

"I'm going to open a clothing boutique!" she announced.

As I left on the stretcher I cast a glance over to my grandma's antique perfume bottles and smiled. "Thank you, Grandma Dixie," I whispered. I peered at the kitchen floor. Oh, my gosh. The perfume bottle that Ronnie had thrown against the wall had not broken.

Zack was called by Detective Zadora, and he raced to the hospital to meet me. I had my mother call Jed to tell him what happened. Jed immediately called Zack and told him not to talk to the police under any circumstances. He needed an attorney, and Jed was already in the process of getting him one.

Zack hugged me tight, but not too tight, as I was all banged up again. "Baby, I am so sorry."

"Zack, please. Just kiss me. Gently." He did.

Eventually, after fully enjoying her moment in the limelight with the police officers, my mother arrived at the hospital and whispered to me, "Do you think I could write a book about this? I bet Oprah would love to feature me in her magazine. 'Woman Saves Her Daughter's Life but Still Maintains Most of Her Manicure.' What do you think?"

"I think it's a bad idea."

She pouted. "You're ruining my fun." Then she actually became all teary eyed again and, for the second time, kissed my cheek, then my forehead. This was a miracle. Four kisses. In one day! "I love you, Natalie."

Oh. My. Goodness. "I love you, too, Mom."

Once he knew I was okay, relatively speaking, Zack left my hospital room and told the police, and Detective Zadora, and the DA, everything. His attorney had arrived, a true ball-banger named Karen Bennett, and advised him not to talk until she had a chance to talk to him. He declined to do as she advised.

In the end, Zack spent hours being grilled by the authorities. The authorities in Portland talked to the authorities in Arkansas. The cold case was reopened. The authorities in Arkansas found Stephanie and talked to her again. There had been another witness, too — the man who had called the police outside the restaurant that night. He was a chef there, and he told the police that he saw Willie slamming Stephanie's head into the hood of a truck and watched Zack protect her as he called the police. He had even seen the knife that Willie wielded.

Stephanie had moved to Seattle after Ronnie beat her up for "causing Willie's death." She thought he was going to kill her the next time around, which he probably would have. Ironically, she had changed her name, too, to hide from Ronnie.

Stephanie owns a coffee shop and sells her paintings on the side. She is married and has five children. She told the police, unequivocally, again, that Zack had saved her life. Her exact words, which Detective Zadora later told us, were, "Willie was bashing my head into the hood of his truck. Do you see my scars? He broke my nose, my jaw, and an eye socket. I still sometimes have pain in my neck. He was furious that I had broken up with him. He told me that if he couldn't have me, no man would, and he was going to kill me. Zack saved my life. And yes, I did see Willie pull the knife on Zack. He tried to stab it right into Zack's heart. Willie tried to kill Zack."

She backed up every inch of Zack's story, even down to telling the police that she had insisted that Zack leave. "I knew that Willie's and Ronnie's dad and uncle would have Zack in jail even though he had saved my life. They would all lie. They would all manipulate the system. They would pull in favors from other people they knew, they would bribe people, and get Zack locked up forever, probably on death row. They were corrupt people, just like Willie and Ronnie."

What also helped Zack's case in terms of running and eluding the law? He was nineteen at the time. Barely more than a kid. His parents were dead. He was scared. He didn't want to go to jail. He didn't trust the system, who did? He lived in Arkansas and had not seen the system work. He ran because it made sense to him at the time and, fortunately, it made sense to the law enforcement officials who heard it. He had led an exemplary, law-abiding, tax-paying life and now was a successful homebuilder. He did have a stolen social security number, and a license based on a fake name, but they would work that part out.

The media got hold of the story. Every single thing came out. People were fascinated. A man had disappeared after a crime for twenty years! He had murdered a man in self-defense! He had saved a woman's life! And here is the woman! Stephanie spoke at every turn, defending Zack, reiterating she would have been dead if not for him. She even went on three talk shows. Zack declined every invitation for an interview, even when the true story came out about how his parents died.

All charges were dropped. Zack was a free man. Forever.

"Should I call you Devon or Zack?" I asked, curled up naked beside him in bed.

"Baby, you can call me anything you want." He smiled at me, and I smiled back.

"I think I will call you, I love you." I laughed.

"That's the perfect name. Love you, too, Natalie. Always have, always will."

■ ■ ■ ■

Detective Zadora had known *almost* everything. They started looking into Zack's history and then found that his history . . . stopped. Right when he was nineteen. His social security number was false, and they started digging. She and her team were simply researching further, amidst the rest of their enormous criminal caseload, before they came to Zack with the information and their decision. She is a smart woman.

She did have a question for me, though. "Your father . . . is he married?"

Stephanie insisted on getting Zack's phone number to thank him. They had a lovely chat. She asked him what he liked to do, and he said he liked to watch the sun set over the coast range with me. She painted him a glowing sunset, the ragged blue and purple mountains in the distance, two deer outlined in the trees, two people, Zack and I, standing with our arms around each other. We loved it.

I told my dad I'd seen his mother in heaven. "She was working on a red 1967 Chevy, Dad."

He choked up. "That was her dream car. Now she's finally got it. She was a dart-throwing, car-fixing, rifle-shooting, deer-hunting, poker-playing, apple-pie-baking son of a gun, and I loved her."

When I was better I made my grandma Dixie's apple pie for Zack wearing a negligee with apples on it. I had to stop in the middle when Zack could not control himself.

This time I did everything right. I didn't burn it. I added the cinnamon and nutmeg and the right amount of brown sugar. The crisscross crust was crunchy and tasty.

I was so proud of that pie. My grandma would have been, too.

"It's delicious," Zack said.

"You're still my apple pie, Zack."

We laughed, hard. It wasn't that funny, but there was victory in that pie baking.

Yes, the Moonshine and Milky Way Maverick Girls were doing it.

I was going to find my former wild and crazy self, apparently, in the dark, on a bike, naked, riding through the streets of Portland with thousands of other naked bike riders. Chick rode my bike, Justine had hers, and they rented me a three-wheeler with a pretty flowered basket. I laughed when I saw it but was relieved, too, as my balance had taken a hit with Ronnie's hit, so to speak.

We all wore long blond wigs and masks, the Mardi Gras-type mask with glitter and sequins and feathers. We also had helmets on. Taped to our helmets were two foot-long purple and pink feathers and purple and pink ribbons, which flowed along behind us.

We attached pink glittery butterfly wings to our backs and, like a few other people, we wore bikini bottoms, as wide and high as we could find. We sprayed them with silver glitter. On our nipples we glued fake flowers. The flowers actually covered part of mine and Justine's boobs. Chick, not so much. She's a chesty gal. We stripped at the park right before they started, shoved our sweats in my flowered basket, and took off into the darkness.

We had had a little too much to drink from our Maverick Girls Moonshine flasks before we started, so we sang through the streets of Portland as our wings flapped, the sequins on our Mardi Gras masks catching a bit of moonlight. The streets were crowded with naked bike riders laughing and talking, some in masks, most not. Some were free and naked and proud of it, and some were slightly less naked.

One man painted himself blue, a woman rode her bike with a bubble machine behind her, and a couple shared a tandem bike and wore clown hair and green glasses. There were tutus and top hats, cowboy boots and capes.

No one, though, had the artistic butterfly wing creations that we did, which we were extremely proud of.

We laughed so hard, we had to stop several times. Chick, with her weak bladder, had to get off her bike and run behind a tree and squat. There wasn't much covering there in the city, but she was desperate. We stopped at the Porta-Potties for her, too. It's hard to fit butterfly wings in those things, so you know.

We waved to people on the sidewalk, princess style. I saw Zack exactly where he said he would be, Braxton and Jed with him.

I waved at him, but Zack could hardly wave back. He was laughing so hard he was almost bent over double, just like Braxton and Jed. I got off my bike, ran over to him, my wings flapping, feathers streaming, boobs bouncing, and planted a kiss on his lips. He couldn't kiss back very well because of the laughter. He smacked me on the butt, and I got back on my three-wheel bike, his laughter following me down the road.

CHAPTER 19

Zack had told me the truth about the occupations of his parents. His father was a homebuilder, his mother a nurse. But their names were not Randall and Cora Shelton, they had never lived in South Carolina, as he'd said, and they did not die in a car accident.

"My parents' names were Tony and Sandy Walton," he said, his voice heavy with sadness. "They were killed by a woman named Bitsy Chandler when I was a junior in high school, seventeen years old. She lived in her home, by herself, out in the woods, and rarely left. The neighbors tried to help her, my mother tried to help her. Sometimes she was receptive, sometimes she wouldn't answer her door. She was a hoarder and had about twenty cats.

"She had a breakdown one winter, screaming outside of her house about people trying to put her in jail, pulling off her arms and legs, and trying to stick her in a possum trap. The neighbors called my mom. My dad and mom went up to help — they cared about Bitsy. Everyone did. It was freezing cold, late at night, and Bitsy raised a gun, told them she wasn't going to let them put her in a possum trap, and shot both of them."

"Oh, Zack. Oh no."

"They both died immediately. Bitsy ran back in her house, and the neighbors ran toward my parents, but it was too late. No one even knew she had a gun. When the police broke in, they found her in a corner, hysterical, crying, saying she hadn't meant to shoot the nice possums." He took a deep breath. "Anyhow, it was a huge story in Arkansas. It brought up a whole slew of issues about the mentally ill, guns, and our mental health system.

"It was probably overly paranoid, but I thought that if anyone knew even my parents' first names, the situation of their deaths, they could look it up. They would see that they had a son, Devon, who could not be located. The suspicion could start right there and my whole new life would unravel. Right from the start, I made up new names for my parents. It was yet another lie. I'm sorry, Natalie."

I hated all the lies between us. I did. But what to do? Divorce him? Leave the love of my life? I understood why he lied. He had to. Would I have done the same thing? Yes.

"What were your parents like?"

His eyes misted up. "I could not have had better parents."

We returned to Zack's hometown of Tallie Springs in Arkansas. His parents had paid off the house, and it was still his. There was a property bill, but it was dismissed when Zack donated the house and land to the city. The small town had grown a lot in the last twenty years, and they needed space for a park. The park would be named after his parents, Tony and Sandy Walton.

Zack was welcomed with open arms. People recognized him at the diner in town, and it was as if a celebrity had returned. They had all read his story in the news and been fascinated. Everyone had loved his parents, especially his mother, who was "a caring and helpful nurse, dedicated to the people of Tallie Springs," the seventy-five-year-old fire chief said, who had been a friend of Zack's parents. "She was better than any doctor there ever was. She cured almost everyone."

It turns out they all suspected that it was

Zack who had killed the "Hotchkiss boy. That troublemaker, that criminal, that drunk," because Zack disappeared after the murder. "We figured you were on the run, son," a man named Cass Leopold said. "And we wished you God's speed and the best of luck. That woman had her face beaten in, all those bones broken, and we knew you weren't guilty at all. We knew you'd protected her. Sure have missed you. Any chance you could move back to Tallie Springs?"

None of them, not one person, called the police and told them that they thought the recently disappeared nineteen-year-old kid named Devon Walton had killed Willie Hotchkiss.

We went to a hastily set-up potluck dinner at a neighbor's, and I think the whole town came, the tables groaning under the home-made food. Many of Zack's friends from school showed up, some arriving throughout the day from hours away, all eager to see Zack again. It was abundantly clear to me how much they loved him and had missed him when he'd left.

"He was my best friend," I kept hearing. "Helped me make the football team . . . helped me with chemistry . . . rescued me when I was getting beat up one day . . .

came to my dad's funeral and sat right next to me . . . helped my mom and me with our fence after my dad walked out . . . made sure no one made fun of my sister. She has Down's syndrome. . . ."

The next day we walked through his family's white farmhouse, on a small hill. Zack still had the key to his house. Zack said it was exactly as he'd left it. The TVs were gone, but nothing else had been stolen. Someone had boarded up the windows to help prevent break-ins.

It was a wrenching, emotional day. We sat on the front porch of that farmhouse for a long time. We walked through the small orchard under a canopy of leaves. We stood over a long-gone garden his father had planted, bordered with a white picket fence. We were quiet in the yellow kitchen where he'd rinsed the vegetables he and his dad had grown and where he'd canned peaches with his mother.

We lay on his bed in his bedroom and looked at all the photographs in frames and in the scrapbooks. We studied all of his mom's paintings, who was a gifted artist. So many were of Zack and his father, their home, their land, their animals, the garden. She'd even done a self-portrait. "She's one of the most gorgeous women I've ever seen," I said.

"She was," Zack answered, running a finger down her cheek. "Inside and out. Like you."

We sat in the chairs in front of his fireplace where he'd played chess with his dad. We had lunch at the dining room table where his father had taught him how houses were built, solidly, so they would stand for a hundred years, and where he'd shown him blueprints and designs.

We had breakfast at the kitchen table where his mother had talked to him about politics and books and social issues. And how, as a nurse, she took care of the most fragile people. "With love and kindness," she'd told him. "You are obligated to help others."

We went to his parents' graves and stayed for a long time. I walked away and let Zack be. It was hard to see those strong, broad shoulders hunched, the devastation still there. He would never stop missing his parents — who could stop missing parents like Tony and Sandy Walton? No one. They clearly loved him with everything they had.

It took several days, but we boxed up what he wanted to take and arranged for shipping, including all of his mother's paintings, a part of the white picket fence, some of his parents' clothes so we could have a quilt made of them later, his mother's china, his father's blueprints to frame, his mother's cookbooks and classics, his father's garden tools and drafting board, and all the scrapbooks.

We dropped the rest at Goodwill. He signed the papers to donate the land and we left after another potluck, which most of the town attended again. We arranged to have Zack's truck, the one he saved his own money to buy and left when he ran off to Alaska, delivered to us in Oregon. It was a classic, it had huge sentimental value, and we couldn't leave it behind.

"We'll come for the dedication ceremony for the park," I said, grief for his parents, whose lives were cut way too short, grief for Zack who had lost such amazing people, clogging my throat. I could hardly talk.

"Yes, we will."

We would come back and honor his loving, dedicated parents, who literally gave their lives to help someone else.

"They would be proud of you, Zack."

He smiled at me. "I hope so."

"I know so." I gave him a long kiss because Tony and Sandy Walton's son is so kissable.

EPILOGUE

The Ronnie incident did it for Zack and me in terms of life in the city. My dad was delighted when I told him we were moving back to Lake Joseph. Zack would build homes out there — the place was booming, and more people were building vacation homes on the lake. I would make my jewelry and sell it in Chick's hardware store, a few stores in Portland I'd contacted, and online. My online store was busy already. I had set up a website, a Facebook page, and Instagram for more marketing.

"Come and build a house on our family land, Hummingbird, please," my dad said. "Keep an old man company. There's twenty acres. Plenty of room for you and Zack and any little Natalies and little Zacks who come along. I'm up for half a dozen! Or more!"

So, we did, with part of the $430,000 that we were able to get back from Ronnie, who had spent $70,000 on fancy hotels, hookers, gambling, and traveling expenses back and forth to Las Vegas while he was torturing poor Zack.

There is space between our homes, but we can see each other in the not-too-far-away distance. We both have panoramic views of the mountains and the town below. The lights twinkle at night, the sunrise is a pink and yellow and purple gift each day, the fields roll around us, the apple orchard neat rows of green and red.

Zack and I used the designs we made together for our dream home that we always planned on building "one day." *One day* was now here.

We have a great room downstairs, with a sunny breakfast nook, a kitchen with an island made from the bar of an old saloon, an office for Zack with a table my dad made for him out of an old wooden wagon, and a workshop for me with floor-to-ceiling windows off the great room. We separated the great room and my workshop with barn doors. Inside the workshop we have a table against the wall for fly-tying for Zack and me.

My dad will be working with me in my jewelry business. Two artists moved to town, and he will also do work for them, and he will do some work for Zack. In every home

Zack has decided he needs an outdoor fountain, and my dad will be creating those. Chick asked my dad if he could make some outdoor garden art for her hardware store, and he said he'd "give it a whirl."

Upstairs we have three large bedrooms. Our master bath has a tub built for two and a shower with two showerheads.

Zack and I are going to plant a garden to honor his father, Tony. Zack hasn't grown a garden since he was seventeen. "I couldn't do it," he said. "It hurt way too much." We're planting tomatoes, carrots, onions, corn, chives, peppers, and pumpkins. We're going to plant a ton of white daisies. We've hung the cleaned white picket fence in our great room, and we've framed two sets of blueprints for homes that Tony built.

We're also taking a painting class together to honor Sandy. I'm painting the yellow house I grew up in, and Zack is painting the white farmhouse he grew up in. We do not have high hopes for our artwork, we are simply hoping the homes don't look haunted or possessed. We have Sandy's paintings up throughout our home.

We hired a woman to make three quilts out of his parents cotton shirts and jeans, his father's ties, and a few of his mother's dresses and skirts. I have hung her aprons in our kitchen. His mother's china is in a hutch that Zack built, and her cookbooks are on open shelving in the kitchen. Sandy's classics are in our bookshelves, and Tony's drafting board is in Zack's office. I have enlarged and framed several photographs of Sandy and Tony and Zack and put them above the drafting board.

Zack built a special shelf to hold all of my grandma Dixie's perfume bottles. I see them and think of her playing poker in heaven and working on her dream car, a red 1967 Chevy.

We're pregnant and we are delighted. We want four kids. They can double up in the bedrooms, as neither one of us wants a large home. As Zack said, "If a fifth baby pops out, we'll keep her, too."

"Oh, gee whiz, Zack. Ya think?"

My mother became all mushy when I told her about the baby, but she tried to fake it. She tilted her coiffed blond head up, then away, her lips trembled, her chin shook, then she turned to me and insisted, "I will not be called Grandma. The child will call me Jocelyn."

"Grandma Jocelyn." I bit my lip so I wouldn't laugh.

"Only Jocelyn. Do I look old enough to be a grandma? No. I don't."

I gently prodded, and she finally told me the story of her childhood. There was some bitterness there and an avalanche of hurt because she had buried it, kept it a secret for all these years.

She had no idea where her parents were or if they were still alive. "And I don't care. I wouldn't talk to them if they came to me, anyhow. They were abusive, they were neglectful, they were hurtful, and they put me out on a street corner for hours at a time to sing to earn money for their alcohol." She rubbed her temples. "I told Dell."

"I'm glad. How did he react?"

"That old farmer. He gave me a hug and told me he would always take care of me."

"And what did you do?"

"I showed him the angel porn outfit I received in the mail that day."

I started singing a song from my childhood. I smiled at her.

She said, "If I'm going to sing, I will sing a real song."

She sang. Loud and throaty and completely on key. "I'm still an outstanding singer," she said, "even after all these years."

It was true. She was.

Her clothing boutique business was going well, surprisingly, after an incredibly bad start. She got rid of all of Evelyn's clothes, which people liked. Evelyn sold what those women needed there. So my mother started over, with another loan from dear Dell, and bought "fashionable farm woman clothing," and showed women how to dress. She was rather rude, but she did know how to fit all body types, and the store made an impressive comeback.

"I tell everyone there, there is no one I can't improve upon. No matter how frumpy you are, I can fix you up."

Lovely.

"And by the way, Natalie." She coughed. She blinked her eyes rapidly. She glanced down, then away, then back to me. Her chin trembled. "Why have you never made me a necklace?"

My jaw dropped. "I didn't think you would want one. You wear real jewels. I use rocks. Beads. Glass. Leather for chains. Charms."

Her voice wavered. "I do want one. I have always wanted one. Ever since you were a little girl and you started making them."

"Mom . . ."

She stuck her trembling chin up. "I have excellent taste, Natalie, and your necklaces are stylish and fashionable."

I was so touched. "I'll make you the most beautiful necklace I can possibly make."

"Thank you." She hugged me close, and for once, for this one time, there was no zinging, critical comment following the hug. Miracles do happen.

My dad's reaction to the baby news was loud, booming, effusive. "I can't believe it! I'm going to be a poppa! A poppa!" He burst into tears, poor man. "I can't wait to tell my hunting group." Then he started to cluck over me. Asked me if I was eating enough, I shouldn't work too hard, I should get off my feet. "Hummingbird, you are making a tiny hummingbird, you must take it easy."

Zack has his hand on my stomach all the time and talks to the baby. He's working with the baby on his alphabet so he'll be "competent at crosswords."

We laugh, we chat, we already know it's a boy. We're going to call him Scott, after my dad. His middle name will be Tony, after Zack's father. My dad doesn't know yet. It'll tear him to pieces.

Detective Zadora is coming to town to go to dinner with my dad.

Zack and I went to Portland to a party at Soldier's house. Frog Lady and Architect were there, too. They all had made progress.

We laughed and chatted, true friends that we are, and I know we will see one another many times in the future.

Before I became pregnant, Chick, Justine, and I were arrested by Justine's father, Chief Knight. One night we drank whiskey out of the Maverick Girls Moonshine flasks. That was not illegal. We got a smidgen drunk and sang songs loudly. That was not illegal, either. We climbed up the water tower. There are signs that say you may not do that. That was illegal.

Chief Knight upholds the law.

We laughed and sang drunkenly all the way to the police station in the back of Chief Knight's car.

We were released an hour later on an unsuspecting public. Chick went home to Braxton and her six quirky kids. I went home to my and Zack's home beside a garden and an orchard, and Justine rode back home with her father.

But our out-of-control wild and crazy behavior was not quite finished!

On the first warm, sunny day, Chick, Justine, and I (still prepregnancy!) went out to The Rocks over the lake. Braxton and the kids were there. Zack, my dad, and his hunting friends were there, too, as were Jed, Rosie, who had done our nails last night, and my mother, who brought Dell. The chief was there with Annabelle and five of Justine's siblings and their kids. I had held four of them shortly after they were born in the pool (no slide!) in the living room, so we have a special connection.

The three of us were in bathing suits. Chick's suit was black and said HOT MAMA. Justine's was a red bikini "to turn Jed on," and I was in my black one-piece with the gold fringe. We climbed up the hill to The Rocks, then we climbed out on The Rocks.

I looked all the way down, down, down to the lake.

Oh no.

Oh, heck.

Why was I doing this? This was unnecessary.

Chick leaned over, her toes clinging to the ledge, and said, "Did this rock get higher? It feels like we're way higher up than we were when we jumped as kids."

Justine said, "We've lost our bleeping minds. What were we thinking?"

"Whose idea was this? This is stupid," I muttered.

Our families hooted at us, cheered. There was a cooler down there that held peppermint ice cream and pickles to eat in celebration of our bravery. I wanted to be down there now.

"We can't back out now," I said.

Justine held out her hands. I grabbed one, Chick grabbed the other. We used to do this all the time when we were younger, and daring and free, wild and adventurous.

"One," I said.

"Two," Justine said.

"Oh, just go!" Chick said.

We all jumped.

Justine and Jed finally got together. Justine said the switch came after I was attacked by Ronnie. She flew to the hospital and met Jed there.

Once Jed and Justine heard the whole story and ascertained that I was okay, that Zack was okay, they left around eleven that night. Jed asked Justine to go to dinner. Justine suggested her place. My gracious! All that pent-up passion!

"It was hours before we limped out of bed, hours," she told me. "I told him about Natalie Chick. He didn't think . . . he doesn't think . . ." She gasped on a cry. "He doesn't think I'm a bad woman. He thinks I made the right choice, but he said he knew it hurt me a lot and still does."

Jed said that after Justine graduated from

college he started to see her differently but was too shy to make a move, especially as she was soon dating the Needle Penis Husband and he thought she was in love with him, especially after they got married. Gee-whiz. Can't blame the guy for thinking that. As he told me, "How could I tell her I loved her when she was engaged? How could I tell her when she was married? Then she divorced, and I was involved with someone else. We missed our time, and I hid how I felt about her. Plus, as you know, I am somewhat shy when it comes to Justine."

Fortunately, they're now on the same clock.

Jed is a judge in our county, and they, too, have moved to Lake Joseph.

Three months ago, Justine received a message on her Facebook page. Justine had no interest in being on Facebook. None. But she signed up years ago in case Natalie Chick wanted to contact her. As she said, "This is how kids talk to each other. If she wants to talk to me, this is the way she'll do it." She was right.

The message was from Natalie Chick. Justine's daughter's real name is McKayla Gilroy.

"Hello. I know this is, like, weird," Mc-

Kayla wrote, "but I didn't really think about being adopted until recently. My parents and I don't talk about it much. But I wanted to get my blood tested because I'm studying biology and genetics and I wanted to find out what countries my ancestors were from and who you are. Anyhow, my parents told me your name again and that I'm your biological daughter. If you don't want to talk to me I totally understand and it's cool. But if you do, I would like to talk to you. Just to say hi."

Needless to say, Justine *absolutely* wanted to "just say hi." She flew out to North Dakota to have lunch with McKayla and her parents that very weekend in their home. Justine was so nervous, and tearful, and told us she didn't want to appear nervous, or tearful, because she was afraid that McKayla would be scared or think she was "creepy or obsessive or overly emotional. A loon. A maniac. A mother mess."

It went well. Remarkably well. McKayla looks exactly like Justine, we saw that through the photos Justine took. The resemblance is uncanny. Thick black hair, gold eyes. She is the same height as Justine.

Justine told us, "The parents I chose for her were perfect. She adores them, and they adore her. They gave her the perfect life, and I love them for it."

The family showed Justine all the scrapbooks. In an incredibly generous gesture, McKayla's parents and McKayla made Justine her own huge scrapbook with copies of McKayla's photos in it from when she was a baby on up.

Justine said she "cried and cried. I was a mother mess."

Later Chick and I cried, with Justine, when we looked through that scrapbook together.

Last weekend McKayla flew out and met Taye, too, who was thrilled that McKayla had contacted them. Taye told me, "I have had a hole in my heart since we gave her up, Natalie. I have never felt completely right without that girl in my life. And now" — he did not bother to contain his tears — "she's here. She's back with us."

Taye's wife, Lauren, welcomed McKayla with open arms, as did Taye and Lauren's six kids. It was cool to have an older sister! Lauren told Justine and me, "I always felt like Taye was hiding something, that he was sad about something, and I would ask him about it and he would brush it off, say it was nothing, blame work, blame other worries, but I knew. I simply knew something else was wrong."

I was familiar with that feeling.

Taye and Justine are open about their daughter in town, and she has been embraced, of course.

Justine now has Jed and she has McKayla and she is at peace.

Chick, however, still continues to lose half her mind every day. Ellie is a "mad scientist" and caused an explosion in chemistry class. Her fellow students found it extremely exciting. Hudson, "not the brightest kid in the herd here, he has a hard time remembering where the plates are located in the cupboard," has had success with his worm-selling business. Joshua continues to sing, "on full throttle, it blows my ears out," in his pink pants. Ally the ballerina tripped over her own feet again and broke her arm. Chick is insisting that she, "Big Foot," try swimming. The twins escaped from prekindergarten and the police were called. Chief Knight found them playing in a nearby field with a mouse.

Chick's life is filled with love and chaos and a husband who carves wooden animals when he gets upset when they have fights.

She and Justine are excited to be Aunt Chick and Aunt Justine to baby Scott.

The Moonshine and Milky Way Maverick

Girls were together again, in Lake Joseph, where our friendship and our pickle and peppermint ice-cream tradition began.

People hide things. My mother hid her past. Justine and Taye hid the daughter they gave up as a baby. Jed hid that he'd fallen in love with Justine. My husband hid that he'd killed a man and changed his identity. I hid that I knew my husband was lying until I figured out why, and I hid my FOA issues as best I could.

Relationships are complicated. People are complicated.

Love is complicated.

But after being in a coma, I know one thing for sure: I will take this crazy life any minute, any day, and be grateful for it.

Zack and I went fishing on the Deschutes one Saturday, my stomach growing each day. I could barely fit in my waders. It was almost dusk, and we were in our drift boat, our lines in the water.

The river had a few fading golden sparkles on it from the sun. The sky above the ridge was turning azure blue, lavender, and dusty rose. A hawk soared overhead. We were near the spot where we'd met. Zack pointed it out. "That's it, honey."

I leaned over and gave him a kiss, both of us careful not to drop our poles. "I remember what you said to me once, Zack."

"When?"

"Let's see if you can remember when. I'll say it exactly as you said it to me." I grinned at my man. " 'When you're on the Deschutes, you can believe there are billions of stars and galaxies. You used to say it made you feel tiny, Natalie, but you have never been tiny to me. You've always been my whole life. My whole life. You are all the stars up in the sky for me.' "

"I said that to you when . . . when . . ." Zack's jaw dropped. "Oh, honey, you're kidding me . . . the whole time?"

I love that man. With all that I am, with all that I will ever be, I love Zack.

ABOUT THE AUTHOR

Cathy Lamb is the acclaimed author of over ten novels, including *No Place I'd Rather Be, A Different Kind of Normal, The First Day of the Rest of My Life, Henry's Sisters* and *Julia's Chocolates,* among others. She has earned advanced degrees in education and brings those insights into her writing. Cathy Lamb currently writes full time and lives with her family in Oregon. Please visit her online at cathylamb.org.

The employees of Thorndike Press hope you have enjoyed this Large Print book. All our Thorndike, Wheeler, and Kennebec Large Print titles are designed for easy reading, and all our books are made to last. Other Thorndike Press Large Print books are available at your library, through selected bookstores, or directly from us.

For information about titles, please call:
  (800) 223-1244

or visit our website at:
  gale.com/thorndike

To share your comments, please write:
  Publisher
  Thorndike Press
  10 Water St., Suite 310
  Waterville, ME 04901